One Night with the Italian Doc

CAROL MARINELLI
ANNIE O'NEIL
KATE HARDY

MILLS & BOON

First Published in Great Britain 2019
By Mills & Boon, an imprint of HarperCollins*Publishers*
1 London Bridge Street, London, SE1 9GF

ONE NIGHT WITH THE ITALIAN DOC © 2019 Harlequin Books S.A.

Unwrapping her Italian Doc © 2014 Carol Marinelli
Tempted by the Bridesmaid © 2017 Annie O'Neil
Italian Doctor, No Strings Attached © 2011 Pamela Brooks

ISBN: 978-0-263-27475-2

0219

Printed and bound in Spain
by CPI, Barcelona

UNWRAPPING HER ITALIAN DOC

CAROL MARINELLI

CHAPTER ONE

'ANTON, WOULD YOU do me a favour?'

Anton Rossi's long, brisk stride was broken by the sound of Louise's voice.

He had tried very hard not to notice her as he had stepped into the maternity unit of The Royal in London, though, of course, he had.

Louise was up a stepladder and putting up Christmas decorations. Her skinny frame was more apparent this morning as she was dressed in very loose, navy scrubs with a long-sleeved, pale pink top worn underneath. Her blonde hair was tied in a high ponytail and she had layer after layer of tinsel around her neck.

She was also, Anton noted, by far too pale.

Yes, whether he had wanted to or not, he had noticed her.

He tended to notice Louise Carter a lot.

'What is it that you want?' Anton asked, as he reluctantly turned around.

'In that box, over there…' Louise raised a slender arm and pointed it towards the nurses' station '…there's some gold tinsel.'

He just stood there and Louise wondered if possibly he didn't understand what she was asking for.

'Tin-sel…' she said slowly, in the strange attempt at an Italian accent that Louise did now and then when she was trying to explain a word to him. Anton watched in concealed amusement as she jiggled the pieces around her neck. 'Tin-sel, go-o-old.'

'And?'

Louise gave up on her accent. 'Could you just get it for me? I've run out of gold.'

'I'm here to check on Hannah Evans.'

'It will only take you a second,' Louise pointed out. 'Look, if I get down now I'll have to start again.' Her hand was holding one piece of gaudy green tinsel to the tired maternity wall. 'I'm trying to make a pattern.'

'You are *trying*, full stop,' Anton said, and walked off.

'Bah, humbug,' Louise called to his departing shoulders.

Anton, had moved to London from Milan and, having never spent a Christmas in England, would have to find out later what that translated as but he certainly got the gist.

Yes, he wasn't exactly in the festive spirit. For the last few years Anton had, in fact, dreaded Christmas.

Unfortunately there was no escaping it at The Royal— December had today hit and there were invites galore for Christmas lunches, dinners and parties piling into his inbox that he really ought to attend. Walking into work this morning, he had seen a huge Christmas tree being erected in the hospital foyer and now Louise had got in on the act. She seemed to be attempting to singlehandedly turn the maternity ward into Santa's grotto.

Reluctantly, *very* reluctantly, he headed over to the box, retrieved a long piece of gold tinsel and returned to Louise, who gave him a sweet smile as she took it.

Actually, no, Anton decided, it was far from a sweet smile—it was a slightly sarcastic, rather triumphant smile.

'Thank you very much,' Louise said.

'You're more than welcome,' Anton responded, and walked off.

Anton knew, just knew that if he turned around it would be to the sight of Louise poking her tongue out at him.

Keep going, he told himself.

Do not turn around, for it would just serve to encourage her and he was doing everything in his power to discourage Louise. She was the most skilled flirt he had ever come across. At first he has assumed Louise was like that with everyone—it had come as a disconcerting, if somewhat pleasant surprise to realise that the blatant flirting seemed to be saved solely for him.

Little known to Louise, he enjoyed their encounters, not that he would ever let on.

Ignore her, Anton told himself.

Yet he could not.

Anton turned to the sight of Louise on the stepladder, tongue out, fingers up and well and truly caught!

Louise actually froze for a second, which was very unfortunate, given the gesture she was making, but then she unfroze as Anton turned and walked back towards her. A shriek of nervous laughter started to pour from Louise because, from the way that Anton was walking, it felt as if he might be about to haul her from the ladder and over his shoulder. Wouldn't that be nice? both simultaneously thought, but instead he came right up to her, his face level with her groin, and looked up into china-blue eyes as she looked down at the sexiest, most aloof, impossibly arrogant man to have ever graced The Royal.

'I got you your tinsel.' Anton pointed at her and his voice was stern but, Louise noted, that sulky mouth of his was doing its level best not to smile.

'Yes, Anton, you did,' Louise said, wondering if he could feel the blast of heat coming from her loins. God knew, he was miserable and moody but her body responded to him as if someone had just thrown another log on the fire whenever he was around.

On many levels he annoyed her—Anton checked and re-checked everything that she did, as if she was someone who had just wandered in from the street and offered to help out for the day, rather than a qualified midwife. Yet, aside from their professional differences, he was as sexy as hell and the sparks just flew off the two of them, no matter how Anton might deny that they did.

'So why this?' Anton asked, and pulled a face and poked his tongue out at her, and Louise smiled at the sight of his tongue and screwed-up features as he mimicked her gestures. He was still gorgeous—olive-skinned, his black hair was glossy and straight and so well cut that Louise constantly had to resist running her hands through it just to see it messed up. His eyes were a very dark blue and she ached to see them smile, yet, possibly for the first time, while aimed at her, now they were.

Oh, his expression was cross but, Louise could just see, those eyes were finally smiling and so she took the opportunity to let him know a few home truths.

'It's the way that you do things, Anton.' Louise attempted to explain. 'Why couldn't you just say, "Sure, Louise," and go and get the tinsel?'

'Because, as I've told you, I am on my way to see a patient.'

'Okay, why didn't you smile when you walked into the unit and saw the decorations that I've spent the last two hours putting up and say, "Ooh, that looks nice"?'

'Truth?' Anton said.

'Truth.' Louise nodded.

'I happen to think that you have too many decorations…' He watched her eyes narrow at his criticism. 'You asked why I didn't tell you how nice they looked.'

'I did,' Louise responded. 'Okay, then, third question, why didn't you say hello to me when you walked past?'

For Anton, that was the trickiest to answer. 'Because I didn't see you.'

'Please!' Louise rolled her eyes. 'You saw me—you just chose to ignore me, as I'm going to choose to ignore your slight about my decorations. You can never have too much tinsel.'

'Oh, believe me Louise, you can,' Anton said, looking around. The corridor was a riot of red, gold and green tinsel stars. He looked up to where silver foil balloons hung from the ceilings. Then he looked down to plastic snowmen dancing along the bottom of the walls. Half of the windows to the patients' rooms had been sprayed with fake snow. Louise had clearly been busy. 'Nothing matches.' Anton couldn't help but smile and he *really* tried to help but smile! 'You don't have a theme.'

'The theme is Christmas, Anton,' Louise said in response. 'I had a very tinsel-starved Christmas last year and I intend to make up for it this one. I'm doing the nativity scene this afternoon.'

'Good for you,' Anton said, and walked off.

Louise didn't poke out her tongue again and even if

she had Anton wouldn't have seen it because this time he very deliberately didn't turn around.

He didn't want to engage in conversation with Louise. He didn't want to find out why she'd had a tinsel-starved Christmas the previous year.

Or rather he *did* want to find out.

Louise was flaky, funny, sexy and everything Anton did not need to distract him at work. He wasn't here to make friends—his social life was conducted well away from the hospital walls. Anton did his level best to keep his distance from everyone at work except his patients.

'Hannah.' He smiled as he stepped into the four-bedded ward but Hannah didn't smile back and Anton pulled the curtains around her bed before asking his patient any questions. 'Are you okay?' Anton checked.

'I'm so worried.'

'Tell me,' Anton offered.

'I'm probably being stupid, I know, but Brenda came in this morning and I said the baby had moved and I'm sure that it did, but it hasn't since then.'

'So you're lying here, imagining the worst?'

'Yes,' Hannah admitted. 'It's taken so long to get here that I'm scared something's going to go wrong now.'

'I know how hard your journey has been,' Anton said. Hannah had conceived by IVF and near the end of a tricky pregnancy she had been brought in for bed rest as her blood pressure was high and the baby's amniotic fluid was a little on the low side. Anton specialised in high-risk pregnancies and so he was very comfortable listening to Hannah's concerns.

'Let me have a feel,' Anton said. 'It is probably asleep.'

For all he was miserable with the staff and kept himself to himself, Anton was completely lovely and open with his patients. He had a feel of Hannah's stomach and then took out a Doppler machine and had a listen, locating the heartbeat straight away. 'Beautiful,' Anton said, and they listened for a moment. 'Have you had breakfast?' Anton asked, because if Hannah had low blood sugar, that could slow movements down.

'I have.'

'How many movements are you getting?'

'I felt one now,' Hanna said.

'That's because I just nudged your baby awake when I was feeling your stomach.'

He sat going through her charts. Hannah's blood pressure was at the higher limits of normal and Anton wondered for a long moment how best to proceed. While the uterus was usually the best incubator, there were times when the baby was safest out. He had more than a vested interested in this pregnancy and he told Hannah that. 'Do you know you will be the first patient that I have ever helped both to conceive through IVF *and* deliver their baby?'

'No.' Hannah frowned. 'I thought in your line of work that that would happen to you all the time.'

'No.' Anton shook his head. 'Remember how upset you were when I first saw you because the doctor you had been expecting was sick on the day of your egg retrieval?'

Hannah nodded and actually blushed. 'I was very rude to you.'

'Because you didn't want a locum to be taking over your care.' Anton smiled. 'And that is fair enough. In Italy I used to do obstetrics but then I moved into reproductive endocrinology and specialised there. In my opinion you can't do both simultaneously, they are completely different specialties—you have to always be available for either. I only helped out that week because Richard was sick. I still cover very occasionally to help out and also because I like to keep up to date but in truth I cannot do both.'

'So how come you moved back to obstetrics?'

'I missed it,' Anton admitted. 'I do like the fertility side of things and I do see patients where that is their issue but if they need IVF then I refer them. Obstetrics is where I prefer to be.'

The movements were slowing down. Anton could see that and with her low level of amniotic fluid, Hannah would be more aware than most of any movement. 'I think your baby might be just about cooked,' Anton said, and then headed out of the ward and asked Brenda to come in. 'I'm just going to examine Hannah,' Anton said, and spoke to both women as he did so. 'Your cervix is thinning and you're already three centimetres dilated.' He looked at Brenda. 'Kicks are down from yesterday.'

Anton had considered delivering Hannah last night and now, with the news that the kicks were down combined with Hannah's distress, he decided to go ahead this morning.

'I think we'll get things started,' Anton said.

'Now?'

'Yes.' Anton nodded and he explained to Hannah his reasoning. 'We've discussed how your placenta is coming to the end of its use-by date. Sometimes the baby does better on the outside than in and I think we've just reached that time.' He let it sink in for a moment. 'I'll start a drip, though we'll just give you a low dose to help move things along.'

Hannah called her husband and Anton spoke with

Brenda at the nurses' station, then Hannah was taken around to the delivery ward.

All births were special and precious but Anton had been concerned about Hannah for a couple of weeks as the baby was a little on the small side. Anton would actually be very relieved once this baby was out.

By the time he had set up the drip and Hannah was attached to the baby monitor, with Luke, her husband, by her side, Anton was ready for a coffee break. He checked on another lady who would soon deliver and then he checked on his other patients on the ward.

Stephanie, another obstetrician, had been on last night and had handed over to him but, though Anton respected Stephanie, he had learnt never to rely on handovers. Anton liked to see for himself where his patients were and though he knew it infuriated some of the staff it was the way he now worked and he wasn't about to change that.

Satisfied that all was well, he was just about to take himself to the staffroom when he saw Louise, still up that ladder, but she offered no snarky comment this time, neither were there any requests for assistance. Instead, she was pressing her fingers into her eyes and clearly felt dizzy.

Not my problem, Anton decided.

But, of course, it was.

CHAPTER TWO

'LOUISE…' HE WALKED over and saw her already pale features were now white, right down to her lips. 'Louise, you need to get down from the ladder.'

The sound of his voice created a small chasm between the stars dancing in her eyes and Louise opened her eyes to the sight of Anton walking towards her. And she would get down if only she could remember how her legs worked.

'Come on,' Anton said. This time he *did* take her down from the ladder, though not over his shoulder, as they had both briefly considered before. Instead, he held his hand out and she took it and shakily stepped down. Anton put a hand around her waist and led her to the staffroom, where he sat her down and then went to the fridge and got out some orange juice.

'Here,' he said, handing the glass to her.

Louise took a grateful gulp and then another and blew out a breath. 'I'm so sorry about that. I just got a bit dizzy.'

'Did you have breakfast this morning?'

'I did.' Louise nodded but he gave her a look that said he didn't believe a word. Anton then huffed off, leaving her sitting in the staffroom while he went to the kitchen. Louise could hear him feeding bread into the toaster.

God, Louise thought, rolling her eyes, here comes the lecture.

Anton returned a moment later with two slices of toast smothered in butter and honey.

'I just told you that I'd already had breakfast,' Louise said.

'I think you should eat this.'

'If I eat that I'll be sick. I just need to lie down for a few minutes.'

'Do you have a photo shoot coming up?' Anton asked, and Louise sighed. 'Answer me,' Anton said.

'Yes, I have a big photo shoot taking place on Christmas Eve but that has no part in my nearly fainting.'

Louise was a part-time lingerie model. She completely loved her side job and took it seriously. Everyone thought that it was hilarious, everyone, that was, except Anton. Mind, he didn't find anything very funny these days.

'You're too thin.' Anton was blunt and though Louise knew it was out of concern, there was no reason for him to be. She knew only too well the reason for the little episode on the ladder.

'Actually, I'm not too thin, I'm in the healthy weight range,' Louise said. 'Look, I just got dizzy. Please don't peg me as having an eating disorder just because I model part time.'

'My sister is a model in Milan,' Anton said, and Louise could possibly have guessed that, had Anton had a sister, then a model she might be because Anton really was seriously beautiful.

Louise lay down on the sofa because she could still see stars and she didn't want Anton to know that. In fact, she just wanted him gone. And she knew how to get rid of him! A little flirt would have him running off.

'Are my hips not childbearing enough for you, Anton?' Louise teased, and Anton glanced down and it wasn't a baby he was thinking about between those legs!

No way!

Louise had used to work in Theatre—in fact, she had been the nurse who had scrubbed in on his first emergency Caesarean here at The Royal. It had been the first emergency Caesarean section he had performed since losing Alberto. Of course, Louise hadn't known just how nervous Anton had been that day and she could not possibly have guessed how her presence had both helped and unsettled him.

During surgery Anton had been grateful for a very efficient scrub nurse and one who had immediately worked well with him.

After surgery, when he'd gone to check in on the infant, Louise had been there, smiling and cooing at the baby. She had turned around and congratulated him on getting the baby out in time, and he had actually forgotten to thank her for her help in Theatre.

Possibly he had snapped an order instead—anything rather than like her.

Except he did.

A few months ago Louise had decided to more fully utilise her midwifery training and had come to work on Maternity, which was, of course, Anton's stomping ground.

Seeing her most days, resisting her on each and every one of them, was quietly driving him insane.

She was very direct, a bit off the wall and terribly

beautiful too, and if she hadn't worked here Anton would not hesitate.

Mind you, if she hadn't worked here he wouldn't know just how clever and funny she was.

Anton looked down where she lay, eyes closed on the sofa, and saw there was a touch of colour coming back to her cheeks and her breathing was nice and regular now. Then Anton pulled his eyes up from the rise and fall of her chest and instead of leaving the room he met her very blue eyes.

Louise could see the concern was still there. 'Honestly, Anton, I didn't get dizzy because I have an eating disorder,' Louise said, and, because this was the maternity ward and such things were easily discussed, especially if your name was Louise, she told him what the real problem was. 'I've got the worst period in the history of the world, if you must know.'

'Okay.' He looked at her very pale face and her hand that moved low onto her stomach and decided she was telling the truth.

'Do you need some painkillers?'

'I've had some,' Louise said, closing her eyes. 'They didn't do a thing.'

'Do you need to go home?' Anton asked.

'Are you going to write me a note, Doctor?'

He watched her lips turn up in a smile as she teased but then shook her head. 'No, I'll be fine soon, though I might just stay lying down here for a few minutes.'

'Do you want me to let Brenda know?'

'Please.' Louise nodded.

'You're sure I can't get you anything?' Anton checked.

'A heat pack would be lovely,' Louise said, glad that her eyes were closed because she could imagine his expression at being asked to fetch a heat pack, when surely that was a nurse's job. 'It needs two minutes in the microwave,' she called, as he walked out.

It took five minutes for Anton to locate the heat packs and so he returned seven minutes later to where she lay, knees up with her eyes closed, and he placed the heat pack gently over her uterus.

'You make a lovely midwife,' Louise said, feeling the weight and the warmth.

'I've told Brenda,' Anton said, 'and she said that you are to take your time and come back when you're ready.' He went to go but she still concerned him and Anton walked over and sat down by her waist on the sofa where she lay.

Louise felt him sit down beside her and then he picked up her hand. She knew that he was checking her nails for signs of anaemia and she was about to make a little tease about her not knowing he cared, except Anton this close made talking impossible. She opened her eyes and he pulled down her lower lids and she wished, oh, how she wished, those fingers were on her face for very different reasons.

'You're anaemic,' Anton said.

'I'm on iron and folic acid…'

'You're seeing someone?'

'Yes, but I…' Louise had started to let a few close friends know what was going on in her personal life but she wasn't quite ready to tell the world just yet. She ached to discuss it with Anton, not on a personal level but a professional one, yet was a little shy to. 'I've spoken to my GP.' His pager went off and though he read it he still sat there, but the moment had gone and Louise decided not to tell him her plans and what was going on.

'He's told you that you don't have to struggle like this.

There is the Pill and there is also an IUD that can give you a break from menstr—'

'Anton,' Louise interrupted. 'My GP is a she, and I *am* a midwife, which means, oh, about ten times a day I give contraceptive advice, so I do know these things.'

'Then you should know that you don't have to put up with this.'

'I do. Thanks for your help,' Louise said, and then, aware of her snappy tone, she halted. After all, he was just trying to help. He simply didn't know what was going on in her world. 'I owe you one.' She gave him a smile. 'I'll buy you a drink tonight.'

'Tonight?' Anton frowned.

'It's the theatre Christmas do,' Louise said, and Anton inwardly groaned, because another non-work version of Louise seared into his brain he truly did not need! Anton had seen Louise dressed to the nines a few times since he had started here and it was a very appealing sight. He had braced himself for the maternity do in a couple of weeks—in fact, he had a date lined up for that night—but it had never entered his head that Louise would be at the theatre do tonight.

'So you will be going tonight?' Anton checked. 'Even though you're not feeling well?'

'Of course I'm going,' Louise said. 'I worked there for five years.' She opened her eyes and gave him a very nice smile, though their interlude was over. Concerned Anton had gone and he was back to bah, humbug as he stood. 'I'll see you tonight, Anton.'

Stop the drip! Anton wanted to say as he went in to check on Hannah, for he would dearly love a reason to be stuck at the hospital tonight.

Of course, he didn't stop the drip and instead Hannah progressed beautifully.

* * *

'Louise, would you be able to go and work in Delivery after lunch?' Brenda came over as Louise added the finishing touches to her nativity scene during her lunch break. She'd taken her chicken and avocado salad out with her and was eating it as she arranged all the pieces. 'Angie called in sick and we're trying to get an agency nurse.'

Louise had to stop herself from rolling her eyes. While she loved being in Delivery for an entire shift, she loathed being sent in for a couple of hours. Louise liked to be there for her patient for the entire shift.

'Sure,' Louise said instead.

'They're a bit short now,' Brenda pushed, and Louise decided not to point out that she'd only had fifteen minutes' break, given the half-hour she'd taken earlier that morning. So, instead, she popped the cutest Baby Jesus ever into the crib, covered him in a little rug and headed off to Delivery.

She took the handover, read through Hannah's birth plan then went in and said hello to Hannah and Luke. Hannah had been a patient on the ward for a couple of weeks now so introductions had long since been done.

Hannah was lying on her side and clearly felt uncomfortable.

'It really hurts.'

'I know that it does,' Louise said, showing Luke a nice spot to rub on the bottom of Hannah's back, but Hannah kept pushing his hand away.

'Do you want to have a little walk?' Louise offered, and at first Hannah shook her head but then agreed. Louise sorted out the drip and got her up off the delivery bed and they shuffled up and down the corridor, sometimes silent between contractions, when Hannah leant against the wall, other times talking.

'I still can't believe we'll have a baby for Christmas,' Hannah said.

'How exciting.' Louise smiled. 'Have you shopped for the baby?''

'Not yet!' Hannah shook her head. 'Didn't want the bad luck.' She leant against the wall and gave a very low moan and then another one.

'Let's get you back,' Louise said, guiding the drip as Luke helped his wife.

Hannah didn't like the idea of sitting on a birthing ball—in fact, she climbed back onto the delivery bed and went back to lying on her side as Louise checked the baby's heart, which was fine.

'You're doing wonderfully, Hannah,' Louise said.

'I can't believe we're going to get our baby,' Hannah said. 'We tried for ages.'

'I know that you did,' Louise said.

'I'm so lucky to have Anton,' Hannah said. 'He got me pregnant!'

Louise looked over at Luke and they shared a smile because at this stage of labour women said the strangest things at times, only Louise's smile turned into a slight frown as Luke explained what she'd meant. 'Anton was the one who put back the embryo…'

'Oh!' Louise said, more than a little surprised, because that was something she hadn't known—yes, of course he would deal with infertility to a point, but it was a very specific specialty and for Anton to have performed the embryo transfer confused Louise.

'He was a reproductive specialist in Milan, one of the top ones,' Luke explained further, when he saw Louise's frown. 'We thought we were getting a fill-in doctor when Richard, the specialist overseeing Hannah's treatment, got sick, but it turned out we were getting one of the best.' He looked up as Anton came in. 'I was just telling Louise that you were the one who got Hannah pregnant.'

Anton gave a small smile of acknowledgement of the conversation then he turned to Louise. 'How is she?'

'Very well.'

Anton gave another brief nod and went to examine Hannah.

Hannah was doing very well because things soon started to get busy and by four o'clock, just when Louise should be heading home to get ready for tonight, she was cheering Hannah on.

'Are you okay, Louise?' Brenda popped her head in to see if Louise wanted one of the late staff to come in and take over but instead Louise smiled and nodded. 'I'm fine, Brenda,' Louise said. 'We're nearly there.'

She would never leave so close to the end of a birth, Anton knew that, and she was enthusiastic at every birth, even if the mother was in Theatre, unconscious.

'How much longer?' Hannah begged.

'Not long,' Louise said. 'Don't push, just hold it now.' Louise was holding Hannah's leg and watched as the head came out and Anton carefully looped a rather thin and straggly umbilical cord from around the baby's neck.

She and Anton actually worked well in this part. Anton liked how Louise got into it and encouraged the woman no end, urging her on when required, helping him to slow things down too, if that was the course of action needed. This was the case here, because the baby was only thirty-five weeks and also rather small for dates.

'Oh, Hannah!' Louise was ecstatic as the shoulders

were delivered and Anton placed the slippery bundle on Hannah's stomach and Louise rubbed the baby's back. They all watched as he took his first breath and finally Hannah and Luke had their wish come true.

'He's beautiful,' Hannah said, examining her son in awe, holding his tiny hand, scarcely able to believe she had a son.

He was small, even for thirty-five weeks, and, having delivered the placenta, Anton could well see why. The baby had certainly been delivered at the right time and could now get the nourishment he needed from his mother to fatten up.

Anton came and looked at the baby. The paediatrician was finishing up checking him over as Louise watched.

'He looks good,' Anton said.

'So good,' Louise agreed, and then smiled at the baby's worried-looking face. He was wearing the concerned expression that a lot of small-for-dates babies had. 'And so hungry!'

The paediatrician went to have a word with the parents to explain their baby's care as Louise wrapped him up in a tight parcel and popped a little hat on him.

'How does it feel,' Louise asked Anton, 'to have been there at conception and delivery?' She started to laugh at her own question. 'That sounds rude! You know what I mean.'

'I was just saying to Hannah this morning that it has never happened to me before. So this little one is a bit more special,' Anton admitted. 'I'm going to go and write my notes. I'll be back to check on Hannah in a while.'

'Well, I'll be going home soon,' Louise said, 'but I'll pass it all on.' She picked up the baby. 'Come on, little man, let's get you back to your mum.'

She didn't rush home then either, though. Louise helped with the baby's first feed, though he quickly tired and would need gavage top-ups. Having put him under a warmer beside his parents, she then went and made Hannah a massive mug of tea. Anton, who was getting a cup of tea of his own, watched as she went into her pocket and took out a teabag.

'Why do you keep teabags in your pocket?'

'Would you want that…' she sneered at the hospital teabags on the bench '…if you'd just pushed a baby out?'

'No.'

'There's your answer, then. I make sure my mums get one nice cup of tea after they've given birth and then they wonder their entire stay in hospital why the rest of them taste so terrible after that,' Louise said. 'It's my service to women.' She went back into her pocket and gave him a teabag and Anton took it because the hospital tea really was that bad. 'Here, but that's *not* the drink I owe you for this morning. You'll get that later.'

He actually smiled at someone who wasn't a patient. 'I'll see you tonight,' Louise said, and their eyes met, just for a second but Anton was the one who looked away, and with good reason.

Yes, Anton thought, she would see him tonight but here endeth the flirting.

CHAPTER THREE

LOUISE LIVED FAIRLY close to the hospital and arrived at her small terraced home just after five to a ringing phone.

She did consider not answering it because she was already running late but, seeing that it was her mum, Louise picked up.

'I can't talk for long,' Louise warned, and then spent half an hour chatting about plans for Christmas Day.

'Mum!' Louise said, for the twentieth time. 'I'm on days off after Christmas Eve all the way till after New Year. I've told you that I'll be there for Christmas Day.'

'You said you'd be there last year,' Susan pointed out.

'Can we not go through that again,' Louise said, regretting the hurt she had caused last year by not telling her parents the truth about what had been going on in her life. 'I was just trying to—'

'Well, don't ever do that again,' Susan said. 'I can't bear that you chose to spend Christmas miserable and alone in some hotel rather than coming home to your family.'

'You know why I did, Mum,' Louise said, and then conceded, 'But I know now that I should have just come home.' She flicked the lights of her Christmas tree to on, smiling as she did so. 'Mum, I honestly can't wait for Christmas.'

'Neither can I. I've ordered the turkey,' Susan said, 'and I'm going to try something extra-special for Boxing Day—kedgeree...'

'Is that the thing with fish and eggs?' Louise checked.

'And curry powder,' Susan agreed.

'That's great, Mum,' Louise said, pulling a face because her mother was the worst cook in the world. The trouble was, though, that Susan considered herself an amazing cook! Louise ached for her dad sometimes, he was the kindest, most patient man, only that had proved part of the problem—the compliments he'd first given had gone straight to Susan's head and, in the kitchen, she thought she could do no wrong. 'Mum, I'd love to chat more but I have to go now and get ready, it's the theatre Christmas night out. I'll call you soon.'

'Well, enjoy.'

'I shall.'

'Oh, one other thing before you go,' Susan said. 'Did you get the referral for the specialist?'

'Not yet,' Louise sighed. 'She says she wants me to have a full six months off the Pill before she refers me...' Louise thought for a moment. She really wasn't happy with her GP. 'I know I said that I didn't want to go to The Royal for this but it might be the best place.'

'I think you're right,' Susan said. 'I didn't like to say so at the time but I don't think she took you very seriously.'

Louise nodded then glanced at the clock. So much for a quick chat!

'I have to get ready, Mum.'

'Well, if you do go to The Royal, let me know when and I'll come with you...'

'I will,' Louise said, and then there were all the *I love you*s and *Do you want a quick word with Dad?*

Louise smiled as she put down the phone because, apart from her cooking, Louise knew that she had the best mum and possibly the best family in the world.

Her dad was the most patient person and Louise's two younger sisters were amazing young women who rang Louise often, and they all got on very well.

This was part of the reason why she hadn't wanted to spoil Christmas for everyone last year and had pretended that something had happened at work. At the time it had seemed kinder to say that they were short-staffed rather than arrive home in such a fragile state on Christmas morning and ruin everyone's day.

Her sisters looked up to her and often asked her opinion on guys; it had been hard, admitting how badly she had judged Wesley. Even a part of the truth had hurt them and her dad would just about die if he knew even half of what had really gone on.

Louise lay on her bed while her bath was running, thinking back to that terrible time. Not just the break-up with Wesley but the horrible lonely time before it.

Louise's wings had been clipped during their relationship. *Seriously* clipped, to the point that she had given up her modelling side job, which she loved. Somehow, she wasn't quite sure how it had happened, her hems had got lower, her hair darker until her sparkle had almost been extinguished.

At a work function Wesley had loathed that she had chatted with Rory, an anaesthetist who was also ex-boyfriend of Louise's from way back.

She and Rory had remained very good friends up to that point.

Louise had given Wesley the benefit of the doubt after that first toxic row. Yes, she'd decided, it wasn't unreasonable for him to be jealous that she was so friendly with her ex. She had severed things with Rory, which had been hard to do and had caused considerable hurt when she had.

It hadn't stopped there, though.

Wesley hadn't liked Emily, Louise's close friend, either. He hadn't liked their odd nights out or their phone calls and texting and gradually that had all tapered off too.

Finally, realising that she had been constantly walking on eggshells and that she'd barely recognised herself any more, Louise had known she had to end things. It had been far easier said than done, though, knowing, with Wesley's building temper, that the ending would be terrible.

It had been.

On Christmas Eve, when Wesley had decided that her family didn't like him and perhaps it should be just the two of them for Christmas, Louise had known she had to get the hell out. An argument had ensued and the gentle, happy Louise had finally lost her temper.

No, he hadn't taken it well.

It would soon be a year to the very day since it had happened, and in the year that had followed Louise had found herself again—the woman she had been before Wesley, the happy person she had once been, though it had taken a while.

Louise's confidence had been severely shaken around men but her dad, her uncles, Rory, Emily's now-husband, Hugh, all the people Wesley had been so jealous of had been such huge support—insisting that Wesley wasn't in the regular mould men were cast from. Finally convincing her that she should simply be her sparkling, annoying, once irrepressible self.

Without her family and friends, Louise did not know how she'd have survived emotionally.

She'd never turn her back on them again.

Anton had appeared at The Royal around March and the jolt of attraction had been so intense Louise had felt her mojo dash back. Possibly because he was so aloof and just so unobtainable that it had felt safe to test her flirting wings on him.

Anton never really responded, yet he never stopped her either. He simply let her be, which was nice.

It was all for fun, a little confidence boost as she slowly returned to her old self, yet in the ensuing months it had gathered steam.

Nope!

Louise got of the bed and looked around her room. It was a sexy boudoir indeed, thanks to a few freebies from a couple of photo shoots. There was a velvet red chair that went with the velvet bedspread, and it made Louise smile every time she sat in it. She smiled even more at the thought of Anton in here but she pushed that thought aside.

In the flirting department he was divine but his arrogance, the way he double-checked everything Louise did at work, rendered him far from relationship material.

Not that she knew if he even liked her.

To Louise, Anton was a very confusing man.

Still, flirting was fun!

Not that she felt particularly sparkly tonight.

After her bath, Louise did her make-up carefully,

topped it off with loads of red lipstick and then started to dry her hair.

It still fell to the right, even after nearly a year of parting it to fall to the left.

Louise examined the shiny red scar on her scalp for a moment. She could still see the needle marks. Thanks to her delay in getting sutured, the stitches had had to stay in for ten days. Unable to deal with the memory, she quickly moved on and tonged her hair into wild ringlets. She put on the Christmas holly underwear that she'd modelled a couple of months ago, along with the stockings from the same range, which were a very sheer red with green sprigs of holly and little red dots for berries.

They were fabulous!

As were the red dress and high-heeled shoes.

Hearing Emily blast the horn outside, Louise pushed out a smile, determined to enjoy all the celebrations that took place at her very favourite time of the year, however unwell she felt.

'God help Anton!' Hugh said, as Louise stepped out of her house and waved to him and Emily.

'Why haven't they got it on?' Emily asked, as Louise dashed back in the house to check that she'd turned off her curling tongs.

'I don't know,' Hugh mused. 'Though I thought that Louise had sworn off men.'

'She's sworn off relationships,' Emily said, 'not joined a nunnery.'

Hugh laughed. No, he could not imagine Louise in a nunnery.

'Is Anton seeing anyone?' Emily asked, but Hugh shook his head.

'I don't think so—mind you, Anton's not exactly friendly and chatty.'

'He is to me.'

'Because you're six months pregnant and his patient,' Hugh pointed out, as Louise came down her path for the second time. 'Maybe you could ask him if he's seeing someone next time you see him.'

'That's a good idea.' Emily smiled. 'I'll just slip that question in while he examines me, shall I?'

She turned and smiled as Louise got into the back of the car.

'Hi, Emily. You make a lovely taxi driver—thank you for this,' Louise said. 'Hi, Hugh, how lucky you are to have a pregnant wife over Christmas!'

'Very lucky,' Hugh agreed, as Emily drove off.

'You look gorgeous, Louise,' Emily said.

'Thank you, but I feel like crap,' Louise happily admitted. 'I've got the worst period and I can only have one eggnog as I'm working in the morning.'

Hugh arched his neck at Louise's openness and Emily smiled.

They both loved her.

As they arrived at the rather nice venue, Louise got her first full-length look at Emily.

'You look gorgeous and I want one…' she said, referring to Emily's six–months-pregnant belly, which was tonight dressed in black and looking amazing.

'You will soon,' Emily said, because Louise had shared with her her plans to get pregnant next year.

'I hope so.'

Louise's eyes scanned the room. It had been very tastefully decorated—there were pale pinkish gold twigs in vases on the tables and pale pinkish gold decorations and lights that twinkled, and there was Anton, talking to Alex, who was Hugh's boss, and Rory was with them as well.

Perfect, Louise thought as the trio made their way over and all the hellos began.

'Aren't the decorations gorgeous?' Emily said, but Louise pulled a face.

'Some colour would be nice. Who would choose pink for Christmas decorations?' As a waiter passed with a tray, she took a mini pale pink chocolate that the waiter called a frosted snowball but even the coconut was pink. 'They have a *theme*,' she said, and smiled at Anton, but it went to the wall because he wasn't looking at her.

'No Jennifer?' Hugh checked with Alex, because normally his wife Jennifer accompanied him on nights such as this.

'No, Josie's got a fever.' Alex explained things a little better for Anton. 'Josie's our youngest child. You haven't yet met my wife Jennifer, have you?'

'Your wife?' Anton said. 'I have heard a lot of nice things.'

Perhaps because Louise was close to PhD level in Anton's facial features, Anton's accent, Anton's words, oh, just everything Anton, she frowned just a little at his slightly vague response. Still, she didn't dwell on it for long because he simply looked fantastic in an evening suit. Her eyes swept his body, taking in his long legs, his very long black leather shoes and then, when her mind darted to rude places, she looked up. His olive complexion was accentuated by the white of his shirt and he was just so austere that it made her want to jump onto his lap and whisper in his ear all the things she wanted him to do to her for Christmas.

Oh, a relationship might not be on the agenda but so pointed was his dismissal of her tonight that they were clearly both thinking sex.

'Is that holly on your stockings?' Rory asked, and everyone looked down to examine Louise's long legs.

Everyone, that was, but Anton.

'Yes, I got them free after that shoot I did a couple of months ago,' Louise said. 'I've been dying to wear them ever since. Got to get into the Christmas spirit. Speaking of which, does anyone want a drink?'

'No, thank you,' Alex said.

'I'll have a tomato juice,' Emily sighed. 'A virgin bloody Mary.'

'Hugh?' Louise asked.

'I'd love an eggnog.'

'Yay!' Louise said. 'Anton?'

'No, thank you.'

'Are you sure?' Louise said. 'I thought I owed you one.'

'I'm fine,' he responded, barely looking at her. 'I think Saffarella is getting me a drink. Here she is…'

Here she was, indeed!

Rippling black hair, chocolate-brown eyes, a figure to die for, and she was so seriously stunning that she actually made Louise feel drab, especially when her thick Italian accent purred around every name as introductions were made.

'Em-il-ee, Loo-ease.'

On sight the two women bristled.

It was like two cats meeting in the back yard and Louise almost felt her tail bush up as they both smiled and nodded.

'Sorry, I didn't catch your name,' Louise said.

Saffarella was already getting on her nerves.

'Saffarella,' she repeated in her beautiful, treacle voice, and then was kind enough to give Louise a further explanation. 'Like Cinderella.'

With a staph infection attached, Louise thought, but thankfully Rory knew Louise's humour and decided to move her on quickly!

'I'll come and help you with the drinks.' Rory took Louise's arm and they both walked over to the bar.

'Good God!' Louise said the second they were out of earshot.

'No wonder you've got nowhere with him.' Rory laughed. 'She's stunning.'

'Oh!' Louise was seriously rattled, she was far too used to being the best-looking woman in the room. 'What sort of name is Saffarella? Well, there goes my fun for the night. I thought I'd at least get a dance with him. I don't have anyone to fancy any more,' Louise sighed. 'And I'm going to look like a wallflower.'

'Don't worry, Louise.' Rory smiled. 'I'll dance with you.'

'You have to now,' Louise said. 'I'm not having him seeing me sitting on my own. I was so positive that he liked me.'

Louise returned with Emily's virgin bloody Mary but then she caught sight of Connor and Miriam and excused herself and headed over for a good old catch up with ex-colleagues. It was actually a good, if not brilliant night—Rory was as good as his word and midway through proceedings he did dance with her.

Rory was lovely, possibly one of the nicest men that a woman could know.

In fact, Rory was the last really nice boyfriend that Louise had had.

There was absolutely nothing going on between them. Their parting, three years ago, had been an amicable one. Though most people lied when they said that, in Rory and Louise's case it had been true. Just a few weeks into their relationship Louise had, while undergoing what she'd thought were basic investigations for her erratic menstrual cycle, received the confronting news that, when the time came, she might not fall pregnant very easily.

It hadn't been a complete bombshell, Louise had known things hadn't been right, but when it had finally dropped Louise had been inconsolable. Rory had put his hands up in the end and had said that, as much as he liked her, there wasn't enough there to be talking baby, baby, baby every day of the week.

They were far better as exes than as a couple.

'How's Christmas behaving?' Rory asked, as they danced.

'Much better this time.'

'You look so much happier.'

'I'm sorry we stopped being friends,' Louise said.

'We never stopped being friends,' Rory said. 'Well, I didn't. I was so worried when you were with him.'

'I know,' Louise said. 'Thanks for being there for me.' She gave him a smile. 'I might have some happy news soon.'

'What are you up to, Louise?'

'I'm going to be trying for a baby,' Louise admitted, 'by myself.'

'How did I not guess that?' Rory smiled.

'Please don't ask me if I've thought about it.'

'I wouldn't. I know that it's all you think about.'

'It's got worse since I've gone back to midwifery,' Louise said. 'My fallopian tubes want to reach out and steal all the little babies.'

'It might end any chance of things between you and Anton,' Rory said gently, but Louise just shrugged.

'He's the last person I'd go out with, he's way too controlling and moody for my taste. I just wanted a loan of that body for a night or two.' Louise smiled. 'Nope...' She had made up her mind. In the three years since she and Rory had broken up she had made some poor choices when it came to men. The news that she might have issues getting pregnant had seriously rocked Louise's world, leaving her a touch vulnerable and exposed. She was so much stronger now, though her desire to become a mother had not diminished an inch. 'I want a baby far more than I want another failed relationship.'

'Fair enough.'

They danced on, Louise with her mind on Anton. She was seriously annoyed at the sight of them laughing and talking as they danced and the way Saffarella ran her hands through his hair and over his bum had Louise burn with jealousy. Worse, though, was the way Anton laughed a deep laugh at something she must have said.

'I don't think I've ever seen him laugh till now, and I know that I'm funnier than her,' Louise grumbled. 'God, why does she have to be so, so beautiful? What did he introduce her as?'

'Saffarella.'

'Did he say girlfriend when he introduced her?' Louise pushed. 'Or my wife...?' She was clutching at straws as she remembered that his sister was a model. 'It's not his sister, is it?'

'If it's his sister then we should consider calling the police!' Rory said. 'Sorry, Louise, they're on together.'

But then a little while later came the good news!

She and Rory were enjoying another dance, imagining things that could never happen to John Lennon's 'Imagine'. Louise was thinking of Anton while Rory was thinking of a woman who couldn't be here tonight. He glanced up and saw that Anton was watching them, and then Anton looked over again.

'Anton keeps looking over,' Rory whispered in Louise's ear.

'Really?'

'He does,' Rory said. 'I don't think he likes me any more—in fact, I'd say from the look I just got he wants to take me out the back and knock my lights out.'

'Seriously?' Louise was delighted at the turn of events.

'Well, not quite that much, but I think you may be be right, Louise, Anton does like you.'

'I told you that he did. Is he still looking?'

'He's trying not to.'

'You have to kiss me,' Louise said.

'No.'

'Please.' Louise was insistent. 'Just one long one—it will serve him bloody right for trying to make me jealous. Come on, Rory,' she said when, instead of kissing her, he still shook his head. 'It's not like we never have before and I do it all the time when I'm modelling. It doesn't mean anything.'

'No,' Rory said.

'I got off with you a couple of years ago when Gina got drunk and was making a play for you!' Louise reminded him.

Gina was an anaesthetist who had had a drink and

drug problem and had gone into treatment a few months ago. A couple of years back Rory had been trying to avoid Gina at a Christmas party. Gina had tended to make blatant plays for him when drunk, so he and Louise had had a kiss and pretended to leave together.

'Come on, Rory.'

'No,' he said, and then he rolled his eyes and reluctantly admitted the reason why not. 'I like someone.'

'Who?' Louise's curiosity was instant.

'Just someone.'

'Is she here?'

'No,' Rory said. 'But I don't want it getting back to her that I got off with my ex.'

'Do I know her?'

'Leave it, Louise,' Rory said. 'Please.'

It really was turning out to be the most frustrating night! First Anton and Saffarella, now Rory with his secret.

Hugh and Emily watched the action from the safety of the tables, trying to work out just what was going on.

'Anton is holding Saffarella like a police riot shield,' Hugh observed, but Emily laughed just a little too late.

'Are you okay?' Hugh checked, looking at his wife, who, all of a sudden, was unusually quiet.

'I'm a bit tired,' Emily admitted.

'Do you want to go home?' Hugh checked, and Emily nodded. 'But I promised Louise a lift.'

'She'll be fine,' Hugh said, standing as Louise and Rory made their way over from the dance floor. 'We're going to go,' Hugh said. 'Emily's a bit tired.'

'Emily?' Louise frowned as she looked at her friend. 'Are you okay?'

'Can I not just be tired?' Emily snapped, and then corrected herself. 'Sorry, Louise. Look, I know that I said I'd give you a lift—'

'Don't be daft,' Louise interrupted. 'Go home to bed.'

'I'll see Louise home,' Rory said, and Hugh gave a nod of thanks.

They said their goodnights but as Hugh and Emily walked off, Rory could see the concern on Louise's face.

'Louise!' Rory knew what she was thinking and dismissed it. 'Emily's fine. It isn't any wonder that she's feeling tired. She's six months pregnant and working. Theatre was really busy today...'

'I guess, but...' Louise didn't know what to say. Rory didn't really get her intuition where pregnant women were concerned. She wasn't about to explain it to him again but he'd already guessed what she was thinking.

'Not your witch thing again?' Rory sighed.

'Midwives know.' Louise nodded. 'I'm honestly worried.'

'Come on, I'll get you a drink,' Rory said. 'You can have two eggnogs.' But Louise shook her head. 'I just want to go home,' she admitted. 'You stay, I can get a taxi.'

'Don't be daft,' Rory said, and, not thinking, he put his arm around her and they headed out, followed by the very disapproving eyes of Anton.

Rory dropped her home and, though tired, Louise couldn't sleep. She looked at the crib, still wrapped in Cellophane, that she had hidden in her room, in case Emily dropped round. It was a present Louise had bought. It was stunning and better still it had been on sale. Louise had chosen not to say anything to Emily, knowing how superstitious first-time mums were about not getting anything in advance.

Emily had already been through an appendectomy at six weeks' gestation, as well as marrying Hugh and sorting out stuff with her difficult family. She was due to finish working in the New Year and finally relax and enjoy the last few weeks of pregnancy.

Louise lay there fretting, trying to tell herself that this time she was wrong.

It was very hard to understand let alone explain it but Emily had had that *look* that Louise knew too well.

Please, no!

It really was too soon.

CHAPTER FOUR

ANTON WAS RARELY uncomfortable with women.

Even the most beautiful ones.

He and Saffarella went back a long way, in a very loose way. They had met through his sister a couple of years ago and saw each other now and then. He had known that she would be in London over Christmas and Saffarella had, in fact, been the date he had planned to take to the maternity Christmas evening.

'Where are we going?' Saffarella frowned, because she clearly thought they were going back to his apartment but instead they had turned the opposite way.

'I thought I might take you back to the hotel,' Anton said.

'And are you coming in?' Saffarella asked, and gave a slightly derisive snort at Anton's lack of response. 'I guess that means, no, you're not.'

'It's been a long day…' Anton attempted, but Saffarella knew very well the terms of their friendship and it was *this* part of the night that she had been most looking forward to and she argued her case in loud Italian.

'Don't give me that, Anton. Since when have you ever been too tired? I saw you looking at that blonde tart…'

'Hey!' Anton warned, but his instant defence of Louise, combined with the fact that they both knew just who he was referring to, confirmed that Anton's mind had been elsewhere tonight. Saffarella chose to twist the knife as they pulled into the hotel. 'I doubt that she's being dropped off home by that Rory. They couldn't even wait for the night to finish to get out of the place.' When the doorman opened the door for her Saffarella got out of the car. 'Don't you ever do that to me again.' She didn't wait for the doorman, instead slamming the door closed.

Anton copped it because he knew that he deserved it.

His intention had never been to use Saffarella, they were actually good together. Or had been. Occasionally.

Anton had never, till now, properly considered just how attracted he really was to Louise. Oh, she was the reason he had called Saffarella and asked if she was free tonight, and Saffarella had certainly used him in the same way at times.

But it wasn't just the ache of his physical attraction to Louise that was the problem. He liked her. A lot. He liked her humour, her flirting, the way she just openly declared whatever was on her mind, not that he'd ever tell her that.

But knowing she was on with Rory, knowing he had taken her home, meant that Anton just wanted to be alone tonight to sulk.

It's your own fault, Anton, he said to himself as he drove home.

He should have asked Louise out months ago but then he reminded himself of the reason he hadn't, couldn't, wouldn't be getting involved with anyone from work ever again.

Approaching four years ago, Christmas Day had suddenly turned into a living nightmare. Telling parents on

Christmas Day that their newborn baby was going to die was hell at the best of times.

But at the worst of times, telling parents, while knowing that the death could have been avoided, was a hell which Anton could not yet escape from and he returned to the nightmare time and again.

The shouts and the accusations from Alberto's father, Anton could still hear some nights before going to sleep.

The coroner's report had pointed to a string of communication errors but found that it had been no one person's fault in particular. Anton could recite it off by heart, because he had gone over and over and over it, trying to see what he could have done differently.

But the year in the between the death and the coroner's report had been one Anton could rarely stand to recall.

He took his foot off the brake as he realised he was speeding and pulled over for a moment because he could not safely think about that time and drive.

His relationship hadn't survived either. Dahnya, his girlfriend at the time, had been one of the midwives on duty that Christmas morning and when she hadn't called him, the continual excuses she had made instead of accepting her part in the matter, had proved far too much for them.

Friends and colleagues had all been injected with the poison of gossip. Everyone had raced to cover their backs by stabbing others in theirs and the once close, supportive unit he had been a part of had turned into a war zone.

Anton had been angry too.

Furious.

He had raged when he had seen that information had not been passed on to him. Information that would have meant he would have come to see and then got the labouring mother into Theatre far sooner than he had.

The magic had gone from obstetrics and even before the coroner's findings had been in, Anton had moved into reproductive endocrinology, immersing himself in it, honing his skills, concentrating on the maths and conundrum of infertility. It had absorbed him and he had enjoyed it, especially the good times—when a woman who had thought she never would get pregnant finally did, and yet more and more he had missed obstetrics.

To go back to it, Anton had known he would need a completely fresh start, for he no longer trusted his old colleagues. He had come to London and really had done his best to put things behind him.

It was not so easy, though, and he was aware that he tended to take over. He sat there and thought about his first emergency Caesarean at The Royal. Louise just so brisk and efficient and completely in sync with him as they'd fought to get the deteriorating baby out.

He had slept more easily that night.

That hurdle he had passed and perhaps things would have got better. Perhaps he might have started to hand over the reins to skilled hands a touch further had Gina not rear-ended him in the hospital car park.

Anton had got out, taken one look at her, parked her car, pocketed the keys and then driven her home.

Twenty minutes later he'd reported her to the chief of Anaesthetics and Anton had been hyper-vigilant ever since then.

Anton looked down the street at the Christmas lights but they offered no reprieve; instead, they made it worse. He loathed Christmas. Alberto, the baby, had missed out on far too many.

Yep, Anton reminded himself as he drove home and then walked into his apartment, which had not a single shred of tinsel or a decoration on display, there was a very good reason not to get involved with Louise or anyone at work.

He took out his work phone and called the ward to check on a couple of patients, glad to hear that all was quiet tonight.

Anton poured a drink and pulled out his other phone, read an angry text from Saffarella, telling him he should find someone else for the maternity night out, followed by a few insults that Anton knew she expected a response to.

He was too tired for a row and too disengaged for an exchange of texts that might end up in bed.

Instead, he picked up his work phone and scrolled through some texts. All the staff knew they could contact him and with texting often it was easy just to send some obs through or say you were on your way.

He scrolled through and looked at a couple of Louise's messages.

BP 140/60—and yes, Santa, before you ask, I've read your list and I've checked it twice—it's still 140/60. From your little helper

He'd had no idea what that little gem had meant until he'd been in a department store, with annoying music grating in his ears, and a song had come on and he'd burst out laughing there and then.

He had realised then how lame his response at the time had been.

Call me if it goes up again.

Her response:

Bah, humbug!

Followed by another text.

Yes, Anton, I do know.

He must, Anton thought, find out what 'bah, hum-bug' meant.

Then he read another text from a couple of months ago that made him smile. But not at her humour, more at how spot-on she had been.

I know it is your weekend off, sorry, but you did say to text with any concerns with any of your patients. Can you happen to be passing by?

Anton had *happened* to be passing by half an hour later and had found Louise sitting on the bed, chatting with the usually sombre Mrs Calini, who was in an un-usually elated mood.

'Oh, here's Anton.' Louise had beamed as he had stopped by the bed for a *chat*.

'Anton!' Mrs Calini had started talking in rapid Ital-ian, saying how gorgeous her baby was, just how very, very beautiful he was. Yes, there was nothing specific but Anton had been on this journey with his patient and Louise was right, this was most irregular.

Twelve hours and a lot of investigations later, Mrs Calini had moved from elation to paranoia—loudly de-claring that all the other mothers were jealous and likely to steal her beautiful baby. She had been taken up to the psych ward and her infant had remained on Maternity.

Two weeks later the baby had been reunited with Mrs Calini on the psychiatric mother and baby unit and just a month ago they had gone home well.

Anton looked up 'bah, humbug' and soon found out she wasn't talking about odd-looking black and white mints when she used that term.

He read a little bit about Scrooge and how he despised Christmas and started to smile.

Oh, Louise.

God, but he was tempted to text her now, by accident, of course. In his contacts Louise was there next to 'Labour Ward' after all.

He loathed that she was with Rory but, then again, she had every right to be happy. He'd had his chances over the months and had declined them. So Anton decided against an accidental text to Louise, surprised that he had even considered sending one.

He wasn't usually into games.

He just didn't like that the games had now ended with Louise.

Louise checked her phone the second she awoke, just in case Emily had called or texted her and she'd missed it, but, no, there was nothing.

It had been a very restless night's sleep and it wasn't even five. Louise lay in the dark, wishing she could go back to sleep while knowing it was hopeless.

Instead, she got up and made a big mug of tea and took that back to bed.

Bloody Anton, Louise thought, a little embarrassed at

her blatant flirting when she now knew he had the stunning Saffarella to go home to.

Had it all been one-sided?

Louise didn't think so but she gave up torturing herself with it. Anton had always been unavailable to her, even if just emotionally.

After a quick shower Louise blasted her hair with the hairdryer, and as a public service to everyone put some rouge on very pale cheeks then wiped it off because it made her look like a clown.

She took her vitamins and iron and then decided to cheer herself up by wearing the *best* underwear in the world to work today. She had been saving it for the maternity Christmas party but instead she decided to debut it today. It was from the Mistletoe range, the lace dotted with leaves of green and embroidered silk cream berries topped with a pretty red bow—and that was just the panties. The bra was empress line and almost gave her a cleavage, and she loved the little red bow in the middle.

It was far too glamorous for work but, then, Louise's underwear was always far too glamorous for work.

Instead of having another cup of tea and watching the news, Louise decided to simply go in early and hopefully put her mind at rest by not finding Emily there.

She lived close enough to walk to work. It was very cold so she draped on scarves and walked through the dark and damp morning. It was lovely to step into the maternity unit, which was always nice and warm.

There was Anton sitting sulking at the desk, writing up notes amidst the Naughty Baby Club—comprising all the little ones that had been brought up to the desk to hopefully give their mothers a couple of hours' sleep.

Louise read through the admission board, checking for Emily's name and letting out a breath of relief when she saw that it wasn't there.

'How come you're in early?' she asked Anton, wondering if he was waiting for Emily.

'I couldn't sleep,' Anton said, 'so I thought I'd catch up on some notes.'

They were both sulking, both jealous that the other had had a better night than they'd had.

'I'm going to make some tea,' Louise said. 'Would you like some?'

'Please.' Anton nodded.

'Evie?' Louise asked, and got a shake of the head from the night nurse. 'Tara?'

'No, thanks, we've just had one.'

Louise changed into her scrubs then headed to the kitchen and made herself a nice one, and this time Anton got a hospital teabag.

He knew he was in her bad books with one sip of his tea.

Well, she was in his bad books too.

'You and Rory left very suddenly,' Anton commented. 'I didn't realise that the two of you…'

'We're not on together,' Louise said. 'Well, we were three years ago but we broke up after a few weeks. We're just good friends now.'

'Oh.'

'Rory took me home early last night because I'm worried about Emily,' Louise admitted. She was too concerned about her friend to play games. 'She hasn't called you, has she? You're not here, waiting for her to come in?'

'No.' Anton frowned. 'Why are you worried? She seemed fine last night.'

'She was at first but then she was suddenly tired and went home. Rory said that she'd had a big day at work but…'

'Tell me.'

'She snapped at me and she had that look,' Louise said. 'You know the one…'

'Yep,' Anton said, because, unlike Rory, he did know what Louise meant and he took her concerns about Emily seriously.

'How many weeks is she now?'

'Twenty-seven,' Louise said.

'And how many days…?' Anton asked, pulling Emily's notes up on his computer. 'No, she's twenty-eight weeks today.' Anton read through his notes. 'I saw her last week and all was fine. The pregnancy has progressed normally, just the appendectomy at six weeks.'

'Could that cause problems now?' Louise asked.

'I would have expected any problems from surgery to surface much earlier than this,' Anton said, and he gave Louise a thin smile. 'Maybe she *was* just tired…'

'I'll ring Theatre later and find out what shift she's on,' Louise said. 'In fact, I'll do it now.'

She got put through and was told that Emily was on a late shift today.

'Maybe I am just worrying about nothing,' Louise said.

'Let us hope so.'

A baby was waking up and Tara, a night nurse, was just dashing off to do the morning obs.

'I'll get him.'

Louise picked up the little one and snuggled him in. 'God, I love that smell,' Louise said, inhaling the scent of the baby's hair, then she looked over at Anton.

'Did Saffron have a good night?'

She watched his lips move into a wry smile.

'Not really,' Anton said, and then added, 'And her name is Saffarella.'

'Oh, sorry,' Louise said. 'I got mixed up. Saffron's the one you put in your rice to make it go yellow, isn't it?' Louise corrected herself. 'Expensive stuff, costs a fortune and you only get a tiny—'

'Louise,' Anton warned, 'I don't know quite where you're going there but, please, don't be a bitch.'

'I can't help myself, Anton,' Louise swiftly retorted. 'If you get off with another woman in front of me then you'll see my bitchy side.'

Anton actually grinned; she was so open that she fancied him, so relentless, so *aaagggh*, he thought as he sat there.

'I didn't *get off*, as you say, with Saffarella. We danced.'

'Please,' Louise scoffed.

Maybe he wanted to share the relief he had felt when he had just heard that she and Rory were only friends but, for whatever reason, he put her out of her misery too.

'I took Saffarella back to the hotel she is staying at last night.'

He gave her an inch and, yep, Louise took a mile.

'Really!' Louise gave a delighted grin and covered the baby's ears. 'So you didn't—'

'Louise!'

'The baby can't hear, I've covered his ears. So you and she didn't…?'

'No, we didn't.'

'Did she sulk?' Louise asked with glee, and he grimaced a touch at the memory of the car door slamming.

'Yes.'

'Oh, poor Saffron, I mean Saffarella—now that I know you and she didn't do anything, I can like her.'

They both smiled, though it was with a touch of regret because last night could have been such a nicer night.

'Thanks so much,' Tara said, coming over and looking at the baby. 'He's asleep now, Louise. You can put him back in his isolette.'

'But I don't want to,' Louise said, looking down at the sleeping baby. He was all curled up in her arms, his knees were up and his ankles crossed as if he were still in the womb. His little feet were poking out of the baby blanket and Louise was stroking them.

'They're like kittens' paws,' Louise said, watching his teeny toes curl.

'You are so seriously clucky,' Tara said.

'Oh, I'm more than clucky,' Louise admitted. 'I keep going over to the nativity scene just to pick up Baby Jesus. I have to have one.'

'It will ruin your lingerie career,' Tara warned, but Louise just laughed.

'I'm sure pregnant women can and do wear fabulously sexy underwear—in fact, my agent's going to speak to a couple of companies to see what sort of work they might have for me if I get pregnant.'

'Surely you're missing something if you want a baby...' Tara said, referring to Louise's lack of a love life, but now she had told her mum, now she'd told Rory and Emily knew too, Louise had decided it was time to start to let the world know.

'No, I'm not missing anything.' Louise smiled. 'In fact, I might have to pay a visit to Anton.'

She was referring to the fact she'd found out he was

a reproductive specialist too and he gave a wry smile at the ease of her double entendre.

'I have an excellent record,' Anton said.

'So I've heard.' Louise smirked.

Then Anton stopped the joking around and went to get back to his notes. 'You don't need to be rushing. How old are you?'

'Thirty next year!' Louise sighed.

'Plenty of time. You don't have to be thinking about it yet,' Anton said, but it turned out that the ditzy Louise ran deep.

'I think about it a lot,' she admitted. 'In all seriousness, Anton,' she continued, as Tara headed off to do more obs, 'I'm actually confused by the whole thing. I recently saw my GP but she just told me to come off the Pill for a few months.'

Anton frowned, fighting the urge to step in while not wanting to get involved with this aspect of Louise, so he was a little brusque in response. 'The fertility centre at this hospital runs an information night for single women,' Anton offered. 'Your questions would be best answered there.'

'I know they do,' Louise said. 'I've booked in for the next one but it's not till February. That's ages away.'

'It will be here before you know it. As I said, there's no rush.'

'There might be, though,' Louise said, and told him the truth. 'A few years ago I found out I'd probably have problems getting pregnant. That's why I'm off the Pill and trying to sort out my cycle. I know quite a bit but even I'm confused.'

'You need a specialist. Perhaps see an ob/gyn and have him answer your questions, but I would think, from the little you've told me, that you would be referred to a fertility specialist. Certainly, if you are considering pregnancy, you need to get some base bloods down and an ultrasound.'

'Can I come and see you?' Louise was completely serious now. 'Make an appointment, I mean, and then if I did get pregnant…'

'There is a long wait to see me.'

'Even for colleagues?' Louise cheekily checked.

'Especially for colleagues,' Anton said, *really* not liking the way this conversation was going.

'What about privately?' Louise asked, and she was serious about that because all her money from modelling was going into her baby fund.

'Louise.' Anton was even brusquer now. 'Why would you want to be a single mother?'

'I'm sure that's not the first thing you ask your patients when they come to see you,' Louise scolded. 'I don't think that's very PC.'

'But you're not my patient,' Anton pointed out, 'so I don't have to watch what I say. Why would you want to be a single mother?'

'How do you know I'm not in a relationship?' Louise said.

'You just told me that you and Rory were only friends.'

'Hah, but I could have an infertile partner at home.'

'Do you?'

'Lorenzo,' Louise teased, kicking him gently with her foot. 'And he's very upset that he can't give me babies.'

He knew she was joking, though he refused to smile, and he wanted to capture her foot as she prattled on.

'Or,' Louise continued, 'I might be a lesbian in a very happy relationship and we've decided that we want to have a baby together.' She loved how his lips twitched as she continued. 'I'm the girly one!'

'You're not a very good lesbian,' Anton said, 'given the way that you flirt with me.'

'Ha-ha.' Louise laughed. 'Seriously, Anton—' and she was '—about seeing you privately. You're right, I need to get an ultrasound and some bloods done. I'm going in circles on my own—fertility drugs, artificial insemination or IVF. I'm worried about twins or triplets or even more...' Louise truly was. 'I want someone who knows what they are doing.'

'Of course you do,' Anton agreed. 'If you want, I can recommend someone to you. Richard here is excellent, I can speak with him and give you a referral and get you seen quickly—' Anton started, but Louise interrupted him.

'Why would I see someone else when we both know you're the best?' she pushed. 'Look, I know we mess around...'

'*You* mess around,' Anton corrected.

'Only at work.'

Louise *was* serious, Anton realised. She had that look in her eyes that Anton recognised on women who came to his office. It was a look that said she was determined to get pregnant, so he had no real choice now but to be honest.

No, this conversation wasn't going well for him at all.

'It would be unethical for me to see you,' Anton said, and stood.

'Unethical?' Louise frowned. 'What, because we work together?'

'Professionally unethical,' Anton said, and rolled his

eyes as a delighted smile spread across her face. 'I can't say it any clearer than that.'

Ooooh!

She hugged the baby as Anton walked off.

'He *has* got the hots for me,' Louise whispered to the baby, and then let out a loud wolf whistle to Anton's departing back.

No, Anton did not turn around but he did smile.

CHAPTER FIVE

'I NEED SOMEONE to buddy this,' Beth called, and Louise went over to the nurses' station to look at the CTG tracing of one of Beth's patients.

The policy at The Royal was that only two experienced midwives could sign off on a tracing and so a buddy system was in place.

It was way more than a cursory look Louise gave to the tracing. They discussed it for a few moments, going over the recordings of the contractions and foetal heart rate before Louise signed off.

It was a busy morning and it sped by. At lunchtime, as Anton walked into the staffroom, had he had sunglasses then he would have put them on. There was a silver Christmas tree by the television and it was dressed in silver balls. There were silver stars hanging from the ceiling—really, there was silver everything hanging from every available space.

'Have you been at the tinsel again?' Anton said to Louise, who was eating a tuna salad.

'I have. I just can't help myself. I might have to go and speak with someone about my little tinsel problem— though I took up your suggestion and went with a theme in here!'

'I cannot guess what it was.'

Anton chose to sit well away from her and, for something to do, rather than listen to all the incessant gossip, he picked up a magazine.

Oh, no!

There she was and Louise was right—the underwear was divine.

'Christmas Holly' said the title and there a stunning Louise was in the stockings she'd had on last night but now he got the full effect—bra, stockings and suspenders. Anton turned the page to the Mistletoe range, and the shots, though very lovely and very tasteful, were so sexy that Anton felt his body responding, like some sad old man reading a porn magazine, and he hastily turned to the problem page, just not in time.

Oh, God, he was thinking about swiping the magazine, especially when he glimpsed the Holly and the Ivy shots.

'Ooooh.' Louise looked over and saw what he was reading. 'I'm in that one.' She plucked it from his hands and knelt at the coffee table and turned to the section in the magazine as a little crowd gathered around.

She was so unabashed by it, just totally at ease with her body and its functions in a way that sort of fascinated Anton.

'You've got a cleavage,' Beth said, admiring the shot.

'I know,' Louise said. 'Gorgeous, isn't it?'

'But how?'

Anton closed his eyes. These were women who spent most of their days dealing with breasts and vaginas and they chatted with absolute ease about such things, an ease Anton usually had too, just not when Miss Louise was around.

'Well,' Louise said as Anton stared at the news, 'they

take what little I have and sort of squeeze it together and then tape it—there's a lot of scaffolding under that bra,' Louise explained. 'Then they pad the empty part and then they edit out my nipples.'

'Wow!'

'I wish they *were* real,' Louise sighed.

'Would you ever get them done?' Beth asked.

'No,' Louise said, as Anton intently watched the weather report. 'I did think about it one time but, no, I'll stick with what I've been given, which admittedly isn't much. Hopefully they'll be *massive* when I get pregnant and then breastfeed.'

'Anton!' Brenda popped her head in to save the day. 'I've got the husband of one of your patients on the phone. Twenty-eight weeks, back pain…'

'Who?'

'Emily Linton.'

'Merda.' Anton cursed under his breath and then took the phone while trying to ignore Louise, who was now standing over him as Hugh brought him up to speed.

'Okay,' Anton said, as Louise hopped on the spot. 'I'll come down now and meet you at the maternity entrance.'

'Back pain, some contractions,' Anton said. 'Her waters are intact…' As Louise went to follow him out Anton shook his head. 'Maybe Emily needs someone who is not close to her,' Anton said.

'Maybe she needs someone who *is* close to her,' Louise retorted. 'You're not getting rid of me.'

Anton nodded.

'Brenda, can you let the paediatricians know?'

'Of course.'

They stood waiting for the car and Anton looked over. Louise was shivering in the weak winter sun and her teeth were chattering. 'Emily isn't the most straightforward person,' Louise said. 'She acts like she doesn't care when, really, she does.'

Anton nodded and watched as, even though she was terrified for her friend, Louise's lips spread into a wide smile as the car pulled up.

'Come on, trouble,' Louise said, helping her friend into a wheelchair.

'I'm sure it's nothing,' Emily said, as Louise gave directions.

'Hugh, go and park the car and meet us there.'

Once Hugh was out of earshot, Emily let out a little of her fear. 'It's way too soon,' Emily said. Her expression was grim but there were no tears.

'Let's just see where we are,' Anton said.

Though Anton would do his level best to make sure that the pregnancy remained intact, Emily was taken straight through to the delivery ward, just in case.

'I had a bit of a backache last night,' Emily admitted. 'At first I thought it was from standing for so long yesterday. Then, late this morning, I thought I was getting Braxton-Hicks…'

Louise was putting on a foetal monitor as Anton put in an IV line and took some bloods, and then, as Hugh arrived, Anton looked at the tracing. 'The baby is looking very content,' Anton said, and then he put a hand on Emily's stomach as the monitor showed another contraction starting.

'I'm only getting them occasionally,' Emily said.

But sometimes you only needed a few with a baby this small.

'Emily,' Anton said when the contraction had passed, 'I am going to examine you and see where we are.'

But Emily kept panicking, possibly because she didn't *want* to know where they were, and nothing Hugh or Anton might say would reassure her.

'I need you to try and relax,' Anton said.

'Oh, it's so easy for them to say that when they come at you with a gloved hand!' Louise chimed in, and Anton conceded Louise was right to be there because Emily let out a little laugh and she did relax just a touch.

'How long are you here for?' Emily asked Louise, because even though Louise had yesterday told her she was on an early today, clearly such conversations were the last thing on Emily's mind at the moment and it was obvious that she wanted her friend to be here.

'I've just come on duty,' Louise lied, 'so I'm afraid that you're stuck with me for hours yet.'

Anton examined Emily and Louise passed him a sterile speculum and he took some swabs to check for amniotic fluid and also some swabs to check for any infection.

'You are in pre-term labour,' Anton said. 'You have some funnelling,' Anton explained further. 'Your cervix is a little dilated but if you think of a funnel…' he showed the shape with his hands '…your cervix is opening from the top but we are going to give you medication that will hopefully be able to, if not halt things, at least delay them.' He gave his orders to Louise and she started to prepare the drugs Anton had chosen. 'This should taper off the contractions,' he said as he hooked up the IV, 'and these steroids will help the baby's lungs mature in case it decides to be born. You shall get another dose of these in twenty-four hours.'

Louise did everything she could to keep the atmosphere nice and calm but it was all very busy. The paediatricians came down and spoke with Anton. NICU was notified that there might be an imminent admission. Anton did an ultrasound and everything on there looked fine. Though the contractions were occasionally still coming, they started to weaken, though Emily had a lot of pain in her back, which was a considerable concern.

'Content,' Anton said again, but this time to the screen. 'Stay in there, little one.'

'And if it doesn't?' Emily asked.

'Then we have everything on hand to deal with that if your baby is born,' Anton said. 'But for now things are settling and what I need for you to do is to lie there and rest.'

'I will,' Emily said. 'First, though, I need a wee.'

'I'll get you a bedpan!' Louise said.

'Please no.'

'I'm afraid so.' Louise smiled. 'Anton's rules.'

Anton smiled as he explained his rules. 'Many say that it makes no difference. If the baby is going to be born then it shall be. Call me old-fashioned but I still prefer that you have complete bed rest, perhaps the occasional shower...'

'Fine.' Emily nodded, perhaps for the first time realising that she was going to be there for a while.

Hugh and Anton waited outside as much laughter came from the room, mainly from Louise, but Emily actually joined in too as they attempted to get a sterile specimen and also to check for a urinary tract infection.

Bedpans were not the easiest things to sit on.

But then Emily stopped laughing. 'Louise, I'm scared if I wee it will come out.'

'You have to wee, Emily,' Louise said, and gave her friend a cuddle. 'And you have to poo and do all those things, but I'm right here.'

It helped to hear that.

'I've got such a bad feeling,' Emily admitted, and Hugh gave a grim smile to Anton as outside they listened to Emily expressing her fears out loud. 'I really do.'

'Okay.' Louise was practical. 'How many women at twenty-eight weeks sit on that bed you're on, having contractions, and say, "I've got a really good feeling"? How many?' Louise asked.

'None.'

'I had a bad feeling last night,' Louise admitted. 'You can ask Anton, you can ask Rory, because I left five minutes after you and I came in early just to look at the board to see if you had been admitted, but I don't have a bad feeling now.'

'Honest?'

'Promise,' Louise said. 'So have a wee.'

'I'm going to give her a sedative,' Anton said to Hugh.

'Won't that relax her uterus?' Hugh checked, and then stopped himself because he trusted Anton.

'I want her to sleep and I want to give her the best chance for those medications to really take hold,' Anton said. 'You saw that her blood pressure was high?'

Hugh nodded—Emily's raised blood pressure could simply be down to anxiety but could also be a sign that she had pre-eclampsia.

'We'll see if there's any protein in her urine,' Anton said. If she did that would be another unwelcome sign that things were not going well.

Louise came out with the bedpan and urine sample, which would be sent to the lab.

'Can you check for protein?' Anton asked.

Louise rolled her eyes at Hugh. 'He thinks that because I'm blonde I'm thick,' she said to a very blond

Hugh, who smiled back. 'Of course I'm going to check for protein!'

'He's blondist,' Hugh joked, but then breathed out in relief when Louise called from the pan room.

'No protein, no blood, no glucose—all normal, just some ketones.'

'She hasn't eaten since last night,' Hugh said, which explained the ketones.

'I've put dextrose up but right now the best thing she can do is to rest.'

It was a very long afternoon and evening.

Louise stayed close by Emily, while Anton delivered two babies but in between checked in on Emily.

At eight, Louise sat and wrote up her notes. It felt strange to be writing about Emily and her baby. She peeled off the latest CTG recording and headed out.

'Can you buddy this?' Louise asked Siobhan, a nurse on labour and delivery this evening.

'Sure.'

They went through the tracing thoroughly, both taking their time and offering opinions before the two midwives signed off.

'It's looking a lot better than before,' Siobhan said. 'Let's hope she keeps improving.'

Around nine-thirty p.m. Anton walked into the womblike atmosphere Louise had created. The curtains were closed and the room was in darkness and there was just the noise of the baby's heartbeat from the CTG. Emily was asleep and so too was Hugh. Louise sat in a rocking chair, her feet up on a stool, reading a magazine with a clip-on light attached to it that she carried in her pocket for such times, while holding Emily's hand. She let go of the magazine to give a thumb's-up to Anton, and then she put her finger to her lips and shushed him as he walked over to look at the monitors—Louise loathed noisy doctors.

All looked good.

Anton nudged his head towards the corridor and Louise stepped outside and they went into the small kitchenette where all the flower vases were stored and spoke for a while.

'She's still got back pain,' Louise said, and Anton nodded.

'We'll keep her in Delivery tonight but, hopefully, if things continue to improve we can get her onto the ward tomorrow morning.'

'Good.'

'You were right,' Anton said. 'There *was* something going on with her last night.' He saw the sparkle of tears in Louise's eyes because, despite positive appearances, Anton knew she was very worried for her friend.

'I'd love to have been wrong.'

'I know.'

'Anton…' Louise spilled what was on her mind. 'I bought a crib for the baby a few days ago.'

'Okay.'

'It was in a sale and I couldn't resist it. I didn't tell Emily in case she thought it bad luck…'

'Louise!' Anton's firm use of her name told her to let that thought go.

She took a breath.

'Louise,' he said again, and she met his eye. 'That's crazy. I've got Mrs Adams in room two, who's forty-one weeks. She's done everything, the nursery is ready…'

'I know, I know.'

'Just put that out of your mind.'

Louise did. She blew it away then but a tear did sneak out because Louise cared so much about Emily and she was also pretty exhausted. 'Why did it have to be now?' she asked.

'I would love to know that answer,' Anton said, and Louise gave a small smile as he continued. 'It would save me many sleepless nights.'

'I wasn't asking a medical question.'

'I know you weren't.'

Anton stood in the small annexe and looked at Louise. Today she had been amazing, though it wasn't just because she was Emily's friend. Every mother got Louise's full attention. It was wrong of him to compare her to Dahnya, Anton realised. It was futile to keep going back to that terrible day.

Louise was too worried about Emily to notice his silence and she rattled on with her fears.

'I know twenty-eight weeks isn't tiny tiny but...'

'It is far too soon,' Anton agreed. 'She's *just* into her third trimester but we'll do all we can to prolong it. It looks like we've just bought her another day and those steroids are in. The night staff have arrived, Evie is on and she is very good.'

Louise nodded. 'I know she is but I'm going to sleep here tonight.'

'Go home,' Anton said, because Louise really did look pale, but she shook her head at his suggestion. 'Louise, you have been here since six.'

'And so have you,' Louise pointed out. 'I didn't think you were on call tonight, Anton, so what's your excuse for being here?'

'I'll be a lot happier by morning. I just want to be close if something occurs.'

'Well, I'm the same. If something happens tonight then I want to be here with Emily.'

'I get that but—Louise, I never thought I'd say this to you, but you look awful.'

It was a rather backhanded compliment but it did make her smile. 'I'll go and lie down soon,' Louise said, and looked over as Hugh came out.

'Is she awake?'

'Yes, they're just doing her obs. Thanks for today,' Hugh said to them both. 'I'm going to text and ring five thousand people now. Emily told her mum and, honestly, it's spread like wildfire…'

'I get it,' Louise said, because she knew about Emily's very complex family and the last thing she needed now was the hordes arriving. 'I've put her down as no visitors.'

'Thanks for that,' Hugh said. 'I'm going to ring for pizza—do you want some?'

'No, thanks.' Louise shook her head and yawned. 'I'm going to go and sleep.'

'Anton?'

'Sounds good.'

Louise handed over to Evie, the night nurse who would be taking care of Emily. 'Promise, promise, promise that you'll come and get me if anything happens.'

'Promise.'

'I'm going to take a pager,' Louise said, 'just in case you're too busy, so if you page him…' she nodded to Anton '…page me too.'

Louise went to the hotbox and took out one of the warm blankets that they covered newly delivered mums in. Brenda would freak if she knew the damage that Louise singlehandedly did to the laundry budget but she was too cold and tired to care about that right now.

'I'll be in the store cupboard if anything happens.'

'Store cupboard?' Anton said.

'Where all the night nurses sleep.' Louise nodded to the end of the corridor. ''Night, guys. 'Night, Hugh. I'll just go and say night to Emily if she's awake.'

She popped in and there was Emily half-awake as Evie fiddled with her IV.

'You've done so well today.' Louise smiled, standing wrapped in her blanket. 'I'm just going to get some shut-eye but I'm just down the hall, though I have a feeling I shan't be needed.'

'Thanks so much for staying,' Emily said.

'Please.' Louise gave her a kiss goodnight on her fore-head. 'Hopefully we'll move you to a room tomorrow. I'm going to have a jiggle with the beds in the morning and give you one of the nice ones.' She spoke then in a loud whisper. 'One of the private ones!'

'You're such a bad girl.' Evie smiled.

'I know.' Louise grinned. 'Sleep!' Louise said to Emily and then stroked her stomach. 'And you, little one, stay in there.'

'Do you know what I'm having?' Emily asked, and Louise just smiled as Emily spoke on. 'Hugh knows and when I said that I didn't want to find out, he said that he wouldn't tell me even if I begged him.'

'Do you want to know?' Louise asked.

'No, yes, no,' Emily admitted. 'But I want to know if you know.'

'I do,' Louise said, and then burst into Abba. '"I do, I do, I do, I do, I do,"' Louise sang, just as Anton and Hugh walked in. 'But I'm not telling. If you want to know you can speak to Anton.'

'She's mad,' Emily said, when Louise had gone but she said it in the nicest way.

'Completely mad,' Anton agreed. 'How are you feeling now?'

'A bit better.'

'Any questions?' Anton checked, but Emily shook her head.

'I think you've answered them all. Presumably you know what I'm having?'

'Of course I do,' Anton said. 'You know you are allowed to change your mind and find out if you want to.'

'I want it to be a surprise.'

'Then a surprise it will be.'

'Are you going home now?' Emily asked, because she had been told he was only here till six and she felt both guilty and relieved when Anton shook his head.

'Stephanie is the on-call obstetrician tonight and she will be keeping an eye on you so that I can get some rest as I am working tomorrow. I am staying here tonight, though, and if anything changes, I have asked her to discuss it with me.'

'Thank you.'

The store cupboard was actually an empty four-bedded ward at the front of the unit and was used to store beds, trolleys, stirrups, birth balls and all that sort of stuff. Louise curled up on one of the beds and lay there with her eyes closed, hoping that they would stay that way till morning.

She was exhausted, she'd barely had any sleep last night, but now that she finally could sleep, Louise simply could not relax. There was that knot of worry about Emily and another knot between her legs when she thought about Anton and the fact that he actually liked her.

In *that* way!

After half an hour spent growing more awake by the minute Louise padded out with her blanket around her.

Anton gave her a smile and she couldn't really remember him smiling like that, unless to a patient. In fact, he didn't smile like *that* to the patients.

'Food should be here soon,' Anton said.

Louise shook her head and instead of waiting for the pizza to arrive she had a bowl of cornflakes in the kitchen. Anton looked up as she returned with a bottle of sparkling water and a heat pack for her cramping stomach and then took two painkillers.

She tossed her now cold blanket into the linen skip and took out a newly warm one.

'If Brenda knew…' Anton warned, because the cost of laundering a blanket was posted on many walls, warning staff to use them sparingly.

'I like to be warm at night,' Louise said, and, no, she hadn't meant it to be provocative but from the look that burnt between them it was.

She headed back to the storeroom but sleep still would not come.

Then she heard the slam of the door. Louise climbed out of the bed to tell whoever it was off for doing that but then a delicious scent reached her nose.

Pizza.

OMG.

She could almost taste the pepperoni.

Louise hadn't said no to Anton because of some diet, she had said no because…

Well.

Because.

No, she did not want to be huddled up at the desk with him—she might, the way she was feeling this moment, very possibly end up licking his face.

God, he was hot.

Her stomach was growling, though, and it was the scent of pizza that was at fault, not her, Louise decided as she smiled and pulled out her phone.

Anton had two phones and one of the numbers she was privy to. It was his work phone and she'd call him on it at times if one of his patients weren't well while he was off duty, or she might text him sometimes for advice.

She wondered if he'd tell her off for using it for something so trivial.

Or if he'd ignore her request, perhaps?

Anton sat eating pizza as Hugh fired off texts to family to let them know that Emily was doing well.

When his work phone buzzed, indicating a text, Anton read it and decided it might be best to ignore it.

For months he had done his best to ignore her yet since he'd see her up that stepladder it had been a futile effort at best.

He did try to ignore it. In fact, he said goodnight to Hugh and then went into the on-call room, grimly determined to sleep.

Then he read her text again and gave up fighting. He went back to the desk, picked up two slices of pizza and headed off to where perhaps he shouldn't.

CHAPTER SIX

'PIZZA MAN!' ANTON said, as he came into the dark room.

'Oh, my, and an authentic Italian one too!' Louise smiled in the dark and sat up and then took out her light from her pocket and shone it up at him. 'And so good looking.'

'You changed your mind about the pizza?'

'I did,' Louise said. 'A bowl of cornflakes wasn't going to cut it tonight.'

'I could have told you that half an hour ago—you need to eat more.'

'I do eat.'

Anton shook his head very slowly. 'With my sister's line of work I know all the tricks, *all* of them,' Anton said. 'Tell me the truth.'

'Okay, I do watch my weight,' Louise admitted, 'a lot! But I am not anorexic.'

'I can see that you're not anorexic but you do seem to live off salad.'

'Ah, so you notice what I eat, Anton, how sweet!' Louise teased, and then she answered him properly. 'I love my modelling work,' Louise said. 'I mean I *love* it and it is my job to present at a certain weight but I don't do the dangerously thin stuff. Yes, for the most part I have to watch what I eat but, in saying that, I eat very well. I'm nearly thirty. I can't believe I'm still working…'

'I can.' Anton smiled.

'Anyway, I've got a huge photo shoot on Christmas Eve,' Louise explained, as she ate warm pizza. 'It's for Valentine's Day and I'm going to pay a small fortune to get dressed up to the nines and have my hair and make-up done so, yes, I'm being careful.' Her slice of pizza was finished and he handed her the other one. 'I'm just not being very careful tonight.'

'If you are looking at trying for a baby…'

'I would never jeopardise that for work, Anton. I'm just eating healthily. What happened this morning is unrelated to that.'

'Good to know.'

He glanced at the stirrups over the bed. 'You really sleep here?'

'Of course,' Louise said, and then she looked to where his gaze fell. 'Do you want me in stirrups, Anton?'

He actually laughed. 'No. It is that I *don't* want you in stirrups that means you can't be my patient.' He explained as best he could. 'Louise, I know I have given mixed messages. Yes, I like you but I never wanted to get involved with someone at work.'

'We're not at work.' Louise smiled a provocative smile. 'Officially we're both off duty.'

'Louise, the thing is—'

'Please, please, don't,' Louise said. 'Please spare me the lecture, because, guess what, I'm the same. The last thing I want now is a full-on relationship, particularly with you.'

Anton frowned in slight surprise. He'd come in having finally given in and deciding that they should perhaps give it a go, only to find out that a relationship with him was far from her mind.

'Why *particularly* not with me?'

'Okay, I think you're as sexy as hell and occasionally funny but I think you'd be very controlling, and that's fine in the bedroom perhaps—'

'I am not controlling,' Anton immediately interrupted.

'Well, I know that I am at work but not when I'm in a relationship.'

'Oh, they all say that.' Louise put on an Italian accent. 'I do not want my woman posing in her underwear...'

'That is the worst Italian accent ever.' He frowned at her opinion of him. 'I happen to think your work is very beautiful.'

'Really?'

'Of course it is.' He was still frowning. 'Have you had trouble in the past—?'

'I have,' Louise said quickly, hurrying over that part of her life, 'and so I keep things on my terms. The only thing I want to focus on right now is myself and becoming a mum. I'm not on a husband shop.'

A flirt, some fun, was all she was prepared to give to a man right now.

Though she had fancied Anton for ages.

Ages.

Pizza done, Louise went into her pocket, peeled off some baby wipes from a small packet she carried and wiped her hands. Then she went into her pockets again and pulled out a breath spray.

'What the hell have you got in those pockets?'

'Many, many things—basically my pockets are designed so that I don't have to get up if I'm comfy.' Louise smiled and settled back on the pillow. 'The breath spay is so that I don't submit a labouring woman to my pizza breath, and,' she added, 'it's also terribly convenient if you want to kiss me goodnight.'

'Louise,' Anton warned. 'We're not going to be skulking around in the shadows.'

'I know,' Louise sighed regretfully. 'How come you left fertility?' She yawned, but was pleased when Anton sat on the edge of the bed.

'I missed obstetrics,' Anton admitted, though he too chose to avoid the dark stuff.

'Is it nice to be back doing it?'

'Some days,' Anton said, 'like yesterday with Hannah's son—that was a really good day. Today…' He thought for a moment. 'Yes, it is still good. Thanks for your help today, you were right to stay—it is good for Emily to have you nearby.'

'You're making me nervous, Anton—you're being too nice.'

Anton smiled and watched as she put her hand under the blanket and turned the hot pack on her stomach.

'Still hurt?'

'Yep.'

He wanted his hand there.

Louise wanted the same thing.

She wanted him to lean forward and Anton actually felt as if her hand were at the back of his head, dragging him down, but it wasn't her hand that was pressuring him, it was want.

'I'm going to go,' Anton said. 'I just wanted to clear the air.'

'It doesn't feel very clear,' Louise said, because it was thick with sexual tension, a tension that had come to a head last night but had had no outlet for either of them.

'You're right, it doesn't,' Anton agreed. 'You are such a flirt, Louise,' he said, his mouth approaching hers.

'I know.' She smiled then asked a question as his lovely mouth approached. 'If you were intending to just pop in to clear the air, why did you brush your teeth before you came in?'

'I was *hoping* to clear the air but you have worn me down.'

They were far from worn down as their mouths finally met. It was supposed to break the tension but instead it upped it as, in the dark, Louise found out how lovely that sulky mouth could be.

The mixture of soft lips and rough stubble had her break on contact.

Anton had decided on one small kiss to chase away a wretched day but small was relative, Anton told himself as he slipped in his tongue and met the caress of hers, for it was still a small kiss if he compared it to the one he really wanted to give.

For Louise, it was bliss. She could not remember a kiss that had been nicer, and her hands moved up to his head and their kiss deepened from intimate to provocative. As he moved to remove her hands and halt things he changed his mind as his thumb grazed her breast. Anton heard the purr and the nudge of her body into his palm, like a cat demanding attention, and so he stroked her through the fabric, until for both of them he had to feel her.

Anton went to lift her top, just to get to her breast, but the heat pack slipped off and she willed his hand to change direction, her tongue urging him on as Anton obliged.

He could feel the ball of tension of her uterus as his

hand slipped down instead of up, stroking her tense stomach as he kissed her more deeply.

Louise lifted her knees to the bliss and the sensation but then she peeled her mouth from his.

'Anton…'

'I know that you do,' he said, not caring a bit. 'What colour underwear?' he asked, as he toyed with the lace.

'Cream and green, with a red bow—it's from the Mistletoe collection.'

She loved his moan in her mouth and the feel of his fingers creeping lower. His warm palm massaged low on her stomach as his finger hit the spot and Louise felt her face become red and hot as she kissed now his neck then his ears. One of his hands was behind her head, supporting it, while beneath the other she succumbed.

The tension hit and his mouth suckled hers as he stroked her through the deepest come of her life and then she felt the bliss abate as her stomach lay soft beneath his palm. Her intimate twitches stilled and Louise lay quiet for a moment.

'Better?' Anton asked.

'Positively sedated.'

She lay in sated bliss, pain free for the first time today, and trying to tell herself it was just the sex she wanted as she moved her hand and stroked his thick erection.

'Poor Anton,' she said.

'There have been way too many poor Antons of late,' Anton said. 'I'm going to go and you're going to sleep and—'

'We never discuss this again.' Louise smiled. 'Got it!'

How was she supposed to sleep after that? Louise thought as Anton made his way out.

It took about forty-seven seconds!

CHAPTER SEVEN

LOUISE AWOKE TO the sound of the domestic's floor polisher in the hallway and the even happier sound of no pager, which meant nothing had happened with Emily and so she padded out to the ward.

'How is she?' Louise asked Evie.

'Very good,' Evie said. 'She's slept mostly through and her back ache has eased and the contractions have stopped.' She looked at Louise, who was yawning. 'Why don't you go home?'

'I'm going to have a shower and then I'll see Emily over to her room before I do just that.'

'Well, the royal suite is empty.' Evie smiled as she used the name they all called it. 'I'll go and set it up.'

'I'll do that when I've had my shower,' Louise said, smiling when she heard Anton's voice.

'Morning, Louise,' Anton said, looking all the more handsome for not having shaven. 'How did you sleep?'

'Oh, I went out like a light,' Louise answered. She headed off to the shower and had to wash with the disinfectant soap used for washing hands. Smelling like a bathroom cleaner commercial, she headed out to set up the room for Emily.

It was hardly a royal suite but it had its own loo and

was more spacious than others and there was a trundle bed if Hugh wanted to stay. Louise checked the oxygen and suction and that there were pads and vomit bowels and suchlike.

Anton checked in on Emily and was very happy with her lack of progress and agreed that she could be moved.

'Every day that you don't go into labour is a good day,' Anton said, as Louise helped her onto the bed. 'For now you are on strict bed rest and that means bedpans.'

'Okay.' Emily nodded. She wasn't going to argue if it meant her baby stayed put. 'I feel much more positive today.' She looked over at Louise. 'You can go home now.'

'I am,' Louise said. 'But you're to text me with anything you want me to bring in for you. I can visit tonight or tomorrow. I'm off for two days now but—'

'I'll text you,' Emily interrupted, because Louise lived by her phone and they texted each other most days anyway.

As they headed out—Anton to start his shift, Louise to commence her days off—he asked if he could have a word with her in his office.

'Sure,' Louise said.

She knew what was coming and immediately she broached it. 'Don't worry, I get that last night was an aberration.' She saw him frown. 'A one-off.'

Anton wasn't so sure. He had no regrets about last night and he looked at the woman standing before him and wanted to get to know her some more, but before he did there was something that he first needed to know.

'This referral, are you sure that now is the right time?'

'Very sure,' Louise said. 'I've been thinking about it for close to a year.'

'Okay…' Anton said, because that alone was enough for him to ensure last night remained an *aberration*, although still he would like to give them a chance. 'Why don't you wait a while? Maybe we can—?'

'Anton, I already have waited a while. I'm twenty-nine years old and for twenty-eight of those years I have wanted a baby. I didn't just dress up my dollies and put them in a pram, Anton, I used to put them up my dress…' Anton smiled as she carried on. 'I'm not brilliant at relationships.'

'Why would you say that?'

'Oh, I've gathered quite a list of the reasons over the years.' Louise started to tick off on her fingers. 'I'm high maintenance, vain, obsessed with having a baby, inappropriate at times… I could go on but you get the drift. And, yes, I am all of those things and shall happily continue to be them. But, while relationships may not be my forte, I do know for a fact that I shall be a brilliant mum. So many women do it themselves these days.'

'Even so…'

'It's not a decision I've come to lightly. I've sat on it for close to a year and so, if I could have that referral, it would be completely brilliant.'

He wrote one out for her there and then. 'I'll let his secretary know this morning. When you call ask to speak to her because Richard is very booked up too.'

'Thank you.'

'Louise…'

'Anton.' She turned round. She did not want to hear now how they might stand a chance, and she did not want to be put off her dream. One of the reasons she was attracted to him perhaps was that he had been so unobtainable and she wanted that to remain the same. 'Don't be such a girl!'

Six feet two of testosterone stood there and smiled as she continued.

'It was fun, there can be more fun, just as long as it's conducted well away from work, but I *am* going ahead with this.'

He said nothing as she stepped out and Louise didn't really want him to. She didn't want to hear that maybe they could give it a go. She had fancied him for ever, since the moment she had first laid eyes on him, and now, when the year she had given herself to come to her decision was almost up, when her dream was in sight, Anton was suddenly interested.

Why couldn't he have left it at sex?

That, Louise could deal with.

It was the relationship part that terrified her.

Louise went and visited her family that morning and told them what was going on with Emily. When she got home Emily texted, asking her to go shopping for some nightwear but that there was no rush. And she added…

Something suitable, Louise!!!

Louise killed a couple of happy hours choosing nightwear for a pregnant, soon-to-be breastfeeding woman, while pretending she was shopping for herself. She did her level best to buy not what she'd like but what she guessed Emily would like, and, finally home, she thought about Anton and what had happened.

Not just their kiss and things, more the revelation that he liked her.

She had always been herself with him. Almost, since the day they had met, she had actually *practised* being herself with him. Anton had no idea just how much he had helped her. Not once had he told her to tone it down as she'd gradually returned to the woman she once had been.

She didn't particularly want Anton to know just how bad things had been. In fact, as her fingers traced the scar on her scalp and her tongue slid over the crown on her front tooth, she could not imagine telling him what had happened in her past—it would be a helluva lot to dump on him.

Louise let out a breath as she recalled her family's and friends' reactions.

It had been Emily she had called on Boxing Day and Rory too.

Rory, whose friendship she had dumped, had, when she'd needed him, patched her up enough to go and face her parents at least.

No, she did not even want to think of Anton's reaction to her tale so she pushed all thoughts of that away and pulled out the referral letter and made the call she had been waiting for ever to make.

Anton must have rung ahead as promised because when Louise spoke to the secretary she was told that there had been a cancellation and that she could see Richard the following Wednesday at ten a.m. Louise checked her diary on her phone and saw that she was on a late that day.

Perfect!

Louise put down the phone and did a little happy dance.

Finally, possibly, her baby was on the way!

CHAPTER EIGHT

EVERY QUESTION THAT Louise had, and there were many, was answered.

Susan had come to Louise's appointment with her and Louise was very glad to have her mother by her side. She knew she would probably forget half of what was said later. Also it was easier if her mother understood what was happening first hand.

Richard ordered a full screening, along with a pelvic ultrasound, and did a thorough examination, as well as looking through the app she had on her phone that charted all her dates.

'We have counsellors here and I really suggest that you take up my suggestion and make an appointment. The next step is to await all the blood results and then I'll see you in the new year and we'll look at the ways we can go ahead.'

Louise nodded.

'But you think I'll probably end up having IVF?' Louise said, because that was the impression she had got during the consultation. She was nervous that the fertility drugs might produce too many eggs but with IVF it was more controlled and Louise only wanted one embryo put back. Richard had even discussed egg sharing, which would give Louise one round of IVF free.

'I'm leaning that way, given your irregular cycle and that you want to avoid a multiple pregnancy, but right now I'd suggest you carry on with the iron and folic acid till we get the results back. We might put you on something stronger once they're in. For now, go and have a good Christmas.'

Louise made an appointment for the second week in January, when Richard returned from his Christmas break, and she made an appointment for an ultrasound and then went and had all the bloodwork done as well.

'Aren't you going to book the counsellor?' Susan asked.

'Why would I need to see one?' Louise said. 'You didn't have to see one before you had your three children.'

'True,' Susan responded, 'but before we went in you said that you were going to do *everything* he suggests.'

'And I am,' Louise said, 'apart from that one.'

Louise's cheeks were unusually pink as they walked down the corridor. Her mind was all ajumble because even as little as a couple of weeks ago she'd have happily signed up to talk to someone. She was one hundred per cent sure that she wanted this.

Or make that ninety-nine point nine per cent positive.

'Have you got time for a quick lunch before your shift?' Susan asked.

She did have time but unfortunately that point one per cent, or rather Anton, was already in the canteen and Louise was very conscious of him as they got their meals. Fortunately the table that Susan selected was quite far away from where Anton sat.

'Well, all I can say is that he was a lot better than the GP,' Susan said. 'Do you feel better for having seen him?'

'I do.'

'You're very quiet all of a sudden.'

Louise didn't know whether or not to say anything to her mum.

Actually, she didn't know if there even was anything to discuss. She and Anton had returned to business as usual after the other night. She was being far less flirtatious and Anton was checking up on her work even more than usual, if that was possible.

'I think I like someone, Mum,' Louise admitted. 'I'm a bit confused, to be honest.'

'Does he know that you like him?'

Louise nodded. 'And he also knows I'm doing this but I think if I continue to go ahead then it takes away any chance for us. I don't even know if I want us to have a chance.'

Susan asked what should have been a simple question. 'What's he like?'

'I don't really know.' Louise gave a wry laugh. 'I know what he's like at work and I find him a bit...' She hesitated. 'Well, he's very thorough with his patients and I'm pretty used to doctors dismissing and overriding midwives...' Louise thought for a long moment before continuing. 'I've just fancied him for a long time but nothing ever happened and now, when I've decided to do this, he seems to want to give us a try.'

'How long have you liked him for?' Susan asked.

'About six months.'

'And if he'd tried anything six months ago, what would you have done?'

'Run a mile.'

'If he'd tried anything three months ago, what would you have done?'

'Run a mile,' Louise admitted.

Only now was she truly healing.

'Do you want to give it a try?'

'I think so,' Louise said, 'but I want this so much too.'

She wanted back her one hundred per cent and her unwavering certainty she was finally on the right path. Unthinkingly she looked across the canteen and possibly the cause of her indecision sensed it, because Anton glanced over and briefly met her gaze.

'I don't see a problem.' Susan picked up her knife and fork and brought Louise back to the conversation. 'You don't have an appointment till the second week of January and Richard did say to go and enjoy Christmas. Have some fun, heaven knows, you deserve it. Maybe just try not to think about getting pregnant for a few weeks.'

Louise nodded, though her heart wasn't in it. Her mum tried, she really did, but she simply couldn't get it. Getting pregnant wasn't something Louise could shove in a box and leave in her wardrobe and drag it out in a few weeks and pick up again— it was something she had been building towards for a very long time.

She glanced over and saw that Anton was walking out of the canteen. There had been so little conversation of late between them that Susan could never have guessed the topic of their conversation had just walked past them.

'Think about counselling,' Susan suggested again.

'Why would I when I've got you?' Louise smiled.

'Ah, but since when did you tell me all that's going on?'

Her mother was right, she didn't tell her parents everything. 'Maybe I will,' Louise said, because this year had been one of so many changes. Even as little as a month or so ago she'd have died on the spot had Anton responded to one of her flirts. She was changing, ever changing, and every time she felt certain where she was heading, the road seemed to change direction again.

No.

Louise refused to let go of her dream.

'I need to get to my shift.'

'And I need to hit the shops.' Susan smiled. 'Come over at the weekend, I'll make your favourite.'

'I shall,' Louise said, and gave her mum a kiss good-bye. 'I'll give you a call. Thanks for coming with me today.'

Louise's patient allocation was a mixed bag between Stephanie and Anton's patients and all were prenatal patients, which meant no baby fix for Louise this shift.

'Hi, Carmel, I'm Louise,' she introduced herself to a new patient. Carmel had been admitted via the antenatal clinic where she had been found to have raised blood pressure. 'How are you?'

'Worried,' Carmel said. 'I thought I was just coming for my antenatal appointment and I find out my blood pressure's high and that the baby's still breech. I'm trying to sort out the other children.'

'This is your third?'

Carmel nodded. 'I've got a three- and a five-year-old. My husband really doesn't have any annual leave left and I can't ask my mum.' Carmel started to cry and, having taken her blood pressure, Louise sat on the chair by her bed.

'There's still time for the baby to turn,' Louise said.

'You're not due till January...' she checked her notes '...the seventh.'

'But Stephanie said if it doesn't turn then I'll have a Caesarean before Christmas.'

Louise nodded because, rather than the chance of the mother going into spontaneous labour, Caesareans were performed a couple of weeks before the due date.

'I just can't be here for Christmas. I know the baby might have come then anyway but at least with a natural labour I could have had a chance to be in and out...' Carmel explained what was going on a little better. 'My mum's really ill—it's going to be her last Christmas.'

Poor Carmel had so much going on in her life at the moment that hospital was the last place she wanted to be. Right now, though, it was the place she perhaps needed to be, to concentrate on the baby inside and let go a little. Louise sat with her for ages, listening about Carmel's mum's illness and all the plans they had made for Christmas Day that were now in jeopardy.

Finally, having talked it out, Carmel calmed a bit and Louise pulled the curtains and suggested she sleep. 'I'll put a sign on the door so that you're not disturbed.'

'Unless it's my husband.'

'Of course.' Louise smiled. 'The sign just says to speak to the staff at the desk before coming in.'

She checked in on Felicity, who was one of Anton's high-risk pregnancies, and then she got to Emily.

'How's my favourite patient?' Louise asked a rather grumpy Emily.

Emily was very bored, very worried and also extremely uncomfortable after more than a week and a half spent in bed. She was relying heavily on Louise's chatter and humour to keep her from the dark hole that her mind kept slipping into. 'I'm dying to hear how you got on at your appointment.'

'It went really well,' Louise said, as she took Emily's blood pressure.

'Tell me.'

'He was really positive,' Louise explained, 'though not in a false hope sort of way, just really practical. I'm going to be seeing him in the new year, when all my results are in, to see the best direction to take, but I think it will be IVF.'

'Really!'

'I think so.' Louise nodded. 'He discussed egg sharing, which would mean I'll get a round of IVF free...'

'You don't feel funny about egg sharing?' Emily asked, just as Anton walked in.

'God, no,' Louise said, happy to chat on. 'I'd love to be able to help another woman to get her baby. It would be a win-win situation. I think egg sharing is a wonderful thing.'

She glanced over as Anton pulled out the BP cuff.

'I've done Emily's blood pressure,' Louise said.

'I'm just checking it for myself.'

Louise gritted her jaw. He did this all the time, *all the time*, even more so than before, and though it infuriated Louise she said nothing.

Here wasn't the place.

'Everything looks good,' Anton said to Emily. 'Twenty-nine weeks and four days now. You are doing really well.'

'I'm so glad,' Emily said, 'but I'm also so...' Emily didn't finish. 'I hate that I'm complaining when I'm so glad that I'm still pregnant.'

'Of course you are bored and fed up.' Anton shrugged. 'Would a shower cheer you up?'

'Oh, yes.'

'Just a short one,' Anton said, 'sitting on a chair.'

'Thank you,' Emily said, but when Anton had gone she looked at Louise. 'What's going on with you two?'

'Nothing,' Louise said.

'Nothing?' Emily checked. 'Come on, Louise, it's me. I'm losing my mind here. At least you can tell me what's going on in the real world.'

'Maybe a teeny tiny thing *has* gone on,' Louise said, 'but we're back to him sulking at me now and double-checking everything that I do.'

'Please, Louise, tell me what has happened between you.'

'Nope,' Louise said, but then relented a touch. 'We got off with each other a smudge but I think the big chill is from my getting IVF.'

'Well, it wouldn't be the biggest turn-on.'

'I guess.'

'Can you put it off?'

'I don't want to put it off,' Louise said. 'Then again, I sort of do.' She was truly confused. 'God, could you imagine being in a relationship with Anton? He'd be coming home and checking I'd done hospital corners on the bed and things…'

'He's nothing like that,' Emily said.

'Ah, but you get his hospital bedside manner.'

'Why not just try?'

'Because I've sworn off relationships, they never work out… I don't know,' Louise sighed, and then she looked at her friend and told her the truth. 'I'm scared to even try.'

'When's the maternity do?' Emily asked.

'Friday, but I'm on a late shift, so I'll only catch the end.'

'If you get changed at work I want to see you before you go.'

'You will.' Louise gave a wicked smile. 'Let's see if he can rustle up another supermodel.'

'Or?'

Louise didn't answer the question because she didn't know the answer herself. 'I'll go and set up the shower for you,' Louise said instead, and opened Emily's locker and started to get her toiletries out. 'What do you want to wear?'

'Whatever makes me look least like a prostitute,' Emily said, because, after all, it was Louise who had shopped for her!

'But you look gorgeous in all of them,' Louise said, 'and I promise that you're going to feel gorgeous too once you've had a shower.'

Emily actually did. After more than a week of washing from a bowl, a brief shower and a hair wash had her feeling so refreshed that she actually put on some make-up and her smile matched the scarlet nightdress that Louise had bought her.

'Wrong room!' Hugh joked, when he dropped in during a lull between patients, please to see how much brighter Emily looked.

In fact, Emily had quite a lot of visitors and Anton glanced into her room as he walked past.

'Is she resting?' Anton asked Louise.

'I'm going to shoo them out soon,' Louise said. 'She's had her sister and mum and now Hugh's boss and his wife have dropped in.'

Alex and Jennifer were lovely, just lovely, but Emily really did need her rest and so, after checking in on Carmel, who seemed much calmer since her sleep and a visit from her husband and children, Louise popped in on Emily, dragging the CTG monitor with her.

'How are you?' Louise asked.

'Fine!' Emily said, but she had that slightly exhausted look in her eyes as she smiled brightly.

'That's good.' Louise turned to the visitors. She knew Alex very well from the five years she had worked in Theatre and she knew Jennifer a little too. 'I'm sorry to be a pain, but I've got to pop Louise on the monitor.'

'Of course,' Jennifer said. 'We were just leaving.'

'Don't rush,' Louise said, while meaning the opposite. 'I'm just going to get some gel.'

That would give them time to say goodbye.

Of course Emily was grateful for visitors but even a shower, after all this time in bed, was draining, and Louise would do everything and anything she had to do to make sure Emily got her rest. By the time she returned with the gel Alex and Jennifer had said their goodbyes and were in the corridor.

'How are you, Louise?' Alex asked. 'Missing Theatre?'

'A bit,' Louise admitted, 'although I simply love it here.'

'Well, we miss you,' Alex said kindly, and then glanced over to the nurses' station, where Anton was writing his notes. 'Oh, there's Anton. Jennifer, I must introduce you—'

'Not now, darling,' Jennifer said. 'We really do have to get home for Josie.'

'It will just take two minutes.' Alex was insistent but as he went to walk over, Jennifer caught his arm.

'Alex, I really am tired.'

'Of course.' Alex changed his mind and they wished Louise goodnight before heading off the ward.

Louise looked at Anton, remembering the night of the theatre do and Anton's stilted response when Alex had said he hadn't yet met his wife. Even if she and Anton were trying to keep their distance a touch, Louise couldn't resist meddling.

'She's gone,' Louise said, as he carried on writing.

'Who?'

'Jennifer.'

'That's good.'

'She's nice, isn't she?' Louise said, and watched his pen pause for a second.

'So I've heard,' Anton responded, and carried on writing.

'Have you met her?'

Anton looked up and met Louise's eyes, which were sparkling with mischief. 'Should I have?'

'I don't know.' Louise smiled, all the more curious, but, looking at him, properly looking at him for the first time since he had handed her the referral, she was curious now for different reasons. 'Why aren't we talking, Anton?'

'We're talking now.'

'Why are you checking everything I do?'

'I'm not.'

'Believe me, you are. I might just as well give you the obs trolley and follow you around and simply write your findings down.'

'Louise, I like to check my patients myself. It has nothing to do with you.'

'Okay.' She went to go but changed her mind. 'We're not talking, though, are we?'

He glanced at the sticking plaster on her arm from where she had had blood tests. 'How was your appointment?'

'He was very informative,' Louise said.

'You're seeing him again?'

'In January.' Louise nodded.

'May I ask…?' Anton said, and Louise closed her eyes. 'Please don't.'

'So I just sit here and say nothing?' Anton checked.

He glanced down the corridor. 'Come to my office.'

Louise did as she wanted to hear what he had to say.

'I want to see if we can have a chance and I don't think we'll get one with you about to go on IVF.'

'Oh, so I'm to put all my plans on hold because you now think we might have a chance.'

'I don't think that's unreasonable.'

'I do,' Louise said. 'I very much do. I've liked you for months,' she said, 'months and months, and now, when I'm just getting it together, when I'm going ahead with what I've decided to do, you suddenly decide, oh, okay, maybe I'll give her a try.'

'Come off it, Louise…'

'No, you come off it,' Louise snapped back. A part of her knew he was right but the other part of her knew that she was. She'd cancelled her dreams for a man once before and had sworn never to do it again and so she went to walk off.

'You won't even discuss it?'

'I need to think,' Louise said.

'Think with me, then.'

'No.'

She was scared to, scared that he might make up her mind, and she was so past being that person. Instead, she gave him a cheeky smile. 'Richard told me to have a *very* nice Christmas.'

Her smile wasn't returned.

'I'm not into Christmas.'

'I meant—'

'I know what you meant, Louise,' Anton said. 'You want some gun for hire.'

'Ooh, Anton!' Louise smiled again and then thought for a moment. 'Actually, I do.'

'Tough.'

Anton stood in his office for a few moments as she walked off.

Maybe he'd been a bit terse there, he conceded.

But it was hearing Louise talk about egg sharing with Emily that had had him on edge. From the little Louise had told him about her fertility issues he had guessed IVF would be her best option if she wanted to get pregnant. Often women changed their minds after the first visit. He had hoped it might be the case with Louise while deep down knowing that it wouldn't be.

He had seen her sitting in the canteen with her mother today—and it had to have been her mum as Anton could see where Louise had got her looks from—but even that had caused disquiet.

Louise had talked this through with her family. It was clearly not a whim.

It just left no room for them.

Anton wanted more than just sex for a few weeks.

Then he changed his mind because a few weeks of straight sex sounded pretty ideal right now.

Perhaps they should try pushing things aside and just seeing how the next few weeks unfolded.

He walked out of his office and there was Louise, walking with a woman in labour. She caught his eye and gave him a wink.

Anton smiled in return.

The tease was back on.

CHAPTER NINE

'I AM SO, so jealous!' Emily said, as Louise teetered in on high heels on Friday night, having finished her shift and got changed into her Christmas party clothes.

'It's fine that you're jealous,' Louise said to Emily, 'because I am so, so jealous of you. I'd love to be in bed now, nursing my bump.'

'You look stunning,' Hugh said.

Louise was dressed in a willow-green dress that clung to her lack of curves and she had her Mistletoe range stockings on, which came with matching panties, bra and suspenders. As they chatted Louise topped her outfit off with a very red coat that looked more like a cape and was a piece of art in itself.

'God help Anton,' Hugh said openly to Louise.

'Sadly, he's stuck on the ward.' Louise rolled her eyes. 'So that was a waste of six pounds.'

As she headed out Hugh turned to Emily, who was trying not to laugh at Hugh's reaction.

'Was she talking about condoms?' Hugh asked.

'She was.'

Oh, Louise was!

As she approached the elevator, there was Anton and his patient must have been sorted because he had changed out of scrubs and was wearing black jeans and a black jumper and looked as festive as one might expect for Anton. He smelt divine, though, Louise thought as she stood beside him, waiting for the lift. 'You've escaped for the weekend,' Louise said.

'I have.'

'Me too!'

She looked at the clothes he was wearing. Black trousers, a black shirt and a very dark grey coat. He looked fantastic rather than festive. 'I didn't know they did out-of-hours funerals,' Louise said as they stepped into the elevator and her eyes ran over his attire.

'You would have me in a reindeer jumper.'

'With a glow stick round your neck,' Louise said as she selected the ground floor. 'It will be fun tonight.'

'Well, I'm just going to put my head in to be polite,' Anton said. 'I don't want to stay long.'

'Yawn, yawn,' Louise said. 'You really are a misery at Christmas, Anton. Well, I'm staying right to the end. I missed out on far too many parties last year.'

She leant against the wall and gave him a smile when she saw he was looking at her.

'You look very nice,' Anton said.

'Thank you,' Louise responded, and she felt a little rush as his eyes raked over her body and this time Anton did look down, all the way to her toes and then back up to her eyes.

She resented that the lift jolted and that the doors opened and someone came in. They all stood in silence but this was no socially awkward nightmare. His delicious, slow perusal continued all the way to the ground floor.

'Do you want a lift to the party?' Anton offered.

'It's a five-minute walk,' Louise said. 'Come back later for your car.'

They stepped out and it was snowing, just a little. It was too damp and not cold enough for it to settle but there in the light of the streetlamps she could see the flakes floating in the night and he saw her smile and chose to walk the short distance.

It was cold, though, and Louise hated the cold.

'I should have worn a more sensible coat,' Louise said through chattering teeth because her coat, though divine, was a bit flimsy. It was the perfect red, though, and squishy and soft, and she dragged it out every December and she explained that to Anton. 'But this is my Christmas party coat. It wasn't the most thought-out purchase of my life.'

'You have a Christmas coat?'

'I have a Christmas wardrobe,' Louise corrected. 'So, you're just staying for a little while.'

'No,' Anton said.

'Oh, I thought you said—'

'You ruined my line. I was going to suggest that you leave five minutes after me but then you said that you were looking forward to it.'

'Oh!'

'I think you are right and that we should enjoy Christmas, perhaps together, and stop concerning ourselves with other things.' He stopped walking and so did she and they faced each other in the night and he pulled her into his lovely warm coat. 'Can you be discreet?'

'Not really,' Louise said with a smile, 'but I am discreet about important things.'

'I know.'

'And having a nice Christmas is a very important thing,' she went on, 'so, yes, I'll be discreet.'

Pressed together, her hands under his coat and around his waist there was nothing discreet about Anton's erection.

'I would kiss you but…' He looked down at her perfectly painted lips for about half a second because he didn't care if it ruined her make-up and neither did she. It had been a very long December, all made worth it by this.

After close to two weeks of deprivation Louise returned to his mouth. His kiss was warm and his lips tender. It was a gentle kiss but it delivered such promise. His tongue was hers again to enjoy. His hands moved under her coat and stroked her back and waist so lightly it was almost a tickle, and when their lips parted their faces barely broke contact and Louise's short breaths blew white in the night. She was ridiculously turned on in his arms.

'We need get there,' Anton said.

'Should we arrive together?' Louise asked. 'If we're going to be discreet?'

'Of course,' Anton said, 'we left work at the same time.'

She went into her bag, which was as well organised as her pockets at work, and did a quick repair job on her face and handed Anton a baby wipe.

'Actually, have the packet,' Louise said, and Anton pocketed it with a smile.

He might rather be needing them.

It was everything a Christmas party should be.

The theme was fun and midwives knew how to have it. All the Christmas music was playing and Louise was the happiest she had been in a very, very long time amongst her colleagues and friends. Anton was there in the background, making her toes curl in her strappy stilettoes as she danced and had fun and made merry with friends while he suitably ignored her. Now and then, though, they caught the other's eye and had a little smile.

It was far less formal than the theatre do and everyone let off a little seasonal steam, well, everyone but Anton.

He stood chatting with Stephanie and Rory, holding his sparkling water, even though he was off duty now until Monday.

'Louise,' Rory called to her near the end of the evening, 'what are you doing for Emily at Christmas?'

'I don't know,' Louise said. 'I've been racking my brains. She's got everything she needs really but I'm going Christmas shopping tomorrow. I might think of something then.'

'Well, let me know if you want to go halves,' Rory said. 'Or if you see something I could get, then could you get it for me?'

'I shall.'

'I'm going to take Stephanie home,' Rory said, and as Stephanie went to get her coat, even though Anton was there, Louise couldn't resist, once Stephanie had gone, asking Rory a question.

'Is it Stephanie?'

'Who?'

'The woman you like.'

'God.' Rory rolled his eyes. 'Why did I ever say anything?'

'Because we're friends.'

'Just drop it,' Rory said. 'And, no, it's not Stephanie.'

He let out a laugh at Louise's suggestion. 'She's married with two children.'

'Maybe that's why you have to keep it so quiet.'

'Louise, it's not Stephanie and you are to leave this alone.' He looked at Anton. 'She's relentless.'

'She is.'

Louise pulled a face at Rory's departing back and then turned and it was just she and Anton.

'Do you want a drink?' Anton asked.

'No, thanks,' Louise said. 'I've had one snowball too many.'

'What *are* you drinking?' Anton asked, because he had seen the pale yellow concoction she had been drinking all night.

'Snowballs—Advocaat, lemonade and lime juice,' she pulled a face.

'You don't like them?'

'I like the *idea* of them,' Louise said, and then her attention was shot as a song came on. 'Ooh, I love this one…'

'Of course you do.'

'No, seriously, it's my favourite.'

It was dance with her or watch her dance alone.

'I thought we were being discreet?' Louise said.

'It's just a dance,' Anton said, as she draped her arms round his neck. 'But Rory's right—you are relentless.'

'I know I am.' Louise smiled.

They were as discreet as two bodies on fire could be, just swaying and looking at each other and talking.

'I want to kiss you under the mistletoe,' Anton said.

'I assume we're not talking about the sad bunch hanging at the bar.'

'No.'

'Did you know these stockings come with matching underwear?'

'I do,' Anton said, 'I saw your work in the magazine.'

'Did you like?'

'I like.' Anton nodded. 'As I said, I want to kiss you under the mistletoe.'

'I am so turned on.' She stated the obvious because he could feel every breath that blew from her lips, he could see her pulse galloping in her neck as well as the arousal in her eyes.

'Good.'

'We need to leave,' Louise said.

'I'm going to go and speak to Brenda and then leave, and you're going to hang around for a little while and then we meet at my car.'

'I live a two-minute walk from here,' Louise said.

'Okay…'

She loved his slow smile as she gave him her address. 'I'll slip the key into your coat pocket,' Louise said. 'You can go and put the kettle on.'

'I shall.'

'Please don't,' Louise said. 'I meant—'

'Oh, I get what you meant.'

Anton said his goodbyes and chatted with Brenda for an aching ten minutes, though on the periphery of his vision he could see Louise near the coats but then off she went, back to the dance floor.

Anton headed out into the night and found her home very easily. Louise had left the heating on. She loathed coming home to a cold house and a furnace of heat hit Anton as he opened the door as well as the dazzle of decorations, which were about as subtle as Louise.

And as for the bedroom!

Anton couldn't help but smile as he stepped inside Madame Louise's chamber. He looked at the crushed velvet bed that matched the crushed velvet chair by the dressing table and he looked at the array of bottles and make-up on it.

Anton undressed and got into her lovely bed. He had never met someone so unabashed and he liked that about her, liked that she was who she was.

Louise had never been more in demand than in the ten minutes at the end of the party. Everyone, *everyone* wanted her to stop for a chat, and just as she finally got her coat on and was leaving, Brenda suggested they drop over to Louise's as some work dos often ended up there.

'I can't tonight,' Louise said. 'Mum's over.'

'Your mum?'

'I think she and Dad had a row,' Louise lied, but she had to, as her mind danced with a sudden vision of a naked Anton in the hallway greeting half of the maternity staff. 'It's a bit of a sensitive point.'

Louise texted him as she walked out.

I just told the biggest lie

Should I be worried that there is a crib in your bedroom? Anton texted back.

She laughed because she had already told him it was for Emily's baby and it was wrapped in Cellophane too, so she continued the tease.

Aren't we making a baby tonight? Louise fired back. Get here!!!

She waved as a car carrying her friends tooted, trying not to run on shaky, want-filled legs, and almost breaking her ankle as she walked far too fast for her stilettoes.

She could barely get the key in the door, just so delighted by the turn of events—that they were going to put other things on hold and simply enjoy. Her coat dropped to the floor as she stepped into the bedroom and there he was, naked in her bed and a Christmas wish came true.

'Who's been sleeping in my bed?' Louise smiled.

'No sleeping tonight,' Anton said. 'Come here.'

Louise was not shy; she went straight over, kneeling on her bed and kissing him without restraint.

It was urgent.

Anton was at the tie of her dress as their mouths bruised each other's. He tried to peel it off over arms that were bent because she was holding his head, tonguing him, wanting him, but there was something she first had to do.

'I have to take my make-up off.'

'I'll lick it off.'

'Seriously.' She could hardly breathe, she was somehow straddling him, her dress gaped open and it would be so much easier not to reach for the cold cream. 'It's not vanity, it's work ethic—I'll look like a pizza for my photo shoot otherwise…'

She climbed off the bed and shed her dress and Anton got the full effect of her stunning underwear, and as beautiful as the pictures had been he far preferred the un-airbrushed version.

Louise sat on her chair and slathered her face in cold cream, quickly wiping it off and wishing she hadn't worn so much mascara. Just as she had finished she felt the chair turn and she was face to groin with a naked Anton.

'Poor Anton,' Louise said.

'Not any more,' Anton said, as she started to stroke him. She went to lower her head but he was starting to kneel.

'Stay…' Louise said, because she wanted to taste him.

'You can have it later.'

He caressed the insides of her thighs through her stockings then the white naked flesh so slowly that she was twitching. He stroked her through her damp panties till he moved them aside and explored her again with his fingers till she could almost stand it no more. Her thighs were shaking and finally his hands went for her mistletoe panties and slid them down so slowly that Louise was squirming. Anton pulled her bottom right to the edge of the chair and then took one stockinged leg and put it over his shoulder and then slowly did the same with the other. Such was the greed in his eyes she was almost coming as finally he did kiss what had been under the silken mistletoe.

Louise looked down but his eyes were closed in concentration and her knees started to bend to the skill of his mouth but hands came up and clamped her legs down, so there was nowhere to go but ecstasy.

She felt the cool blowing of his breath and then the warm suction of his mouth and then another soft blow that did nothing to put the fire out. In fact, her hips were lifting, but his mouth would not allow them to.

'Anton…' She didn't need to tell him she was coming, he was lost in it too, moaning, as her thighs clamped his head and she pulsed in his mouth. Anton reached for his cock on instinct. He was close to coming too. He raised himself up, and was stroking himself at her entrance.

They were in the most dangerous of places, two people who definitely should know better.

Louise was frantically patting the dressing table behind her, trying to find a drawer, while watching the silver bead at his tip swelling and drizzling.

'Here...' She pulled out a foil packet and ripped it open. She slid it onto his thick length and there was no way they could make it to the bed, but Anton took a turn in the lucky chair and she leapt on his lap. His mouth sucked her breast through her bra as she wriggled into position.

She hovered provocatively over his erection, revelling for a brief moment in the sensation of his mouth and the anticipation of lowering herself. Anton had worked the fabric down and was now at her nipple, her small breast consumed by his mouth, and then his patience expired. His hands pulled her hips down and in one rapid motion Louise was filled by him, a delicious searing but, better still, his hands did not leave her. Her bedroom was like a sauna and the sheen on her body had her a little slippery but his hands gripped her and did not relent, for she would match his needs.

It had her feeling dizzy—the sensation of being on top while being taken. Louise rested her arms on his shoulders as he pulled her down over and over, and then his mouth lost contact with her breast as he swelled that final time. Her hands went to his head and she ground down, coming with him, squealing in pleasure as they hit a giddy peak. They shared a decadent, wet kiss as he shot inside her, a kiss of possession as she pulsed around his length and her head collapsed onto his shoulder.

Louise kissed his salty shoulder as her breathing finally slowed down.

She could feel him soften inside her and she lifted her head and smiled into his eyes.

'Ready for bed?'

CHAPTER TEN

AFTER ONE HOUR and about seven minutes of sleep they woke to Louise's phone at six.

'I thought you were off today,' Anton groaned.

'I am, but I'm going Christmas shopping.'

'At six a.m.?'

'I want to get a book signed for Mum so I have to line up,' Louise said. 'Stay,' she said, kissing his mouth .'Get up when you're ready, or you can come shopping with me.'

'I'll give it a miss, thanks.'

'Have you done your Christmas shopping?'

'I'll do it online. The shops will be crazy.'

'That's half the fun.' She gave him a nudge. 'Come on.'

She went into the shower and Anton lay there, looking up at the ceiling. He had a couple of things to get. Something for the nurses and his secretary and, yes, he might just as well get it over and done with.

'We'll stop by my place and I can get changed,' Anton said, as she came out of the shower.

'Sure.' Naked, she smiled down at him and lifted her hair. 'Check me for bruises,' she said, while craning her neck and looking down at her buttocks where his fingers had dug in, but, no, they were peachy cream too.

'No need to check,' Anton said, for he had been careful, knowing that she had her photo shoot coming up.

Neither could wait till it was over!

Louise dressed while Anton showered. She pulled on jeans and boots and a massive cream jumper and then she tied up her hair and added a coat.

Anton put on the clothes he had worn last night, though they were stopping by his place so he could get changed.

'Ready to do battle?' she asked, thrilled that Anton had agreed to come along with her. She was determined to Christmas him up, especially when they arrived at his apartment.

'You really are a misery,' Louise said, stepping in. She didn't care about the view or the gorgeous furnishings in his apartment—what she cared about was that there wasn't a single decoration. There were a few Christmas cards stacked with his mail on the kitchen bench but, apart from that, it might just as well have been October, instead of just over a week before Christmas.

'Aren't you even going to get a tree?' Louise asked.

'No.'

'Don't you have Christmas trees in Italy?'

'Some,' Anton said, 'but we go more for nativity scenes and lights.'

'You have to do something.'

'I'm hardly ever here, Louise,' Anton said.

'It's not the point. When you come home—'

'I don't like Christmas,' Anton said, but then amended, 'Although I am starting to really enjoy this one.'

'What do you have to get today?'

'I need to get something for my secretary,' Anton said. 'Perfume?'

'Maybe,' Louise said. 'What sort of things does she like?'

Anton spread out his hands—he really had no idea what Shirley liked.

'What sort of things does she talk about?'

'My diary.'

'God, you're so antisocial,' Louise said.

'Oh, she likes cooking,' Anton recalled. 'She's always bringing in things that she's made.'

'Then I have the perfect present,' Louise said, 'because I'm getting it for my mum. That's what we're going to line up for.'

It wasn't just a book. The first twenty people had the option to purchase a morning's cooking lesson with a celebrity chef. It was fabulous and expensive and with it all going to charity it was well worth it.

Celebrating their success at getting the signed books and cookery lessons, at ten a.m., having coffee and cake in an already crowded department store, they chatted.

'If your mother can't cook, why would you spend all that money? Surely it will be wasted?'

'Oh, no.' Louise shook her head. 'If she learns even one thing and gets it right, my dad will be grateful for ever—the poor thing,' she added. 'He has to eat it night after night after night. I usually wriggle out of it when I go and visit. I'll go over tomorrow and say I've just eaten, but you can't do that on Christmas Day.'

'How bad is it?'

'It's terrible. I don't know how she does it. It always looks okay and she thinks it tastes amazing but I swear it's like she's put it in a blender with water added, burnt it and then put it back together to look like a dinner again...' She took out her list. 'Come on, off we go.'

Louise was a brilliant shopper, not that Anton easily fathomed her methods.

'I adore this colour,' Louise said, trying lipstick on the back of her hand. 'Oh, but this one is even better.'

'I thought we were here for your sisters.'

'Oh, they're so easy to buy for,' Louise said. 'Anything I love they want to pinch, so anything I love I know they'll like.'

Make-up, perfume, a pair of boots… 'I'm the same size as Chloe,' she explained, as she tried them on. 'It's so good you're here, I'd have had to make two trips otherwise.'

Bag after bag was loaded with gifts. 'I want to go here,' Louise said, and they got off the escalator at the baby section. 'I'm going to get something for Emily and Hugh's baby,' Louise said. 'Hopefully it will be a waste of money and I can give it to NICU.' She looked at Anton. 'Do you think she'll get to Christmas?'

'I hope so,' Anton said. 'I'm aiming for thirty-three weeks.'

Louise heard the unvoiced *but* and for now chose to ignore it.

They went to the premature baby section and found some tiny outfits and there was one perk to being the obstetrician and midwife shopping for a pregnant friend, they knew what colour to get! Louise said yes to giftwrapping and they waited as it was beautifully wrapped and then topped with a bow.

'I'll keep it in my locker at work,' Louise said.

It was a lovely, lovely, lovely day of shopping, punctuated with kisses. Neither cared about the grumbles they caused as they blocked the pavement or the escalators when they simply had to kiss the other and by the end Louise was seriously, happily worn out.

'You want to get dinner?' Anton offered.

'Take-out?' Louise suggested. 'But we'll have it at my place. I'm not going to your miserable apartment.'

'I have to go back,' Anton said. 'I have to do an hour's work at least.'

'Fine,' Louise conceded, 'but we'll drop these back at my place first and I'll get some clothes.'

'You won't need them,' Anton said, but Louise was insistent.

All her presents she put in the bedroom. 'I can't wait to wrap them,' Louise said. 'I'll just grab a change of clothes and things, you go and make a drink.'

Louise grabbed more than a change of clothes. In fact, she went into her wardrobe and pulled out some leftover Christmas decorations and stuffed them all into a not so small overnight bag. She also took the tiny silver tree that she'd been meaning to put up at the nurses' station but kept forgetting to take.

'How long are you staying for?' Anton asked, when she came out and he saw the size of her overnight bag.

'Till you kick me out.' Louise gave him a kiss. 'I like to be prepared.'

Anton really did have work to do.

A couple of blood tests were in and he went through them, and there was a patient at thirteen weeks' gestation who was bleeding. Anton went into his study and rang her to check how things were.

Louise could hear him safely talking and quickly set to work.

The little tree she put on his coffee table and she draped some tinsel on the window ledges and put up some stars, a touch worried she might leave some marks on his walls but he'd just have to get over it, Louise decided.

She took out her can and sprayed snow on his gleaming windows, and oh, it looked lovely.

'What the hell have you done?' Anton said, as he came into the lounge, but he was smiling.

'I need nice things around me,' Louise said, 'happy things.'

'It would seem,' Anton said, looking not at her handiwork now but the woman in his arms, 'that so do I.'

CHAPTER ELEVEN

'WHAT HAPPENED LAST Christmas?' Anton asked, late, late on Sunday night. They'd started on the sofa and had watched half a movie and now they lay naked on the floor bathed by the light from the television. 'You said it was tinsel-starved.'

She really would prefer not to talk about it. They had had such a lovely weekend but there were so many parts of so many conversations that they were avoiding, like IVF and Anton's loathing of Christmas, that when he finally broached one of them, Louise answered carefully. There was no way she could tell him all but she told him some.

'I broke up with my boyfriend on Christmas Eve.'

'You said it was tinsel-starved before then, that you didn't go to many parties.'

'It wasn't worth it.'

'In what way?'

'I know you think I'm a flirt…'

'I like that about you.'

'But I'm only really like that with you,' Louise said. 'I mean that. I used to be a shocking flirt and then when I started going out with Wesley…well, I got told off a lot.'

'For flirting with other men?'

'No!' Louise said, shuddering at the memory. 'He decided that if I flirted like that with him, then what was I like when he wasn't there? I don't want to go into it all, but I changed and I hate myself for it. I changed into this one eighth of a person and somehow I got out—on Christmas Eve last year. It took months, just months to even start feeling like myself again.'

'Okay.'

'Do you know the day I did?' Louise asked, smiling as she turned to face him.

'No.'

'We were going to Emily's leaving do and I saw you in the corridor and I asked you to come along…'

'You were wearing red,' Anton easily recalled. 'You were with Emily.'

'That's right, it was for her leaving do. Well, even when I asked if you wanted to come along, I deep down knew that you wouldn't. I was just…' She couldn't really explain. 'I was just flirting again…sort of safe in the knowledge that it wouldn't go anywhere.'

'But it has,' Anton said.

'I guess.' Louise smiled. 'Have you ever been married?' Louise asked.

'Why do you ask?'

'I just wondered.'

'No,' Anton said. 'Have you?'

'God, no,' Louise said.

'Have you ever come close?'

'No,' Louise admitted.

'You and Rory?'

Louise laughed and shook her head. 'We were only together a few weeks. Just when we started going out I found that it was likely that I was going to have issues getting pregnant. It was terrible timing because it was all I could think about. Poor Rory, he started going out with a happy person and when the doctor broke the news I just plunged into despair. It wasn't his baby I wanted, just the thought I might never have one. It was just all too much for him…' She looked at Anton. 'I think I was just low at that time and that's why I must have taken my bastard alert glasses off. I've made a few poor choices with men since then.' She closed her eyes. 'None worse than Wesley, though.'

'How bad did it get?' Anton asked, but Louise couldn't go there and she shook her head.

'What about you?' Louise asked. 'Have you been serious with anyone?'

'Not really, well, there was one who came close…' It was Anton who stopped talking then.

Anton who shook his head.

He simply couldn't go there with someone who might just want him for a matter of weeks.

CHAPTER TWELVE

'CAN YOU KEEP a close eye on Felicity in seven?' Anton asked. 'She's upset because her husband has been unable to get a flight back till later this evening.'

Felicity was one of Anton's high-risk pregnancies and finally the day had arrived where she would meet her baby, but her husband was in Germany with work.

'How is she doing?' Louise asked.

'Very slowly,' Anton said. 'Hopefully he'll get here in time.' He picked up a parcel, beautifully wrapped by Louise. 'I'm going to give this to Shirley now. She's only in this morning to sort out my diary before she takes three weeks off. Then I will be in the antenatal clinic. Call me if you have any concerns.'

'Yes, Anton,' Louise sighed.

Anton heard her sigh but it did not bother him.

Things were not going to change at work. In fact, he was more overbearing if anything, just because he didn't want a mistake to come between them.

'This is for you,' Anton said, as he went into Shirley's office. 'I just wanted to thank you for all your hard work this year and to say merry Christmas.'

'Thank you, Anton.' Shirley smiled.

'I hope you have a lovely break.'

He went to go, even as she opened it, but her cry of surprise had him turn around.

'How?'

Anton stared. His usually calm secretary was shaking as she spoke.

'How did you manage to get this—there were only twenty places.'

'I got there early.'

'You lined up to get me this! Oh, my…'

Anton felt a little guilt at her obvious delight. It really had been far from a hardship to be huddled in a queue with Louise, but it was Shirley's utter shock too that caused more than a little disquiet.

'I never thought…' Shirley started and then stopped. She could hardly say she'd been expecting some bland present from her miserable boss. 'It's wonderful,' she said instead.

God, Anton thought, was he that bad that a simple nice gesture could reduce a staff member to tears?

Yes.

He nodded to Helen, the antenatal nurse who would be working alongside him, and he saw that she gave a slightly strained one back.

Things had to change, Anton realised.

He had to learn to let go a little.

But how?

'How are things?' Louise asked, as she walked into Felicity's room with the CTG machine.

'They're just uncomfortable,' Felicity said. She was determined to have a natural birth and had refused an epidural or anything for pain. 'I'm going to try and have a sleep.'

'Do,' Louise said. 'Do you want me to close the curtains?'

Felicity nodded.

Brenda popped her head in the door. 'Are you going to lunch, Louise?'

'In a minute,' Louise said. 'I'm just doing some obs.' Both Felicity and the baby seemed fine. 'I'll leave this on while I have my lunch,' Louise said about the CTG machine, and Felicity nodded. 'Then later we might have a little walk around, but for now just try and get some rest.'

She closed the curtains and moved a blanket over Felicity, who was half-asleep, and left her to the sound of her baby's heartbeat. Louise would check the tracing when she came back from her break and see the pattern of the contractions.

'Press the bell if you need anything and I'll be here.'

'But you're going to lunch.'

'Yep, but that buzzer is set for me, so just you press it if you need to.'

'Thanks, Louise,' Felicity said. 'What time are you here till?'

Louise thought before answering. 'I'm not sure.'

Louise left the door just a little open so that her colleagues could easily pop in and out and could hear the CTG, then headed to the fridge and got out her lunch.

'Fancy company?' Louise asked Emily as she knocked on her open door.

'Oh, yes!' Emily sat up in the bed. 'How was the party?'

'Excellent.'

'Why didn't you text me all weekend?'

'I did!' Louise said.

'Five-thirty on a Sunday evening suggests to me you were otherwise engaged.'

'I was busy,' Louise said, 'Christmas shopping!'

'You lie,' Emily said.

'Actually, I need to charge my phone,' Louise said, because she hadn't been back home since being at Anton's. 'Can I borrow your charger?'

'Sure.' Emily smiled. 'That's not like you.'

Louise said nothing. She certainly wasn't going to admit to Emily her three-night fest with Anton. As she plugged in her phone and sat down, the background noise of Felicity's baby's heartbeat slowed. Louise was so tuned into that noise, as all midwives were, and she didn't like what she had just heard.

'Are you okay?' Emily asked.

'I think I've got restless leg syndrome.' Louise gave a light response. 'I'm just going to check on someone and then I'll be back.'

She went quietly into Felicity's room. Felicity was dozing and Louise warmed her hand and then slipped it on Felicity's stomach, watching the monitor and patiently waiting for a contraction to come.

'It's just me,' Louise whispered, as Felicity woke up as a contraction deepened and Emily watched as the baby's heart rate dipped. She checked Felicity's pulse to make sure the slower heart rate that the monitor was picking up wasn't Felicity's.

'Turn onto your other side for me,' Louise said to the sleepy woman, and helped Felicity to get on her left side and looked up as Brenda, alerted by the sound of the dip in the baby's heart rate, looked in.

'Page Anton,' Louise said.

Even on her left side the baby's heart rate was dipping during contractions and Louise put some oxygen on Felicity. 'We'll move her over to Delivery,' Brenda said.

'Have you heard from Anton?'

'I've paged him but he hasn't answered,' Brenda said. 'I'll see if he's in the staffroom.'

Louise raced around to check but Anton wasn't there.

She paged him again and then they moved Felicity through to the delivery ward. They were about to move her onto the delivery bed but Louise decided to wait for Anton before doing that as she listened to the baby's heart rate. The way this baby was behaving, they might be running to Theatre any time soon.

She typed in an urgent page for Anton but when there was still no response Louise remembered her phone was in Emily's room. 'Text him,' Louise said to Brenda, and, ripping off a tracing, Louise left Felicity with Brenda and swiftly went to a phone out of earshot.

'Are the pagers working?' she asked the switchboard operator. 'I need Anton Rossi paged and, in case he's busy, I need the second on paged too, urgently.'

She then rang Theatre and, because she had worked there for more than five years, when she rang and explained they might need a theatre very soon, she knew she was being taken seriously and that they would immediately be setting up for a Caesarean.

'I can't get hold of Anton,' Louise said, but then she saw him, his phone in hand, racing towards them. 'Anton! Felicity's having late decelerations. Foetal heart rate is dropping to sixty.'

'How long has this been going on?'

'About fifteen minutes.'

'And you didn't think to tell me sooner! Hell! If Brenda hadn't texted me…' Anton hissed, taking the tracing and looking at it in horror, because time was of the essence. With pretty much one look at the tracing the decision to operate was made. For Anton it was a done deal.

It was like some horrific replay of what had happened two years ago.

'I paged you when it first happened,' Louise said, but there wasn't time for explanations now. As Anton went into the delivery room the overhead speakers crackled into life.

'System error. Professor Hadfield, can you make your way straight to Emergency? Mr Rossi, Delivery Ward, room two.'

Anton briefly closed his eyes.

'Mr Rossi, urgently make your way to Delivery, room two. System error—pagers are down.'

And so it repeated.

'Is that for me?' Felicity cried, terrified by the urgency of the calls overhead.

'Hey…' Louise gave Felicity a cuddle as Anton examined her. 'It's just that the pagers are down and so I had to use my whip a bit on Switchboard to get Anton here.'

'Felicity.' Anton came up to the head-end of the bed. 'Your baby is struggling…' Everything had been done. She was on her side, oxygen was on and she was still on the bed so they could simply speed her to Theatre. 'We're going to take you to Theatre now and do a Caesarean section.'

'Can I be awake at least?'

'We really do need to get your baby out now.'

'I'll be there with you,' Louise said, as the porter arrived. 'I am not leaving your side, I promise you. I can take some pictures of your baby if you like,' Louise offered, and Felicity gave her her phone.

'Can you let Theatre know?' Anton said, before he raced ahead to scrub.

It took everything she could muster to keep the bitterness from her voice. 'I already have, Anton.'

Louise and the porter whisked the bed down the corridor. There was no consent form to be signed—that had been taken care of at the antenatal stage.

'I'm so scared,' Felicity said, as they wheeled her into Theatre.

'I know,' Louise said, cleaning down her shoes and popping on shoe covers, then she put on a theatre hat and gown. 'You've got the best obstetrician,' Louise said. 'I've seen him do many Caesareans and he's brilliant.'

'I know.'

The bed was wheeled through and Louise's old colleagues were waiting. Connor and Miriam helped Louise to get Felicity onto the theatre table and she smiled when she saw Rory arrive. He was a bit breathless and as he caught his breath Louise spoke on. 'You've got an amazing anaesthetist too. Hi, Rory, this is Felicity.'

Rory was lovely with Felicity and went through any allergies and previous anaesthetics and things. 'I'm going to be by your side every minute,' he said to Felicity. 'Till you're awake again, here is where I'll be.'

'I'll be here too,' Louise said.

Theatre was filling. The paediatric team was arriving as Rory slipped the first drug into Felicity's IV.

'Think baby thoughts,' Louise said with a smile as Felicity went under.

Louise was completely supernumerary at this point. She was simply here on love watch for one of her mums. And so, once Felicity had been intubated, Louise simply closed her mind to everything, even bastard Anton. She just sat on a stool and thought lovely baby thoughts.

She heard the swirl of suction and a few curses from Anton as he tried to get one very flat baby out as quickly as possible.

Then there was silence and she looked up as a rather floppy baby was whisked away and she kept thinking baby thoughts as they rubbed it very vigorously and flicked at its little feet. She glanced at Rory as another anaesthetist started to bag him.

But then Rory smiled and Louise looked round and watched as the baby shuddered and she watched as his little legs started to kick and his hands started to fight. His cries of protest were muffled by the oxygen mask but were the most beautiful sounds in the world.

Louise didn't look at Anton, she just told Felicity that her baby was beautiful, wonderful, that he was crying and could she hear him, even though Felicity was still under anaesthetic.

Anton did look at Louise.

She did that, Anton thought.

She made all his patients relax and laugh, and though Felicity could not know what was being said, still Louise said it.

He could have honestly kicked himself for his reaction but, God, it had been almost a replica of what had happened back in Italy.

'He's beautiful,' Louise said over and over.

So too was Louise, Anton thought, knowing he'd just blown any chance for them.

Louise *was* beautiful, even when she was raging.

Not an hour later she marched into the male changing room and slammed the door shut.

'Hey, Louise,' called Rory, who was just getting changed. 'You're in the wrong room.'

'Oh, I'm in the right room,' Louise said. 'Could you excuse us, Rory, please?'

'We will do this in my office,' Anton said. Wet from the shower, a towel around his loins, he did not want to do this now, but Louise had no intention of waiting till he got dressed. She was far, far beyond furious.

'Oh, no, this won't keep.'

'Good luck,' Rory called to Anton as he left them to it.

And then it was just Louise and Anton but even as he went to apologise for what had happened earlier, or to even explain, Louise got in first.

'You can question my morals, you can think what you like about me, but don't you ever, ever—'

'Question your morals?' Anton checked. 'Where the hell did that come from?'

'Don't interrupt me,' Louise raged. 'I've had it with you. What you accused me of today—'

'Louise.'

'No!' She would not hear it.

'I apologise. I did not realise the pagers were down.'

'I did,' Louise said instantly. 'When you didn't come, or make contact, it was the first thing I thought—not that you were negligent and simply couldn't be bothered to get here...'

Her lips were white she was so angry. 'I'm going to speak to Brenda and put in an incident report about the pagers today, and while I'm there I'm going to tell her I don't want to work with you any more.'

'That's a bit extreme.'

'It's isn't extreme. I've thought about doing it before.' She saw him blink in surprise. 'Everything I do you check again—'

'Louise...' Anton wasn't about to deny it. He checked on her more than the other midwives, he was aware of that. In trying to protect her, to protect *them*, from what had happened to him and Dahnya, he had gone over the top. 'If I can explain—'

But Louise was beyond hearing him. She lost her temper then and Louise hadn't lost her temper since that terrible day. 'You don't want a midwife,' Louise shouted, 'you want a doula, rubbing the mums' backs and offering support. Well, I'm over it, Anton. Have you any idea how demoralising it is?' she raged, though possibly she was talking more to Wesley than Anton. 'Have you any idea how humiliating it is…?'

Anton took a step forward, to speak, to calm her down, and then stood frozen as he heard the fear in her voice.

'Get off me!' She put her hands up in defence and there was a shocked moment of silence when she realised what she had said, what she had done, but then came his calm voice.

'I'm not touching you, Louise.'

She pressed her hands to her face and her fingers to her eyes. 'I'm sorry,' Louise said, 'not for what I said before but—'

'It's okay.' Anton was breathless too, as if her unleashed fear had somehow attached to him. 'We'll talk when you've calmed down.'

'No.' Louise shook her head, embarrassed at her outburst but still cross. 'We won't talk because I don't want to hear it, Anton.' And then turned and left.

She was done.

CHAPTER THIRTEEN

'WHAT HAPPENED?' EMILY asked, when Louise returned a couple of hours later to the ward.

'Sorry, I just got waylaid.'

'Louise?'

'I'm fine.'

'You've been crying.'

'There's nothing wrong.'

'Louise?' Emily frowned when she saw Louise's smile was wavering as she took Emily's blood pressure. 'What's going on? Look, I'm bored out of my mind. I mean, I am so seriously bored and I'm fed up with people thinking I can't have a normal conversation, or that they only tell me nice things.' Emily was truly concerned because she hadn't seen red eyes on Louise in a very long time. 'Wesley isn't contacting you again?'

'No, no.' Louise sat down on the bed, even though Brenda might tell her off.

'Tell me.' Emily took her hand.

'Anton.' Louise gulped. Certainly she wasn't going to scare Emily and tell her all that had gone on with Felicity's baby but they really were speaking as friends.

'Okay.'

'Personal or professional?'

'Both,' Louise admitted. 'He checks and double-checks everything, you know what he's like…'

'I do,' Emily said.

'It's like he doesn't trust any of the staff but he does it more with me.'

'Louise.' Emily didn't know whether she should say anything but it was pretty much common knowledge what had happened a few months ago. 'Remember when Gina had her meltdown and went into rehab?'

'Yep, I know, Hugh reported her…' Louise looked at Emily, remembering that there had been more than one complaint, or so the rumours went. 'Did Anton report her as well?'

'I'm saying nothing.'

'Okay.' Louise squeezed her hand in gratitude as Emily spoke on.

'So maybe he feels he has reason to be checking things.'

'Hugh doesn't, though,' Louise pointed out. 'Hugh isn't constantly looking over the nursing staff's shoulders and assuming the worst.'

'I know.' Emily sighed. She adored Anton but had noticed that he was dismissive of the nurses' findings and she could well understand that things might have come to a head. 'So, what's the personal stuff?'

'Do you really need to know that your obstetrician got off with your midwife?'

'Ooh.' Emily gave a delighted smile. 'I think I did really need to know that.'

'Well, it won't be happening again,' Louise said. 'We just had the most terrible row, or rather I did…'

'And what did Anton do?' Emily gently enquired.

'He apologised,' Louise said, and then she frowned

because she wasn't very used to a guy backing down. For too long it had been the other way around. 'Emily…' Louise's eyes filled with tears. 'I shouted for him to get off me and the poor guy was just standing there.'

'Oh, Louise…' Emily rubbed Louise's shoulder. 'It must have been terrifying for you to have a big row. Rows are normal, though. What happened to you wasn't.'

'I know.' Louise blew her nose and recovered herself and gave Emily a smile. 'I really let rip.' Louise let out a small shocked laugh.

'She really did!' Anton was at the door and came over to the bed. 'Your latest ultrasound is back. All looks well, there is a nice amount of fluid.' He had a feel of Emily's stomach.

'Nice size,' Anton said.

'Really?'

'Really.' Anton nodded. 'Now is the time they start to plump up and your baby certainly is.'

They headed out of Emily's room and he turned to Louise. 'What is her blood pressure?'

'Ha-ha,' Louise said. 'Check it yourself.'

Anton gave a wry smile as Louise flounced off but it faded when he saw she went straight up to Brenda.

Louise hadn't been lying when she had said she didn't know when she'd be going home.

Something, something had told her she'd be around for the delivery, which meant she wanted to be around when Felicity was more properly awake, and at four she sat holding a big fat baby who had given everyone a horrible scare.

'Your husband just called and he's at Heathrow and is on his way,' Louise said. 'And your mum is on her way too.' Felicity smiled. 'And you have the cutest, most gorgeous baby. In fact, he's so cute I don't think I can hand him over…'

Felicity smiled as Louise did just that and placed the baby in her arms.

'He's gorgeous.'

'I was so scared.'

'I know you were but, honestly, he gave us a fright but he's fine.' She stared at the baby, who was gnawing at his wrist. 'He's beautiful and he's also starving,' Louise said.

'Can I feed him?'

'You can,' Louise said, 'because he's trying to find mine and I've told him I've got nothing…' She looked up as Anton came in and then got back to work, helping a very hungry baby latch on.

'Louise, can I have a word before you leave?' Anton asked.

Louise's response was a casual 'Sure', but Anton knew that was for the sake of the patient.

'Felicity,' Anton said. 'Your mother has just arrived…'

'Do you want me to tell her to wait while you feed?' Louise checked, but Felicity shook her head.

'No, let her in.'

Louise stayed for the first feed. She just loved that part and then when finally the baby was fed and content and in his little isolette she gave Felicity a cuddle. 'I'll come by tomorrow and we'll talk more about what happened today, if you want to. I took some photos with your phone, if you want to have a look through them with me.'

'Thank you.'

She popped in to see Emily on her way out, as she always did, but she was just about all smiled out. She just wanted to go home for a good cry, a glass of wine and then bed.

She didn't even pretend to smile when she knocked on Anton's office door and went in.

'Can we talk?'

Louise shook her head. 'I don't want to talk to you, Anton,' Louise said. 'I'm tired. I just want to go home.'

'Louise, what happened today was not about you. I had an incident in Milan…'

'I don't want to hear it, Anton,' Louise said, and then relented. 'Imelda's, then,' Louise said. 'I'm just going to get changed.'

'Sure.'

'I'll meet you over there.'

There was Anton with his sparkling water but there was a glass of wine and some nachos waiting for Louise. Really, she shouldn't because she had the bloody photo shoot in less than a week but Louise shovelled them in her mouth, getting hungrier with each mouthful.

'Do you want to get something else?'

'These are fine,' Louise said, and then looked at him. 'Well?'

'I am so very sorry for today. You did everything right, from ringing Theatre to keeping her on the bed. She was very lucky to have you on duty and I apologise for jumping to the worst conclusion.'

Louise gave a tight shrug. It wasn't just today she was upset about. 'What about the other days?' she challenged. 'I don't think you trust me.'

'No.' Anton shook his head. 'That is not the case.'

'It's very much the case,' Louise said. 'Everything I do you double-check, or you simply dismiss my findings…

Aside from the repeated wallops to my ego, it's surely doubling up for the patient.' Louise let out a breath. 'So what happened in Milan?'

'A few years ago, on Christmas morning, I took a handover, and I was told everything was fine, but by lunchtime I had a baby dead—' Louise was about to say something but Anton spoke over her. 'It *was* the hospital's fault,' Anton said. 'Apparently the night midwife had told a junior doctor she had concerns; I took the handover from the registrar and those concerns hadn't been passed on to her. It was just complete miscommunication. I went in to see my patient at ten, and there were many things that I should have been paged about but hadn't been. I took her straight to Theatre and delivered the baby but he only lived for a couple of hours.

'The coroner did not blame me, thank God, but I have never seen friendships fall so rapidly. There was blame, accusations, it was hell. So much so that when the finding came in I no longer trusted anyone I worked with, and I knew I had to make a fresh start, which was why I moved into fertility.'

'But you came back.'

'Yes, I never thought I would but the last months I was there, the parents of Alberto, the baby who had died, came in to try for another baby. It was a shock to us all. I offered to step aside but by then I had quite a good reputation and they asked that I remain. I was very happy when they got pregnant and it was then that I realised how much I had missed obstetrics. I knew I needed a fresh start so I applied to come here. I had always had a good rapport with colleagues until Alberto's death. I wanted to get that back and I tried, but within a few weeks of being here there was an incident…' He looked at Louise and she was glad that Emily had filled her in about Gina because Anton didn't. 'I'm not giving specifics but it shook me and from that point I have been cautious…'

'To the extreme,' Louise said.

'Yes.'

'Terrible things happen, Anton. Terrible, terrible things…'

'I know that. I just wish I had not taken a handover that morning and had checked myself…'

'You can't check everyone, you can't follow everyone around.'

'I'm aware of that.'

'Yet you do.'

'I've spoken to Brenda and I have told her what went on, not just today but in the past. I also told her that I am hoping things will be different in the future.'

'Did you get her "There's no I in team" lecture?' Louise asked, and Anton smiled and nodded.

'I've had it a few times from Brenda already and, yes, I got it again today.'

'Well, I disagree with her,' Louise said. 'There should be an I in team. I am responsible, I am capable, I know I've got this, and if I stuff up then I take responsibility. If we all do that, which we seem to do where I work, then teams do well. We look out for each other,' Louise said. 'We have a buddy system. I don't just glance at CTGs when they're given to me and neither do my colleagues. We take ages discussing them, going over them…'

'I know that.'

'It doesn't feel like it,' Louise said.

'I am hoping things will be different now.'

'Good,' Louise said. 'Is that it?'

'No, I want to know what you meant about me judging you on your morals.'

'This isn't a social get-together, Anton. I'm here to talk about work.'

'Louise.'

'Okay, just because I'm not on a husband hunt, just because I fancied you…'

'Past tense?'

'Oh, it is so past tense,' Louise said. 'So very past tense.'

'Louise,' Anton said, and she must have heard the tentative tone to his voice because immediately her eyes darted away, even before his question was voiced. 'What happened that made you so scared back there?'

'That isn't about work either.' She got up and hoisted up her bag. 'I'm sorry you went through crap and I'm so sorry for the baby and its family.'

'Louise.' He halted her as she went to go. 'The midwife on that morning, I was going out with her. She was busy, meant to go back and check, meant to call, but got waylaid. Can you see why I was very reluctant to get involved with you?'

'I can.' She stood there but didn't give him the answer he was hoping for. 'Well, at least you don't have that problem with me now—we're no longer involved.' She gave him a tight smile. 'Goodnight, Anton.'

Louise got home, closed the door and promptly burst into tears. Despite her tough talk with Anton she could think of nothing worse than losing a baby under those circumstances and at Christmas too.

Then she went into the bath and cried some more. She'd been raging at him and he'd simply stood there.

She was beyond confused and all churned up from her loss of control.

Why couldn't it just be sex? Louise thought. Why did she have to really, really like him?

As she got out of the bath her phone bleeped a text from Emily.

U OK?

Louise gave a rapid reply.

Bloody men! How's baby?

Kick-kicking, or maybe he's waving to you.

Louise sent back a smiley face, knowing what was to come.

Maybe SHE'S waving???? Emily texted, hoping that Louise would give her a clue.

Not telling, came Louise's reply. Ask Hugh.

He won't tell me, Emily replied. Bloody men!

CHAPTER FOURTEEN

ANTON REALLY DID make an effort at work, though Louise wasn't sure if it was temporary. At least he had stopped double-checking everything that she did. Brenda had a word with some of the staff, as Anton had asked her to do. They in turn rang him a little sooner than usual with concerns, and slowly the I in team was working, except Louise was no longer a part of his team.

'Phone for you, Louise,' someone called, and Louise headed out to the desk. It was the IVF clinic, which had been unable to reach her on her mobile or at home, and Louise took out her phone and saw that the battery was flat.

'Are you okay to talk, or do you want to call us back?'

'No, now's fine,' Louise said.

'Richard wanted to let you know that your iron levels are now normal but to keep taking the supplements, especially the folic acid.'

'I shall. Thank you,' Louise said.

'Have a lovely Christmas and we'll see you in the new year.'

Louise's stomach was all aflutter as she ended the call.

'Good news?' Brenda asked, but Louise didn't answer. Her *lovely Christmas* was walking past and this time when he sat down and ignored her it was at Louise's request.

Of course, she still dealt with his patients—after all, Emily was one of them—but the distance she had asked for was there. As far as was reasonable she was allocated other patients and when they spoke it was only about work.

'Can you buddy this?' Beth asked, and Louise nodded and sat down. 'What are you working over Christmas?' Beth asked.

'Tomorrow's my last shift,' Louise said, 'and then I'm off till after New Year.'

'Lucky you!'

'I know.' Louise smiled. 'I can't wait.'

She lied.

They looked at the CTG together and Anton could hear them discussing it, Louise asking a couple of questions before they both signed off on it.

What a mistrusting fool he had been.

He had never worked anywhere better than here. The diligence, the care, was second to none but he'd realised it all too late.

'Do you need anything, Anton?' Beth asked, as Anton signed off on a few prescriptions and then stood.

'Nope, I'm heading home. Goodnight, everyone.'

When Anton stepped into his apartment a little later he felt like ripping the bloody tinsel down, yet he left it.

Louise had been in his apartment for three nights in total yet she was everywhere.

From lipstick on the towels and sheets to long blonde hairs in his comb.

Even the bed smelt of her perfume and Anton woke to his phone buzzing at three-thirty a.m. and, for a second, so consuming was her scent he actually thought she was in bed beside him.

Instead, it was the ward with news about Emily.

'I'm so sorry...' Emily said, as Anton came into the room at four a.m.

'No apologies,' Anton said, taking off his jacket, and then smiled at Evie, who had set up for Anton to examine Emily.

'I thought I'd wet myself,' Emily said. 'Maybe I did...'

'It is amniotic fluid,' Anton said, taking a swab. 'Your waters are leaking. We will get this swab checked for any signs of infection and keep a close eye on your temperature.'

'How long can I go with a leak?'

'Variable. Do you have any discomfort?'

'My back aches,' Emily said, 'but I'm not sure if that's from being in bed...'

'Have you told Hugh?'

'Not yet,' Emily said. 'He was paged at midnight and he's in Theatre. He'll find out soon enough.'

When Louise came on for her shift she saw Anton sitting at the desk and duly ignored him. She headed around to the kitchen and made herself a cup of tea, trying to ignore the scent and feel of him when he walked into the kitchen behind her.

'Emily's waters are leaking,' Anton said. 'I just thought I'd tell you now, rather than you hear it during handover.'

Louise turned round.

'I've ordered an ultrasound to check the amniotic levels and she is on antibiotics...'

'But?'

'Her back is hurting again. There are no contractions but her uterus is irritable.'

'She's going to have it.'

'You don't know that's the case…'

'I do know that this baby is coming soon,' Louise said, and Anton nodded.

'I don't think she'll hold off for much longer.'

Louise felt her eyes fill up when Anton spoke on.

'I miss working with you, Louise.'

Louise didn't say anything.

'I miss *you*,' Anton said.

She looked at him and, yes, she missed him too.

'Can we start again?' Anton said.

'I don't know.'

'Louise, you seem to have it in your head that I'm controlling. I get that I have been at work, I still will be…' He looked at her. 'Do you know why I've been on water at all the parties over Christmas? It's because I have Hazel who is due to deliver soon and I believe Emily will have that baby any day. I want to be there for them both. Yes, I am fully in control at work, and I get you have seen me at my worst here, but you know why now.'

Louise breathed out and looked at him, the most diligent person she knew, and then he continued speaking.

'You explained you are dieting because you have a photo shoot, that you know what you're doing with your weight, and not once since then have I said anything. I was worried about you because my sister has been there but when you said you knew what you were doing, I accepted that.'

He had.

'My ex…' she didn't want to say it here but it was time to tell him a little, if not all. 'He was so jealous, he didn't get that I could be friends with Rory. He didn't even like Emily…'

'And…?' Anton pushed, but Louise shook her head so he pushed on as best he could, but he was a non-witness after the fact and Louise kept him so.

'I would never come between you and your friends.'

'You weren't exactly friendly towards Rory on the night of the theatre do—you were giving him filthy looks.'

'Oh, that's right,' Anton said. 'And you were so sweet to *Saffron*. I was jealous when I thought you were on together, just as you were with me.'

Louise swallowed, she knew he was right.

'I like your friends. I like it that you can be friendly with an ex. And you can flirt, you can be funny, and I have no issue with it, but what I will not do is go along with the notion that I like you going for IVF so early in our relationship.'

Louise turned to go.

'Wrong word for you, Louise?'

It was.

'I need to think, Anton,' Louise said, and possibly the nicest thing he did then was not to argue his case or demand that they speak. He simply nodded.

'Of course.'

Louise took handover and she was allocated Stephanie's patients, all except for Emily, who was asleep when she went in to her.

'Just rest,' Louise said. 'I'm only doing your blood pressure.'

'When are you going for lunch?' Emily asked sleepily.

'About twelve. Do you want me to have it here with you?'

Emily nodded. 'Unless you need a break from the patients.'

'Don't be daft—of course I'd love to have lunch with you.'

When lunchtime came Louise went and got her salad from the fridge and it was so nice to close the door and sit down with her friend.

'It's going to be strange, not having you around,' Emily admitted.

'I'll be visiting, texting…'

'I know,' Emily said, 'it just won't be the same. Are you excited about your photo shoot tomorrow?'

'I am, though you're to promise you'll text me if anything happens.' Louise went into her pocket and handed Emily a business card. 'This is the hotel I'm at, just in case there's nowhere to put my phone!'

'Louise, you are not leaving your photo shoot,' Emily said, handing her back the card.

'But I want to be here if anything happens.'

'I know you do and I'd love you to be here, but I've got Hugh.'

Louise took back the card and stared at it.

Emily had Hugh.

Yes, Louise could do this alone and she would, but for a moment there she reconsidered. Hugh had been here every day, making Emily laugh, letting her relax, an endless stream of support.

It would be so hard to do this alone.

Louise cleared her throat. She didn't like where her mind was heading. 'Well, if you can hold off tomorrow,

Christmas Day would be fine.' Louise gave her friend a wide smile as she teased her. 'At least that would get me out of dinner at Mum's.'

Emily laughed,

'Have you seen what you're wearing for the photo shoot?' Emily asked.

'Oh, it's so nice, all reds and black—Valentine's Day stuff, seriously sexy,' Louise said. 'We've got the presidential suite and I think I'm his girlfriend or wife, the model's Jeremy...' Louise rattled on as, unseen, Anton came in and checked Emily's CTG. 'He's so gorgeous but so gay. Anyway, we wake up and why I'm wearing a bra and panties and shoes at six a.m. I have no idea, but then there are to be photos with me waving him off to work...'

'Still in your undies and shoes?' Emily asked, and Louise nodded.

'Then he comes home with flowers and I'm in my evening stuff then, and I think he takes me over the dining table...'

Emily wished Louise would turn around and see Anton's smile as she spoke.

'Everything is looking good,' Anton said, and Emily watched as Louise jumped, wondering how much he had heard. Emily's heart actually hurt that Louise expected to be told off for being herself, and she watched her friend make herself turn around and smile.

'Hiya,' Louise said. 'I'm just asking Emily to cross her legs tomorrow, but any time after that is fine.'

'How Emily's temperature?'

'All normal. I'm actually on my lunch break.'

'Oh,' Anton said, and left them to it. 'Sorry for interrupting.'

'Why won't you give the two of you a chance?' Emily said. 'Why can't you believe—?'

'Because I stopped believing,' Louise said. 'I want to believe—I want to believe that we might be able to work, that we're as right for each other, as I sometimes feel we are. I just don't know how to start.'

'Have you told him what happened last Christmas?'

'I don't know how to.'

'He needs to know, Louise. If you two are to stand a chance then you have to somehow tell him.'

Louise shook her head. 'I don't want to talk about it ever again.'

'Why don't you ask Anton to come along tomorrow?'

'Good God, no!'

'Think about it—you at your tarty best. What would Wesley have done?'

'I shudder to think,' Louise said. 'Look, I know Anton's not like that. I'm just so scared because I'd have sworn Wesley wasn't like that either.'

'Well, there's one very easy way to find out.'

'I think he's working tomorrow,' Louise said. 'Anyway, don't you want him here?'

'Oh, believe me, if I go into labour I'll be calling him, so you'd know anyway, but please don't leave your photo shoot for me. I know how important it is to you.'

'Okay,' Louise said. 'I still want to know, though.'

'Ask Anton.'

Louise shook her head. 'He's not going to take a day off for that.'

'He's not going to if you don't ask him.'

Louise checked on a patient who was sleeping but in labour and she put her on the CTG machine and took a footstool and climbed up onto the nurses' station where she sat, watching her patient from a distance, listening to the baby's heartbeat.

Anton walked onto the unit and saw Louise sitting up on the bench, back straight, ears trained, like some elongated pixie.

'What are you doing?' Anton asked, as he walked past.

'Watching room seven,' Louise said, and smiled and looked down.

'Are you okay?' Anton said, referring to their conversation in the kitchen that morning.

'I don't know.'

'I know you don't and that's okay.'

'Can you help me down?' Louise asked cheekily, and watched as he glanced at the footstool. 'Whoops!' She kicked away the footstool and Anton smiled and helped her down. The brief contact, the feel of his hands on her waist stirred her senses and made her long to break her self-imposed isolation. She just didn't know how.

'I know we need to talk,' Louise said. 'I just don't know when.'

'That's fine.'

A patient buzzed and he let her go.

'Hello, Carmel,' Louise said, and then saw that Carmel wasn't in bed but in the bathroom, and the noise she was making had Louise instantly push the bell before even going to investigate.

'There's something there,' Carmel said. She was deep-squatting and Emily pulled on gloves with her heart in her mouth. Carmel's baby was breech, and if it was a cord prolapse then it was dire indeed.

Louise pressed the bell in the bathroom in three short bursts as she knelt.

Thankfully it wasn't the cord. Instead two little legs

were hanging out. 'Call Stephanie,' Louise said, as Brenda popped her head in the door.

'She's delivering someone,' Brenda said. 'I'll get Anton and the cart.'

'You,' Louise said to Carmel, 'are doing amazingly.' The baby was dangling and it was the hardest thing not to interfere. Instinct meant you wanted traction, to get the head out, but Louise breathed through it, her hands hovering to catch the baby.

She heard or rather sensed that it was Anton who had come in and she went to move aside but he just knelt behind Louise. 'Well done, Carmel,' Anton said.

Louise felt his hand on her shoulder as patiently they waited for Mother Nature to take her course.

It was just so lovely and quiet. Brenda came in with the cart and stood back. There was a baby about to be born and everyone just let it happen.

Patience was a necessary virtue here.

'That's it,' Louise said. 'Put your hands down and feel your baby,' she said, as the baby simply dropped, and Carmel let out a moan as her baby was delivered into her own and Louise's hands.

'Well done,' Anton said, as Brenda went and got a hot blanket and wrapped it around the mother and infant.

Stephanie arrived then, smiling delightedly.

'Well done, Carmel!'

It had been so nice, so lovely and so much less scary with Anton there—a lovely soft birth. Louise's eyes were glittering with happy tears as finally Carmel was back in bed with her husband beside her and her baby in her arms.

It was lovely to see them all cosy and happy.

'It looks like you might get that Christmas at home after all.' Louise smiled.

'Oh, I'm going home tomorrow,' Carmel said. 'Nothing's going to stop us having the Christmas we want now.'

Later, in the kitchen, pulling a teabag from her scrubs to make Carmel her only fantastic cup of hospital tea, she saw the hotel card that she had brought in to give Emily.

Was it a ridiculous idea to ask him to be there tomorrow? Did she really have to put him through some strange test?

Yet a part of Louise wanted him to see the other side of her also.

She walked out and saw Anton sitting at the desk, writing up his notes.

'Are you working tomorrow?' Louise asked.

'I am.'

She put the card down.

'It's my photo shoot tomorrow from ten till seven—see if you can get away for an hour or so. I'll leave your name at Reception.'

Anton read the address and then looked up but Louise was gone.

CHAPTER FIFTEEN

IT REALLY WAS the best job in the world.

Well, apart from midwifery, which Louise absolutely loved, but this was the absolutely cherry on the cake, Louise thought as she looked in the mirror.

Her hair was all backcombed and coiffed, her eyes were heavy with black eyeliner and she had lashings of red lipstick on.

All her body was buffed and oiled and then she'd had to suffer the hardship of putting on the most beautiful underwear in the world.

It was such a dark red that it was almost black and it emphasised the paleness of her skin.

And she got to keep it!

Louise smiled at herself in the mirror.

'Okay, they're ready for you, Louise.'

Now the hard work started.

She stepped into the presidential suite and took off her robe and there was Jeremy in bed, looking all sexy and rumpled but very bored with it all, and there, in the lounge, was Anton.

Oh! She had thought he might manage an hour, she hadn't been expecting him to be here at the start.

He gave her a smile of encouragement and Louise let out a breath and smiled back.

'On the bed, Louise,' Roxy, the director said.

'Morning, Jeremy.' Louise smiled. She had worked with him many times.

'Good morning, Louise.'

It was fun, though it was actually very hard work. There were loads of costume changes and not just for Louise—Jeremy kept having to have his shirt changed as Louise's lipstick wiped off. Cold cream too was Jeremy's friend as her lips left their mark on his stomach.

And not once did Anton frown or make her feel awkward.

As evening fell, the drapes were opened to show London at its dark best, though the Christmas lights would be edited out. This was for Valentine's Day after all.

'He's just home from work,' Roxy said. 'Flowers in hand but there's no time to even give them...'

'Okay.'

Jeremy lifted her up and she wrapped her legs around his hips and crossed her ankles as Roxy gave Jeremy a huge bouquet of dark red roses to hold.

'A bit lower, Louise.'

Louise obliged and as she wiggled her hips to get comfortable on Jeremy's crotch she made everyone, including Anton, laugh as she alluded to his complete lack of response. 'You are so-o-o gay, Jeremy!'

Anton had stayed the whole day. Louise could not believe he'd swapped shifts for her and, better still, clearly Emily's baby was behaving.

At the end of the shoot she put on her robe, feeling dizzy and elated, clutching a huge bag of goodies and ready to head to a smaller room to get changed. Anton joined her and they shared a kiss in the corridor.

'Do you want me to hang up my G-string?' Louise asked, between hot, wet kisses.

'God, no,' Anton said.

'You really don't mind?'

'Mind?' Anton said, not caring what he did to her lipstick.

They were deep, deep kissing and she loved the feel of his erection pressing into her, and then she pulled back and smiled—they must look like two drunken clowns.

'I've booked a room,' Anton said.

'Thank God!'

They made it just past the door. Her robe dropped, her back to the wall, Louise tore at his top because she wanted his skin. Louise worked his zipper and freed him, still frantically kissing as she kicked her panties off. Anton's impatient hands dealt swiftly with a condom and then he lifted her. Louise wrapped her legs around him and crossed her ankles far more naturally this time. She was on the edge of coming as she lowered herself onto him but he slowed things right down as he thrust into her because what he had to say was important.

'I am crazy for you, Louise, and I don't want to change a single thing.'

'I know,' Louise said, 'and I'm crazy about you too.'

She couldn't say more than that because her mouth gave up on words and gave in to the throb between her legs. The wall took her weight then as Anton bucked into her, a delicious come ensuing for them both. Then afterwards, instead of letting her down, he walked her to the bed and let her down there.

'We're going to sort this out, Louise.'

'I know we will.' Louise nodded, except she didn't want to ruin their day with tales of yesterday and it was Christmas tomorrow and Louise didn't want to ruin that again, so instead she smiled.

'I need carbs.'

They shared a huge bowl of pasta, courtesy of room service, and then Louise, who had been up since dawn, fell asleep in his arms. Better than anything, though, was the man who, when anyone else would have been snoring, lay restless beside her and finally kissed her shoulder.

'I'm going to pop into the hospital,' Anton said. 'I've got two women—'

'Go,' Louise said, knowing how difficult it must have been to swap his shift today. 'Call me if something happens with Emily.'

'You don't mind me going in?'

She'd have minded more if he hadn't.

CHAPTER SIXTEEN

TWO PATIENTS WERE on his mind this Christmas Eve and Anton walked into the ward and chatted with Evie.

'Hazel's asleep,' Evie said, as he went through the charts. 'I'd expect you to be called in any time soon, though.'

'How about Emily?'

'Hugh's in with her, he's on call tonight. Stephanie looked in on her an hour ago and there's been no change.'

'Thanks.'

He let Hazel sleep. Anton knew now he would be called if anything happened but, for more social reasons, he tapped on the open door of the royal suite.

'Hi, Anton,' Hugh said. 'All's quiet here.'

'That's good.'

'How was your day off?' Emily asked.

'Good.'

'I was just going to check on a patient.' Hugh stood and yawned.

'I could say the same,' Anton said, 'but I wanted to check in on Emily too.'

'Is this a friendly visit, Anton?' Emily asked when Hugh had left.

'A bit of both,' Anton said, and sat on the bed. 'How are you?'

'I don't know,' Emily admitted. 'I think I've given up hoping for thirty-three weeks.'

'Thirty-one weeks is considered a moderately premature baby,' Anton said. 'Yours is a nice size. I would guess over three pounds in weight and it's had the steroids.'

'How long would it be in NICU?'

'Depends,' Anton said. 'Five weeks, maybe four if all goes well.' He knew this baby was coming and so Anton prepared Emily as best he could. 'All going well with a thirty-one-weeker means there will be some bumps—jaundice, a few apnoea attacks, runs of bradycardia. All these we expect as your baby learns to regulate its temperature and to feed…' He went through it all with her, and even though Emily had been over and over it herself he still clarified some things.

Not once had she cried, Anton thought.

Not since he had done the scan after her appendectomy had he seen Emily shed a tear.

'You can ask me anything,' Anton offered, because she was so practical he just wanted to be sure there was nothing on her mind that he hadn't covered.

'Anything?' Emily said.

'Of course.'

'How was the photo shoot?'

Anton smiled. 'I walked into that one, didn't I?'

'You did.'

'Louise was amazing.'

'She is.'

'Yet,' Anton ventured, 'for someone who is so open

about everything, and I mean *everything*, she's very private too…'

'Yes.'

'I'm not asking you to tell me anything,' Anton said.

'You just want her to?'

Anton nodded and then said, 'I want her to feel able to.'

CHAPTER SEVENTEEN

LOUISE OPENED HER eyes to a dark hotel room on Christmas morning and glanced at the time. It was four a.m. and no Anton.

She lay there remembering this time last year but even though she was alone it didn't feel like it this time, especially when the door opened gently and Anton came in quietly.

'Happy Christmas,' Louise said.

'Buon Natale,' Anton said, as he undressed.

'How's Emily?'

'Any time now,' Anton said. 'I was just about to come back here when another patient went into labour.'

'Hazel?' Louise sleepily checked.

'A little girl,' Anton said. 'She's in NICU but I'm very pleased with how she is doing.'

'A nice way to start Christmas,' Louise said, as he slid into bed and spooned into her.

His hands were cold and so was his face as he dropped a kiss on her shoulder.

'Scratch my back with your jaw.'

He obliged and then, without asking, scratched the back of her neck too, his tongue wet and probing, his jaw all lovely and stubbly, and his hand stroking her very close to boiling.

'Did you stop for condoms?'

'No,' Anton said. 'We have one left.'

'Use it wisely, then.' Louise smiled, though she didn't want his hand to move for a second and as Anton sheathed himself Louise made the beginning of a choice—she would have to go on the Pill. They were both so into each other that common sense was elusive, but she stopped thinking then as she felt him nudging her entrance. Swollen from last night and then swollen again with want, it was Louise who let out a long moan as he took her slowly from behind. His hand was stroking her breast and she craned her neck for his mouth.

He could almost taste her near orgasm on her tongue as it hungrily slathered his. He was being cruel, the best type of cruelty because she was going to come now and he'd keep going through it. She almost shot out of her skin as it hit, and she wished he would stop but she also wished he wouldn't. It was so deliciously relentless, there was no come down. Anton started thrusting faster, driving her to the next, and then he stilled and she wondered why because they were just about there...

'No way,' Louise said, hearing his phone. 'Quickly...'

Oh, he tried, but it would not stop ringing. 'Sorry...' Anton laughed at her urgency, because sadly it was his special phone that was ringing. The one for his special Anton patients. And a very naked Louise lay there as he took the call.

'Get used to it,' Anton said as he was connected, and then he hesitated, because if he was telling Louise to get used to it, well, it was something he'd never said before. There was no time to dwell on it, though, as he listened to Evie.

'I'll be there in about fifteen minutes. Thank you for letting me know.' He ended the call. 'Are you coming in with me to deliver a Christmas baby?'

'Emily!'

'Waters just fully broke...'

'Oh, my goodness...'

'She's doing well. Hugh's on his way in but things are going to move quite fast.'

They had the quickest shower ever and then Anton drove them through London streets on a wet, pre-dawn Christmas morning and he got another phone call from the ward. He asked for them to page the anaesthetist for an epidural as that could sometimes slow things down and also, despite the pethidine she'd been given, Emily was in a lot of pain.

'She'll be okay,' Louise said, only more for herself. 'I'm so scared, Anton,' Louise admitted. 'I really am.'

'I know, but she's going to be fine and so is the baby.' There was no question for Anton, they *had* to be okay. 'Big breath,' Anton said.

'I'm not the one in labour.'

It had just felt like it for a moment, though.

Oh, she was terrified for her friend but Louise was at her sparkly best as she and Anton walked into the delivery ward.

'Oh!' Emily smiled in delighted surprise because it was only five a.m. after all.

'The mobile obstetric squad has arrived,' Louise teased. 'Aren't you lucky that it's us two on?' She smiled and gave Emily a cuddle. 'Oh, hi, Hugh!' Louise winked and noted he was looking a bit white. 'Merry Christmas!'

'Hi, Louise.' Hugh was relieved to see them both too.

'I want an epidural,' Emily said.

'It's on its way. I've already paged Rory. We want to slow this down a little,' Anton explained while examining her, 'and an epidural might help us to do that. You've got a bit of a way to go but because the baby is small you don't have to be fully dilated.'

'I'm scared,' Emily admitted.

'You're going to meet your baby,' Louise said, and she gave Emily's hand a squeeze. 'Let us worry for you, okay? We're getting paid after all.'

Emily nodded.

'NICU's been notified?' Anton checked, and then gave an apologetic smile when Evie rolled her eyes and nodded, and Anton answered for her. 'Of course they have.'

There was a knock on the door and Emily's soon-to-be-favourite person came in.

'Hi, lovely Emily,' Rory said. 'We meet again.'

'Oh, yes,' Louise recalled. 'Rory knocked you out when you had your appendix.'

'Hopefully this will slow things down enough that I miss Christmas dinner,' Louise joked, though they all knew this baby would be born by dawn.

A little high on pethidine, a little ready to fix the world, very determined not to panic about the baby, Emily decided she had the perfect solution, the perfect one to show Louise how wonderful and not controlling or jealous Anton was.

And the man delivering your premature baby had to be seriously wonderful, Emily decided!

'Tell them about your Christmas dinner last year,' Emily said, as Louise sat her up and put her legs over the edge of the bed and then pulled Emily in for an epidural cuddle.

'Relax,' Hugh said, stroking Emily's hair as she leant on Louise, while Rory located the position on Emily's spine.

But Emily didn't want to relax, she wanted this sorted now!

'Tell them!' Emily shouted, and Louise shared a little 'yikes' look with Hugh.

Never argue with a woman in transition!

'I'm going to have a word with you later,' Louise warned. She knew what Emily was doing.

'Okay!' Louise said, as she cuddled Emily. 'Well, I'd broken up with Wesley and I checked myself into a hotel—the most miserable place on God's earth, as it turned out, and I couldn't face the restaurant and families so I had room service and it was awful. I think it was processed chicken...'

'Stay still, Emily,' Rory said.

'She's having a contraction,' Anton said, and Louise rocked her through it and after Rory got back to work she went on with her story.

'Well, I was so miserable but I cheered myself up by realising I'd finally got out of having Christmas dinner at Mum's.'

'It's seriously awful food,' Rory said casually, threading the cannula in.

'You wouldn't know,' Louise retorted. 'The one time you came for dinner you pretended you'd been paged and had to leave. Anyway, I arrived at Mum's on Boxing Day and she'd *saved* me not one but about five dinners, and had decided I needed a mother's love and cooking...'

Anton laughed. 'That bad?'

'So, so bad,' Louise said, and her little tale had got them through the insertion of the epidural and she'd managed not to reveal all.

She looked at Anton and there wasn't a flicker of a ruffled feather at her mention of Rory once being at her family's home.

He was a good man. She'd always known it, now she felt it.

'You'll start to feel it working in a few minutes, Emily,' Rory said.

'I can feel it working already.' Emily sighed in relief as Louise helped her back onto the delivery bed.

Rory left and Louise told Evie she'd got this and then suggested that Anton grab a coffee as she set about darkening the room.

'Sure,' Anton said, even though he didn't feel like leaving, but, confident that he would be called when needed and not wanting to make this birth too different for Emily, he left.

The epidural brought Emily half an hour of rest and she lay on her side, with Hugh beside her as Louise sat on the couch out of view, a quiet presence as they waited for nature to take its course, but thirty minutes later Louise called Anton in.

The room was still quiet and dark but it was a rather full one—Rory and the paediatric team were present for the baby as the baby began its final descent into the world.

'Do you feel like you need to push?' Anton asked, and Emily shook her head as her baby inched its way down.

'A bit,' she said a moment later.

'Try not to,' Anton said. 'Let's do this as slowly as we can.'

'Head end, Hugh,' Louise said, because he looked a bit green, and she left him at Emily's head and went down to the action end, holding Emily's leg as Anton did his best to slow things down.

'Do you want a mirror?' Louise asked.

'Absolutely not.'

'Black hair and lots of it.' Louise was on delighted tiptoe.

'Louise, can you come up here?' Emily gasped. 'I don't want you seeing me...'

'Oh, stop it.' Louise laughed and then Emily truly didn't care what anyone could see because, even with the epidural, there was the odd sensation of her baby moving down.

'Oh!'

'Don't push,' Anton said.

'I think I have to.'

'Breathe,' Hugh said, and got the F word back, but she did manage to breathe through it as Anton helped this little one get a less rapid entrance into the world. And then out came the head and Louise gently suctioned its tiny mouth as its eyes blinked at the new world.

'Happy Christmas,' Anton said, delivering a very vigorous bundle onto Emily's stomach.

Emily got her hotbox blanket wrapped around her shoulders and then another one was placed over a tiny baby whose mum and dad were starting to get to know it.

Anton glanced over at the paediatrician and all was well enough to allow just a minute for a nice cuddle.

'A girl,' Emily said.

The sweetest, sweetest girl, Louise thought. She stood watching over them, holding oxygen near her little mouth as Emily and Hugh got to cuddle her and Louise cried happy tears, baby-just-been-born tears, but then she did what she had to.

'We need to check her…'

And finally Emily started to cry.

CHAPTER EIGHTEEN

LOUISE TOOK THE baby over to the warmer and she was wrapped and given some oxygen and a tube put down her to give her surfactant that would help with her immature lungs.

'We're going to take her up,' Louise said, as Emily completely broke down.

'Can't I go with her?'

'Not yet,' Anton said, 'but you'll be able to see her soon.'

'I'll go with her,' Hugh assured his wife, but Louise could see how upset Emily was. She had been holding onto her emotions for weeks now, quietly determined not to love her baby too much, though, of course she did.

'Hugh, you stay with Emily and I'll stay with the baby,' Louise suggested. 'She's fine, she's beautiful and you'll see her very soon, Emily. I promise I am not going to leave her side.'

Louise did stay with her, the neonatal staff did their thing and Louise watched, but from a chair, smiling when an hour or so later Hugh came in.

'Hi, Dad,' Louise said, watching as Hugh peered in. 'How's Emily?'

'Upset,' Hugh said. 'She'll be fine once she sees her

but Anton says she needs to have a sleep first and she won't.' He took out his phone and went to film the baby, who was crying and unsettled.

'Why don't you go and get some colostrum from her?' Ellie, the neonatal nurse, suggested to Louise. 'Mum might feel better knowing she's fed her.'

'Great idea.' Louise smiled and headed back to the ward.

Emily was back in her room, the door open so she could be watched, but the curtains were drawn.

'Knock-knock,' Louise said, and there was her friend, teary and missing her baby so much. 'She's fine, Hugh's with her,' Louise went on, and explained her plans.

'You just need to get a tiny bit off,' Louise said, 'but she's hungry and it's so good to get the colostrum into them.'

'Okay.'

Emily managed a few drops, which Louise nursed into a syringe, but Louise reassured her that that was more than enough. 'This is like gold for your baby.' Louise was delighted with her catch.

As Louise headed out she glanced at the time and re-alised she would have to ring her mum, who was going to be incredibly worried, given what had happened last year.

As Anton walked into the kitchen on the maternity unit it was to the sight of Louise brightly smiley and taking a selfie with her phone.

'Forward it onto me,' Anton said.

Louise smiled. He didn't care a bit that she was vain, though in this instance he was mistaken. 'Actually, this is for Mum. She's all stressed and thinks I've made up Emily's baby. Well, she didn't say that exactly…' She texted her mum the photo and then picked up the small syringe of colostrum. 'Christmas dinner for Baby Linton. I can't believe she's here.'

'Relieved?' Anton asked.

'So, so relieved. I know she's going to get jaundice and give them a few scares but she is just so lovely and such a nice size...'

'Louise.' Anton caught her arm as she went to go. 'How come you didn't go home last Christmas?'

'I told you, I was pretty miserable.'

'Your family are close.'

'Of course.' She shrugged. 'I just didn't want to upset them...'

'You couldn't put on an act for one day?'

'No...' Her voice trailed off. She hadn't wanted to upset her family on Christmas Day and neither did she want to upset him now. Yet her family had been so hurt by her shutting them out. Louise looked into his eyes and knew that her silence was hurting him too. Everyone in the delivery room except Anton knew what had happened last year and if they were going to have a future, and she was starting to think they might, then it was only fair to tell him.

'I couldn't cover up the bruises. I waited till Boxing Day and called Emily, who came straight away. When I wouldn't go to hospital she called Rory and he came to the hotel and sutured my scalp.'

Louise didn't want to see his expression and neither did she want to go into further details of the day right now. She had told him now and she could feel his struggle to react, to suppress, possibly just to breathe as he fathomed just what the saying meant about having the living daylights knocked out of you. The light in Louise had gone out that day and had stayed out for some months, but it was fully back now. 'I'm going to get this up to the baby.' She kissed his taut cheek. 'You need to shave.'

They had a small, fierce cuddle that said more than words could and then Louise said she was heading up to NICU, still unable to meet his eyes.

Hugh watched and Louise did the filming as Baby Linton was given the precious colostrum and a short while later was asleep.

Have a sleep now, Louise texted. Your daughter is and she attached the film and sent it.

A few moments later Hugh's phone buzzed and he smiled as Emily gave him the go-ahead.

'Thanks,' Hugh said, and then he took out a pen and crossed out the 'Baby' on 'Baby Linton'. He wrote the word 'Louise' in instead.

Louise Linton.

'Two Ls means double the love,' Louise said, trying not to cry. 'Thanks, Hugh, that means an awful lot.'

More than anyone could really know.

When Hugh went back to Maternity to be with Emily, Louise sat there, staring at her namesake, and the thought she had briefly visited that morning returned.

She'd have to go back on the Pill. It wouldn't be fair to Anton if there were any mistakes, however unlikely it was that she might naturally fall pregnant. But that ultimately meant, when she came off the Pill again, another few months of the horrible times she'd just been through simply trying to work out her cycle.

Louise knew she was probably looking at another year at best. Could she do it without sulking? Louise wondered. Just let go of her hopes for a baby and chase the dream of a relationship that actually worked?

She walked over and looked at the little one who had

caused so much angst but who had already brought so many smiles.

'How's Louise?' Anton came up a couple of hours later and saw Louise standing and gazing into the incubator.

'Tired,' Louise said, still not able to meet his eyes after her revelation. 'Oh, you mean the baby? She's perfect.' She glanced over to where Rory and several staff were gathered around an incubator. Louise knew that it was Henry, a baby she had delivered in November. He had multiple issues and was a very sick baby indeed. She looked down at little Louise, who was behaving beautifully. 'You're a bit of a fraud really, aren't you?'

'Emily's asleep,' Anton said. 'When she wakes up she can come and visit.'

'I'll stay till then.' Louise smiled. 'Can you just watch Louise while I go to the loo?'

Anton glanced over at the neonatal nurse but that wasn't what Louise meant. 'No, you're to be on love watch,' Louise said.

Anton took a seat when usually he wouldn't have and looked at the very special little girl.

'Thank you!' Louise was back a couple of minutes later. 'I really needed that!'

Anton rolled his eyes as Louise, as usual, gave far too much information. When Anton didn't get up she perched on his knee, with her back to him, watching little Louise asleep. She had nasal cannulas in but she was breathing on her own and though she might need a little help with that in the coming days, for now she was doing very well.

'Emily's here,' Anton said, and Louise jumped up and smiled as Emily was wheeled over.

Yes, Louise was far from the tiniest infant here but

the machines and equipment were terrifying and Ellie talked them through it.

'I'm going to go,' Louise said, and gave Emily a kiss. 'I'll come and see you tomorrow. Send me a text tonight. Oh, and here…' She handed over a little pink package. 'Open it later. Just enjoy your time with her now.'

She gave her friend a quick cuddle then she and Anton left them to it.

'Do you want to come to Mum and Dad's?' Louise asked, as they stopped by his office to get his laptop.

'Will it cause a lot of questions for you?'

'Torrents,' Louise said, but then the most delicious smell diverted her and she peeked out the door, to see Alex and Jennifer heading onto the ward with two plates and lots of containers.

'Alex,' Louise called, and they turned round.

'They're up seeing the baby,' Louise explained.

'Oh, we didn't come to see them,' Jennifer said, and Louise jumped in.

'How sweet of you to bring Christmas dinner for the obstetrician and midwife,' Louise teased, watching Jennifer turn purple as Anton stepped out.

'Anton.' Alex smiled warmly. 'Merry Christmas.'

'Merry Christmas,' Anton said.

'You haven't met Jennifer…'

'Jennifer.' Anton smiled. 'Merry Christmas.'

'Merry Christmas,' Jennifer croaked, and then turned frantic eyes to Louise. 'We don't want to disturb Emily and Hugh, we were just going to leave them a dinner for tonight…' She was practically thrusting the plates at Louise. 'We'll leave these with you.'

But Louise refused to be rushed.

'That's so nice of you,' Louise said, but instead of taking the plates she peeked under the foil. 'Jennifer, Emily didn't just give birth to a foal—there's enough here to feed a horse.'

It looked and smelt amazing and Louise was shameless in her want for a taste, not just for her but for Anton too. 'That's what a traditional Christmas dinner looks like, Anton.' Louise smiled sweetly at Jennifer. 'It's Anton's first Christmas in England,' Louise explained, and of course she would get her way. 'What a shame he's never tasted a really nice one.'

'I'm sure there's enough for everyone,' Alex said, oblivious to his wife's tension around Anton, and Jennifer gave in.

'Luckily my husband's good with a scalpel!'

It was a very delicate operation.

They went into the kitchen and got out tea plates.

Louise and Anton got two Brussels sprouts each, one roast potato and two slivers of parsnips in butter as Anton watched, fascinated by the argument taking place.

'I don't think Emily needs six piggies in blankets,' Louise said.

'Piggies in blankets?' Anton checked.

'Sausages wrapped in bacon,' Alex translated.

'Two each, then,' Jennifer said, and Alex added them to the tea plates.

'How much turkey can they have?' Alex asked.

'A slice each,' Jennifer said. 'Emily needs her protein.'

Louise shook her head.

'Okay, one and a half,' Jennifer relented.

Alex duly divided.

They got one Yorkshire pudding each too, as well as home-made cranberry and bread sauce, and finally dinner was served!

'You can go now.' Louise smiled. 'Merry Christmas.'

She put sticky notes on Hugh and Emily's plates, warning everyone to keep their greedy mitts off, then Louise closed the kitchen door.

She found a used birthday candle among the ward's Christmas paraphernalia and stuck it in a stale mince pie as their Christmas dinners rotated in the microwave and then she turned the lights off.

'Do you want to pull a cracker?'

'Bon-bon,' Anton said, but they cracked two and sat in hats and, oh, my, Jennifer's cooking was divine, even if you had to fight her to taste it.

'How do you know Jennifer?' Louise asked, as she smeared bread sauce over her turkey.

'I don't.'

'Anton!' Louise looked at his deadpan face. 'No way was that the first time you two have met. Is she pregnant again?' Louise frowned. 'She must be in her midforties…'

'I don't know what you're on about,' Anton said, though his lips were twitching to tell.

'Are you having an affair with Jennifer?' Louise asked, smiling widely.

'Where the hell did you produce that from?' Anton smiled back.

'Anton, Jennifer went purple when she saw you and I just know you've seen each other before.'

'I don't know if I like this bread sauce,' was Anton's response to her probing.

'It's addictive,' Louise said, and gave up fishing.

It was the nicest Christmas dinner ever—perfect food, the best company and a baby named Louise snug and safe nearby. After they had finished their delectable meal

Louise went over and sat on his knee. 'Thank you for a lovely Christmas, Anton.'

'Thank you,' Anton said, because what she'd told him, though upsetting, hadn't spoiled his Christmas. Instead, it had drawn them closer.

'We both deserve it, I think.'

She felt his arms on her back, lightly stroking the clasp of her bra and as she rested her head on his shoulder it felt the safest place in the world.

'Do you understand why I'm so wary?'

'Now I do,' Anton said. 'I'm glad you were able to tell me and I am so sorry for what happened to you.'

It was then Louise let her dreams go; well, not for ever, but she put them on hold for a while.

'I'm going to cancel my appointment,' Louise said, and she didn't lift her head, not now because she couldn't look him in the eye but because she didn't want Anton to see her cry. 'Well, I'm going to go and get the test results back but I'm not going to go for the IVF.'

He could hear her thick voice and knew there were tears and he rubbed her back.

'Thank you,' Anton said, and they sat for a moment, Anton glad for the chance for them, Louise grateful for it too but just a bit sad for now, though she soon chirped up.

'When I say cancelling the IVF I meant that I'm postponing it,' Louise amended. 'No pressure or anything but I'm not waiting till I'm forty for you to make up your mind whether you want us to be together.'

'You have to make your mind up too,' Anton pointed out.

'Oh, I did yesterday,' Louise said, and pulled her head

back and smiled into his eyes. 'I'm already in.' She gave him a light kiss before standing to head for home.

'You're stuck with me now.'

CHAPTER NINETEEN

As THEY WALKED out they bumped into Rory, who was on his way up to NICU to check in on a six-week-old who was doing his level best to spoil everyone's Christmas.

'You look tired,' Louise said.

'Very,' Rory admitted. 'I'm just off to break some bad news to a family.'

'What time do you finish?' Louise asked.

'Six.'

'Do you want to come for a rubbish dinner at Mum's?' Louise asked.

'God, no.' Rory smiled.

'Honestly, if Anton and you *both* come then Mum will assume I'm just bringing all the strays and foreigners who are lonely…' she pointed her thumb in Anton's direction '…rather than grilling me about him.' She knew Rory's family lived miles away. 'You don't want to be on your own on Christmas night.'

'I won't be on my own,' Rory said. 'Thanks for offering, though. I'm going to Gina's to help her celebrate her first sober Christmas in who knows how long.'

'Gina?' Louise checked. 'Is she the one you're—?'

'She's always been the one,' Rory said. 'It's nearly killed me to watch her self-destruct.' He stood there on the edge of breaking down as Anton's hand came on his shoulder. 'Nothing's ever happened between us,' Rory explained. 'And nothing can.'

'Why?' Louise asked.

'Because she's in treatment and you're not supposed to have a relationship for at least a year.'

'Does she know how you feel?' Louise asked.

'No, because I don't want to confuse her. She's trying to sort her stuff out and I don't want to add to it.'

'She's so lucky to have you,' Louise said, 'even if she doesn't know that she has.' Louise let out a breath. 'Who's going to speak to the parents with you?'

'Just me,' Rory said. 'They're all busy with Henry.'

'I know the parents,' Louise said to Rory. 'You're not doing that on your own. Is there any hope?'

'A smudge,' Rory said, and they headed back to NICU and Anton stood and waited as Louise and Rory went in to see the parents.

Anton loved her love.

How she gave it away and then, when surely there should be nothing left, she still gave more.

How she walked so pale out of a horrible room and cuddled her ex as Anton stood there, the least jealous guy in the world. He was simply glad that Rory had Louise to lean on as Anton remembered that horrible Christmas when he'd been the one breaking bad news.

He would be grateful to Rory for ever for being there for Louise last year.

As they walked out into the grey Christmas afternoon and to Anton's car, Louise spoke.

'Rory's right not to tell Gina how he feels,' Louise said.

'Do you think?'

'I do.' Louise nodded. 'I think you do need a whole year to recover from anything big. Not close to a year, you need every single day of it, you need to go through each milestone, each anniversary and do them differently, and as of today I have.'

It had been a hard year, though the previous one had been harder—estranged from family and friends and losing herself in the process. But now here she was, a little bit older, a whole lot wiser, and certainly Louise was herself.

Yes, she was grateful for those difficult years.

It had brought her here after all.

CHAPTER TWENTY

'Ooh…' Louise reached for her phone as it bleeped. 'We do need to stop on our way to the hotel for condoms because it would seem that I just ovulated.'

'You get an alert when you ovulate?' Anton shook his head in disbelief.

'Well, I put in all my cycles and temperatures and things and it calculates it. It's great…'

'You're going to be one of those old ladies who talks about her bowels, aren't you?'

'God, yes.' Louise laughed at the thought. 'I'll probably have an app for it.'

The thing was, Anton wanted to be the old man to see it.

'Where's a bloody chemist when you need one?' Louise grumbled, going through her phone as Anton drove on and came to the biggest, yet ultimately the easiest decision of his life.

'We could stop at a pub,' Louise suggested. 'Nip in to the loos and raid the machines.'

'We're not stopping, Louise. You need to get to your mum's.'

Louise sulked all the way back to the hotel and even more so when they came out of the elevator and she swiped her entry card to their room. 'I've got the hotel room, a hot Italian and no bloody condoms. Where's the justice, I ask you…'

And then the door opened and she simply stopped speaking. For a moment Louise thought she had the wrong room because it was in darkness save for the twinkling fairly-lights reflecting off the tinsel. She had never seen a room more overly decorated, Louise thought. There was green, silver, red and gold tinsel, there were lights hanging everywhere. It was gaudy, it was loud and so, so beautiful.

'You did this?'

'I don't want you ever to think of a hotel room on Christmas Day and be sad again. I want this to be your memory.'

'How?'

'I rang them,' Anton said. 'They were worried it looked over the top, but I reassured them you can *never* have too much tinsel.'

'It's the nicest thing you could have done.'

'Yet,' Anton said, for he intended many nice things for Louise.

They started to kiss, a lovely long kiss that led them to bed. A kiss that had them peeling off their clothes and Louise stared up at the twinkling lights as slowly he removed her underwear, kissing her everywhere.

'Anton…' She was all hot and could barely breathe as he removed her bra and kissed her breasts. Louise unwrapped her presents with haste; Anton took his time.

'Anton…' she pleaded, touching herself in frustration as he slid down her panties, desperate for the soft warmth of his mouth.

'Your turn next,' Louise said, as, panties off, he kissed

up her thigh. Right now she just wanted to concentrate on the lovely feel of his mouth there, except his mouth now teased her stomach and then went back to her breasts, swirling them with his tongue and then working back up to her mouth.

His erection was there, nudging her entrance, teasing her with small thrusts, and her hands balled in frustration.

'We don't have any—'

'Do you want to try for a baby?' Anton said, throwing caution to a delectable wind that had chased him for, oh, quite a while now.

'Our baby?' Louise checked.

'I would hope so.' Anton smiled.

'You're sure?'

'Very,' Anton said. 'But are you?'

He didn't need to ask twice, but the ever-changing Louise changed again, right there in his arms.

'I'm very sure, but it isn't just a baby I want now. I want to have a baby with you,' Louise said.

'You shall,' Anton said, and it brought tears to her eyes because here was the man she loved, who would do all he could to make sure her dream came true.

The feel of him unsheathed driving into her had Louise let out a sob of pleasure. For Anton, it was heady bliss. Sensations sharpened, and he felt the warm grip and then the kiss of her cervix, welcoming him over and over again, till for Anton that was it.

The final swell of him, the passion that shot into her tipped Louise deep into orgasm. Her legs tight around him, she dragged him in deeper and let out a little scream. Then she held him there for her pleasure, just to feel each and every pulse and twitch from them as his breathing made love to her ear.

She looked up at the twinkling lights and never again would she think of Christmas and not remember this.

'What are you doing?' Anton spoke to the pillow as, still inside her, Louise's hand reached across the bed.

'Taking a photo,' Louise said, aiming her camera at the fairy-lights. And capturing the moment, she knew she'd found love, for ever.

CHAPTER TWENTY-ONE

'WILL IT BE a problem, us working together?' Louise asked. They were back at her home, with Louise grabbing everyone's presents from under her tree. 'Honestly, it's something we need to speak about.'

'We'll be fine,' Anton said. 'Louise, the reason I came down harder on you than anyone is because of what happened in Italy that day when it did all go wrong…but you're an amazing midwife, over and over I've seen it. Aside from personally, I love working with you. I know that the patients get the very best care.'

'Thank you,' Louise said. 'Still, if we get sick of each other…' She stopped then and looked at the amazing man beside her. She could never get tired of looking at him, working alongside him, getting to know him.

'I got you two presents,' Louise said.

He opened the first annoying slowly. It was beautifully wrapped and he took his time then smiled at black and white sweets wrapped in Cellophane.

'Humbugs,' Louise said, and popped one in her mouth and then gave him a very nice kiss.

'Peppermint,' Anton replied, having taken it from her mouth.

He opened the other present a little more quickly, given its strange shape, to find a large pepperoni.

'Reminds me of,' Louise teased, 'my first kiss with the pizza man and I'm also ensuring that if we ever do break up then you will never be able to eat pepperoni, or taste mint, without thinking of me. I've just hexed you orally.'

'You *are* a witch!'

'I am!' Louise smiled.

'Then you would know already that I love you.'

'I do.' Louise's eyes were misty with tears as he confirmed his feelings.

'And, if you are a witch, you would know just *how much* I love you and that I would never, ever hurt you.'

'I do know that,' Louise said. 'And if you're my wizard you'll already know that I love you with all my heart.'

'I do.'

'But I'm about to make you suffer.' She smiled at his slight frown. 'We need to get to Mum's.'

Louise's family were as mad as the woman they had produced.

Anton watched as they tore open their presents.

'A cookery book?' Susan blinked. 'Oh, and a lesson. It's a lovely thought, Louise, but I don't need a cookery lesson…'

'It's for charity, Mum.'

'I could teach her a thing or three,' Susan said, 'but I suppose if it's for charity…' She smiled a bright smile. 'Time for dinner. It's so late, you must all be starving.'

They headed to the dining room, which was decorated with so much tinsel that Anton realised where Louise's little problem stemmed from.

At first Anton had no idea what Louise was talking about when she had moaned about her mother's cooking.

It looked as good as Jennifer's, it even smelt as good as Jennifer's, but, oh, my, the taste.

'That,' Anton said, after an incredibly long twenty minutes, putting down his knife and sweating in relief that he'd cleared his plate, 'was amazing, Susan.'

'There's plenty more.' Susan smiled as she collected up the plates.

Anton looked over at Louise's dad, who gave him a thumbs-up.

'Christmas pudding now,' he said. 'Home-made!'

'If you get through this,' Chloe, Louise's younger sister, whispered to him, 'you're in.'

The lights went down and a flaming pudding was brought in and they all duly sang, except for Anton because he didn't know the words.

It looked amazing, dark and rich and smothered in brandy crème, though had he not had a taste of Jennifer's delectable one then Anton would, there and then, have sworn off Christmas pudding for life.

It was a very small price to pay for love, though.

'Family recipe.' Susan winked, as she sat down to eat hers.

'It's wonderful, Mum,' Louise said.

In its own way it was, so much so that Louise decided to share the smile.

'I'm going to take a photo and send it to my friends,' Louise said, as her mother beamed with pride. 'They don't know what they're missing out on!'

Later they crashed on the sofa and watched a film. Anton sat and Louise lay with her head in his lap. Her sisters were going through the Valentine bras she had left over from the shoot. 'There's your namesake,' Louise said, munching on chocolate as Ebenezer Scrooge appeared on screen. Anton smiled. He had never been happier.

He even smiled as Louise's sister wrinkled her nose. 'What's that smell?'

'Mum's making kedgeree for Boxing Day.' Louise yawned.

'What's kedgeree?' Anton asked.

'Rice, eggs, haddock, curry powder.' Louise looked up and met his gaze.

'How about tomorrow we go shopping for a ring?' Anton said.

'Did you just propose?'

'I did.'

'Louise Rossi…' she mused. 'I like it.'

'Good.'

'And I love you.'

'I love you too.'

'But if you're buying my ring in the Boxing Day sales, I expect a really big one, and if we're engaged, then you can tell me what's going on with you and Jennifer.'

'When I get the ring I'll tell you.'

'Mum,' Louise called, 'Dad, we just got engaged.'

There were smiles and congratulations and after a very dry December Anton enjoyed the champagne as he pulled out his phone. 'I'd better ring my family and tell them the news. They're loud,' he warned.

There were lots of 'complimentes!' and 'salute!' on speaker phone as glasses were raised. Much merriment later they came to the rapid decision they would go over there for the New Year and see them and, yes, it would seem they were officially engaged.

Louise checked her own phone and there was a picture of Hugh and Emily sharing a gorgeous Christmas dinner, courtesy of Jennifer and Alex. There was a text too, thanking them for the little pink outfit and hat, which they were sure Baby Louise would be wearing very soon.

There was also a text from Rory and it made her smile.

'How's that smudge of hope?' Anton asked, referring to little Henry.

'Still smudging.' Louise smiled as she read Rory's text. 'It's sparkling apple juice his end and I've been given strict instructions that we're not to say anything, ever, to anyone, about what he said today.'

'I am very glad that Gina has Rory with her,' Anton said.

'And me,' Louise said, and then looked up at the man she would love for ever. 'You do know that you're going to be sleeping on the sofa tonight?'

'Am I?'

'My parents would freak otherwise.' She smiled again. 'Did you know that I'm a twenty-nine-year-old virgin?'

'Of course you are,' Anton said, and stroked her hair. He'd sleep in the garden if he had to.

Louise lay there, her family nearby, Anton's hands in her hair, and all felt right with the world.

Just so completely right.

'I think that I might already be pregnant,' Louise whispered.

'Don't start.' Anton smiled.

'No, I really think I am. I feel different.'

'Stop it.' Anton laughed.

But, then, Anton thought, knowing Louise, knowing how meant to be they were, she possibly was.

They might just have made their own Christmas baby.

* * * * *

TEMPTED BY THE BRIDESMAID

ANNIE O'NEIL

This book could go to no other than Jorja and Grissom—my own fluffy hounds who are always there when I need them...and sometimes when I don't! Furry friends...simply the best

CHAPTER ONE

IT FELT AS if she were watching the world through a fishbowl. Everything was distorted. Sight. Sound. Fran would have paid a million dollars to be anywhere else right now.

Church silence was crushing. Especially under the circumstances.

Fran looked across to the groomsmen. Surely there was an ally within that pack of immaculately suited Italian gentry who…?

Hmm... Not you, not you, not you... Oh!

Fran caught eyes with one of them. Gorgeous, like the rest, but his brow was definitely more furrowed, the espresso-rich eyes a bit more demanding than the others… Oh! Was that a scar? She hadn't noticed last night at the candlelit cocktail party. *Interesting.* She wondered what it would feel like to—

"Ahem!" The priest—or was he a bishop?—cleared his throat pointedly.

Why had she raised her hand? This wasn't school— it was a church!

This wasn't even Fran's wedding, and yet the hundreds of pairs of eyes belonging to each and every esteemed guest sitting in Venice's ridiculously beautiful basilica were trained on *her*. Little ol' Francesca "Fran" Martinelli, formerly of Queens, New York, now of…well…

nowhere, really. It was just her, the dogs, a duffel bag stuffed to the hilt with more dog toys than clothes and the very, *very* pretty bridesmaid's dress she was wearing.

Putting it on, she'd actually felt girlie! Feminine. It would be back to her usual jeans and T-shirt tomorrow, though, when she showed up for her new mystery job. In the meantime, she was failing at how to be a perfect bridesmaid on an epic scale.

Fran's fingers plucked at the diaphanous fabric of her azure dress and she finally braved looking straight into the dark brown eyes of her dearest childhood friend, Princess Beatrice Vittoria di Jesolo.

The crowning glory of their shared teenage years had been flunking out of finishing school together in Switzerland. That sun-soaked afternoon playing hooky had been an absolute blast. Sure, they'd been caught, but did anyone really *care* if you could walk with a book on your head?

Their friendship had survived the headmistress dressing them down in front of their more civilized classmates, grass stains on their jeans, scrapes on their hands and knees from scrabbling around in the mountains making daisy chains and laughing until tears shot straight out of their eyes… But this moment—the one where Fran was ruining her best friend's wedding in front of the whole universe—this might very well spell the end of their friendship. The one thing she could rely on in her life.

Fran squeezed her eyes tight against Bea's inquiring gaze. The entire veil-covered, bouquet-holding, finger-waiting-for-a-ring-on-it image was branded onto her memory bank. Never mind the fact that there were official photographers lurking behind every marble pillar, and hundreds of guests—including dozens of members of Europe's royal families—filling the pews to overflowing, not to mention the countless media representatives waiting outside to film the happy power couple once they had been pronounced husband and wife.

Which they would be doing in about ten minutes or so unless she got her act together and did something!

"What exactly is your objection?" asked the man with the mystery scar through gritted teeth. In English. Which was nice.

Not because Fran's Italian was rusty—it was all she and her father ever spoke at home…when she *was* at home—but because it meant not every single person in the church would know that she'd just caught Bea's fiancé playing tonsil tennis with someone who wasn't Bea.

She stared into the man's dark eyes. Did *he* know? Did he care that the man he was standing up for in front of Italy's prime guest list was a lying cheat?

"If you could just speak up, dear," the priest tacked on, a bit more gently.

Maybe the priest didn't want to know specifically what her objection was—was choosing instead just to get the general gist that everything wasn't on the up-and-up. That or he would clap his hands, smile and say "Surprise! I saw them, too. The wedding's off because the groom's a cheat. He's just been having it off with the maid of dishonor in the passage to the doge's palace. So…who's ready for lunch?"

After another quick eye-scrunch, Fran eased one eye open and scanned the scene.

Nope. Beatrice was still standing next to her future husband, just about to be married. All doe-eyed and… well…maybe not totally doe-eyed. Beatrice had always been the pragmatic one. But—*oh, Dio! C'è una volpe sciolto nel pollaio*, as her father said whenever things were completely off-kilter. Which they were. Right now.

Right here. A fox was loose in the hen house of Venice's most holy building, where a certain groom should have been hit by a lightning bolt or something by now.

On the plus side, Fran had the perfect position to give the groom the evil eye. Marco Rodolfo. Heir apparent to some royal title or other, here in the Most Serene Republic of Venice, and recent ascendant to the throne of a ridiculously huge fortune.

Money wasn't everything. She knew that from bitter experience. Truth was a far more valuable commodity. At least she hoped that was what Bea would think when she finally managed to open her mouth and speak.

Maybe she could laser beam a confession out of him…

The groom looked across at Fran…caught her gaze… and smiled. In its smarmy wake she could have sworn that a glint, a zap of light striking a sharp blade, shot across at her.

Go on, the smile said. *I dare you.*

Marco "The Wolf" Rodolfo.

The wolf indeed. He hadn't even bothered with the sheep's clothing. If she looked closely, would she see extra-long incisors? *All the better to eat you—*

"*Per favore, signorina?*"

A swirl of perfectly coiffured heads whipped her way as the priest gave her an imploring look. Or was he a cardinal? She really should have polished up her knowledge of the finer details of her Catholic childhood. Church, family dinners, tradition… They'd all slipped away when her mother had left for husband number two and her father had disappeared with a swan dive into his work.

"Francesca!" Bea growled through a fixed smile. "Any clues?"

Santo cielo! This was exactly the reason her father had held her at arm's length all these years. She couldn't keep her mouth shut, could she? Always had to speak the truth, no matter what the consequences.

"Francesca?"

"He's—" Fran's index finger took on a life of its own and she watched as it started lifting from her side to point at the reason why Bea's wedding shouldn't go ahead. She couldn't even look at the maid of honor he'd been having his wicked way with. What was her name? Marina? Something like that. The exact sort of woman who always made her feel more tomboy than Tinker Bell. Ebony tresses to her derriere. Willowy figure. Cheekbones and full lips that gave her an aloof look. Or maybe she looked that way because she actually *was* aloof.

She was insincere and a fiancé thief—that much was certain. Since when did Bea hang out with such supermodelesque women anyhow?

Society weddings.

Total. Nightmare.

Last night, in their two seconds alone, Bea had muttered something about out-of-control guest lists, her mother and bloodline obligations. All this while staring longingly at Fran's glass of champagne and then abruptly calling it a night. Not exactly the picture of a bride on the brink of a lifetime of bliss. A bride on the brink of disaster, more like.

"Francesca, say something!"

All Fran could do was stare wide-eyed at her friend. Her beautiful, kind, honest, wouldn't-hurt-a-fly, take-no-prisoners friend. This was life being mean. Cruel, actually. When she'd seen Mommy kissing someone who definitely hadn't been Santa Claus and told her father about it, how had she been meant to know that her mother would leave her father and break his heart?

Would Bea stay friends with the messenger now, or

hate her forever? A bit like Fran's father had hated her since his marriage blew apart no matter how hard she'd tried to gain his approval. A tiny hit of warmth tickled around her heart. They were going to try again. *Soon.* He'd promised.

The tickle turned ice-cold at another throat-clearing prompt from Mr. Sexy.

Why, why, why was *she* the one who caught all the cheaters in the world?

All the eyes on her felt like laser beams.

Including the eyes of the mystery groomsman who she really *would* have liked to get to know a bit better if things had been different. *Typical.* Timing was definitely not her forte. What was his name? Something sensual. Definitely not Ugolino, as her aunt had mysteriously called her son. No…it was something more…*toothsome.* A name that tantalized your tongue, like amaretto or a perfectly textured gelato. Cool and warming all at once. Something like the ancient city of…

Luca! That was his name.

Luca. He was filling out his made-to-measure suit with the lean, assured presence of a man who knew his mind. His crisp white shirt collar highlighted the warm olive tone of his skin and the five-o'clock shadow that was already hinting at making an appearance, despite the fact it was still morning. He looked like a man who would call a spade a spade.

Which might explain why he was staring daggers at her. Strangely, the glaring didn't detract from his left-of-center good looks. He wasn't one of those calendar-ready men whose perfection was more off-putting than alluring. Sure, he had the cheekbones, the inky dark hair and brown eyes that held the mysteries of the universe in them, but he also had that scar. A jagged one that looked as if it could tell a story or two. It dissected his left eyebrow, skipped the eye, then shot along his cheek. If she wasn't wrong, there were a few tiny ones along his chin, too. Little faint scars she might almost have reached out and touched—if his lips hadn't been moving.

"*Per amor del cielo!* Put these poor people out of their misery!"

Fran blinked. Enigmatic-scar man was right.

She looked to his left. The priest-bishop-cardinal was speaking to her again. Asking her to clarify why she believed this happy couple should not lawfully be joined in marriage. Murmurs of dismay were audibly rippling through the church behind her. Part of her was certain she could hear howls from the paparazzi as they waited outside to pounce.

Clammy prickles of panic threatened to consume her brain.

Friends didn't let friends marry philandering liars. Right? Then again, what did *she* know? She was Italian by birth, but raised in America. Maybe a little last-minute nookie right before you married your long-term intended was the done thing in these social circles filled with family names that went back a dozen generations or more. It wasn't illegal, but… Oh, this was ranking up there in worst-moments-ever territory!

Fran sucked in a deep breath. It was the do-or-die moment. Her heart was careening around her chest so haphazardly she wouldn't have been surprised if it had flown straight out of her throat, but instead out came words. And before she could stop herself, she heard herself saying to Beatrice, "He's… You can't marry him!"

CHAPTER TWO

"BASTA!" QUICK AS a flash, Luca shuttled the key players in this farce to the back of the altar, then down a narrow marble passageway until they reached an open but mercifully private corridor.

"Her dress was up and Marco—"

"Per favore. I implore you to just...*stop.*" Luca whirled around, only to receive a full-body blow from the blonde bridesmaid. As quickly as the raft of sensations from holding her in his arms hit him she pressed away from him—*hard.*

"I'm just trying—" Bea's friend clamped her full, pink lips tight when her eyes met his.

The rest of the party was moving down the corridor as Luca wrestled with her revelation. "Do you have *any* idea what you've done? The damage you've caused?"

Stillness enveloped her as his words seemed to take hold.

Such was the power of the moment, Luca was hurtled back to a time and place when he, too, had been incapable of motion. Only there had been a doctor *and* a priest then.

Stillness had been the only way to let the news sink in.

Mother. Father. His sister, her husband—all of them save his beautiful niece. Gone. And *he'd* been the one behind the wheel.

He closed his eyes and willed the memory away, forcing himself to focus on the bridesmaid in front of him. Still utterly stationary—a deer in the headlights.

Another time, another place he would have said she was pretty. Beautiful, even. Honey-gold hair. Full, almost-pouty lips he didn't think had more than a slick of gloss on them. Eyes so blue he would have sworn they were a perfect match to the Adriatic Sea not a handful of meters from the basilica.

"Don't you dare—" She took in a jagged breath, tears filming her eyes. "Don't you *dare* tell me I don't understand what speaking up means."

Luca's gut tightened as she spoke. Behind those tears there was nothing but honesty. The type of honesty that would change everything.

His mind reeled through the facts. Beatrice was one of his most respected friends. They'd known each other all their lives and had been even closer during med school. Their career trajectories had shot them off in opposite directions, much to their parents' chagrin. He'd not missed their hints, their hopes that their friendship would blossom into something more.

Beautiful as Beatrice was, theirs would always be a platonic relationship. When she'd taken up with Marco he'd almost been relieved. *Si*, he had a playboy's reputation, but he was a grown man now. A prince with an aristocratic duty to fulfill—a legacy to uphold. When Marco had asked him to be best man he'd been honored. Proud, even, to play a role in Beatrice's wedding.

Cheating just minutes before he was due to marry? What kind of man would *do* that?

He shot a glance at Marco, who was raising his hands in protest before launching into an impassioned appeal to both Bea and the cardinal.

Marco and a bridesmaid in a premarital clinch? As much as he hated to admit it, he couldn't imagine it was the type of thing a true friend would conjure up just to add some drama to Italy's most talked-about wedding.

He glanced down at her hands, each clutching a fistful of the fairy-tale fabric billowing out from her dress in the light wind. No rings.

A Cinderella story, perhaps? The not-so-ugly stepsister throwing a spanner into the works, hoping to catch the eye of the Prince?

Each time she pulled at her dress she revealed the fact that she was actually wearing flip-flops in lieu of any Italian woman's obligatory heels. No glass slippers, then. Just rainbow-painted toes that would have brought the twitch of a smile to his lips if his mind hadn't been racing for ways to fend off disaster.

She'd be far less high maintenance than his only-the-best-will-do girlfriend.

He shook off this reminder that he and Marina needed "a talk" and forced himself to meet the blonde's gaze again. Tearstained but defiant. A surge of compassion shot through him. If what she was saying was true she was a messenger who wouldn't escape unscathed.

"I saw them!" she insisted, tendrils of blond hair coming loose from the intricate hairdo the half-dozen or so bridesmaids were all wearing. All of the bridesmaids including *his* girlfriend. "It's not like you're the one who's been cheated on," she whisper-hissed, her blue eyes flicking toward Beatrice, who, unlike her, was remaining stoically tear-free.

Luca took hold of her elbow and steered her farther away from the small group, doing his best to ignore how soft her skin felt under the work-hardened pads of his fingertips. Quite a change from the soft-as-a-surgeon's hands he'd been so proud of. Funny what a bit of un-expected tragedy could do to a man.

"Perhaps we should leave the bride and groom to chat with the cardinal." A shard of discord lodged in his spine as he heard himself speak. It had been in the icy tone he'd only ever heard come out of his mouth once before. The day his father had confessed he'd gambled away the last of the family's savings.

"I'm Francesca, by the way," she said, as if adding a personal touch would blunt the edges of this unbelievable scenario. Or perhaps she was grasping at straws, just as he was. "I think I saw you at the cocktail party last night."

"I would say it's a pleasure to meet you, but…"

She waved away his platitudes. They both knew they were beyond social niceties.

"Francesca…" He drew her name out on the premise of buying time. He caught himself tasting it upon his tongue as one might bite into a lemon on a dare, surprised to find it sweet when he had been expecting the bitterness of pith, the sourness of an unripe fruit.

Focus, man.

Luca clenched his jaw so tightly he saw Francesca's eyes flick to the telltale twitch in his cheek. The one with the scar.

Let her stare.

He swallowed down the hit of bile that came with the thought. He knew better than most that nothing good came from a life built on illusion.

"I don't think I need to remind you what our roles are here. I promised to be best man at this wedding. To vouch for the man about to marry our mutual friend."

He moved closer toward her and caught a gentle waft of something. Honeysuckle with a hint of grass? His eyes met hers and for a moment…one solitary moment…they were connected. Magnetically. Sensually.

Luca stepped back and gave his jaw a rough scrub, far too aware that Francesca had felt it, too.

"There is no one in the world I would defend more than Bea." Francesca's words shattered the moment, forcing him to confront reality. "And, believe me, of all the people standing here I *know* how awful this is."

Something in her eyes told him she wasn't lying. Something in his heart told him he already knew the truth.

"I'd want to know," she insisted. "Wouldn't you?"

Luca looked away from the clear blue appeal in her eyes, redirecting the daggers he was shooting toward her to the elaborately painted ceiling of the marble-and-flagstone passageway. The hundreds of years it had taken to build the basilica evaporated to nothing in comparison to the milliseconds it had taken to grind this wedding to a halt.

A wedding. A marriage. It was meant to last a lifetime.

"Of course I'd want to know," he bit out. "But your claims are too far-fetched. The place where you're saying you saw them is not even private."

"I know! It doesn't mean it didn't happen."

Francesca's eyes widened and the tears resting on her eyelids cascaded onto her cheeks before zipping down to her chin and plopping unceremoniously into the hollow of her throat. Luca only just stopped himself from lifting both his hands to her collarbone and swiping them away with his thumbs. First one, then the other… Perhaps tracing the path of one of those tears slipping straight between the soft swell and lift of—

Focus!

"Which one was it? Which woman?"

Francesca's blue eyes, darkened with emotion, flicked up and to the right. "She had dark hair. Black."

The information began to register in slow motion. Not Suzette…a flame-bright redhead. And the others were barely into their teens.

Elimination left him with only one option.

A fleeting conversation with his girlfriend came back to him. One in which he'd said he was going to be too busy with the clinic to come to the wedding. Marina had been fine with it. Had agreed, in fact. *So* much work at the clinic, she'd said. And then it all fell into place. The little white lies. The deceptions. The ever-increasing radio silences he hadn't really noticed in advance of the clinic's opening day.

A coldness took hold of his entire chest. An internal ice storm wrought its damage as the news fully penetrated.

"My girlfriend was *not* having sex with Marco."

Francesca's eyes pinged wide, a hit of shock shuddering down her spine before she managed to respond.

"Your girlfriend? That's… *Wow.*" She shook her head in disbelief. "For the record, she is an idiot. If you were *my* boyfriend, lock and key might be more—"

Luca held up a hand. He didn't want to hear it.

It was difficult to know whether to be self-righteous or furious. In Rome, his relationships had hardly warranted the title. Since moving back to Mont di Mare…

The home truths hit hard and fast. Sure, Marina had been complaining that she wasn't the center of his universe lately, but any fool—anyone with a heart beating in their chest—could have seen that his priorities were not wooing and winning right now.

He owed every spare ounce of his energy to his niece.

The one person who'd suffered the most in that horrific car accident. His beautiful, headstrong niece, confined to a wheelchair evermore.

He looked across at Marco. The sting of betrayal hit hard and fast.

He and Marina had never been written in the stars—but *Beatrice*? A true princess if ever there was one. She was shaking her head. Holding up a hand so that Marco would stop his heated entreaty. From where Luca was standing it didn't look as if the wedding would go ahead.

He swore under his breath. He had trusted Marco to treat Bea well—cautioned him about his rakish past and then congratulated him with every fiber of his being when at long last he'd announced his engagement to Princess Beatrice Vittoria di Jesolo.

The three of them had shared the same upbringing. Privileged. Exclusive. Full of expectation—no, more than that, full of *obligation* that they would follow in their ancestors' footsteps. Marry well. Breed more titled babies.

Luca might have considered the same future for himself before the accident. But that had all changed now. Little wonder Marina had strayed. He'd kept her at arm's length. Farther away. It was surprising she had stayed any time at all.

"Why don't you go and get her? Ask her yourself?" Francesca wasn't even bothering to swipe at the tears streaking her mascara across her cheeks.

"You're absolutely positive?"

Even as the hollow-sounding words left his mouth he knew they were true. There weren't that many women wandering around the basilica in swirls of weightless ocean-blue fabric. And there was only one bridesmaid with raven hair. The same immaculate silky hair he'd been forbidden from touching that morning when Marina had popped into the hotel suite to grab the diamante clutch bag she'd left while she was at the hairdresser's. Not so immaculate when she'd appeared at the altar, looking rosy cheeked and more alive than he'd seen her in months, if he was being honest.

"I—I can go get her for you, if you like," Francesca offered after hiccuping a few more tears away.

He had to hand it to her. The poor woman was crying her eyes out, but she knew how to stand her ground.

"Why don't I go find her?" Her fingers started doing a little nervous dance in the direction of the church, where everyone was still waiting.

"No offense, but you are the *last* person I would ever ask to help me."

"Isn't it better to know the truth than to live a lie?"

Luca swore softly and turned away. She was hitting just about every button he didn't care to admit he had. Truth. Deceit. Honesty. Lies. Weakness.

He had no time in his life for weakness. No capacity for lies.

He forced himself to look Francesca in the eye, knowing there wasn't an iota of kindness in his gaze. But he still couldn't give in to the innate need to feel empathy for the position she'd been put in. Or compassion for the tears rising again and again, glossing her eyes and then falling in a steady trickle along her tear-soaked face. How easy it would be to lift a finger and just…

Magari!

Shooting the messenger was a fool's errand, but he didn't know how else to react… A knife of rage swept through him. If he never thought about Marina or Marco again it would be too soon.

"It didn't seem like it was the first time," Francesca continued, her husky voice starting to break in a vain attempt to salve the ever-deepening wound. "I'm happy to go and get her if you want."

"Basta! Per favore!"

No need to paint a picture. He almost envied Francesca. Seeing in an instant what he should have known for weeks. He should have ended it before she'd even thought to stray.

"If you want, I'll do it. Go and get her. I would do it for any friend."

Francesca shifted from one foot to the other, eyes glued to his, waiting for his response. He'd be grateful for this one day, but right now Francesca was the devil's messenger and he'd heard enough.

The words came to him—jagged icicles shooting straight from his arctic heart. "I know you mean well, Francesca, but you and I will *never* be friends."

Shell-shocked. That was how Bea had looked for the rest of the day. Not that Fran could blame her. Talk about living a nightmare. She knew better than most that coming to terms with deception on that kind of scale could take years. A lifetime, even, if her father's damaged heart was anything to go by.

From the look on Luca's face when they'd finally parted at the basilica he was going to need *two* lifetimes to get over his girlfriend's betrayal. Good thing they wouldn't be crossing paths anytime soon.

"Want me to see if I can find a case of prosecco lying around? A karaoke machine? We could sing it out and down some fizz."

Fran scanned the hotel suite. The caterers had long been sent away, the decorations had been removed and the staff instructed to keep any and all lurking paparazzi as far away as possible…

"No, thanks, *cara*. Maybe some water?" Bea asked.

"On it."

As she poured a glass of her friend's favorite—sparkling water from the alpine region of Italy—Fran was even more in awe of her friend's strength. All tucked up in bed, makeup removed, dress unceremoniously wilting like a deflated meringue in the bathroom, Bea looked exhausted, but not defeated.

"Want to tell me anything about this mystery job I'm due to start tomorrow?"

"No." Bea took a big gulp of water and grinned, obviously grateful for the change of topic. "Although it *will* make use of both your physio skills and the assistance dogs."

Fran frowned. "I thought you said she had a doctor looking after her?"

Bea blinked, but said nothing.

"The girl's in a wheelchair, right? Lower extremities paralyzed?"

"Yeah, but…" Bea tipped her head to the side and gave her friend a hard look. "You're not going to waste all those years of practicing physio are you?"

"What? Because the person I was stupid enough to go into business with saw me as a limitless supply of cash?"

"You're clear of that, though, aren't you?"

Fran grunted.

People? Disappointing. Dogs? They never asked for a thing. Except maybe a good scratch around the ears.

"Are you sure you're all right?" Fran flipped the topic back to Bea. "Don't you want to stay in the palazzo with your family?"

"And listen to my mother screech on about the disaster of the century? How I've ruined the family's name. The family's genetic line. Any chance of happiness for

the di Jesolos forever and ever. Not a chance. Besides—"
she scanned the sumptuous surroundings of the room
"—your suite is great and I'd much rather be with you,
even if the place *does* smell all doggy."

"Does not." Fran swiped at the air between them with
a grin. She'd washed the dogs to within an inch of their
lives before they'd checked into Venice's fanciest hotel.
A little trust-fund treat to herself before heading out to
this mystery village where Bea had organized her summer job.

"You don't need to watch over me, you know," Bea
chided gently. "I'm not going to do anything drastic. And
you *are* allowed to take the dress off. Don't know if
you've heard, but the wedding's off!"

"Just wanted to get my money's worth!" Fran said,
knowing the quip was as lame as it sounded.

The truth was, she hadn't felt so pretty in…*years*, really. When your workaholic dad bought your clothes from
the local menswear shop, there was only so much ironic
style a girl could pull off. When she'd graduated to buying her own clothes it had felt like a betrayal even to
glance at something pink and frilly. It wasn't *practical*.

*"Not exactly what a proper engineer would wear,
Frannie!"*

So much for *that* pipe dream! It had died along with
a thousand others before she'd found her niche in the
world of physiotherapy and then, even more perfectly, in
assistance-dog training. *Dogs*. They were who she liked
to spend her time with. They were unconditionally loyal
and always ridiculously happy to see her. When she had
to hand over these two dogs to her mystery charge at the
end of the summer…

Fran swallowed down another rush of tears. Bea
shouldn't have to be the one being stoic here. "I'm so

sorry, Bea. About doing things the way I did. There just wasn't time to catch you after I'd seen them, and before I knew it, we were all up there at the altar and—"

"I'm not sorry at all." Bea said. "I'm glad you said something. Grateful you had the courage when no one else did."

"That's pretty magnanimous for someone who just found out they were being cheated on!"

"Others knew. All along. Even my mother." Bea chased up the comment with a little typical eye roll.

Fran's hands flew to cover her mouth. *Wow.* That was just… *Wow.*

"They were all so desperate for me to be one half of the most enviable couple in Europe. Even if it came at a cost." She shuddered away the thought. "You were the only one today who was a true friend."

Fran's tear ducts couldn't hold back any longer.

"How can you be so nice about everything when I've ruined the best day of your life?"

"*Amore!* Stop. You were *not* the one who ruined the day. Besides, I'm pretty sure there will be another best day of my life," Bea added, with a hint of something left unsaid in her voice.

"Since I barely see you once a year, it would've been nice to be honest about something else. Like how ridiculously beautiful you looked today."

Fran's heart rose into her throat as at long last Bea's eyes finally clouded with tears.

"Everyone has their secrets," Bea whispered.

"Including you?"

Bea looked away. Fair enough. There had to be a full-blown tropical storm going on in that head of hers right now, and if she wanted to keep her thoughts to herself, she was most deserving. Thank heavens her family had the financial comfort to sort out the mess The Wolf's infidelity would leave in its wake.

"You all ready for your new job?" Bea turned back toward her with a soft smile.

"Yes!" She gave an excited clap of her hands. The two dogs she had trained up for this job were amazing. "Not that you've told me much about the new boss, apart from the pro bono bit. I can't *believe* you offered to pay me."

Beatrice scrunched her features together. "Best not to mention that."

"I have no problem doing it for free. You know that. If I could've lived in one place for more than five minutes over the past few years, I would've set up a charitable trust through Martinelli Motors years ago, but..."

"*He* was too busy making his mark?"

"As ever. We don't have ancient family lineage to rely on like you do."

"*Ugh.* Don't remind me."

"Sorry..." Fran cringed, then held her arms open wide to the heavens. "Please help me stop sticking my foot in my mouth today!" She dropped her arms and pulled her friend into a hug. "Ever wished you'd just stayed in England?"

Bea's eyes clouded and again she looked away. This time Fran had *definitely* said the wrong thing, brought up memories best left undisturbed.

"That was..." Bea began, stopping to take a faltering breath. "That was a very special time and place. Those kinds of moments only come once in a lifetime."

Fran pulled back from the hug and looked at her friend, lips pressed tight together. She wouldn't mention Jamie's name if Beatrice didn't. The poor girl had been through enough today without rehashing romances of years gone by.

"Right!" Fran put on a jaunty grin. "Time to totally change the topic! Now, as my best friend, won't you please give me just a teensy, tiny hint about my new boss so I don't ruin things in the first five minutes?"

"*You're* the one who wanted a mystery assignment!"

"I didn't want them to know who *I* was—not the other way around!" Fran shot Bea a playful glower.

She'd already been burned by a business partner who had known she was heiress to her father's electric-car empire. And when it came to her social life, people invariably got the wrong idea. Expected something…*someone*…more glamorous, witty, attention seeking, party mad.

It was why she'd given up physio altogether. Dogs didn't give a damn about who she was so long as she was kind and gave them dinner. If only her new boss was a pooch! She giggled at the thought of a dog in a three-piece suit and a monocle.

"What's so funny?" Bea asked.

"C'mon…just give me a little new-boss hint," Fran cajoled, pinching her fingers together so barely a sheet of paper could pass between them.

Bea shook her head no. "I've told you all you need to know. The girl's a teenager. She's been in a wheelchair for a couple of years now. Paraplegic after a bad car accident. Very bad. Her uncle—"

"Ooh! There's an enigmatic *uncle*?"

"Something like that," Bea intoned, wagging her finger. "No hints. They need the dog so she can be more independent."

"*She* needs the dog."

"Right. That's what I said."

"You said *they* need the dog," Fran wheedled, hoping

to get a bit more information, but Bea just made an invisible zip across her lips. *No more.*

"That's not tons to go on, you know. I've been forced to bring two dogs to make sure I've got the right one!"

"Forced?" Bea cackled. "Since when have you had to be *forced* to travel with more than one dog?"

"C'mon…" Fran put her hands into a prayer position. "Just tell me what her parents are like—"

Beatrice held up her hand. "No parents. They both died in the same accident."

"Ouch." Fran winced. She'd lost her mother to divorce and her father to work. Losing them for real must be devastating.

"So does that mean this devilishly handsome uncle plays a big role in her life?"

"No one said he was handsome!" Bea admonished. "And remember—good things come to those who wait!"

Bea took on a mysterious air and, if Fran wasn't mistaken, there was also an elusive something else she couldn't quite put her finger on. How could a person *glow* when their whole life had just been ripped out from beneath them? Bea was in a league of her own. There weren't too many people who would set up a dream job for a friend who was known to dip in and out of her life like a yo-yo.

"Well, even if her uncle is a big, hairy-eared ogre, I can't wait. Nothing beats matching the right pooch to the right patient." Fran couldn't stop herself from clapping a bit more, drawing the attention of her two stalwart companions. "C'mere, pups! Help me tuck in Her Majesty."

Bea batted at the air between them. "No more royal speak! I don't want to be reminded."

"What?" Fran fell into their lifelong patter. "The fact that you're so royal you'd probably bleed fleurs-de-lys?"

"That's the French, idiot!"

"What do Italian royals bleed, then? Truffles?"

"Ha!" Bea giggled, reaching out a hand to give Fran's a big squeeze. "It's not truffle season. It's tabloid season. And they're *definitely* going to have a field day with this. I can't even bear to think about it." She threw her arm across her eyes and sank back into the downy pillow. "What do you think they'll say? Princess left at the altar, now weeping truffle tears?"

Fran pulled her friend up by her hands and gave her a hug. It was awful seeing her beautiful dark eyes cloud over with sadness. "How about some honey?" she suggested, signaling to the two big dogs to come over to the bedside. "That mountain honey you gave me from the Dolomites was amazing."

"From the resort?" Bea's eyes lit up at the thought. "It's one of the most beautiful places in the world. Maybe…"

"Maybe what?" Fran knew the tendrils of a new idea when she saw one.

"Maybe I'll pull a Frannie!"

"What does *that* mean?" She put on an expression of mock horror, fully aware that it wasn't masking her defensive reaction.

She knew exactly what it meant. A lifetime of trying to get her father's attention and failing had turned her into a wanderer. Staying too long in any one place meant getting attached. And that meant getting hurt.

"Don't get upset. I envy you. Your ability to just pick up and go. Disappear. Reinvent yourself. Maybe it's time *I* went and did something new."

Fran goldfished for a minute.

"That phase of my life might be over," she hedged. "Once this summer's done and dusted I'm going home."

"*Home*, home?" Bea sat up straight, eyes wide with shock. "I thought you said you'd never settle down there."

"Dad's offered to help me set up a full-time assistance-dogs training center—"

"You've never accepted his money before! What's the catch?"

"You mean what's going to be different this time?" Fran said, surprised at the note of shyness in her voice.

Bea nodded. She was the one who had always been there on the end of a phone when Fran had called in tears. *Again*.

"We spent a week together before I came over."

"A *week*?" Bea's eyes widened in surprise. "That's huge for you two. He wasn't in the office the whole time?"

"Nope! We actually went to a car show together."

Bea pursed her lips together. Not impressed.

"I know. I know," Fran protested, before admitting, "He had a little run-in with the pearly gates."

"Fran! Why didn't you *tell* me?"

"It turned out to be one of those cases of indigestion disguising itself as a heart attack, but it seems to have been a lightbulb moment for him. Made him reassess how he does things."

"You mean how he's neglected his only daughter most of his life?"

"It wasn't *that* bad."

"Francesca Martinelli, don't you *dare* tell me your heart wasn't broken time and time again by your father choosing work over spending time with you."

Fran met her friend's gaze—saw the unflinching truth in it, the same solid friendship and loyalty she'd shown her from the day they'd met at boarding school.

"I know. But this time it really *is* different."

"Frannie…" Bea's brow furrowed. "He took you to a *car* show. You *hate* cars!"

"It was an antique car show. Not a single electric car in sight."

Bea gave a low whistle. "Will wonders never cease?"

"Martinelli Motors is doing so well it could probably run itself."

"No surprise there. But I'm still amazed he took time off. It must've been one heck of a health scare."

Fran nodded. She knew Bea's wariness was legitimate. The number of times Fran had thought *this* would be the time her father finally made good on his promise to spend some quality father-daughter time…

"It was actually quite sweet. I got to learn a lot more about him as we journeyed through time via the cars." She smiled at the memory of a Model T that had elicited a story about one of his cousins driving up a mountainside backward because the engine had only been strong enough in reverse. "Even though we all know cars aren't my passion, I learned more about him in that one weekend than I have…*ever*, really."

He'd thought he was going to die—late at night, alone in his office. And it had made him change direction, hadn't it? Forced him to realize a factory couldn't give hugs or bake your favorite cookies or help you out when you were elderly and in need of some genuine TLC or a trip down memory lane.

"We've even been having phone calls and video-link chats since I left. Every day."

Bea nodded. Impressed now. "Well, if those two hounds of yours are anything to go by, it'll be a successful business in no time. Who knows? I might need one of those itty-bitty handbag assistance dogs to keep me chirpy!"

"Ooh! That's their specialty. Want a display?" Without waiting for an answer, she signaled directions at her specially trained pooches, "Come on, pups! Bedtime for Bea!"

Fran was rewarded with a full peal of Beatrice's giggles when the dogs went up on their hind legs on either side of the bed and pulled at the soft duvet until it was right up to her chin.

Snuggled up under her covers, Bea turned her kind eyes toward Fran. "*Grazie*, Francesca. You're the best. Mamma has promised caffe latte and your favorite *brioche con cioccolata* if we head over to the palazzo tomorrow morning."

"I'll be up early, so don't worry about me. I'll just grab something from this enormous fruit bowl before I shoot off." She feigned trying to lift the huge bowl and failing. "Better save my back. I've got to be there at nine. Fit and well!"

"At Clinica Mont di Mare?"

"Aha! I *knew* I'd get something from you beyond the sat-nav coordinates!"

Bea gave her a sidelong glance, then shook her head. "All I'm going to say is keep an open mind."

"Sounds a bit scary."

Bea gave her hand a squeeze. "Of all the people in the world, I know you're the best one for this particular job."

"Thanks, friend."

Fran fought the tickle of tears in her throat. Bea was her absolute best friend and she trusted her implicitly. The fact Bea was still speaking to her after today's debacle made her heart squeeze tight.

"*Un bacione.*" She dropped a kiss on her friend's forehead and gave her hand a final squeeze before heading to her own bedroom and climbing into the antique wrought iron–framed bed.

"Freda, come! Covers!" *Might as well get as much practice in as possible.*

The fluffy Bernese mountain dog padded over, did as she had been bid, then received a big ol' cuddle. Fran adored Freda, with her big brown eyes. The three-year-old dog was ever patient, ever kind. In contrast to the other full-of-beans dog she'd brought along.

"Edison! Come, boy!"

The chocolate Lab lolloped up to the side of the bed to receive his own cuddle, before flopping down in a contented pile of brown fur alongside Freda.

The best of friends. Just like her and Bea. It would be so hard to say goodbye.

Never mind. Tomorrow was a new beginning.

Exactly what she needed after a certain someone's face had been burned into her memory forever.

"You and I will never be friends."

Luca's hardened features pinged into her mind's eye. No matter the set of his jaw, she'd seen kindness in his eyes. Disbelief at what was happening. And resignation. A trinity of emotions that had pulled at her heartstrings and then yanked hard, cinching them in a tight noose. No matter how foul he'd been, she knew she would always feel compassion for him. Always wonder if he'd found someone worthy of his love.

CHAPTER THREE

"*How* much?" Luca's jaw clenched tight. He was barely able to conceal his disbelief. Another *five million* to get a swathe of family suites prepared?

He looked at the sober-faced contractor. He was the best, and his family had worked with the Montovano family for years. In other words, five million was a steal.

Five million he didn't have, thanks to his father's late nights at the poker table. Very nice poker tables, in the French Riviera's most exclusive casinos. Casinos where losing was always an option.

Luca's eyes flicked up to the pure blue sky above him. Now that his father was pushing piles of chips up there, somewhere in the heavenly hereafter, it wasn't worth holding on to the anger anymore. The bitterness.

His gaze realigned with the village—his inheritance… his millstone. Finding peace was difficult when he had a paraplegic niece to care for and a half-built clinic he was supposed to open in a week's time.

Basta! He shook off the ill will. Nothing would get in the way of providing for Pia. Bringing her every happiness he could afford. Be it sunshine or some much-needed savings—he would give her whatever he had. After the losses she'd suffered…

"Dottore?" The contractor's voice jarred him back into the moment.

"Looks like we're going to have to do it in phases, Piero. *Mi perdoni.*"

Luca didn't even bother with a smile—they both knew it wouldn't be genuine—and shook hands with the disappointed contractor. They walked out to the main gate, where he had parked. Luca remained in the open courtyard as the van slowly worked its way along the kilometer-long bridge that joined the mountaintop village to the fertile seaside valley below.

He took in a deep breath of air—just now hinting at all the wildflowers on the brink of appearing. It was rare for him to take a moment like this—a few seconds of peace before heading back into the building site that needed to be transformed into an elite rehabilitation clinic in one week's time.

He scanned the broad valley below him. Where the hell was this dog specialist? Time was money. Money he didn't have to spare. Not that Canny Canines was charging him. Bea had said something about fulfilling pro bono quotas and rescue dogs, but it hadn't sat entirely right with him. He might have strained the seams of his bag of ducats to the limit, but he wasn't in the habit of accepting charity. Not yet anyway.

The jarring clang of a scaffolding rail reverberated against the stone walls of the medieval village along with a gust of blue language. Luca's fists tightened. He willed it to be the sound of intention rather than disaster. There was no time for mistakes—even less for catastrophe.

Sucking in another deep breath, Luca turned around to face the arched stone entryway that led into the renamed "city." Microcity, more like. Civita di Montovano di Marino. His family's name bore the legacy of a bustling medieval village perched atop this seaside mountain—once thriving in the trades of the day, but now left to fade away to nothing after two World Wars had shaken nearly every family from its charitable embrace.

Just another one of Italy's innumerable ghost towns—barely able to sustain the livelihood of one family, let alone the hundred or so who had lived there so many years ago.

But in one week's time all that would change, when the Clinica Mont di Mare opened its doors to its first five patients. All wheelchair bound. All teenagers. Just like his niece. Only, unlike his niece, *they* all had parents. Families willing to dedicate their time and energy to trying rehabilitation one more time when all the hospitals had said there was no more hope.

A sharp laugh rasped against his throat. After the accident, that was exactly what the doctors at the hospital working with Pia had said. "She'll just have to resign herself to having little to no strength."

Screw that.

Montovanos didn't resign themselves to anything. They fought back. *Hard*.

His hand crept up to the thin raised line of his scar and took its well-traveled route from chin to throat. A permanent reminder of the promise he'd made to his family to save their legacy.

"Zio! Are they here yet?"

Luca looked up and smiled. Pia might not be his kid, but she had *his* blood pumping through her veins. Type A positive. Two liters' worth. Montovano di Marino blood. She was a dead ringer for her mother—his sister—but from the way she was haphazardly bumping and whizzing her way along the cobbled street instead of the wheelchair-ready side path to get to their favorite lookout site, he was pretty sure she'd inherited her bravura from him.

Pride swelled in him as he watched her now—two years after being released from hospital—surpassing each of his expectations with ease.

Breathless, his niece finally arrived beside him. "Move over, Zio Luca. I want to see when she gets here."

"What makes you so sure the trainer is a she?"

"Must be my teenage superpowers." Pia smirked. "And also Bea told me it was a she. Girl power!"

Another deep hit of pride struck him in the chest as he watched her execute a crazy three-point turn any Paralympian would have been hard-pressed to rival and then punch up into the morning sunshine, shouting positive affirmations.

"Never let her down. You're all she has now."

The words pounded his conscience as if he'd heard them only yesterday. His sister's last plea before her fight for survival had been lost.

His little ray of sunshine.

A furnace blast of determination was more like it.

Pia wanted—*needed*—to prove to herself that she could do everything on her own. Her C5 vertebra fracture might have left her paralyzed from the waist down, but it hadn't crushed her spirits as she'd powered through the initial stages of recovery at the same time as dealing with the loss of her parents and grandparents all in one deadly car crash. She had even spoken of training for the Paralympics.

And then early-onset rheumatoid arthritis had thrown a spanner in the works. Hence the dog.

They both scanned the approaching roads. One from the north, the other from the south and their own road—a straight line from the *civita* to the sea, right in the middle.

There was the usual collection of delivery vehicles and medical staff preparing the facility for its opening. And inspectors. Endless numbers of inspectors.

He was a doctor, for heaven's sake—not a bureaucrat.

"Just think, Pia…in one short week that road and this sky will be busy with arriving patients. Ambulances, helicopters…"

She let out a wistful sigh. "Friends!"

"Patients," he reminded her sternly, lips twitching against the smile he'd rather give.

"I know, Uncle Luca. But isn't it part of the Clinica Mont di Mare's ethos that rehab covers all the bases. And that means having friends—like me!"

"Remember, *chiara*, they won't all be as well-adjusted and conversation starved as you."

He gave her plaits a tug, only to have his hand swatted away. She was sixteen. Too old for that sort of thing. Too young to find him interesting 24/7. Having other teens here would be good for her.

"They're all in wheelchairs, right?"

"You know as well as I do they are. And thank you for being a guinea pig for all the doctors here in advance of their coming."

"Anything for Mont di Mare!" Pia's face lit up, then just as quickly clouded. "Do you think they'll try to take my dog? The other patients, I mean? What if they need the dog more than I do?"

Luca shook his head. "No. Absolutely not. This is solely for *you*."

"What if they get jealous and want one, too?"

"That's a bridge to cross further down the line, Pia. Besides," he added gently, "they'll have their families with them."

"I have *you*!" Pia riposted loyally.

"And I have you." He reached out a hand and she met it for a fist bump—still determined to make him hip.

Hard graft for Pia, given everything he'd been dealing with over the past few months in the lead-up to opening the clinic. Endless logistics. Paint samples. Cement grades. Accessibility ramps. Safety rails. And the list went on. It was as if he was missing a part of himself, not being able to practice medicine.

It's what your family would have wanted. You're doing it for them. Medicine will wait.

"Do you think that's her?" Pia's voice rose with excitement.

In the distance they could see a sky blue 4x4 coming along the road from the north, with a telltale blinking light. It was turning left.

"Can't you remember anything about her at all?" Pia looked up at him, eyes sparkling with excitement.

"Sorry, *amore.* Beatrice didn't say much. Just said it was a friend she'd stake our own friendship on."

"Wow! Beatrice is an amazing friend. That means a lot. Not like—" Pia stopped herself and grimaced an apology. "I mean, Marina was never really very nice anyway! You deserve better."

He grunted. There wasn't much to say on the matter. Not anymore. His thoughts were all for Bea and her privacy. He'd offered her a cottage up here at Mont di Mare, but she'd said she needed some serious alone time.

"Do you know what Dr. Murro and I called Marina?" Pia asked, a mischievous smile tweaking at the edges of her sparkle-glossed lips.

He shook his head. "Do I *want* to know?"

"Medusa!" She put her hands up beside her head and turned them into a tangle of serpents, all the while making creepy snake faces.

"Charming, *chiara*. Next time you go to the gym to work with Dr. Murro, please do tell him that perhaps a bit less chat about my defunct love life and a splash more work might be in order."

"Zio!" Pia widened her big puppy-dog eyes. "We can't help it if she was horrible."

Luca gave one of her plaits another playful tug. Just what a man needed. To find out that no one liked his girl-friend all along. Then again…being upset about Marina was pretty much the last thing on his mind. Making the clinic a running, functioning entity was most important.

Six months. That was how far what little money he had left would last before the bank made good on their promise to repossess what had been under his family's care for generations.

Pia shrugged unapologetically, then pulled the pair of binoculars she always had looped around her neck up to her eyes, to track the car that was still making its way toward the turnoff to Mont di Mare.

"I hope Freda looks exactly like she did in the pic-tures Bea forwarded. And Edison. He's *definitely* a he, and Freda's a she, but I'm glad the trainer is a she, too."

"Why's that?"

"It'll be nice to have a grown-up friend."

"You have me!"

"I know, but…" Her eyes flicked away from his.

She'd always been so good about making him feel worthy of the enormous role of caring for her. And yet at moments like these…he knew there were gaps to be filled.

"It'll be nice to have a girl to talk to about…you know…*things*."

Luca looked away. Of *course* she could do with a woman in her life. Someone to fill even a small portion of the hole left when her mother had been killed in that insane accident. A massive truck hurtling toward them from the other side of the tunnel with nowhere else to go…

"Zio! I think I see Freda!"

"Who's Freda?"

"Freda's the *dog*!"

"Right."

"And it *is* a her! She's a *her*!"

"Who? The dog?"

"The *trainer*!"

Pia was clapping with excitement now and Luca couldn't help but crack a smile. His first genuine one in the last twenty-four hours.

"*Zio!* Comb your hair. She's almost here!"

Luca laughed outright. Fat lot of good a comb would do with the rest of him covered in sawdust and paint.

A far cry from his Armani-suited and booted days at his consultancy in Rome. The one none of his colleagues had been able to believe he'd just up and leave for a life in the hinterlands. He wouldn't have wished the life lessons he'd had to learn that night on anyone. His cross to bear. The suits were moth food as far as he was concerned.

He tugged both hands through his hair and messed it up werewolf-style.

"Suitable?"

Pia gave his "makeover" the kind of studious inspection to which only a sixteen-year-old could add gravitas, then rolled her eyes.

"It's not *my* fault if you're a fashion plate," he teased.

"I'm trying to save you from yourself," Pia shot back. "What if she's a beautiful blonde and you fall in love?"

"Nice try, Pia. I'm officially off the market."

"Officially off your rocker, more like," she muttered with an eye roll. "Look! They're turning onto the bridge!"

He spotted the vehicle, then looked out beyond the road and took in the sparkle of the sun upon the Adriatic Sea. Italy's most famed coastline. Croatia and Montenegro were somewhere out there in the distance. Dozens of ports where the world's billionaires parked their superyachts. The price tag of just one of those would have him up and running in no time.

He gave himself a short sharp shake. This wasn't the time for self-pity or envy. It was time to prove he was worthy of the name he'd been given. The name he hoped would stay on this village he now called home.

"Shall we go and greet our new guest?" Luca flourished a hand in the direction of the approaching vehicle, even though his niece already had the wheels of her chair in motion.

Fran had to remind herself to breathe. Way up there on the hilltop was the most beautiful village she'd ever seen. Golden stone. Archways everywhere. The hillsides were terraced in graduated "shelves." If one could define countless acres of verdant wildflower meadows and a generous sprinkling of olive trees to be the "shelves" of a mountainside.

It was almost impossible to focus on driving, let alone the figures coming into view in the courtyard at the end of the bridge. She rolled down the window to inhale a deep breath of air. Meadow grass. The tang of the sea. The sweetness of fruit ripening on trees.

Heaven.

For the first time in just about forever, Fran wondered how she was going to find the strength to leave.

Was that…? *Wait a minute.*

All the air shot out of her lungs.

Long, lean and dark haired was no anomaly in Italy, but she recognized this particular long, lean, dark-haired man. As she clapped eyes on the tall figure jogging alongside the beaming girl in the wheelchair, her heart rate shot into overdrive.

Fight or flight kicked in like something crazy. Her skin went hot and cold, then hot again. Not that it had *anything* to do with the picture-perfect jawline and cheekbones now squaring off in front of her SUV.

No *wonder* Beatrice had been all mysterious and tight-lipped last night.

Un-freakin'-believable.

Mr. You-and-I-Will-Never-Be-Friends was her new boss.

Chills skittered along her arms as their gazes caught and locked.

From the steely look in his eyes he hadn't exactly erased her from *his* memory either.

From the flip-flop of warmth in her tummy, her body hadn't forgotten all that glossy dark hair, tousled like a lusty he-man ready to drag her into a cave and—

Silver linings, Fran. Think of the silver linings. He hates you, so flirting isn't something you need to worry about.

The dogs were both standing up in the back now, mouths open, tongues hanging out as if smiling in anticipation of meeting Pia. Trust *them* to remember they were here to help—not ogle the local talent.

Take a deep breath... One...two...three... Here goes nothing.

She pulled the car up to where the pair were waiting, then jumped out and ran around the back to the dogs. The dogs would be the perfect buffer for meeting—

"Francesca."

Gulp! His voice was still all melted chocolate and a splash of whiskey. Or was it grappa because they were in Italy? Whatever. It was all late-night radio and she liked it. Precisely the reason to pretend she didn't by saying absolutely nothing.

"We meet again."

Mmm-hmm. All she could do was nod. Luca had looked a treat in his fancy-schmancy suit yesterday, but now, with a bit of sawdust… *Mmm.* The sleeves of his chambray shirt were rolled up enough to show forearms that had done hard graft…and he wore a pair of hip-riding moleskin trousers that looked as if they'd seen their fair share of DIY…

Mamma mia!

Of all the completely gorgeous, compellingly enigmatic Italians needing an assistance dog for his…

"Allow me to introduce my niece, Pia."

Fran shook herself out of her reverie.

Niece! Nieces were nice.

"Yes! Pia—of course." She swept a few stray wisps of hair behind her ear and turned her full attention on the teenager whose smile was near enough splitting her face in two. "I bet you're far more interested in meeting these two than me."

They all turned to face the back of her SUV, where two big furry heads were panting away in anticipation of meeting their new charge. Fran deftly unlocked the internal cage after commanding the two canines to sit.

"If you'd just back your chair up a bit, Pia. They are both really excited to meet you."

"Both?" Luca's voice shuddered down her spine.

"Yes, both," she answered as solidly as she could. "Not everyone gets off on the right foot when they first meet."

She lifted her gaze to meet his.

Luca's eyebrow quirked.

"Is that so? I thought dogs were instinctive about knowing a good match."

"*Dogs* are," Fran parried, with a little press and push of her lips. "People sometimes need a second chance to get things right."

Luca's eyebrow dipped, then arced again, and just when she was expecting a cutting remark she saw it— the kindness she'd knew she'd seen lurking somewhere in those smoky brown eyes of his.

"Zio! Leave Francesca alone. I want to see the dogs!"

Grateful for the reprieve from this verbal fencing, Fran turned her focus to a starry-eyed Pia as her eyes pinged from one dog to the other.

"Aren't they a bit…big?" Luca stepped forward, his presence feeling about a thousand times more powerful than either dog did to Fran.

"Zio Luca! No!" Pia protested. "They are perfect. Both of them!"

"She's actually right." Fran shrugged an apology. "When Bea explained that your village offered unique challenges in the navigating department, I thought a mountain dog would be perfect."

"You mean the big one?" Pia pointed at Freda, the Bernese.

"I sure do." She shot a glance toward Luca, who had moved back from his protective position but still held a wary look in his eye.

She always forgot that to a person who wasn't used to dogs a Bernese could seem enormous. *Baby pony* was an oft-heard phrase when mountain dog "virgins" first saw them.

"Come along, Freda. Let's say hello to Pia."

"Surely Labs are more reliable. In terms of character." Luca stepped forward again, just managing to slot himself between Fran and Pia before she asked the dog to jump out.

Fran bit down hard on the inside of her cheek before replying. "Both dogs are extremely gentle and come with my one hundred percent guarantee."

"And what exactly is *that* worth?" Luca arced an eyebrow, daring her to name a number.

Fran's blood boiled. She wasn't here to prove herself to anyone. She was here to help. How *dare* he put her to some sort of ridiculous test of worth?

"I'll leave right now, if you think that's what's best. But I can guarantee that by the end of the day you will see a change in your niece's life. And as it is Pia's life we're talking about, perhaps *she* should be the one who is deciding."

They both turned to look at her, but when his niece opened her mouth to interject, Luca held out a hand to stop her.

"As her guardian, I make all the decisions for Pia's welfare."

"As an experienced trainer, I know you'd be making a mistake by turning me away."

Luca's inky, dark eyes stayed glued to hers, his face completely immovable. She felt as if she was clashing with a gladiator. One false move and—*crack!*—down she'd go. It didn't stop her from wanting to reach out and touch that salt-and-pepper stubble of his, though. Soft or scratchy…?

"You and I will never be friends."

"So?" Defiance saturated Fran's posture, but she didn't care. "Are you happy for me to unload them? Start bringing some empowerment to your niece's life?"

Without a backward glance Fran quickly clipped leads onto the dogs, and silently commanded them to jump down, approach Pia and present their paws for a handshake.

Pia laughed, delightedly taking each dog's paw for a shake, then giving their heads an adoring pat.

"Zio! *Per favore!* Can they all stay forever?" Pia's plaits flipped from one shoulder to the next as she looked between the two dogs and then beamed up at Fran as if she were a fairy godmother, complete with a magic wand. Which was nice. It was good to have someone rooting for her when the other person looked as if he'd happily tip her off the side of the mountain.

Fran turned toward Luca and crossed her arms. "Two against one?"

"Four against one," Pia said, then quickly tacked on in a gentler plea. "If that's okay, Zio? Can they at least stay until the end of the day?"

Luca's hands slipped to his hips as if he were reaching for invisible holsters. A small gust of wind rustled his already tousled hair. Off in the distance, Fran saw a rising plume of dust, as if a band of horses and *banditos* were heading their way to intervene. A showdown at dawn—minus the weapons and the sunrise.

"I promise you'll see a difference. In an hour, even."

Luca's eyelids lowered to half-mast as his glance skidded away from her toward the dogs and then back to her.

Too much? *Oh, jinks.* How was she going to tell her father she'd messed up Canny Canines before she'd even had a chance to begin? Yes, she wanted to go back—but not with her proverbial tail between her legs.

"*Per favore*, Francesca." Luca affected a courtly bow, though the charm didn't quite make it to his eyes. "My niece seems to want to give you a tour. Please. Allow us to show you around our humble abode."

He stood up to his full height, brow furrowed tight at the bridge of his aquiline nose.

"Then we'll talk."

CHAPTER FOUR

FRAN'S GAZE CAUGHT with Luca's. If he wasn't being sincere, she was out of here.

What? And run home to Daddy a failure before you've even begun?

She forced herself to look deep into the mahogany darkness of his irises and seek answers. He didn't look away this time. He held his ground—eyes glued to hers—as if he knew what she was looking for.

Somewhere between the crackle of "I dare you to fail" and the burn of "she's all I've got," Fran found what she needed. The answer. How she knew that Luca was hiding a good man deep within that flinty exterior of his was beyond her—but she did.

"Luca, I just wanted—"

Of all the times for her backside to vibrate!

"Can you excuse me for just a moment?" Fran tugged her cell phone out of her back pocket, instructed the dogs to stay with Pia and Luca, then scooted off to the far end of the village's central plaza, where their tour of the "humble abode" was just wrapping up.

"Beatrice?" She didn't wait for a reply. "You are truly the evilest friend I have ever had the privilege of knowing."

Bea's wicked cackle trilled down the line. "I guess you've met the baron, then?"

"The baron?"

"Luca. Il Barone Montovano di Marino. Didn't I tell you he was a baron?"

She'd been at her lippiest, sassiest best with a *baron*?

"Princess Beatrice, you know blinking well you didn't tell me *anything*! And, yes. Since you ask, we *have* met, formed an instant kinship, become blood siblings and vowed to be the absolute best of friends forever and ever."

There was a beat.

Too sarcastic?

"Well, make sure you use an antiseptic wipe. It would be a shame if your new BFF had to chop off your finger because of a case of sepsis," Bea said without a hint of apology. Then she added, "I *knew* you two would get along."

"Yeah. Like water and oil."

"Oh, don't be ridiculous. He enjoys being a baron as much as you love being sole heiress to Martinelli Motors, so cool your jets. You two will hit it off. Mark my words."

Hmm… Time would have to be the arbiter on that one.

"Everything okay with you?"

"What do you think of Mont di Mare? Pretty impressive, eh?"

"Nice dodge, my friend." Fran tugged at her pony-tail before deftly knotting it into a bun at the base of her neck. "Tell me you're all right and then I'll tell you how meeting Luca really went. Thunder and lightning are your two clues."

She glanced across at Luca and her eyes went wide. He was kneeling beside the dogs, calling out half-hearted protests as Edison gave him a good old-fashioned face cleaning while Freda kept trying to put her paws on his shoulders for a hug. Pia's eyes were lit up bright. Not so brooding and glowering after all, then…

"Everything's fine, Fran. I'm planning an escape under the cover of darkness!"

Hearing Bea add melodramatic dum-dah-dum-dum noises was all the reassurance Fran needed. She was smarting, but she'd be fine.

"Any clues about where you're headed? I hear Transylvania's nice this year."

"Ha-ha. Vampires aren't my style."

"*No one* has your amount of style. Or class," Fran insisted.

"No need to fluff my ego, Fran. I'm going to be fine."

"You're amazing, Bea. Seriously. I don't think I'd be as calm and collected in your shoes."

"It's…it's a relief, really. My only goal is to get through the next few months with no paparazzi. Yours should be to get Luca to cook his stuffed pumpkin flowers for you. *Delicioso!*"

"He cooks?"

"Like a dream."

Fran grinned at the sound of Beatrice kissing the tips of her fingers.

"And just remember, Frannie, his bark is worse than his bite. He's a pussycat, really,"

Fran muttered a few disbelieving words to the contrary, but something in her fluttered as she caught sight of Luca trying—and failing—to get the dogs to stop chasing him.

Maybe he was just taking out his frustration about Marina on her. He wouldn't be the first man she'd met who'd dealt with a broken heart by taking it out on her.

Dads are different, Fran.

Besides. Something told her Luca wasn't exactly brokenhearted about Marina.

"Steel exterior. Molten heart," Beatrice insisted. "You two'll be friends before you know it."

Humph. Doubtful.

She looked over and saw Luca, lying flat on his back, with the dogs appearing to give him some sort of chest compressions. Seeing him all silly and smiley made him...

"Beautiful..."

"He *is* a hottie, isn't he?" Bea teased.

"The place—not the man," Fran swiftly corrected.

"As I said," her friend teased, "time will change all that. You'll be fine. Just remember—Luca's the hawk... Pia's his fledgling. She's his number one concern. You get that right, your summer will be golden."

Fran shot a look up to the pure blue sky, hoping there was someone up there watching out for her. She had a feeling she'd need all the help she could get this summer.

"You *sure* you don't want to come up here to Mont di Mare? Luca told me he'd offered you an invitation."

"No, *chiara*. I'm all right. Just be there on the end of the phone if I need you?"

"Always."

"*Un bacione*, Fran. *Ciao!*"

"*Ciao, ciao!* Be safe."

She clicked the phone off and cast a final wish up to the heavens that Bea would find somewhere beautiful and private to heal. When she dropped her gaze, her eyes met and clashed with Luca's. Goose bumps ran across her arms as she watched the shutters slam down, cloaking the warm, loving man she'd just caught a glimpse of.

Never you mind, Il Barone. I'll show you everything I'm made of and then some.

"Bea." Fran held up the phone, toward him, as if it would prove their mutual friend had been on the line.

"Ending your friendship after yesterday's debacle?"

From the sharp intake of breath and the hollowing of Francesca's cheeks Luca knew he'd pushed it too far. Been too brusque. *Again.*

"Quite the opposite," she replied evenly, her eyes darting about the courtyard until they lit on some bloodred roses. A beautiful contrast to her honey-tanned skin. She bent forward, then stopped herself, giving him a sidelong glance. "I trust there aren't any rules against smelling the roses here?"

Her blue eyes widened, daring him to say otherwise.

He looked away as she called the dogs to heel, only to catch a don't-be-so-grumpy glare from his niece. A sharp reminder of who he was doing this for. All of it. When life ripped your entire family away from you except for one precious soul you cherished it. And he was making a hash of that, as well. Too out of practice. Too many of his earlier years spent being intent on the wrong goals. If he'd known the learning curve to making things right would be so hard…

He'd still be doing it. Even if it meant putting up with Little Miss Ray of Sunshine for the next two months. Pia seemed smitten and that was what counted.

Despite himself, Luca's eyes were drawn to Francesca like a feline to catnip. The fullness of her lips was darkened to a deep emotional red. Not a speck of any other makeup. Jeans and a baseball shirt that teased at the edges of her shoulders. Her blond hair was pulled back from her face in a thick ponytail that swished between her shoulder blades when she walked. Not that he'd been watching her closely… Her shoes were practical leather ankle boots, similar to the boots horsey types wore. Funny… He could easily picture her riding a horse along the mountain trails. Something he and his sister had often done, disappearing for hours at a time, stuffing themselves with wild berries and drinking straight from the mountain streams.

Those days were gone now. Long gone. Just as Francesca's fripperies from yesterday's wedding had all but disappeared. No more soft pink nail polish. No eye shadow, mascara. All of it cleared away to show off her distinct natural beauty. The countryside suited her. Mont di Mare suited her—as if an Old Master had painted her there and just changed her clothing with the passage of time…

"Freda. Edison." Fran commanded the dogs to sit with a gesture, shot Luca an over-the-shoulder wait-for-it-look, then a mischievous grin to Pia. She whipped out her fingers pistol-style and "shot" each of the dogs, who instantly rolled over and played dead.

Pia was consumed by gales of laughter and Fran's lips had parted into a full-fledged smile. One a movie star would have paid a lot for.

"Is there anything *useful* they can do?"

"Zio Luca!" Pia swiped at the air between them. "What *has* got into you today?"

"I'm just waiting to see if Francesca has something helpful to show us. What was it? An hour, she said, and we'd see a change?"

"She made me laugh," Pia growled.

He opened his mouth to protest. Surely he and Pia had laughed… No. Not so much. Especially in the weeks since the bank had slapped the deadline on him. Six months or *finito*.

"Pia—" Fran took a couple of steps forward "—could I use your binoculars for a minute?"

"*Si*, of course." She untangled the strap from her plaits and handed them to Fran.

Without a second glance at Luca, Fran took a scan around the plaza.

"Can you distract the dogs for a minute?"

Pia obliged as Fran jogged over to a small olive tree and hung the binoculars on a low branch, then jogged back.

"Freda." She signaled to Pia's neck. "Where are the binoculars?"

Luca watched wordlessly as the dog took a quick sniff of Pia, did a quick zigzag around the courtyard, abruptly loped over to the olive tree, spotted and tugged down the binoculars by their strap, then padded back, offering the binoculars to a delighted Pia.

"Impressive," he acquiesced. "But hardly a life changer."

Fran pushed her lips forward into a little moue. One that said, *You ain't seen nothin' yet, cowboy.*

He folded his arms and rocked his weight back onto his heels. *Go on*, his stance said. *Prove it.*

A flare of irritation lit up her eyes, bringing a smile to his lips. He got to her as much as she got to him. A Mutual Aggravation Society.

In quick succession Fran ran both dogs through a number of tasks. She had Pia wheel around the courtyard, dropping various items. The dogs picked them all up. They found exits from the courtyard on command. The dogs pushed the wheelchair from one point to another, navigating it around the low-slung branches of the various fruit trees dappling the area.

Fran slipped each dog into a harness and had them take turns pulling Pia on various routes around the courtyard, stopping at one point to pick up a set of keys that had slipped from Luca's pocket. The display culminated in each dog barreling out of the courtyard and returning two minutes later, triumphant, with their water bowls tucked in their mouths, and then dropping them at Fran's feet.

She turned to him, arms crossed in satisfaction. "Proof enough for you?" The arc in her eyebrow dared him to say otherwise.

He made a noncommittal noise, his eyes glued to Fran's, as sharp hit after hit of connection exploded in his chest. He rammed the sensations to the background. Work and Pia. His only two concerns. Francesca brought chaos in her wake. She teased too cruelly at his instinctive urges to pull her in close and taste exactly what those full lips of hers—

"They're *amazing*, Zio! Aren't they amazing? We should get dogs for all the patients! Wouldn't that be just the best?" Pia reeled off her praises, failing to notice the crackle of electricity surging between her uncle and Fran.

He took a step back to break the connection. "Bravo, Francesca." Luca gave a stilted clap, trying to ignore his niece's ebullient response. "I'm sorry to bring the display to an end, but I'm afraid my niece has to spend some time with her tutor."

"It's English lessons, Zio. I could practice with Francesca, *si*?"

"No," he answered in his most pronounced Italian accent. The role of cantankerous uncle was coming to him a bit too fluidly, but needs must. Their world had mayhem enough without a canine-training Mary Poppins running around the place with fairy dust and moonbeams.

Although it was better than Marina's preference, that the village be revamped into an exclusive hotel. Little wonder she'd chosen Marco. He had glitz and glamour down to a T.

Pia gave an exasperated sigh but turned her wheelchair toward the arched stone passageway that led to their private quarters before abruptly spinning around. "Can they—will the dogs be able to come with me?"

"Absolutely." Fran nodded with a quick backward glance to check that it was okay with Luca.

He nodded.

"They are *your* buddies now. Freda is the one I thought might best suit your needs, but it's a good idea to spend time with both of them. We can meet later and talk about things you specifically need help with and start to set up a training routine. Sound good?"

"Cramp!" Pia screamed suddenly, her hands seizing into gnarled fists. "Cramp!"

Without a second glance Fran was on her knees in front of Pia, cupping her hands together, kneading one, then the other, tension knotting her brow as tears formed in Pia's eyes.

"Do you have any heat wraps?" She glanced up at Luca, completely oblivious to the shock in his eyes.

"Let me." Luca reached out to take his niece's slender hands, noting as he did the expert efficiency with which Fran massaged Pia's fingers.

"I'm a physiotherapist. It's fine," Fran said.

"Certified by the University of Life?"

"Harvard," she snapped back. "Good enough for you?" She continued massaging Pia's hands. "You'd be best getting those heat wraps."

"*I* decide what's best for my niece—not you."

"Zio, *please*," Pia pleaded through her tears. "Francesca is doing fine. Please can you get the wraps?"

"I've got a sock filled with rice in my car, if there's a microwave nearby. You just throw the sock in for a—"

"I have appropriate heat wraps. I just—" *I just don't want to leave her with you.* Though unspoken, the words crackled in the air between them.

Francesca continued her fluid movements, but turned her head to face him. "She will be safe with me," she said, more solidly than he'd thought possible. "I will take care of her."

He looked at his niece, her features crumpled in pain, and made the decision.

He ran.

The sooner he left, the sooner he would be back.

A dog trainer *and* a physio? There was a story there. But it was one that would have to wait.

A few minutes later he returned, astonished to see Pia's face wreathed in smiles, her hands lodged in the Bernese mountain dog's "armpits."

"Stand-in heat pads." Fran shrugged, pushing up from her knees at the foot of Pia's wheelchair.

"Rendering these unnecessary?" Luca held up the hot packs he'd already cracked so that they'd be ready for action.

"Sorry." Fran shrugged again and turned to her dogs with a grin, seemingly oblivious to the thousands of dark thoughts that had run through his head as he'd raced to the clinic, pawed through the storage cupboards, then raced back only to find his efforts had been for naught.

"I brought you some electrolyte water, too, Pia. In case you were dehydrated."

"Is she on any medication?"

Luca's eyes widened. "I have brought her what she needs. Pia's on a couple of things for her paraplegia, but other than that has made the choice not to start on any medication until she absolutely has to."

"Right *here*, Zio Luca. No need to talk about me as if I'm invisible!"

"I've got some great cream recipes we can make up that might help," Fran said to Pia, barely acknowledging

Luca. "I bet there are loads of medicinal herbs and flowers growing out there. The dogs and I can forage for you!"

"That'd be great!" Pia enthused.

"Here." Luca took his niece's hands in his and wove the heat pad between them. "Better?"

Pia nodded, then turned away.

"Fran?"

Luca watched as Pia looked up at Fran with a shy look he rarely saw from his niece.

"I'm glad you're here."

"Me, too," Fran replied straight away, then looked up, her azure eyes meeting Luca's as powerfully as a bolt of lightning. There was a connection there. A vivid, primal, deep-seated connection.

One he was going to have to bury in order to survive.

Once Pia had left, her hands wrapped around a heat pad, the tutor in control of the wheelchair and the dogs trotting merrily behind, Fran and Luca eyed each other warily.

A lion and a tigress vying for supremacy. Or a truce?

Fran broke the silence "It's very beautiful up here."

"Far too much room for improvement," he countered, wincing when he saw she'd taken it personally.

Luca put on his "bright" voice, knowing it would sound a bit strangled, but he wasn't ready for making nice with Fran. Might not ever be.

"Shall we get you and your things to your quarters?"

"If that means I'm staying?"

He shot her a noncommittal look. "It's a long walk. Plenty of time to change my mind."

The incident with Pia had shaken him. He was his niece's warrior—her defense against the countless aches and pains she'd had to tackle and overcome since the accident. Getting her an assistance dog was one thing. Seeing her reach to someone else for help...

It hurt.

More than leaving his exclusive reconstructive surgery clinic in Rome to bring his niece here had hurt. More than discovering, once he'd arrived, that his father had leveraged Mont di Mare to within an inch of its life. More than staring daily at the scar he would never fix, keeping it as a reminder—a vivid, daily reminder—of the promises he'd made to do his very best for Pia.

"Hello? Luca?" Fran was waving her hand in front of his face. "You've obviously got things on your mind, and about *this* much patience for me—" She pinched at a smidgen of air, then crushed it between her fingers. "So if you'd just point the way, I'm sure I can find it myself."

"No, you can't."

He bit back a smile as Fran bridled at his pronouncement.

"I happen to have a very good sense of direction."

"I'm sure you do, but we haven't put any signs up on the doors, so it'll be tricky for you to find your cottage."

"Cottage?" Fran's eyes widened in delight as she tugged a couple of medium-sized tote bags out of the truck onto the stone plaza.

She did that a lot. As if everything new was a pleasure rather than a burden. Each corner turned was a moment of thrilling excitement rather than full of the dread that enveloped him whenever a foreman or a staffer headed his way with a purposeful gait and an I-need-to-bend-your-ear-for-a-minute look in his eye.

Fatigue. That was all it was. The clinic was a massive project. The ramifications of failing were too weighty to bear.

"Shall we?"

Fran gave him a wary look, shifting her weight so that her crossed arms formed a protective shield. "Look. I know we didn't get off to a very good start yesterday."

"That would be putting it mildly." They were past niceties. She might as well know she could count him out of her new-friend posse.

"I'm really, truly, incredibly sorry about what happened, but—no offense—I'm much sorrier for Bea, who has to deal with all the mess left by that ratbag fiancé of hers."

"Ratbag?" Luca quirked an eyebrow. Honesty. He liked that in a woman.

"Ratbag," Beatrice replied solidly.

"At last." He picked up one of her bags from the ground where she'd let them drop. "Something we agree on."

"Phew!" She gave a melodramatic swipe of her brow before picking up the other tote bag and running along after him. "And I just want to say I am genuinely grateful for the chance to experiment up here with Pia and the dogs."

"Experiment?" Luca dropped the bag and turned on her. "I don't have time for *experiments*! I need exacting, perfect, unrelentingly driven, skill-based superiority in *everything*. In *everyone* who comes through these gates! Doctors, nurses, cleaners and, most of all, *you*! You are the one person I'm relying on most to help!"

Fran's jaw dropped open, her eyes widening as the stream of vitriol continued.

As the words poured out and he felt his gestures grow more emphatic Luca abruptly clamped his lips tight and stuffed his fists into his pockets. Baring his heart to Bea in the form of this tirade was as good as…as good as showing his hand.

He almost laughed at the irony. His poker face was as

poor as his father's. His father had lost the family fortune. Had *he* just lost Pia's shot at a bit of independence? Some much-deserved fun?

Extraordinarily, Francesca just stood there. Dry-eyed. Patient. Listening to his tongue-lashing as if in fact he was calmly explaining that he was terribly sorry, but he'd been under tremendous pressure owing to the imminent launch of the clinic and, as a result, his concern for his niece and her welfare was escalating. That it pained him to admit it, but he needed support. He needed *her*.

"Feel better?" Fran finally asked after the silence between them had grown heavy with expectation.

"Not really," Luca answered, furious with himself for letting down his guard. He reached for her bags again. "Let's get on with this, shall we? I've already wasted too much time today."

Fran held her ground. "I want you to know I'm willing to stake everything I am on those dogs."

"And what *is* that exactly? Beyond, of course, wedding whistle-blower and circus-trick performer?"

"That's not fair."

"My time is precious, signorina—I'm afraid I didn't catch your surname."

Fran's eyes narrowed. Her teeth took part of her full lip captive, unfurling it bit by bit.

"Martinelli."

When she said it, he saw a change in her. A hint of something he knew *he* saw when he bothered to look at his own reflection in the mirror. Not the scar. The pain. The pain that came from no longer being part of something he should have cherished so much more than he had.

Family.

One simple word that equaled a heady combination

of love, guilt, trying to do better and not getting a single damn thing right.

"Looks like there's a story there," Luca said.

She shrugged.

"Complicated?"

"Very." Her lips pressed forward before thinning into a tight smile.

Luca tipped his chin in understanding. "Looks like we've found *two* things in common."

If there was anyone who grasped *complicated*, it was him.

"Let's cut across here." Luca pointed toward a short covered alley. "It's the long way around."

Fran arched an eyebrow at him.

"I like to get to know my staff."

"I'm not charging you, so technically I'm not staff."

"I can fire you, so technically you *are*. My niece is the single most important person to me in this world. If I'm not happy, you're gone."

Free or not, he wasn't letting just *anyone* get involved with Pia.

"My niece seems to like you. I have yet to be persuaded. With the clinic opening, and no time to look for someone else, I'll give you a chance to prove me wrong."

"And for that I humbly thank you, my lord." An effervescent laugh burbled up and out of Fran's throat as she went into a deep curtsy. "Or is it *Your Excellency*? How *does* one address a baron?"

If he hadn't been so irritated, he would have laughed. She was right to mock him. The arrogance! Since when had he become such a stuck-up prig?

"It's Luca," he said finally, willing himself not to smile. "That's all you need to know."

"Got it." Fran winked, tapping the side of her nose. "Your undercover name."

"Something like that."

He pointed her toward the path they'd need to take to her cottage. Close to his cottage. *Too* close, he realized now. Yet another note for his to-do list: *don't get attached. She'll be gone soon enough.*

CHAPTER FIVE

"DID BEA TELL you anything about me?" Fran asked once they'd walked for a bit in silence, stopping at a bench overlooking the peaks and folds of the surrounding countryside. She focused on a field full of sunflowers. A reminder of all the good she hoped would come of moving back home.

"No. Why?" Luca eyes narrowed, interesting little crinkles fanning out from the corners of his eyes as he tried to figure it out on his own.

"Well, for starters, my full name is Francesca Lisbetta Martinelli." Fran gave him a moment before asking, "Nothing?"

"I've not got all day, Francesca." A flicker of impatience crossed his features.

"Vincente Martinelli... Lui è mio padre."

Saying it in Italian seemed to come more naturally. She and her father spoke it at home. She might as well pronounce her paternity in his native tongue.

"Basta! No? Really?"

A panoply of reaction passed across Luca's face. It was a little bit like watching a short film. Such an interesting face. Not just the scar, which she was aching to touch. There were other stories there. Stories she'd love to hear if only her presence didn't drive him so batty.

"So that makes you…?"

"The daughter of a billionaire."

A flash of understanding lit up his eyes, then disappeared so quickly she thought she'd imagined it.

"And your point is…?" Luca spun his finger in a keep-talking swirl, then gave his watch a sharp tap.

Not the usual reaction. That was nice. Most people wanted to know why she didn't walk around dripping in jewels and designer labels.

"I'm moving home at the end of the summer."

"And…?" Luca's impatience was growing.

"I've not lived there for a long time. Or ever accepted my father's help. But this time…this time he's going to invest in my business."

"The dogs?" Luca's eyebrows lifted.

He obviously thought it was a weird choice, but it wasn't his money, so…

"The point being I've never accepted money from him. *Ever.* And I'm not going home with a fail on my books before I've even started."

Luca blinked, processing that.

"Why are you accepting his help now?"

"Because I want my dad back in my life. And I want him to be proud of me. I believe in what I'm doing this time."

"*This* time?" A flash of concern darkened his features.

"I used to be a physiotherapist. Well, physio and hydrotherapy."

"Why did you give it up?"

She considered him for a moment. He didn't need to know the whole story. Going into business with a "friend" only to discover he'd thought being partners with her meant tapping into her father's wealth.

"One of my patients asked me to help a dog with arthritis. Working with dogs seemed more…"

"Satisfying?" Luca suggested.

"Sounds like the voice of experience," she countered, unwilling to tell Luca how betrayed she'd felt. How hurt. She'd wanted to go to her father, but had felt too ridiculous to confess how foolish she'd been. The last thing she expected from Luca—or anyone—was sympathy. Being an heiress was hardly tragic. Just…*tricky*.

"So you just abandoned your patients? Left on a whim?"

"No. I oversaw their treatment until I could transfer them all to someone I trusted."

"A boyfriend?"

Where had *that* come from?

"My mentor. She took on each and every patient."

"And once you'd shaken off your responsibilities—"

"I didn't shake them off!" Fran protested.

"You left."

"I was young."

"And why should I believe you won't do the same to Pia?"

"You're just going to have to trust me."

Luca's jaw tightened. *Trust.* That was what it was going to boil down to.

"Why should I trust you?"

"I did what was right yesterday, even though it could have cost me the friendship I hold dearest in my heart." Fran's eyes clouded with more emotion than she'd hoped to betray. She swallowed it down and continued, "That, and the second I saw *you* were the person I'd be working for I could've turned the car around and left right then and there. But the dogs seemed excited. They like Pia.

Which makes sense. They seem to like *you*. Which makes less sense. But I trust them. Dogs are loyal."

"Three," Luca said grimly.

"Three?"

"Three things we agree on. Dogs are the only sentient creatures who have any loyalty. Excluding, of course, my niece. If she can stick with me, she can stick with anyone."

"Ah! Finally admitting you're a bit of a Mr. Cranky Pants, then?"

Fran teased at the corner of her T-shirt. Had she overstepped the mark with that one?

"Not a chance, *carina*."

Fran looked up at his change of tone and was caught completely off balance as Luca flashed her a wicked smile.

Santo cielo! A swirl of sparks swept through Fran's tummy, lighting up all sorts of places she'd rather not think about when she was trying to be serious and grown-up. Sort of. Maybe…

"Whatever." She clucked dismissively, feeling a bit more like herself. "Just you wait. Beatrice has assured me we'll be friends. That'll be my summer challenge."

Luca grunted. "We're a long way from friends, *bellissima*. And we're nearly at your cottage." He tipped his head toward a wooden door.

Shame she couldn't convince him to stand there all day. Backlit by the sun. Hair tousled by the gentle breeze. The outline of his body looking rugged and capable. The perfect alpha male to have a summer romance with and then get on with the rest of her life.

As if *that* would ever happen.

"Any final tidbits of wisdom about assistance dogs you want to impart before I drop you off at your cottage?"

"So you're going to let me stay?"

She watched as he processed her question—his teeth biting together, his jaw giving that telltale stress twitch along the line of his scar, his lips parting to demand one last task.

"Give me one word to describe the change you see in your customers once they have a Fran Special."

One word?

"Wait—give me a minute." She scrunched her eyelids tight in order to think and came up blank. In a panic, she looked up into Luca's espresso-dark gaze and it came to her. "Breathtaking."

Just like you, bellissima.

The words popped into Luca's mind and near enough escaped his lips as Fran's blue eyes lit up, her cheeks flushing with pleasure and undiluted pride in what she did.

It was the same sensation *he* felt when a reconstruction surgery had gone to plan. Particularly when a patient picked up a mirror for the first time and, eyes brightening, exclaimed, "It's the old me!" That was far better than the enhancement surgeries that paid the bills. If Mont di Mare could one day do charitable cases, that would be a dream come true.

He shook the thought away. An impossibility right now. A far-off dream.

"So, what's your decision?"

Luca shook his head, temporarily confused. "What decision?"

"Are you going to let me stay—" she swung her thumb toward the village entryway "—or do we have to drag these bags back to my car and pick up the dogs so I can hoof it?"

Pragmatics told him to send her away.

Fran was chaos. He needed peace.

But a splinter of doubt pierced through his more reasoned side.

Perhaps it *wasn't* chaos she brought. Perhaps it was… possibility. And that meant change. Never easy, but sometimes necessary.

The look of glee on his niece's face when she'd seen not only the dogs but Fran had tugged at his sensibilities. Not to mention the sheer expectation on Fran's face now, which was making too great a play on his heartstrings. The strings of the heart he was beginning to realize had never quite regained its usual cheerful cadence since the accident. The very same heart he felt opening, just a sliver, to this ray of joy standing before him. Besides, *he* didn't have to spend time with her. Pia did.

"Si." He gave Fran a quick nod before adding wryly. "Pia might disown me if I say otherwise."

A whoop that might have filled a football stadium flew out of Fran's throat and she immediately launched into some sort of whirling happy dance, the likes of which, he was quite sure, the streets of Mont di Mare had never seen.

Oh, Dio!

Had he *really* just welcomed Hurricane Fran into their lives?

Dance finished, Fran eventually came to a standstill, chest heaving with excitement, eyes alight with the power of that single yes.

"Really?" Endearingly, her voice hit the higher altitudes of her range and her fingers went all pitter-patter happy. "I promise you won't regret it. And when Pia's at school I will *totally* help with painting or putting up

wallpaper or making beds—anything you need. I'll even change bedpans when the patients arrive if it will help."

"We have moved a bit beyond bedpans in terms of patient care."

"Cool." Fran was unfazed. "Whatever the least favorite jobs are, count me in."

He began to shake his head no, but she stopped him with a finger on his lips.

"I won't take no for an answer. You're helping me more than you know, and from what I've gleaned—" they both turned to watch yet another delivery truck begin its way up the bridge toward the clinic "—you have a lot to do. Another pair of hands isn't going to hurt anything, is it? Three years of boarding school has ensured my hospital corners are excellent in the bed-making department."

"How's your grouting?" he asked, in a tone more suited to a master tiler than a doctor doing his best to bring a thousand loose ends together into one beautiful tapestry.

"Unparalleled!" she shot back without the blink of an eye. "My sanding skills are a bit rusty, but I know my way around a mop and bucket something serious."

A sudden urge to pull Fran into his arms seized Luca. If he had Fran on his side she'd no doubt start spreading her pixie dust and turn the entire workload from a burden into an adventure. Why *shouldn't* he have a partner in crime?

Because the bank was threatening to take it all away.

If you'd paid more attention to your father, seen how low he was feeling...

Their gazes connected, meshing in a taut sensation of heightened awareness, powerful currents of electricity surging between the pair of them. Holding them together as one. Sensations he hadn't felt for a long time charged through him, lighting up parts of his body to a wattage he hadn't felt in even longer.

The buzzing of his phone checked the sensations. The raw attraction.

He glanced at the screen.

Work.

The consultant for one of his patients who'd be flying in by helicopter a week from today.

Fun and spontaneity would have to wait.

The first hit of genuine attraction he'd felt in years would have to go untended.

He had bills to pay.

"*Scusi.* I've got to take this."

"Of course." Fran's smile bore the same shade of disappointment he felt in his marrow. "Patients come first."

He took a few steps away, the smile he'd so recently worn eradicated without a trace. "*Si*, Dr. Firenze. How can I help you?"

CHAPTER SIX

THE WEEK HAD passed in a blur. An adrenaline-fueled blur that was about to culminate in the arrival of his first five patients. T minus eighteen hours and counting.

Luca pulled the weights out of their packaging and began lining them up on the rack. These would all be in use soon.

He sat back on his heels and scanned the rehab gym. Gleaming weights machines. Several pairs of handrails ready to bear the weight of patients ready to be put to the test.

The doctor in him itched to get back to work. Not the doctor who'd worn the fancy suits and tended to Rome's image-conscious elite. The doctor who'd retrained at night after working all day with his niece. The doctor who'd poured every last cent he had into getting to this point.

At least Pia and Fran had been so engrossed in working with the dogs that Luca hadn't had to add the guilt of neglecting his niece to everything else he was feeling. And, in fairness to Fran, she'd gone above and beyond being an assistance-dog trainer this past week. Any spare moment she'd had away from Pia and the dogs had, true to her word, been spent doing anything and everything she could to get the clinic to the gleaming, immaculate state of readiness it was in now.

"Are you ready for the big reveal?" Fran appeared in the doorway, a mischievous smile making her look more imp than workhorse.

"Does Pia really need to do this *now*? Half of Mont di Mare still isn't renovated. I haven't checked the patients' rooms or the family quarters yet, and there are still—"

"C'mon!" Fran held up a hand, then arced her arm, waving for him to join her. "This means a lot to her—and I have an idea about the other thing. The unrenovated tidbits."

"How unusual," he answered drily.

Tidbits.

Half the village, more like: ten family houses, ten more patient rooms and the same number again for common rooms and treatment facilities. *Tidbits*. Only an American! He checked himself. Only an *optimist* like Fran would call the amount of work left to be done tidbits. The same projects that buoyed her up near enough pinned him to the ground with worry. What had *possessed* him to turn one of the least disabled-friendly places in the universe into a specialized clinic for disabled people?

Optimism?

Necessity?

"All right." He pushed up from the floor once the final row of weights had been laid out. "Let's hear it, Little Miss Creativity."

"Ha-ha. Very funny, Signor White-Walls-or-Bust." She fluttered her lashes. "It's not *my* fault the spirit of Italy's esteemed relationship with beauty and art courses through my veins and not yours."

Luca watched, unexpectedly transfixed as Fran struck a modeling pose, swooshing her hair up and over one shoulder as she skidded her slender fingers along the length of her athletic figure, eventually coming to rest on her thigh.

He tried to tamp down the flare of heat rising within him.

A lab coat would be most convenient right about now.

He cleared his throat. There were things to do. A clinic to open. This mysterious "reveal" to witness. No doubt another one of Pia's feats with her dogs rather than Francesca reenacting Salome's Dance of the Seven Veils.

He considered the swish of her derriere as she turned to walk down the hall.

Pity.

Where *had* he put those lab coats?

She glanced over her shoulder. "I'll spell out my idea on the way, and you can let me know if it's a yea or a nay by the time we get there." Fran glanced back again, eyes widening as he remained glued to the spot for no apparent reason. "It's our *thing*! Walking, talking, deciding. Remember?"

Just one week together and they had a "thing"? He rolled his eyes.

She dropped him a wink.

A flirtatious wink.

Was that the tip of her tongue peeking out between her teeth, giving the bow and dip of her top lip a surreptitious lick?

Sleep. That was what he needed. A good night's sleep and he'd be seeing things more clearly.

"All right, then. What's this grand idea of yours?"

"Well!" She wove her hands together underneath her chin. "I know you're rehab royalty—"

"Along with a team of highly trained experts," Luca interrupted.

She didn't need to know he'd been dubbed the King

of Collagen before the accident had pushed him away from plastics to spinal injury rehabilitation. He probably would have carried on with plastics forever until—*bam!* In thirty horrifying seconds his life had changed.

He shook his head against the rising bile, forcing himself to focus on what Fran was saying.

"I read all of the bios for your clinicians last night, and there is some serious brainpower in play here." She dropped her hands. "Anyhow, I was thinking about the psychological advantages of being part of things here."

Luca gave her a sidelong look. "Do you mean you or the patients? All your chipping in has been much appreciated, Francesca. The painting, making the beds as promised… But if you read the résumés properly you will have noticed we have two very experienced psychiatrists on the team."

"I'm not talking about me and a paint roller. I'm thinking more hands-on stuff for the patients. There *is* the itty-bitty problem of half your village needing a splash more work done to it."

Her lips widened into an apologetic wince-smile.

"How very…politic, Signorina Martinelli. I presume your plan includes *you* wrapping everything up nicely before your intended departure date?"

The smile dropped from Fran's face as quickly as the light fled from her eyes.

Luca could have kicked himself. Still shooting the messenger. Fran had been a trouper, working as hard as his paid staffers—if not harder—to get everything shipshape for the opening. She didn't deserve to be on the sharp end of his mood. Particularly seeing as he wasn't entirely sure he wasn't behaving like a boor in order to fight off the deepening attraction he felt to his resident sunflower.

"*Per favore*, Francesca." He forced himself to grind out the plea. "Please tell me your idea."

"Why, thank you very much!" She rubbed her hands together excitedly. "I can't really take credit for the idea, though. The other day I was watching online videos— you know, those feel-good ones where human spirit triumphs over adversity and you end up crying because people are so amazing?"

She looked across at the dubious expression he knew he was wearing and qualified her statement.

"The ones that make *me* cry anyway. So, there was this huge pile of bricks and a guy in a wheelchair—totally hot. Completely good-looking. Like you. But he was more…uh…*Nordic*."

She stopped, took a step back to consider him, and as their eyes caught a streak of pink blossomed on her cheeks.

"Let's not get carried away, here, Fran. Shall we?"

He gestured that they should continue along the stone-slab route they were making short work of. Fran scuttled ahead, rabbiting on about the video and only occasionally looking back at him. He was surprised to find he was smiling. At her unquenchable thirst for life? Or the fact she thought he was good-looking?

Foolish, really.

He shoved the thoughts away and forced himself to listen to her suggestion. It was the least he could do after his abrupt behavior.

By the time they reached the archway leading out to the bridge he'd been more than persuaded. Her idea was a good one.

"So what you're saying is if the patients—no matter what their background—put some actual graft into refurbishing the rest of the village, they'll be happier?"

"Precisely. I mean, this guy—totally paralyzed from the waist down—made just about the coolest fireplace out of bricks and mortar that I've ever seen. He *made* something. Crafted it with his own hands. Something many able-bodied people wouldn't even dream of starting, let alone finishing. I'm completely happy to oversee the project, of course. I know your team's hands are full."

She stood before him, blue eyes bright with expectation. Hope.

Tempting…

Pragmatics forced his hand.

"I hate to rain on your parade, Francesca, but there are thousands of other considerations. Health and safety, for one. You don't know how many inspections I have to deal with already—if I were to add patients to the mix of some already dangerous situations, I—"

He stopped himself. He'd been about to say he couldn't afford the insurance. Truth was he could hardly afford *any* of this. But turning it all over to the bank just so it could be demolished was out of the question. The clinic simply *had* to be a success.

"Look—" Fran raised her hands in a hear-me-out gesture "—I know what you're saying, and the idea definitely needs to be fleshed out. Especially as a lot of your patients are on the young side, right?"

"All of them." Luca nodded. "Teenagers."

"I'm not talking about everyone building stone walls or pizza ovens—although that *would* be a totally great idea. Can you imagine it? Pizza under the stars! What teenager doesn't love pizza?"

Luca glanced at his watch and spun his finger in a let's-get-on-with-it gesture, all the while trying his best not to get caught up in her enthusiasm.

His focus had to be X-ray machines. Crucial rehabilitation equipment being properly installed. Clipboards! If he'd known just how many clipboards he'd need when he'd started this pie-in-the-sky project…

"Sorry." She threw him an apologetic look. "I've just—I've just fallen a little bit in love with this place and it's hard to fight the enthusiasm, you know?"

Of course he knew. And her enthusiasm—despite his best efforts to be stoically distant—had touched his heart. His passion for the place was why he'd started the project in the first place. But now, with bills to pay and the bank breathing down his neck…

"I'm afraid it'll have to go on the pipe dreams list, Francesca."

Fran's disappointed expression soon brightened into something else. Inspiration.

"I've got an even better idea. I bet you there are any number of craftsmen who would love to come up here and work. True Italian craftsmen who wouldn't mind passing on some of their expertise to willing apprentices. Leather. Glass. Embossing. Calligraphy. I once saw an entire wall done in a painted leather wallpaper. It was amazing."

"We are *not* covering the walls in leather wallpaper, Fran."

"All right Mr. Grumpy. They don't have to be leather. Who cares what the patients do as long as they're happy? Even if it's just throwing a bit of paint on a wall. In the nicest way possible, of course," she finished with a polished smile.

"And what makes you think working on a building site will be an effective remedy for their ailments in comparison with the unparalleled medical attention they will be receiving here—*if* you ever let me get back to work, that is?"

Fran looked at him as if he was crazy.

"Who *doesn't* feel the satisfaction of a job well-done? Of knowing you've made an actual difference to somewhere this special. I mean, you must be *bursting* with pride."

A crackle of irritation flared in him.

"Francesca, the only thing I'm bursting with is the desire to untangle myself from this ridiculous conversation and get back to—"

Luca stopped in his tracks as they turned the corner of the archway into the main courtyard. Emotions ricocheted across his chest in hot thuds of recognition.

Humility. Pride. Achievement.

All the staff were assembled in the center of the broad arc—an impressive crowd of applauding doctors, rehab therapists, X-ray technicians and countless others. In the center was Pia and the two dogs. When her eyes lit on him she whispered a quick command to the dogs, each holding the end of a thick blue ribbon in their mouths, and they went in separate directions until it was taut and he could read the message on it. *"Bravo! I nostri migliori auguroni, Dr. Montovano!"*

The unfamiliar tickle of emotion teased at the back of Luca's throat.

Congratulations on a job well-done.

No one had done anything like this for him. *Ever.* His partners at the plastic surgery clinic had always mocked him for his pro bono cases. For bringing a bit of pride back into the life of a child with a birth defect or a scar that might have changed their lives forever. *Money!* they'd said. *The high life!*

He looked across at Fran. A flush of pleasure played across her cheeks as she watched him take it all in. The ridiculous conversation they'd been having made sense now. A distraction. Typical Fran. Perfection and mayhem in one maddening and beautiful package.

He felt torn. The sentiment of the moment was pure kindness.

"Zio! Come! Look at the food Fran has organized! It's all from artisan specialists in Tuscany!" Pia wheeled over to him and took his hand.

Behind the doctors and other medical practitioners— a team of about thirty, who were now reliant on him and the success of the clinic—were two trestle tables heaving under the weight of a bounty of antipasti, salads, savory tarts. All the regional specialties—and the people who had made them. Anything and everything a red-blooded Italian would crave if he were away from home.

He gruffly cleared his throat, giving them all a nod of thanks for their contributions.

More cries of *"Bravo!"* and *"Auguroni!"* filled the air.

He waved off the applause with a quick comment about how they were a team. How they all deserved a pat on the back for pulling together in the same way generations of villagers had back in the day when someone had been fool enough to start carving into the side of this blasted mountain and call it home.

Looking around at the smiling faces, hearing the laughter, feeling the buzz of anticipation in the air, he allowed himself a brief moment of elation. If he could hold on to that feeling—

Luca's eyes lit upon Fran, the only woman in the world who would have bothered to make this moment happen.

Something deep within him twisted and ached. Longed to have a spare ounce of energy, an unfettered moment to explore…test the waters and see what would happen if he and Fran were to—

Enough.

He couldn't even hold on to a girlfriend he'd no plans to marry, let alone pay enough attention to his niece.

Pia and the clinic. His two priorities. Everything else—everyone else—would have to wait.

Fran saw the lift in Luca's eyes as he scanned the team. The glint of renewed energy. The gratifying blaze of pride. She hoped he knew just how proud all of these people were of *him*. Of the life he'd brought not only to Mont di Mare but to the community as a whole. A center of excellence, right here in their own little hideaway nook of Italy!

"Cut the ribbon!"

The call originated from Pia, but soon everyone was chanting it.

A nurse ran up to Luca with a small pair of surgical scissors from her hip kit when Pia put out a panicked call that she'd remembered the ribbon but not the scissors. The dogs were instructed to stand at either side of the archway in front of Luca, and as the scissors swept through the silken sash, marking this historic moment, Luca's eyes met Fran's.

It was impossible to read his expression, but the effect his gaze had upon her body was hard to deny. The explosion of internal fireworks. Her bloodstream soaring in temperature. The roar in her ears while the rest of her body filled with a showering cascade of never-ending sparks. The feeling that she was less mortal than she had been before.

She gave herself a sharp shake.

She was here to do a job. Not to get all doe-eyed over the boss man. And yet…was that a hint of softness in Luca's gaze? A concession that she might *not* be the thorn in his side he'd initially pegged her to be.

Little sparkles of pleasure swirled around her belly at the thought. Sparkles she was going to have to round up and tame if doing her job and leaving this place with her heart intact were her intentions.

She felt a set of familiar fingers giving her hand a tug.

Pia. Her golden-hearted charge. The entire point of her being there.

"What do you say we get some food?" Fran asked.

"Sounds good to me." Pia swirled her chair around then looked up at her. "Fran?"

"Mmm-hmm?" Fran pulled her attention back from another surreptitious glance in Luca's direction.

"You're good for him, you know."

"Beg pardon?" Fran's attention was fully on Pia now.

"Uncle Luca. He's a bit like me, I think."

Fran swallowed a disbelieving laugh out of respect for Pia's serious tone. "In what way?"

Pia's expression turned suddenly shy, and her fingers teased at the belt that held her petite torso in place against the low back of her chair.

"He's a bit lonely, I think. He works so hard. And with all the pressure my…my condition must put on him I can't help but worry that he's going to work himself to death. I know he loves medicine and everything, but what if this is all too much for him? What if…?" Pia's voice broke, though she maintained eye contact and tried again. "What if…?"

Fran's heart felt as though it were going to burst with compassion when Pia's eyes filled with tears. The amount of loss the poor girl had endured and now she feared losing her uncle, as well? She saw that Luca was trying to spend time with Pia, but she also knew the long hours he put in with the clinic. It was exactly what had happened with her father and his cars. Even when he was at home

he wasn't really there. And getting access to his heart
was near impossible.

Fran pulled Pia's hands into hers and gave each set
of the girl's knuckles a quick kiss. "Don't you worry,
amore. As long as I'm here we'll make sure your uncle
is looked after."

No matter how hard a task it was.

They both looked across to where Luca was standing.
He'd stepped away from the crowd now, and a smattering of antipasti was near enough tipping off the plate he
barely seemed to notice he was holding.

The team of doctors and support staff had all formed
groups, or were crowding around the table, piling deli-
cacies onto their own plates. Luca's body was drawn up
to his full height. Six feet of *leave me alone*. His attention was utterly unwavering as he gazed upon the clinic's
entryway. His expression was hooded, once again, heavy
with the burden of all that had yet to be done.

CHAPTER SEVEN

LUCA SAW THE helicopter before he heard it. A tiny speck heading in from Florence—the whirring blades, the long body of a medical helicopter with its telltale red cross on the undercarriage coming into view as it crested the "hills," as Francesca insisted upon calling them.

As if his thinking her name had conjured her up, she appeared by his side. "Are you excited?"

"Focused. I have my first surgery today. Shouldn't you be working with Pia? Where are the dogs?"

Fran gave him a sidelong look, clearly unimpressed by his curt tone. "They're with her algebra tutor. Pia wanted me to give you this." She handed him an envelope, but not before shooting him a ha!-take-that look. "She wanted to wish you luck," she continued. "As do I."

Luca pushed the card into his pocket, returning his gaze to the approaching helicopter.

This is work. Fran is...pleasure. There's no room for pleasure in my life.

Despite himself, he turned and watched Fran as she tracked the arrival of the *elicottero*, her chin tipped up toward the sky, the movement elongating the length of her slender neck, the fine outline of her face, the sweet spot where her neck met her jaw. If he were to kiss her there would she groan or whimper with pleasure? Would her legs slip up and around his waist, tugging him in deeper, more fully into her, so that with each thrust he took—

"Dr. Montovano?"

"*Si*, Elisa?" He stopped and corrected himself. "Dr. Sovani. What can I do for you?"

Luca forced his attention to narrow and focus as the doctor rattled through the plans for their patient's arrival and presurgical procedures. He didn't miss Fran's fingers sweeping up to cover the twist of her lips—a snigger at his obviously divided attentions.

She'd obviously caught him staring. Seen the desire in his eyes.

Something in him snapped. Didn't she *know* how vital today was for him and the clinic? The bank had already been on the phone that morning to remind him. *Tick-tock.*

"Miss Martinelli, do you mind? We've got a surgery to prepare for."

She didn't say a word. Didn't have to. Disdain for his dismissive tone was written all over her face.

"Did you want Paolo to go up to the main buildings first, or to his quarters?" Dr. Sovani asked.

"We should get him straight to a prep room." Luca blinkered his vision, forced himself to train his eyes on Elisa's clipboard. "He'll be tired after his journey, and his family would no doubt like to see him settled. The operation isn't for a couple of hours, and we'll need him at his strongest. Are his parents in the chopper with him?"

"They're arriving by car."

As if on cue, a couple appeared in the archway leading to the helicopter landing area, two young children alongside them, all eyes trained on the sky as their loved one approached.

The instant the helicopter touched down, the air was filled with rapid-fire instructions, questions and action.

Fran was nowhere to be seen.

"*Ciao*, Paolo." Luca strode to the teenager's side once the heli-medics had lifted him into his wheelchair and ensured the helmet protecting his skull was in place. "What do you say we head to the clinic and get you settled?"

If Pia hadn't asked, Fran wouldn't have dreamed of stepping foot anywhere near the clinic. But she'd pleaded with Fran to let her take a break from her studies and watch her uncle in surgery. Now that they were here, in the observation room, she had to admit it was amazing.

"Can you turn the speaker up, please, Francesca?" Pia's fingers were covering her mouth, and her body was taut, as if she were watching a blockbuster movie, not a surgery meant to restore a portion of a patient's skull.

"Do you know what happened to him?" Fran asked.

"I don't know the whole story, but he was in a *moto* accident, I think. A year ago. They had to take out part of his skull because of the swelling. The surgeons in Florence said Zio Luca would be the best person to replace it, so they've waited until now. The last thing he needed was a terrible surgeon *and* to be left with a dent in his head!"

Fran smiled at the pride in Pia's voice. Of *course* she was proud. Her surgeon uncle was finally doing what he loved best. Fran could see that now. Sure, he had held his own with a hammer, and seemed to have no problem understanding complicated spreadsheets—but this... Seeing him here in the operating theater was mesmerizing.

The assured sound of his voice as he spoke to the nurses turned her knees to putty, and the exacting movement of his hands was both delicate and confident. It was little wonder he'd seemed like a pent-up ball of frustration in the week leading up to the clinic's opening. He hadn't been doing what he obviously did best: medicine.

"Francesca?" Pia was tapping a finger on her hand.

"Yes—sorry. What is it, *amore*?"

Pia giggled, then singsonged, "Someone's got a crush on Zio Luca!"

"I do *not*!" Fran protested. A bit too hotly, maybe. Just a little. But in a never-ever-going-to-happen kind of way. A flight of fancy.

"Just as well." Pia returned her gaze to the OR window as if she saw that sort of thing all the time. "He's a terrible boyfriend. Too bad you're the only girlfriend I like."

"And you can carry on liking me. Just not as your uncle's girlfriend."

"Maybe not *now*..." Pia teased, her eyes still glued to her uncle.

Maybe not *ever*, Fran told herself, refusing to let the seeds of imagination take root. It was far too easy to imagine those hands touching her body. His full lips, now hidden behind a surgical mask, touching and tasting her own...

She froze when she realized Luca was looking at her. His eyebrows cinched together in confusion. He obviously hadn't been aware he had an audience. Then they lifted, and little crinkles appeared at the corners of his eyes as if he were smiling behind his mask.

A whirl of something heated took a tour around her chest and swirled lazily in her stomach.

All she could think of to do was to point at Pia, then give him a double thumbs-up and a cheesy grin as if he'd just managed to flip a pancake, not perform an incredibly intricate reconstructive surgery.

What an idiot!

If she'd stood even the tiniest chance of being Luca's girlfriend a second ago—not that she *wanted* to be his girlfriend—she'd definitely closed the door of opportunity right down. Luca only took people seriously if *they* were serious. Whether he thought she was cute or not was beside the point. She wanted him to take her as seriously as she took him.

Pia and the dogs. She needed to repeat it like a mantra. *Pia and the dogs.* They were her only focus. Not the other patients. Not the beautiful village. Not the tall, dark and enigmatically talented surgeon putting the final stitches into his first surgery at his new clinic.

He was a picture of utter concentration.

There wasn't room for her in his life.

Never had been.

Never would be.

The best thing she could do now was focus on getting Pia up to speed, then going home and mending fences with her father. He was the only man she should be worrying about impressing.

CHAPTER EIGHT

A SURGE OF pride filled Luca's heart on seeing the new ramps and pathways being put to use as they'd been intended.

Just a few days in and Mont di Mare felt *alive*. More dynamic than it had in years.

His sister would be so proud of what they'd done with the place. If only bank loans could be repaid with good feelings…

Never mind. Treatments were underway. However slowly, payments were starting to come in to counterbalance the flood of outgoing costs.

The surgery with Paolo had gone as smoothly as he'd hoped. The teenager was already out of Recovery, and at this very moment discussing the litany of tests he would be going through to combat further deterioration in the wake of his paralysis.

Luca itched to join Paolo's team, to be part of adding more movement to the young man's upper body after his motor scooter accident had paralyzed him from the waist down. It was a similar injury to his niece's, only he'd received next to no physio in the wake of his accident.

The lack of strength in his upper body was startling. Just thinking about the various avenues of treatment they could explore made him smile.

"Dr. Montovano?" Elisa appeared at the doorway. "We've got Giuliana, ready to discuss her case with you."

"Great! Is she in her room?"

"No, she's over by the pool, speaking with your... your friend?"

Luca's brow cinched. "Friend?"

"You know—the one with the dogs."

"Ah. Francesca. No, she's not a friend. She's here to work with Pia."

The words hit false notes even as they came out. A familiar feeling began to take hold of him. The feeling that he'd started to let someone in and then, slowly but surely, had begun to push her away again. Just as he'd done with Marina. Just as he'd done with the women before her.

Elisa shifted uncomfortably, a soft blush coloring her cheeks. "Apologies... We weren't sure..."

"We?" Luca's alarm bells started ringing.

"The team. We didn't—she just..." Elisa's eyes scanned his office in a panic. "She seems to do a lot more than someone who is just here with the assistance dogs would."

"Yes, she's very...*American*," he said, as if it explained everything.

Elisa nodded, clearly none the wiser.

"Va bene," he said, in a tone he knew suggested otherwise. "Shall we go and have a chat with Giuliana?"

"It's all right. You can pet him if you like." Fran smiled at the teen, well aware that Giuliana's fingers had been twitching on her wheelchair arm supports ever since she and Edison had appeared in the courtyard adjacent to the infinity pool.

The pool she was absolutely dying to jump into now that summer had well and truly made an appearance.

When Giuliana's parents had mistaken her for medical staff and asked if she would look after their daughter while they went to see her room, she had said yes.

Foolish? Perhaps.

But everyone was operating at full capacity now that the clinic was open, and with Pia already busy with her studies what harm could a little babysitting do?

The dark-haired girl looked across at her with a despondent look. "It's my arms. They're just so weak."

"You've got to start somewhere," Fran reminded her gently. "Not to mention the fact you're in the perfect place to start rebuilding that strength."

Fran tried to shake away the problem with a smile, hiding an internal sympathy twinge. Giuliana's arms were strapped to stabilizing arm troughs and wrist supports on her chair. They were so thin it was almost frightening.

"Edison." Fran issued a couple of commands and the Lab bounded over and sat alongside Giuliana, so that his head was directly in line with the armrest. "Is it all right if I undo your strap?"

A hint of anxiety crossed the girl's eyes. "Are my parents back yet?"

Fran looked around, vividly aware of how restricted the poor girl's movement was. Her neck was being cradled by two contoured pads and it didn't seem as if she had the strength—let alone the capacity—to turn it left or right.

"They don't seem to be. They were going to look at your room, right?"

"Si..." Giuliana replied glumly. "They have to approve every single little thing before I am even allowed to see it. I can hardly believe they left me alone with *you*."

Tough for any teen to have helicopter parents. Even harder when there was zero choice in the matter.

Fran bit her cheek when Giuliana gave the telltale eye roll of an exasperated teen. She didn't know how many times *she'd* rolled her eyes behind her dad's back when he'd made yet another unilateral decision on her behalf.

Her hand slipped to her back pocket to check her phone was still there. They hadn't talked yet today.

Time zones.

She'd call him later. Just knowing he'd pick up the phone now, close his laptop and really talk to her, made such a difference. Giuliana might find her parents annoying, but at least they were *there* for her.

"It doesn't really hurt when my hands are out of the supports…" Giuliana was saying.

"Do you mind me asking what happened?"

"Skiing." The word sounded as lifeless as the faraway look in Giuliana's eyes.

"Where was the injury?" Fran asked.

When she'd been a physio being straightforward with her questions had usually paid dividends. No need to tiptoe around patients who were facing a life of paralysis.

"Grade-four whiplash. Cervical spine fracture."

"C1?" Francesca asked, her jaw dropping. Most people would have died.

"C2."

"Oof! That must've hurt." Fran's features widened into a "youch" face. She was still lucky. C2 fractures often resulted in fatalities.

"Quite the opposite," Giuliana answered drily. "I didn't feel a thing."

"Ha! Of course you didn't!"

Fran hooted with laughter before registering the look of disbelief on Giuliana's face. *Oops.*

"I'm sorry, *amore.* You'll have to forgive me. I'm used

to talking to dogs, not humans. I am a class-A expert in Open Mouth, Insert Foot."

Giuliana considered her for a moment, then gave a wry smile. "Actually, it was my test. You just passed."

"Oh!" Fran gave a little wriggle of pride that morphed into a hunch of concern. "Wait a minute. What kind of test?"

"A test to see who will laugh at the poor crippled girl's joke."

"A joke test?"

"A litmus test," Giuliana answered solidly. "Most people don't even ask me what happened. They just look at me with big sad eyes, like I'm on the brink of death or something. I'm paralyzed. Not deaf or blind!"

And not bereft of spirit either, from the looks of things.

Fran let loose an appreciative whoop of respect. "You go, girl!" She put her hand up in a fist bump, rolled her eyes at her second idiotic move within as many minutes, then put her fist to Giuliana's anyway. "Forgive me. *Again.* You're here for the summer?"

Giuliana nodded, amusement skittering through her eyes.

"Well, I don't know what your doctor's plans are, but by the end of our stay what do you say we work toward a proper fist bump?"

"What? So you can be 'down with the kids'?" Giuliana giggled, as if the idea of Francesca being down with the kids was quite the challenge.

"Yeah!" Fran parried, striking a silly pose. "That's how I roll. Hey! I have an idea." She positioned herself so she was at eye level with Giuliana. "How crazy are you feeling today?"

"In what way?"

The teen's brow crinkled and it was all Fran could do

not to reach out and give it a soothing caress. She couldn't promise the girl that everything would be all right, and nor did she have the right to do anything other than what Luca had hired her to do, but…

"Well, Edison here is my number one gentle dog…"

It wasn't a lie. Not really. Her *other* number one dog was already completely under Pia's command.

"If you'd like to pet him, it seems to me the easiest way to do it would be if we unstrapped you. I would be right behind you, supporting your elbow, and Edison is very good at holding his head still."

The glimmer of excitement in Giuliana's eyes was all the encouragement Fran needed. Ever so gently, Fran lifted the girl's frail arm out of the rest and settled it in her lap for a moment.

"Is it all right if I put a treat in your hand?" Fran asked. "It's a sure-fire way to get Edison's full attention."

"I don't know how well I'll be able to hold it."

"Not a problem. I'll support you."

Fran pinched a treat out of her belt pouch, placed it between Giuliana's fragile fingers with Edison sitting at full attention at her feet. Then Fran shifted around behind the wheelchair, so she could provide support for the girl's elbow. It surprised her to feel how rigid the poor thing's arm was—similar to some of the elderly people she'd worked with years ago. Something deep within her bridled. How awful to have to live like this with your whole life in front of you!

Don't get attached, Fran! You gave up on people for a reason. First, fix things with your father…

Her thoughts faded as instinctively she began to massage the girl's arm. Stroking and smoothing her fingers along the length of the musculature, teasing some suppleness into the brittle length of her arm.

"Come, Edison. Want a treat?"

Giuliana's hand jerked as she spoke. The treat went flying. As it arced up so, too, did Edison's snout, his jaw opening wide as he jumped up to catch it.

"What the *hell* do you think you're doing?"

Luca was thundering across the patio, his face dark as midnight.

By the time he arrived Edison was contentedly swallowing the treat he'd caught, with no detriment to Giuliana whatsoever.

"We were just—" Fran began, then she stopped as memory swept her back to her sixteenth birthday. The one her father had forgotten because it had been the same day his first car had rolled off the production line.

All day she had stayed at the factory. Doing homework…idly peeking into the kitchen at the canteen to see if anyone was secretly whipping up a birthday cake. Wandering through the advertising section on the off chance that someone had made a little—or an enormous—birthday banner to mark the day. Hanging around in the mailroom on the pretense of helping to sort the large bundle of post, only to discover that her mother had, as usual, neglected to send anything.

When at long last the first car had come off the assembly line—that first amazing vehicle—she had been so excited she'd run up to touch it, to press her face to the window. The second her hand had touched the car her father had seized her wrist and pulled her away so hard it had hurt for a week.

He hadn't meant to hurt her. She knew that. But it was in that instant that she'd forced herself to take her first significant emotional step away from him.

That same week she had been signed up for her first round of finishing school in Switzerland. And then another and another, until the thick wedge of her self-protection had been permanently driven between them.

The flash of ire lighting up Luca's eyes was near enough identical to the one she'd seen in her father's eyes when she'd dared lay her hand on something that wasn't hers.

In Luca's eyes she'd just crossed the line.

His patient. His clinic. His future.

Her mistake.

"Dr. Montovano! Did you *see* that?"

Luca could just hear Giuliana's voice through the static roaring in his ears. He was still reeling at how careless Fran was. *Reckless!*

"*Scusi*, Giuliana. See what?" Luca forced himself to turn to his new patient, hastily removing from his eyes the daggers he'd been shooting at Fran.

This was a clinic for people with *spinal injuries*, for heaven's sake. Had she no respect for what he was trying to do here? No understanding that the slightest mishap could shut him down?

"The dog!" Giuliana said, the smile so broad across her face he hardly recognized her as the same girl captured in the glowering, unhappy photos her parents had sent. "Did you see how when I threw the treat he caught it?"

"He was catching a treat?"

"*Si, Dottore.* Of course. What did you think he was doing?"

Fran turned to him, arms crossed defensively across her chest, with a look that said, *I'd certainly like to know what it was you thought Edison was doing.*

The dog had been jumping, its mouth wide-open, teeth bared. It had looked as if it had been launching himself at the girl's hand. Which—on went a lightbulb—of *course* he had. She had been throwing a treat.

Another lightbulb joined the first.

"I thought you didn't have any movement in your arm."

"I didn't…" Giuliana replied, her expression changing as she, too, began connecting the dots of an enormous puzzle.

"Mind if I have a quick feel?" Luca knelt, and with his young patient's consent he took her arm in his hands and began to run his fingers along the different muscle and ligament groups in her forearm. Her fingers responded to a few of his manipulations. Fingers that were, according to her physio at home, completely atrophied from disuse.

"Shall we get you into one of the treatment rooms? See what may have happened there?"

"*Si.* Can Edison come, too? And Francesca? She massaged my arm before I fed Edison."

A flash of ire blinded him again for an instant.

Why couldn't Fran keep to herself?

He hesitated for a moment before looking up, forcing himself to take a slow breath. She was a trained physio. This was meant to be a place of innovation. And now that he was repainting the scene into what it had actually been, it was very likely Fran and Edison had each played a role in eliciting movement in Giuliana's arm.

By the time he lifted his eyes to offer an invitation he saw that none was necessary. Fran and Edison were disappearing through an archway leading to the wildflower meadows.

A sour twist of enmity tightened around his heart. He didn't need to push Fran away. She had already gone.

CHAPTER NINE

A KNOCK SOUNDED on the door frame of Fran's cottage. It was so unexpected she nearly jumped out of her skin. And she was half-naked. More than half-naked, really.

The baby-doll nightgown had been a spontaneous, lacy gift to herself when she'd gone bridesmaid-dress shopping with Bea. A nod to the femininity she knew lurked somewhere inside her but that she'd never quite had the courage to explore.

"*Scusi*, Francesca, do you have a moment?"

Little frissons of awareness tickled up along her neck when she heard Luca's voice. Sprays of goose bumps followed in their wake when she turned the corner and saw him. One hand flew to cover her chest and the other stupidly groped for and tugged at the bottom-skimming hemline.

"Yes, of course. What can I help you with?"

"I think I owe you an apology."

"Ah, well…"

Please quit staring at my half-naked body.

"No need. I understand—"

"No. I was too sharp. The truth is…" Luca paused and looked up toward the stars just beginning to shine out against the night sky.

The truth is what? An icy chill spread through her. Was he going to send her away?

She nodded, tugging at the spaghetti straps of her nightdress as if the soupçon of flesh they covered would disguise the fact that the plunging neckline and tiny triangles of lace barely covering her breasts were advertising the fact she hadn't had sex in… Oh…who was counting anyway? Celibacy was the "in" thing, right? Or did the nightdress say the opposite? That she was a floozy and had been hanging out with her front door open just waiting for him to—

Stop. Just stop. Act normal. Relaxed. As if gorgeous Italian doctors who can't bear the sight of you are always popping by for a casual you're-fired chat.

"I think I know why you're here." Fran decided to fill the growing silence. "Making sure we continue in the same vein as we started, right? Frenemies forever!"

Luca's brows hitched closer together.

"Frenemies?" She tried again. "Friends who are enemies?"

He shook his head.

She shifted her shoulder straps again, trying to feel less naked.

This whole standing-here-in-silence thing was getting a little annoying. She had dignity. Brains. Self-esteem.

C'mon, Frannie. Pull it together.

"Luca, is there anything I can help you with? Some last-minute painting…?"

Still too chirpy. Dial back the cheerleader… Bring in the helpful canine-assistance trainer.

Tough when Luca was just standing there staring at her, refusing to engage in her inane one-sided conversation.

"I was not thinking frenemies. I was thinking employee."

"What?" *Unexpected.* "You want me to *work* for you?"

He nodded—yes.

"One of my physios has returned to Rome. The rural location didn't seem to suit him."

"Is he nuts?" Fran was shocked. "I mean Rome is great, but this place is just about as close to heaven as it gets! I'd stay here forever if I could. I mean, not *forever*, forever…just…"

"Francesca. *Per favore*, will you just answer the question?"

"Of course. I'll do anything to help." She held up a finger. "On one condition."

A crease of worry deepened the scar on his cheek—the one she was dying to ask about but already had a pretty good guess had something to do with his orphaned niece being in a car accident. They all added up to a picture no one would keep in their wallet.

But now wasn't the time.

"Luca, listen. I would love to do the work—but only if you let me do it gratis."

"Oh, no—"

Francesca held up a hand to protest.

"Don't take it the wrong way. This would be helping *me*."

Luca laughed, but not because he thought she was funny. "I hardly think not paying you is *helping*."

"It would." She reached out to the side table and wiggled her phone between them. "See…my dad and I have been having daily talks in advance of my return. I've been trying to convince him for years to let me do charitable work in the name of his company. If you'd let me work on the patients and make little video diaries of their

progress as I went—with their permission, of course—
I think it might be a way to persuade him to let me do
more of the same when I get home."

"I thought you were through with treating people?"

She shrugged. "Some people are worth changing your
mind for."

The words hit their mark. Luca's dark eyes sought her
own and when their gazes caught and cinched tight she
could hardly breathe. She'd meant *patients*. But from all
the tiny hairs standing up on her arms, something was
telling her there had just been a shift between them.

As suddenly as the air had gone taut between them
it relaxed. As if Luca had sought and found the answer
to the questions racing through his eyes. She sucked in
a breath of mountain air, her heart splitting wide-open.
More than she'd allowed for anyone else.

He looked tired, his hair all helter-skelter, as if he'd
been repeatedly running a worried hand through it.
Though he wore smart attire, he still had on paint-stained,
sawdust-covered work boots.

Her eyes were trained on his boots because she wasn't
brave enough to look up into those dark eyes of his again.
And then she dared.

A flush of heat struck her cheeks like a slap when she
realized the flash of emotion she'd seen in his eyes was
the same one alight in hers.

Desire.

"I also wanted a quick word about Pia…" Luca began.

"Pia! Yes. Good. All's going blue blazes in *that* camp."
She tried to strike a casual pose. Tricky when she was
half-naked in front of a man whose mere presence made
her nipples tighten. "I think Freda's the dog for her. Those
two seem inseparable."

"Is that a good thing? Being so close?" Luca uncrossed his arms. "What about boundaries?"

Was he still talking about Pia and her dog?

"Well, boundaries are gray areas."

Luca's eyebrow arched. "Oh?"

"But they need to be clear. Boundaries definitely need to be very, very clear."

"Clear enough so that each party knows exactly what they're getting into?"

Luca reached up and rested a crooked arm along the wooden beam above her door frame. Where had stern-faced, humorless Luca gone? There wasn't time to think. Sexy Luca's sun-heated man scent was invading her senses, whooshing through her like a drug.

He definitely wasn't talking about the dogs anymore.

Just as well. There was no room for any thought in her head other than the knowledge that she wanted him. She wanted to jump into his arms, wrap her legs around his trim waist and kiss the living daylights out of him. Touch his scar. Get stubble burn. Ache between her legs from hours of lovemaking. *Hell!* She'd dance around on tiptoe for the next three weeks if he would just scoop her up and have his wicked way with her.

"How does one *establish* these boundaries?" Luca asked, the tension between them thickening with each passing moment.

Gone was the uptight, form-filling timekeeper. In his place was a sensualist. His shoulders shifted, rolling beneath the thick cotton of his shirt with the grace of a mountain lion, and his eyes were alight with need. With hunger.

Heat tickled and teased across Fran's skin, swirling and pooling between her legs.

Per amor del cielo!

Luca let the door frame take some of his weight, bringing him even closer to her.

There was no disguising her body's response to him. Goose bumps shot up her arms. Her breasts were taut, arching toward him as if they had a will of their own.

Did she really want this? Him? Maybe he was right. Clear-cut boundaries were exactly what they needed if either of them was to survive the summer. Then again, sex was an excellent way to cut tension…

No. They needed to talk this out. Like grown-ups. With clothes on.

"Did you want to…um…?"

She pointed toward the bedroom, where her bathrobe was hanging. It was a scrubby terry-cloth number covered in images of Great Danes wearing nerdy spectacles. Her gaze returned to Luca's. As the hit of electricity that only seemed to grow each time their eyes met took effect she lost the power of speech. She'd meant "should she go get her robe and so they could sit down for a talk and a coffee." Or a nightcap. Not "should they go for a roll in the hay"!

Before Fran's brain could comprehend what was happening Luca had pulled her into his arms and was lowering his mouth to hers with a heated passion she had never felt before. There was an urgency in his kisses. A thrilling assurance in his touch. As if they were long-lost lovers separated by oceans, reunited by their unquenchable thirst for each other.

The ardor pouring from his body to hers began to flow between them in an ever-growing circle—floodwaters unleashed. There was nothing chaste about their kisses. They were needy, insatiable. Words escaped her as he tasted and explored first her lips and then her mouth with every bit as much passion as she put into touching and experiencing him. The occasional brush of stubble. The burr of a growl as she nibbled and then softly bit his lower lip before opening her mouth as he teased her lips apart with his tongue.

A soft groan escaped Fran's already kiss-bruised lips as one of Luca's hands slid to the small of her back and tugged her in tight to him; the other slipped around to the nape of her neck. She felt his fingers weave through the length of her hair, then tug it back so that her neck lay bare to him. It wasn't cruelty or domination. It was unfettered desire. The same ache rendering her both powerless and energized in his arms.

Willing away the millions of thoughts that might have shut the moment down, Fran closed her eyes and allowed the sensations of Luca's touch to spread through her veins. With the pad of his thumb he tipped her head to the side. His lips pulled away from hers. Before she had a chance to experience any loss she could feel their heated presence again, tasting and kissing the sensitive nook between her chin and neck.

His fingers moved from the back of her head to the other side of her neck, his thumb drawing along the length of her throat as his lips did the same on the exposed length of her neck. She could feel the pads of his fingers tracing from her shoulder to her collarbone, dipping down to the swell of her breasts. She couldn't help it. She arched into his hands, her body longing for more.

Unexpectedly, Luca cupped her face in both his hands and tipped his forehead to hers, his breath coming as swiftly as her heartbeat, which was racing to catch up with what was happening.

"*Scusi*, Francesca. I'm so sorry."

She heard the words but his body told a different story as his hands tugged her ever so slightly closer toward him. Her hands rose to his chest and confirmed what she'd suspected. His heart was racing as quickly as her own.

"I'm not…" she managed to whisper.

"This isn't why I came here."

"Stay." The word was out before she could stop it.

"I have nothing to offer you." Luca's voice was raw, as if the words had scraped past his throat against his will.

"I don't remember asking for anything," Fran said, her feet arching up onto tiptoe, her lips grazing his as she spoke.

"I need boundaries."

"So do I."

Fran meant the words with all her heart. She felt as if her whole body was on fire, and without protecting her heart she'd never survive the summer.

Luca held her out at arm's length, examining her face as if his life depended upon it.

"What did you say we were?"

Fran ran their conversation through her head at lightning speed, then laughed. "Frenemies?"

Luca nodded. "Will that do?"

"Colleagues by day, lovers by night?" she countered.

He nodded his assent. "No more talking."

Their lips met again, to explosive effect. In just those few moments his touch had already changed. Where there had been tentative exploration now there was fire behind his kisses. Intimacy. As if each erotically charged touch was laying claim to her, physically altering the chemical makeup of her bloodstream. What had once felt heavy now became light. Effervescent, even. In each other's arms they were no longer bound to the earth. They were in orbit—two celestial bodies exploring, teasing, coaxing, arousing.

Fran's breasts were swollen with longing, her nipples taut against the sheer lace of her nightgown. As Luca's hand swept across her bottom his fingers just grazed the sensitive pulsing between her legs, forcing her to bite back a cry of pleasure. He drew his fingers up and along her spine, rendering her core completely molten. She'd experienced lust in the past, but now she became vividly aware that she had never known desire. Not like this. She'd never craved a man's touch as much as she yearned for Luca's.

"Mio piccola passerotta..."

Fran felt Luca's breath glide along her neck as he whispered into her ear. *His little sparrow.* If anyone in the world could make her feel like a delicate bird in flight...

Don't think. Just be.

Abruptly she tugged her fingers down the back of his neck, the pressure of her nails eliciting a groan of pleasure as once again he tipped her head back and dropped kisses along the length of her neck, his fingers tracing the delicate dips and swells of her décolletage.

Fran inhaled deeply—everything about this moment would form the scent palate she would return to when the day came she had to leave. Late-night jasmine. Pepper. Wood shavings. The sun-warmed heat of early summer and tanned skin.

She tipped her head forward as Luca's hands slid along her sides and pulled her close to his chest. Another scent she'd remember forever. One very particular chest, attached to the most intriguing man she had ever laid eyes on.

A particle of insecurity lodged itself in her heart as she became aware of his hands sweeping along the curve of her shoulders to her arms. It took a second to connect mind and body. He was holding her out—away from him—so that he could tip her chin up and their eyes would meet.

And when they did it was like a lightning strike.

One so powerful she knew what she was feeling was more than chemical.

"You must want something. Everyone does."

Respect. Love. Of course she wanted love. Marriage. Family. The whole nine yards one day. But Luca was the worst person in the world to start *that* sort of craziness with. And the last.

"We couldn't have met at a worse time," he continued.

"Or in a less promising way," she reminded him, unable to keep that moment at the basilica from popping into her mind. "You and I will never be friends."

Oh, the irony! And look at them now, woven into one another's arms as if their being together had been pre-destined.

And that was when it hit her. What it was she wanted from a relationship.

To be lit up from within as she had been these last few precious moments. To feel elemental. Woven into the very fabric of someone else's being.

She lowered her eyelids to half-mast. Luca didn't need access to the tempest flaring between her heart and mind.

Her heart was near enough thumping out of her chest. She'd never done anything this...*intentional* before. Offering herself to him only to zip up what was left of her heart and take it away at the end of the summer.

She looked at Luca, all super masculine and reserved. Every bit the courtly gent by day, but by night a wild boy up for a bit of rough and tumble, if his kisses were anything to go by. His five-o'clock shadow was thick with the late hour, cheekbones taut, lips bloodred from their kisses. The scar she was longing not only to trace with her finger but her tongue…

"Let's do it." She moved her hand into the thin wedge of space between them. "Frenemies. Boundary hunters. Whatever you like. Shake on it?"

Luca didn't want to shake hands. He wanted to take possession of her. Become intimately acquainted with every particle of Francesca he could get his hands on. He wanted to touch and caress all that he could see and all that he couldn't beneath the tiny bits of fabric that made up her excuse for a nightgown. To disappear in her beauty and reemerge fortified and vital. Ready to take on anyone and anything.

Fran's hand pressed against his chest as he pulled her tight to him so she could feel the effect she had on him. Her eyes widened and a distinctly saucy laugh burbled up from her throat. She wanted him as much as he wanted her. He could see it in her eyes, feel it in the tipped points of her nipples as they abraded his chest when she wriggled in his arms.

"I've got something better than a handshake in mind for you," he murmured.

"Oh, *do* you now?"

Fran's feline eyes were sultry. She tipped her chin toward him with a smile edging onto the corners of her lips. A naughty smile.

Dio! She was beautiful.

In one swift move he kicked the door shut with his booted foot, swept her up into his arms and carried her without further ceremony straight to her bedroom.

She whooped when he all but tossed her onto the mattress, showing scant restraint as he stretched out alongside her. He was clearly enjoying the soft groan of pleasure he elicited when he ran a hand over the tips of her breasts before brusquely pushing aside the tiny triangles of lace and lowering his lips onto first one, then the other taut nipple, his tongue circling the deep pink of her areolae as he leisurely slid his hand across her belly and down to rest between her legs.

Luca's breath caught, his lips just barely touching her nipple, as Fran pressed against his fingers. She grabbed for his free hand, drawing each of his fingers, one at a time, into her mouth, giving each one a wicked swirl of the tongue, a teasing lick and a suck.

Forcing himself to ignore the growing intensity building below his waistline, Luca slid his fingers beneath the thin strip at the base of Fran's panties, delighting in the heated dew of her response to his touch. He had become utterly consumed with bringing her pleasure.

So responsive to his touch was she, he had to check himself again and again not to move too rapidly. To draw out her pleasure for as long as he could. When at last her body grew taut with expectation and desire, he unleashed his hands from their earlier restraint, let his mouth explore the most tender nooks of her belly, licking and teasing at the very tip of her most sensitive area until she cried out with pleasure and release.

Fran grabbed the sides of his face and roughly pulled his mouth toward hers. "Naked. Now!" were the only two words he could make out between her cries of pleasure as he dipped his fingers in farther, teasing and tempting her to reach another climax.

"Protection?"

An impressive stream of Italian gutter talk flowed as Fran lurched out of the bed, ran to the bathroom, clattered through who knew what at a high rate of knots and reappeared in the doorway, framed by the soft light of the bathroom, with a triumphant smile on her face and a small packet held between two fingers.

"Bridesmaid favors! Now, take off your clothes," Fran commanded, already taking deliberate steps toward the bed. *"Now."*

A broad smile peeled his lips apart. This made a nice change from the needy women he tended to attract. The ones who wanted the title, the property, but not the work that came along with the mantle he'd been forced to wear.

"Is this how it's going to work?" Luca asked, propping himself up on an elbow as he watched her approach like a lioness about to pounce for the kill. "You giving me orders?"

"Tonight it is." Fran straddled him in one fluid move, the bold glint in her eyes hinting at pleasures yet to unfold.

He needed this. He needed *her*.

"Well, then…" Luca arched an eyebrow at her and began unbuttoning his shirt. "I suppose it would be foolish not to oblige."

Fran batted his hands away and ripped off the rest of the buttons of his shirt, her hands swirling possessively across the expanse of his chest.

"Yes," she murmured as she pushed him back on the bed and began lowering herself along the full length of his body, exploring with her lips as much as with her hands. "It would."

Two, maybe three hours later—Luca didn't know; he'd entirely lost track of time—he slipped out from beneath the covers, trying his best not to disturb Francesca.

All the tiptoeing came to nothing when he picked up his trousers and his belt buckle clattered against the tile flooring. A quick glance toward the bed and he could see one bright blue eye peeking out at him amidst a tangle of blond hair.

"Pia?" she asked.

Luca nodded.

The single word had contained no animosity. Only understanding. His main priority was his niece. Luxurious mornings in bed would never be on his menu, and Fran would have to understand that was his reality.

He swept his fingers through her hair, dropped a kiss on her forehead and left without saying a word.

Outside, he sucked in the night air as if he'd been suffocating.

A night like that…

He wanted more.

Much more.

He tried as best he could to push the thoughts—the desire—away. There was no chance he could make peace with giving in to these precious green shoots, the chance at something new blossoming in a place where he'd thought love would only wither and die.

With his niece to provide for, wanting and having had become two very different things. He could want, but he definitely couldn't have. Fran would just have to understand that.

CHAPTER TEN

A SHOT OF irritation lanced through Luca's already frazzled nerves. Spreadsheets taunted him from his computer screen. Stacks of bills sat alongside ledgers he knew he couldn't reconcile. He barked a hollow laugh into the room.

This must be how his father had felt when his business was failing. Alone. Horrified by the ramifications of what would happen if he admitted his failure to his family. To those he loved the most in the world.

Another peal of hysterics echoed down the corner.

Since when did hydrotherapy sessions contain so much *laughter*?

He pushed back from his desk in frustration. He knew the exact moment. Ever since he'd gone to Francesca. Vulnerable. Heart in hand. Needing help. Needing *her*.

A shot of desire coursed through him and just as quickly he iced it.

Their nights together were…otherworldly. Never before had he met his match as he had with Francesca. The pure alpha male in him loved hearing her call his name as he pleasured her. Loved teasing and taunting just a little longer as she begged him to enter her. Even now, fully clothed, he could conjure up the sensation of Fran's nails scratching along the length of his back as he thrust deeply into her until the pair of them both cried out in a shared ecstasy.

If only he hadn't gone to her to ask for help. Help she'd given willingly. Gladly, even. But it made him feel weak. It ate at his pride and filled him with yet another measure of self-loathing he'd yet to conquer.

He was meant to be shouldering the load. Righting wrongs *he* had set in motion.

Paolo's triumphant cry of "I did it!" pierced through to his consciousness.

Pride was his enemy. The devil on his shoulder drowning out the man he'd buried somewhere deep inside him, who knew having Fran here was exactly what the patients needed. What *he* needed.

The Francesca Effect, the staff were calling it.

Yes, the patients worked hard, but they also laughed and cheered, and a few had even cried in moments of triumph they had never thought they'd achieve.

Like a moth to a flame he found himself drawn to the hydrotherapy room.

He looked through the glass window running the length of the indoor pool and ground his teeth together.

Even in a functional one-piece swimsuit she was beautiful. Her hair was in Heidi plaits, trailing behind her in the water as she faced Paolo in his chair, stretching from side to side of the pool along with him, keeping up a steady flow of encouragement. Silly jokes. Pointing out every time he'd done well. Reached further. Done more. Aimed higher.

Luca pressed his head to the glass and as he did so, Fran turned to him, her blue eyes lighting up and her smile growing even broader.

He wanted to smile, too. His heart pounded in his

chest, demanding some sort of response, yet all he could do was grind his teeth tighter together.

How could he let her know? This beautiful, care-free, intelligent, loving woman to whom he could lay no claim... How could he let her know the simple truth?

He turned away before he could see the questions deepen in her pure blue eyes and strode to his office, slamming the door shut behind him and returning to his desk.

Try as he might, the columns and figures blurred together. He pressed his fingertips to his forehead, trying to massage some sort of meaning into them.

It was pointless, really. No matter which way he rear-ranged them—no matter how many times he added them up—the answer was always the same.

It wouldn't last.

Couldn't last.

And the sooner he came to terms with that, the better.

"How's your grip? Still strong?" Fran wheeled herself around in Pia's wheelchair to the edge of the pool.

Pia looked up at Fran from where she was being towed along the shallow end of the pool's edge and grinned. "I think Freda is doing most of the work here, but I'm still hanging on." She faked letting go of the mop head Fran had rigged up as a steering wheel between her and Freda.

"Ha-ha. Better not let your uncle see that."

"You mean Zio the Thundercloud?"

"Yeah." Fran did her best to stay neutral. "Him."

She and Luca had rigorously stuck to their boundar-ies over the past week.

Lover by night—ridiculously fabulous.

Physio and hydrotherapist by day—so much more re-warding than she'd remembered. Teenagers were a hoot.

And, of course, assistance-dog trainer by afternoon.

Although Pia was doing well, Fran had resorted to inventing hybrid physio-hydro-canine combo therapies. If the teen kept it up, Fran would be extraneous before long and would be able to go home.

Home.

Three weeks ago it had been all she could dream of. Her dad. Her new business. But now leaving Mont di Mare seemed more punishment than pleasure.

"How are your wheelchair skills coming along?" Pia teased, openly laughing when Fran tried to mimic her teenage charge and pop a wheelie but failed.

"I've still got a way to go to be on par with you."

"You could always get in a car accident that pretty much ruins your life. Then you'd catch up pretty quick," Pia shot back.

From the shocked look on Pia's face Fran knew the teen hadn't meant the words as they'd sounded. Dark. Angry.

"*Scusi*, Francesca. I didn't mean—"

"Hey…" Fran held up her hands. "This is a safe zone." She drew an invisible circle around the pool area, where she knew it would just be the two of them for the next hour or so as Luca and the rest of the staff were still neck-deep in appointments in the main clinic buildings. "You can say whatever you like. Better out than in, right?"

"Anything?" Pia asked incredulously.

"Anything." Fran gave a definitive nod.

What *she* wouldn't have done to have had an older woman in her life when she was growing up. Someone to confide in. To ask those awkward girl questions that adolescence unearthed.

"Do you think I will ever be able to do more in this pool than be dragged back and forth by Freda?" Pia's face shifted from plaintive to apologetic in an instant. "Not that I don't totally love her. Or this. Or being here with you. It's just…sometimes it's really frustrating."

Fran nodded. It was impossible to imagine. She could just step up and out of the wheelchair whenever she chose and dive into the pool. Do a cartwheel. Anything.

She considered Pia for a moment, then focused on the path Freda was taking, back and forth along the length of the pool.

"It's too bad we can't get Edison in there. He would tow you around like a motorboat!"

The second the words were out of her mouth Fran regretted saying them. From the ear-to-ear grin on Pia's face it was more than obvious that to her being pulled around at high speed sounded great.

"That would be amazing! Zio Luca would—"

"Go apoplectic with rage," Francesca finished for her.

"It's not like anyone else is using the pool." Pia splashed a bit of water toward her.

"Yet," Fran intoned meaningfully, lifting her face up to the sun. "But once everyone's properly settled this place will be more popular than the walk-in refrigerator."

"You mean wheel-in, don't you, Fran?" Pia teased.

"Si. Of course. Wheel-in fridge. Either way, I don't think your uncle would be happy to know the pool maintenance guy might be scooping dog hair out of the filters."

"We could do it! *I'd* do it. All I'd have to do is lie on the ground before I get in my chair and just fish it all out. Excellent upper body strengthening opportunity." Pia smiled cheekily. "He would never have to know."

Fran gave her a sidelong glance. "I think you know as well as I do that your uncle is all seeing, all knowing."

She pointed up to the security camera she was praying he wasn't keeping an eye on.

"He's a pussycat, really."

"Mountain lion, more like."

A sexy mountain lion, with far too much weight on his shoulders.

He shouldn't have to do all this alone. If only she could stay. Share the load.

She wheeled the chair around in a few idle circles, unable to stop a sigh heaving out of her chest. Edison appeared with a ball in his mouth, his permanently worried-looking eyebrows jigging up and down above his amber eyes.

"Don't worry, boy," she whispered into the soft fold of his ear. "I'm not sad. I'm...*perplexed*. Wanna play catch?"

Back and forth went the ball and the dog. Back and forth. Just like her thoughts.

It wasn't as if she wanted to win Luca's heart or anything. She just really believed in everything he was doing here at the clinic.

Boundaries.

A sudden frisson swept through her as her thoughts slipped far too easily back to the bedroom. Had she actually bitten into his shoulder last night, when the explosion of their mutual climax had hit the heavens and returned her to earth in thousands of glittery, grinning pieces?

She threw the ball again. Harder this time.

Edison duly loped off. Returned. Totally obedient.

"C'mon, boy. Drop the ball. There's a good boy," she cooed. "You *always* do everything I ask."

Her eyes pinged wide. Was that why she'd switched to dogs? Because they always did what she wanted? That couldn't possibly be what she was hoping for in a man. *Obedience?*

No! Ridiculous. She wanted a man with his own mind, his own interests—but his heart? She wanted that to beat solely for *her*. And no matter how smitten Luca seemed between the hours of 10 p.m. and whenever they'd exhausted each other, she knew his heart was well and truly off-limits.

"Good boy. Drop the ball." This time she threw it extra hard, her eyes widening in horror when she saw where it had landed. At the far end of the very pristine, very new, entirely immaculate swimming pool...now getting dive-bombed by a thrilled Labrador.

Pia was nearly crying with laughter.

"Can he pull me around now, Francesca? *Per favore? Bravo*, Edison! *Vieni qui*."

"No way!" Fran whispered as if it would make the scenario disappear.

She pulled off the sundress she was wearing over her bikini and dove into the pool, as if she would be able to magnetically draw any loose hairs Edison might be leaving in his wake.

"Edison! *Out!*"

"Edison, *vieni qui*!" Pia repeated. More adamantly this time. "You know..." Pia went on slowly, avoiding eye contact with Fran as she spoke, "Zio Luca didn't say *specifically* that I was meant to have just one assistance dog. You said yourself you'd brought two to see which one I hit it off with the best, and, well...it's not like everyone has just *one* best friend, right?"

"It is pretty standard. Having just the one."

"*What* about life up here at Mont di Mare is standard?" Pia appealed.

Fran couldn't help laughing. She knew exactly where Pia was coming from. It *was* otherworldly up here.

She took a few strokes in Pia's direction, to where Edison was merrily paddling around her. She watched as the teen lay back in the water, her slim legs floating up to the surface. Her fingers pitter-patted on the water's surface, and all the while she was humming a pop tune as she worked on her argument. She looked like any normal kid having a float in a pool—if you ignored the harness and pole contraption she was still holding on to, the life vests, and the float around her neck for an extra "just in case."

"Won't Edison miss Freda?" Pia asked eventually. "I mean, they both spend most of their time with me now, so it wouldn't be like keeping both would be that strange."

"What? And leave me all alone?" Fran had meant it as a jest, but the reality of returning to the States alone...

Ugh. Boundaries, Francesca. Boundaries!

She dunked herself under the surface of the water to mask the rush of emotion. She was meant to be Pia's sounding board, not the other way around. She whooshed up and out of the pool, pulled a huge bath towel around her and plonked herself down in Pia's chair, calling Edison out of the pool.

Staying or going, Luca would kill her if he saw a dog in his fancy pool.

"Just remember, Fran, *you* can get up out of that chair anytime you want and just walk away," Pia sternly reminded her. "I'm stuck in it forever."

The words all but ejected Fran straight out of the chair and into the pool.

She looked from Pia to Edison, his furry legs pedaling at the sky as he rolled on the grass, rubbing the pool water off his back. Then to Freda, who always looked as if she was smiling, happy as ever to stand or walk by Pia's side.

The thought of life without Freda and Edison was so-bering. But that was how it worked.

You train them, you hand them over, you move on.

Normally she was fine with it. But this time it didn't feel right.

"Don't you think you should try asking?" Pia let go of the mop handle and folded her hands in the prayer position before quickly grabbing it again. "It'd be better coming from you."

"Me?" A cackle of disbelief followed the wide-eyed yeah-right look Fran threw Pia's way. "I think pleading for favors from your uncle is more *your* turf."

Pia made a pouty face, then quickly popped on a smile. "Take me to the edge!"

"What? The far edge?" The one overhanging the sheer drop of the mountain. "Not a chance!"

"I bet Edison would do it if we were here alone," Pia grumped.

"And what makes you think your uncle would be thrilled about you being in the pool on your own."

"That's exactly the point! I wouldn't *be* on my own. Edison could tow me around, and if anything went wrong, Freda could run for help." Pia's features wid-ened, then threatened to crumple. "For once I could feel like a normal kid. Just *once*."

"Pia, I really don't think…"

Once more Pia pressed her hands into the prayer posi-tion. "*Per favore*, Francesca. Help the poor little orphan girl on the mountaintop."

"Just the once?" Fran finally conceded.

She knew she was supposed to be the older, wiser per-son in this scenario. At twenty-nine years old she was hardly old enough to be her mother, but she felt protective of Pia. She could say, hand on her heart, that she loved her. Even if she *was* extra cheeky. Demanding. Unbelievably capable of getting her to take risks she knew Luca would frown upon.

She glanced at the sheer drop at the edge of the infinity pool.

Luca was going to kill her. Well and truly kill her.

"C'mon, you wily minx. I'm going to get you out of here. Let go of the pole and grab hold of my neck."

"I'm not wily!" Pia feigned a hurt look. "I'm...*cunning.*"

"That you are." She reached out to Pia and unclipped the pole from Freda.

"You promised!"

"What exactly did you promise?"

Pia and Fran froze, then slowly shifted their gazes from each other to the pair of leather shoes attached to a familiar pair of long legs, which were, in turn, supporting a terrific torso—lovely clothed or unclothed—topped off by one very unamused face.

"Francesca? What did you promise my niece?"

"I promised to keep her hair dry!" Fran chirped.

"*Si*, Zio. That's exactly what she promised. And to keep me safe and out of harm's way." Pia added, tightening her hold on Fran's neck as she did.

"That's us! Two little safety nuts!" Fran grinned while Pia maintained a frantic nodding, as if it would erase everything else from Luca's mind.

Two inane, grinning bobbleheads, still neck-deep in the pool. Which was another issue. If she stepped out any farther, he would see her breasts had pinged to full Luca-alert position.

She narrowed her gaze and dared a quick scan. Damn, that man was head to toe desirable. Even when he was glowering at her.

"And the dog?" Luca couldn't resist tipping his head toward the Lab merrily paddling around the pool. "Is he part of the safety plan?"

"Absolutely...not..."

Fran slipped Pia's arms more securely around her neck and walked her toward the shallow end of the pool. With each step she took, Luca couldn't help but think he was watching a beach-rescue video. In slow motion.

With that barely there bikini on—

Dio mio.

"What *were* your plans to get Pia out of the pool?" Luca heard the bite in his voice and detested himself for it. But he'd been scared. He'd heard screams and had feared the worst.

Lungs heaving with the effort of reaching the pool to save his niece, he felt the burn as he surveyed the scene now. His niece had been in gales of laughter. All because of Fran. Of course. Francesca wasn't just a ray of sunshine—she was a cascade of light. Wherever she went.

"We actually practiced it a lot at the beginning of the session," Fran said, rattling off a technique she'd seen on the internet.

"Aren't you meant to be studying?" He zeroed in on Pia, feeling less like a loving uncle and more like an officer in the Gulag.

"I finished early. Fran helped me with my trigonometry. And it was such a lovely day..."

"How did you get her in?" Luca asked Fran, not entirely certain he wanted to know.

Pia peeked out from behind Fran's head once again. "I swan-dived."

"You *what*?" His voice dropped in disbelief. "The only way you could have done that is if—"

"I tipped her in," Fran interjected, her expression every bit as stoic as an elite soldier caught going a step too far by the drill sergeant.

"Pia said she knew how to swim—that it was her favorite part of rehab when you were still in Rome—so I tipped her in. And because she's such an amazingly graceful girl she turned it into a swan dive!"

"She could've been—"

"What? Paralyzed?" Pia cut in. "Uncle Luca, it's okay. There is no way Edison, Freda or Fran would've let me drown. Besides, it felt amazing. Like I was whole again."

He looked to Fran, saw her teeth biting down on her lip so hard the flesh paled around it. Then he saw the defiance in her eyes.

C'mon. Do it. I dare you to take away this moment from your niece.

Didn't she realize his niece was the only person he had left in the world, and that to chuck her into a swimming pool without the necessary precautions was sheer madness?

"Don't move. I'll go and get one of the portable hoists. I hope I can trust you to respect my wishes for just a few moments?"

His back stiffened as a peal of nervous giggles followed him when he about-faced and began stomping off. Then it struck him. Fran had done it again. Found exactly the sort of moments he'd been hoping for Pia would have here at Mont di Mare. Happy ones. Discovery. Trying new things. Making the village a home as well as his place of work.

His pace slowed. What sort of life was he giving his niece here? Did he even know what Pia wanted to do when she grew up? When was the last time they'd sat down and eaten a normal dinner together? As a family?

An image of the three of them sitting down—Fran, Pia and Luca—enjoying a meal together put a lift in his step. And then just as quickly weighed it down. They weren't a family. It was just him and Pia, and he was barely succeeding at that. And as for the clinic—the bank was still nipping at his heels, getting ever closer.

When he returned a few minutes later with the hoist he saw Pia on the top step at the side of the pool, tugging herself into her wheelchair with a small grunt and a smiley, "Voilà!" She looked him in the eye as he approached. "See? I didn't need you after all."

He forced a smile, knowing full well it didn't reach his eyes. Not because he wasn't happy for her, but because he was furious with himself for being so blind.

Letting her fend for herself was the only way to build Pia's confidence. It was the entire raison d'être of the clinic. How had he lost sight of the endgame so quickly?

When his eyes met and meshed with Fran's a rush of emotion hit him so hard he could barely breathe. Half of him resented her for being there for his niece. The other half was grateful. If only he'd had a chance to grieve for all that he had lost—not just in the accident, but in the years that followed. His spontaneity. His voracious appetite for experimental treatments. His passion for life. His capacity to love.

Perhaps then he would be whole again.

"Would you like to take Pia back to the house?" Fran finally asked. "I'm happy to bring the hoist back to the clinic."

It was an olive branch. She was trying to bring him

closer to Pia, not divide them. He was grateful for the gesture.

"*Grazie*, Fran. See you tomorrow at the clinic?"

She knew what he was saying. They wouldn't meet tonight. He simply couldn't. Not with the demons he was battling.

"Of course," she replied, her eyes darting away in an attempt to hide the hurt he'd seen in an instant. "Tomorrow at the clinic."

He just caught Pia rolling her eyes at him, then putting her hands out. *Do something! Fix it!* her expression screamed.

But all he was capable of was letting Francesca walk away.

CHAPTER ELEVEN

"HERE'S THE BREAK POINT."

Luca followed Dr. Murro's finger as he pointed out the T11 vertebra on the X-ray.

"Hard to miss, isn't it?" he replied grimly. "Severed right in two. No chance of recovering function below the waist." Luca shook his head. Off-road vehicles could be dangerous things. "She's lucky the vertebra didn't rupture her aorta."

"Has Francesca done any work with her?"

"I don't think so." Luca shook his head. "She usually submits a report as soon as she's worked with a patient, and I haven't seen one for Maria yet."

"She'll be staying on?"

"Who? Maria? Of course. She's only just arrived."

"Francesca," Dr. Murro corrected.

Ah. That was a more complicated answer.

"The whole staff seem to have really taken to her," Dr. Murro continued.

So have I. Too much.

"She has commitments back in the States, making it impossible."

"Shame. Someone like that—a triple threat—is going to be difficult to replace."

"Triple threat?" He'd not heard that turn of phrase before.

"Physio, hydro and canine therapist in one. She's a league above most. A real asset to Mont di Mare."

"That she is," Luca conceded. "That she is..."

A sharp knock sounded on the exam room door. "Dr. Montovano? It's Cara Bianchi. Francesca has found her out by the meadows, indicating with possible autonomic dysreflexia."

Luca shot from his chair. "Where is she? Have you brought her in?"

"*Si.* One of the doctors is seeing her now, in the Fiore Suite, but it's probably best if *you* take a look."

"On my way." He stopped at the doorway, "Dr. Murro, are you all right to meet with Maria? Talk through her treatment program?"

"Absolutely, Doctor. And if you could send Francesca to meet me when you're done, that'd be great. Well-done for hiring her, by the way. She's a real catch."

Luca nodded, striding out of the office before the scowl hit his lips.

Francesca was more than an asset. She was a woman. One who once you caught hold of, you'd be a fool ever to let go. But he would have to do just that if he was ever going to stand on his own two feet. Provide for his niece. Be the man his family had always believed him to be.

Doctors and nurses were already surrounding Cara on an exam table, where Francesca and a nurse were holding the girl in an upright position.

"She's bradycardic. Blood pressure is one-four-five over ninety-seven," the nurse said as soon as she saw Luca enter.

"Any nasal stuffiness? Nausea?" Luca asked.

"No, but she's complained to Francesca about a head-ache."

He glanced to Fran, who gave a quick affirmative nod.

"When I saw the goose bumps on Cara's knees and felt how clammy her skin was I brought her in here."

"My head is killing me! And my eyes feel all prickly!" Cara wailed from the exam table. "All I wanted to do was lie in the meadow!"

"It's all right... We'll ease the pain. Can we get an ice compress for Cara's face, please?" Luca smiled when he saw that one was being slipped in place before he'd finished speaking. "Autonomic dysreflexia." He gave Fran a grateful nod. "You were right. Can we strap her in and tilt the exam table up?"

"Has anyone checked her urinary bag?"

"Just emptied it. She had a full bladder."

"Bowels need emptying? Any cuts, bruises? Other injuries?"

"Nothing that I could see," said Fran. "But Cara hadn't voided her bladder in a while and was lying down, which I'm guessing exacerbated the symptoms."

She looked to Luca for confirmation. A hit of color pinked up her cheeks when their eyes met.

"Exactly right," Luca confirmed grimly.

It sounded like a simple enough problem, but for a paraplegic it was potentially lethal. Francesca had done well. His eyes met hers and he hoped she could read the gratitude in them.

"That's all it was?" Cara's voice turned plaintive as she scanned the faces in the room. "I just had to pee but it felt like I was going to die?"

"That's the long and short of it, Cara. If you like..." Luca flashed the group a smile, trying to bring some levity to the room, and dropped Cara a quick wink. What he had to say next was a hard bit of information to swallow. Something she'd have to live with for the rest of her life. "Tell the others it was autonomic dysreflexia. Sounds much cooler." The smile dropped from his lips. "But you should also tell them how quickly it can turn critical. All those symptoms are warning signs of a much more serious response."

"Like what?" Her eyebrows shot up.

"Internal bleeding, stroke and even death." He let the words settle before he continued. These kids already had so much to deal with. Worrying about dying simply because their brain couldn't get the message that they needed to pee seemed cruel. Cara had been snowboarding less than a year ago, and now the rest of her life would involve wheelchairs, assistance and terrifying moments like these that, if she were left unattended, might lead to her death.

"You use intermittent catheterization, right?" Luca asked.

Cara nodded, a film of tears fogging her eyes.

Luca turned to the staff. No need for an audience. "I think we're good here. Cara and I might just have a bit of a chat and then..."

He scanned the collected staff including Gianfranco Torino—a GP who had retrained in psychotherapy when he'd suffered his own irrecoverable spinal injury. He, too, would be in a wheelchair for the rest of his life.

"Dr. Torino, would you be able to meet up with Cara later today? Maybe for an afternoon roll around the gardens?"

"Absolutely." Dr. Torino gave Cara a warm smile. "Three o'clock at the pergola? Is that enough time?"

Cara nodded. "*Si*, Dr. Torino. *Grazie*."

"*Prego*, Cara. See you then."

Luca scanned the staff, everyone of them focused on Cara as a unit.

This is the Mont di Mare I imagined.

His eyes lit on Francesca, who lifted her gaze from Cara's hair. She'd been running her fingers through the girl's long dark locks. Soothing. Caressing. When she saw him looking at her and smiled, it felt as if the heat of the sun was exploding in his chest.

Perfection.

And perfectly distracting. Smiles didn't pay bills. Patients did.

He moved his hands in a short, sharp clap. Too loud for the medium-sized exam room. Too late to do anything about it.

"All right, everyone. I think Cara and I need to chat over a couple of things."

Cara reached over her shoulder and grabbed Francesca's hand, shooting Luca an anxious look. "Can Fran stay? She was going to plait my hair—right, Francesca?"

"Ah! You're a hairdresser now?"

He saw the flutter of confusion in Fran's eyes and then the moment she made her decision.

"One of my hidden talents." She gave Cara a complicit wink and gathered her hair together as if it were a beautiful bouquet of wildflowers. "I promise I won't distract you from what you two are talking about."

Her pure blue eyes met his. There were a thousand reasons he should say no, she couldn't stay, and one single reason to say yes. His patient.

The motivation behind everything. Not Fran. Not desire. Not love.

The thought froze him solid for an instant, but quickly he forced himself into motion.

"I may need you to help for a moment before the hair-styling session begins."

"Of course," Fran replied. "Anything you need."

Despite himself, he risked another glance into her eyes and saw she meant it. She wasn't there to take. To demand. To change him. She was simply there to help.

Removing the cold compress from Cara's face, Luca ran a hand across the girl's brow, satisfied the hot flush was now under control. With Fran's help, they triple-checked for bedsores and ensured her clothing was fitting comfortably. A tight drawstring on a pair of trousers could trigger one of these potentially deadly incidents.

Once they were settled, and Fran had magicked a hairbrush from somewhere, he brought over the portable blood-pressure gauge, straddled a stool and wheeled himself over to Cara.

"Arm." He gave her a smile and held out the cuff.

"You already took my blood pressure."

"It's good to do it every five minutes or so when this happens. Here—let's slip your legs over the edge of the table to help your blood pressure. C'mon. Stretch your arm out."

Cara obliged him with a reluctant grin and soon he was pumping up the pressure in the cuff.

"I know you've had a lot to get used to since the accident, and this is another one of those scary learning curves. Basically, your bladder can't tell your brain it's full, so it's best if you have some sort of schedule. Have you ever set up a regular voiding timetable?"

"I did for the couple of months I was back in school, but over the summer I guess I let it lapse a bit." She shot him a guilty look.

"Did your doctors explain what might happen if your bladder was full and you didn't empty it?"

Another guilty look chased up the first. "I forget…"

"They're pretty strong symptoms—as you just found out. I know you've only been here a few days, but if you have a voiding timeline in your schedule it's a good idea to follow it."

"I was just waiting for my parents to go. You know—making the most of the time they were here."

"I thought you were out in the field on your own? That Francesca found you?"

Instinctively, his eyes flicked up to Fran's. The soft smile playing on her lips as she listened to them talk reminded him to do the same. A smiling doctor was much easier to listen to than the furrowed-brow grump he'd been of late.

Cara was remaining stoically tight-lipped.

"Either way, here's what's happening. Autonomic dysreflexia is your body's response to something happening below your injury level. You're a C6, C7 complete, right?"

Cara gave him a wry grin. "Can't get anything past you, can I, Dr. M?"

"Let's hope not, if it means getting you to a place where you're in charge of your own life. So." He gave the reading on the gauge a satisfied nod and took off the cuff. "I'm sure you've heard it before, but this time let it sink in. There are any number of things that can kick off an AD response. Overfull bladder or bowel."

"Ew!"

"I know—it's gross."

"No grosser than picking up dog poop who knows how many times a day!"

Fran's fingers flew to cover her mouth. *Oops!* So much for staying out of the doctor-patient talk!

Cara gave her a toothy grin. One Fran was pretty sure contained a bit of bravura.

"Actually…do you think an assistance dog would be able to remind me?" Cara had switched from doleful teen to bargaining expert.

Ah! *That* was why the teen had asked her to stay. Not for her sure-handed approach to a fishtail braid.

"That's not really my terrain." Luca pressed his lips together. "Francesca?"

Fran shook her head in surprise. Was Luca *including* her in this?

"Sorry, hon. What exactly is it you want to know?"

"If an assistance dog—one like Edison, maybe—were to help me, couldn't he remind me of things?"

Fran's instinct was to look to Luca, seek guidance. But to her surprise he just smiled, then widened and raised his hands, as if opening the forum to include her.

She gulped. This was… This was getting *involved*. Becoming interwoven in the fabric of things here on a level she'd told herself was a danger zone. A little dog training here. A bit of physio there. But advising a patient…?

"Francesca?" Luca prompted. "This is your area of expertise."

Dropping her gaze from his, she stared at the plait her fingers was weaving by rote and started speaking.

"Of course assistance dogs can certainly respond to alarms, and help you to remain upright in your wheelchair if you were ever to slump down. They can do a lot. But this sounds to me like something you and Dr. Montovano had better work out."

"But couldn't a dog have told you if I was dead or dying?"

"You mean when I found you out in the field? Absolutely. It would've barked. Tried to get someone to come and see you straightaway."

"Like Lassie?" Cara's voice squeaked with excitement. "If you hadn't found me then a dog could have saved my life!"

"Well…" Fran's fingers finished off the plait and she swirled a tiny elastic band she'd dug out of her pocket onto the end.

She'd overstepped the boundaries before. She really didn't want to do it again.

"Cara, you're with us for the rest of the summer, right?" Luca interjected. *Mercifully.*

Cara nodded.

"How about you and Fran spend a bit of time with Pia's dogs—if it's all right with Pia, of course. See how you go. I'm sure assistance dogs suit some people and aren't quite right for others. Am I right, Francesca?"

She'd expected to see some sort of triumph in his eyes. A way to catch her out. But there was nothing there but kindness. Possibility. Respect.

And for one perfect moment she was lost in the dark chocolate twinkle holding her rapt like a… Ha! The irony. Like a giddy teen.

Her phone buzzed. She glanced at the screen and frowned. Her father didn't normally ring this early.

"Sorry, I've just—"

Luca waved her apologies away. "I think Cara and I have plenty to talk about."

She gave Cara a quick wave, then accepted the call, closing the door softly behind her as she went.

"Si, Papa? Va tutto bene?"

CHAPTER TWELVE

"GOT A MINUTE?"

Fran looked up to find Luca at her doorway, striking the pose that had reduced her to a pool of melted butter a handful of weeks ago—arm resting on the low sling of the beam above her door frame, body outlined by the setting sun.

If she knew how, she'd let out a low whistle of appreciation and give him a one-liner an old-time Hollywood starlet would envy.

Somehow she found her voice. "I was just opening a bottle of wine. Fancy a glass?"

Luca didn't answer straight away, his eyes narrowing slightly as if inspecting her for ulterior motives. Which only succeeded in making her think of all the illicit things she could do with him right here and now, if only he'd duck his head, step inside her cottage and kick the door shut behind him.

Desire flared up hot and intense within her.

Bad brain. Naughty thoughts. Quit staring at the sexy doctor.

"*Grazie.* I'd love a glass of wine."

Good, brain. Excellent thoughts. Run to the bedroom to check it doesn't look like a hurricane has hit it.

"Mind if we sit out here? On the bench?"

What? Does not compute.

Then again, not a lot of what passed between them computed. Their tempestuous nights of lovemaking chased up by…absolutely nothing. No talks. No explanations. Just complicated silences.

Perhaps a talk was exactly what they needed.

"Here." Fran threw him a couple of pillows from the sofa. "Makes it comfier."

She pulled on a light sweater, grabbed another glass and cascaded an arc of gorgeous red wine into the goblet, all the while rearranging her features into something she hoped looked like casual delight that Luca had chosen sitting outside on a bench over ripping off his clothes.

"Everything all right with your phone call?" he asked.

"Mmm, yes." She quickly swallowed down a spicy gulp of Dutch courage, then topped up her glass. "It was my father."

"All's going well on the home front?"

"Very. So good, in fact, he'd like to come over."

She stepped outside the cottage in time to see Luca's eyes widen in surprise.

"I know. It freaked me out, too. My dad's never visited me before. Must be all these video calls we've had. I've been showing him Mont di Mare."

"Oh?" Luca's tone was unreadable. "Did he like what he saw?"

"Very much."

She looked up into Luca's eyes as she handed him his glass. His hand brushed hers, lingering just a fraction of a second longer than necessary, and with the connection a rush of heated sparks raced up her arm and circled around her heart.

"How did your day go with Pia?"

Luca stared deep into his wineglass before taking a

thoughtful draught, tasting it fully before swallowing it down.

Had he felt it, too?

"Really well," Fran managed as nonchalantly as she could, tucking her feet up under her on the broad wooden bench. "She and the dogs have a whale of a time together."

"I meant as regards the training."

Killjoy! It wasn't her fault that their being together made them all fizzy and full of lust and desire and… and other things.

"Getting along with the dogs is part of the training," Fran began carefully. "If they don't sync—you know, make a love match as it were—the relationship isn't going to work out."

"A love match?"

"For lack of a better turn of phrase," Fran mumbled. Could she be digging herself into a bigger hole? It wasn't as if she—*oh, no.*

She looked at him, then away and back again, before realizing what had been happening to her for these past few weeks.

She had fallen in love with Luca. It was mad. And foolish. And totally never going to happen. But—

Did he feel the same way?

She turned to him, seeking answers, only to catch Luca's gaze dropping to her mouth as her lips grazed the edge of her wineglass. An urge to throw caution to the wind took hold of her. Why shouldn't she just go for it? Fling her glass away and climb onto his lap so he could claim what was already his?

His lips parted.

For an instant she was certain she could see it in Luca's eyes, too. The exact same exhilarating rush of realization that he'd found love in the least likely of places. With the least likely of people.

He hesitated.

Was he...? Was he about to tell her he loved her, too?

"What are the actual *practical* things Pia is taking away from this? What, *precisely*, are you enabling her to do by having a dog?"

Fran's heart plummeted, finding itself on all too familiar terrain. She was a solitary girl, seeking her place in the world, only to realize she'd read the wrong page. *Again.*

She scrunched her eyes tight, conjuring up an image of Freda and Edison. She could do with a dose of canine cuddles right now.

"If you'd been spending any time with Pia, you probably would've noticed for yourself," she snapped.

Luca's eyes widened at the level of heat in her voice. *Tough. You just broke my heart.*

She looked away, drew in a deep lungful of mountain air and forced it out slowly before continuing.

"Pia and Freda have already mastered a lot of the drop-and-retrieve tasks that will help in her day-to-day life. Right now we're working on Freda responding to very specific verbal commands."

"Like what?" Luca asked—with genuine interest rather than the disdain she'd been expecting. *Good.* At least she'd made some sort of a mark.

Ha! Take that, you doubting...sexy Italian, you.

"Freda can go and get other patients, for example. By name. Scent, really. It's amazing how quickly they learn who is who."

"Why would Pia want her to fetch other patients?"

"Oh...I don't know." Fran took a big gulp of wine before answering that one. "Maybe she's enjoying having some people to spend time with. Friends."

"What would she—" Luca began, then stopped himself, his jaw tensing as his lips pressed together and thinned.

Fran gulped down the rest of her wine, then stood up, hands on hips, to face Luca.

"It may not be my place to say this, but you're letting your niece grow up without you. Take it from me. Once that opportunity is gone, it's hard to claw it back."

A complication of emotions crossed Luca's face as he looked up at her. As if he was having a fight with himself.

"You're right. It's not your place."

Something deep within her flared, hot and fierce.

"That may be so, but let me tell you this. Crush the hearts of all the women you want, Luca Montovano. I'll be fine. *We'll* be fine. But Pia…? You're all she has. You lose this chance to show her you love her and you might lose her for good."

Luca looked away, a searing blast of emotion pounding the breath out of his chest in one sharp, unforgiving blow.

Lose Pia?

Unthinkable.

And what had Fran meant about crushing hearts? Marina wasn't crushed—

"I'll be fine," she'd said.

Did Fran *love* him? Had she invested her heart in those nights they had spent together? Nights he hadn't acknowledged since…since she had become a vital part of his work team. One of the people he kept at arm's length in preparation for the bank's inevitable foreclosure.

He knew she enjoyed sparring with him, working with

him—but love? It wasn't something he had ever allowed himself to consider. Not with so much at stake.

He looked back at her, saw her eyes blazing with indignation. The fury of a child who had been where Pia was now. The rage of a woman who loved a man who could never love her in return.

He pushed himself up to standing after placing his drained glass on the floor and faced her. "You're a very brave woman, Francesca Martinelli."

She shifted her feet, eyes held wide-open as they had been on the very first day they'd met. When she'd been the only one courageous enough to stop her friend from doing something she'd regret forever.

"You never shy away from hard truths, do you, Francesca?"

She gave her head a little shake in agreement.

Luca couldn't help but give a self-effacing laugh. "I suspect moments like these are why Beatrice always speaks so highly of you. Why she insisted you come up here. She said you'd be good for me."

"She did?" Fran's eyes brightened, endearing her to him more than he should allow.

"Often," he said. "And with great affection."

He fought the urge to reach out and touch Fran. Stroke a finger along the length of her jawline. Smooth the back of his hand along the downy softness of her cheek.

"That's good," Fran whispered.

Whether she was referring to Beatrice or to the frisson fizzing between them, Luca couldn't tell. How it had shifted from rage to zingy chemistry, he didn't know, but it had.

Luca took a step back, intentionally breaking the moment in two, and gave his thoughts over to Beatrice—his dear friend who'd all but had the world ripped out from under her feet and yet had remained true, kind. A loving friend who had never, even in her darkest hour, withdrawn her emotions as he so often did. Barring his heart from the aches and pains that loving someone entailed.

"If you don't mind me saying something…" Fran began tentatively.

"Why stop now?" He opened his palms. An invitation for her to continue.

Fran blushed, but continued, "Marina didn't really seem your type. Or deserve you, for that matter."

Before he thought better of it, he asked, "And what exactly is it that *I* deserve?"

They both stopped and stared at each other in a moment of mutual recognition. Of course Francesca was a better choice. The natural choice.

A choice he didn't have the freedom to make.

"Marina just seemed… She seemed to be after something more…*fantasy*. Like in a fairy tale. With cocktails and fast cars."

"That sounds about right," Luca conceded. "You're not like that, though, are you?"

Fran squirmed under his gaze and he didn't blame her. He didn't have the ability to disguise the desire he knew was burning in his eyes. But he couldn't offer her what she deserved. His heart.

He turned to face the view, breaking a moment that would only have led to more heartache. "It's probably just as well we're talking about my relationship failures."

"Why's that?" Fran looked away, then dropped down onto the bench, carefully rearranging the pebbles at her feet with her toe.

"I know my behavior over the past few weeks or so has been…confusing, to say the least."

"Are you saying our being together was a mistake?"

Defensiveness laced her words and tightened the folding of her arms across her chest.

"No. No, *chiara*." He joined her on the bench and reached out a hand to cup her chin, so that she could see straight into his heart when he spoke. "Being with you was…bittersweet."

She swallowed. He forced himself to hold his ground, letting his hand shift from her chin to her arms, which he gently unlaced, taking both of her hands in his.

"I liked the idea of having a summer romance with you."

"Past tense?" she asked, with her usual unflinching desire to hear the truth.

"Yes." He owed it to her.

"I thought…I thought you enjoyed being with me."

Little crinkles appeared at the top of her nose as the sparks in her eyes flared in protest. A swell of emotion tightened in his throat. "I did. More than I should have, given the circumstances."

"Which are…?" Francesca barely got the words out before choking back a small cry of protest.

His fingers twitched and his hands balled into fists. He didn't want to cause her pain. Far from it.

"You said yourself you have to go home."

"Not for another few weeks!"

"Francesca, Mont di Mare may not *be* here in a few weeks."

A silence rang between them so powerfully Francesca felt her skin practically reverberate with the impact of his words.

"What do you mean?"

"The bank." He spat the word out as if it were poison, then swept an arm along the length of the village. "The bank will own all of this in a few weeks if I don't turn things around."

She shook her head as if he'd just spoken in a foreign tongue. "I don't understand…"

"You don't need to." He bit the words out one by one, as if he were actually shouldering the weight of the mountain as he did so. "My focus needs to be entirely on the clinic, and what little time I have left in my day—as you so rightly pointed out—I need to give to Pia. She's all I have."

"You know you could have more," Fran asserted.

"Only to have you disappear at the end of the summer, along with Mont di Mare?" He didn't pause to let Fran answer, and his voice softened as he offered her what little consolation he could. "I've experienced enough loss to last a lifetime, *amore*. I don't think I could bear any more."

A dog's bark filtered into the fabric of the night sounds. It reminded him that he'd delivered the death knell to any future between them. The least he could do was soften the blow.

"I meant to say the reason I was asking so much about the dogs is that after our session with Cara a couple of other patients were asking whether or not they might have one, too. If it suits you, you could look into supplying them with assistance canines before the summer is out."

Fran didn't know whether to be elated or furious, given the circumstances. Shell-shocked was about as close as she could come.

Luca was about to lose the entire village and still his thoughts were on his patients?

Her heart bled for him, and then just as quickly tightened in a sharp twist of anguish.

Why couldn't he afford *her* the same courtesy?

Take a risk.

Chance his heart on love.

She stared at him, searching his dark eyes for answers.

How could he just stand there like that? All business and attention to detail when everything he'd worked so hard for was slipping away.

Wasn't he full of rage? Of fight? *Why* wouldn't he let her love him? Take the blows of an unfair world along-side him?

She stared at Luca, amazed to see the light burning in his eyes turn icy cold.

Perhaps he was right. He was giving her a chance to cut her losses. Preserve what was left of her heart. Do her job, then get on with her life—just as she'd planned.

She forced on her most businesslike tone. He wanted facts? He could *have* facts.

"You know it takes more than a couple of weeks to find the right dogs, let alone train them up, right? It re-quires skill. Precision. Plus, I adopt dogs from local shel-ters, so sometimes there are additional factors to consider. What if the patient doesn't take to the dog and I can't bring it back to the States? I could hardly return it to the shelter afterward, could I? Having given it a glimpse of another life?"

Luca stared at her. Completely unmoved.

Fran continued. "Dogs are loyal, even if people aren't, and I don't play emotional bingo. With anyone."

It was vaguely satisfying to finally see a glint of dis-cord in Luca's eyes.

Vaguely.

There was no glory in one-upping a man whose world was about to collapse in on him.

She bent and picked up his wineglass from the ground,

then took a definitive step toward her doorway before turning to address him again.

"I *will* speak with your administrator about patients looking to work with an assistance dog and see if there's someone local who can be brought in. It would be foolish to invest in something I won't be able to see through to the bitter end. If you'll excuse me?"

She scooted around Luca and into her cottage before she could catch another glimpse of those beautiful dark eyes of his, silently cursing herself, her life—anything she could think of—as she shut the door behind her.

Leaning against the thick, time-worn oak, she let a deep sigh heave out of her chest.

As painful as it was for her to admit, Luca was right. There was too much at stake for him to worry about foolish things like a summer romance. She was going home. She'd promised her father—just as he had promised her.

The only thing she could do now was follow the advice she'd given to Luca. Spend her time building a life she wouldn't regret.

A flicker of an idea came to her, but just as quickly as it caught and flared brightly, she blew it out.

She wasn't ready to ask her father for help. Not yet.

But a talk…

She could do with a talk right now.

She swiped at the number and smiled as the phone began to ring.

Before, she had always turned to Bea, but now, hearing her father's voice brighten when he picked up the phone, she let gratitude flood into her heart that, step by step, they were forging a real relationship.

CHAPTER THIRTEEN

LUCA FROWNED. HE'D caught a glimpse of her. As per usual, no matter how stealthily Fran passed, he always knew when she was near. It was a sixth sense he'd grown all too aware of.

He glanced up at the clock. It was past seven. A lovely evening. Well after rehab hours. The residents were all back in their villas, Pia was tucked up with the dogs, watching a film, and here he was hunkered over a pile of papers, brow furrowed, one hand ramming his hair away from his forehead, the other spread wide against the mahogany sheen of the large desk he commanded. Taut. Ready for action. Poised like a reluctant but honorable admiral, helming a ship when duty called.

"Fran!"

He called out her name before he thought better of it. Unlike Francesca, who, true to her word, had maintained an entirely professional demeanor in the weeks following their talk, Luca had behaved like a bear with a sore head.

A golden halo of hair appeared, then her bright eyes peeped around the edge of his door frame like a curious kitten—tempted, but not quite brave enough to enter the lion's lair.

Luca gazed at her for a moment, just enjoying the chance to drink her in. Those blue eyes of hers were skidding around his office as if trying to memorize it. Or maybe that was just him hoping. It wouldn't be long now before she left.

Her loose blond curls rested atop the soft slope of her bare shoulders. The tiny string straps of her sundress reminded him of…too much.

He pushed the pile of papers away, against his better judgment, and rose. "Fancy a walk? I could do with some fresh air."

She shot him a wary look, then nodded. Reluctantly.

They strolled for a few minutes in a surprisingly comfortable silence. Strands of music, television and laughter ribboned out from the villas along with wafts of home-cooked food.

Fran broke the silence. "That smells good."

"My mother used to call the scents up here 'the real Italy.'" Luca laughed softly at the memory.

"In my house that was store-bought macaroni and cheese!" Fran huffed out a laugh that was utterly bereft of joy.

Her response to his throwaway comment was a stark reminder to Luca that he did have blessings to count. Proper childhood memories. Family, laughter, love and joy.

"So what were they? Those scents of the real Italy?" Fran asked.

"Oh, let's see…" He stopped and closed his eyes for a moment, letting the memories comes to him. "Torn basil leaves. The ripest of tomatoes. Freshly baked focaccia. *Dio*, the bread alone was enough to bring you to your knees. Signora Levazzo!" The memory came to him vividly. "Signora Levazzo's focaccia was the envy of all the villagers. She had a secret weapon."

"Which was…?" Fran asked.

"Her son's olive oil. He had a set of olive trees he always used. Slightly more peppery than anyone else's. No one knows how he did it, but—oh!" He pressed his fingers to his lips and kissed them. *"Delicioso!"*

"Sounds lovely."

He didn't miss the hint of wistfulness in her voice. Or the pang in his heart that she hadn't enjoyed those simple but so-perfect pleasures in her own childhood. From the smattering of comments he'd pieced together, she hadn't had much of a childhood at all.

"They were unforgettable summers." Luca looked up to the sky, unsuccessfully fighting the rush of bitterness sweeping in to darken the fond memories. "And to think I told them to sell it all."

"Who? Your family?" Fran's brow crinkled.

He nodded. "We spent all our summers here. Well…" He held up his index finger. "Everyone but me once I'd turned eighteen."

"What happened then?" Fran asked, her eyes following the line of his hand as he indicated that they should follow a path leading to the outer wall of the village.

"The usual things that happen to an eighteen-year-old male. Girls. Motorcycles. University. Medicine."

Fran laughed, taking a quick, shy glimpse up toward him. "I don't think most eighteen-year-old males are drawn to medicine."

"Well…I always like to be different."

"You definitely are that," Fran said, almost swallowing the words even as she did. "And it was plastics you went into?"

"Reconstructive surgery," he corrected, then amended

his brusque answer. "I did plastics to feed my taste for the high life. Reconstructive surgery to feed my soul."

Fran shot him a questioning glance.

"I did a lot of pro bono cases back then. Cleft palates. Children who'd been disfigured in accidents. That sort of thing."

He felt Fran's eyes travel to his scar and turned away. He'd never remove his scar. Not after what he'd done.

Abruptly Fran stopped and knelt, plucking at a few tiny flowers. She held them up when he asked if she was making a posy.

"Daisy chain," she explained, turning her focus to joining the flowers together. "It's fun. You should try it."

"I don't do *fun*," Luca shot back.

"I know." Fran pressed her heels into the ground and rose to her full height. "That's why I said it."

Luca turned away to face the setting sun.

He shouldn't have to live like this, she thought. All stoic, full of to-do lists and health-and-safety warnings. He was a kind, generous man who—when he dared to let the mask drop—was doing his best to stay afloat and do well by his niece. And failing at both because he insisted upon doing it alone.

She placed the finished daisy chain atop her head, then reached out to grab his hand before he strode off beyond her reach. His heart might not be free to love her, but he didn't have to do this alone.

"Talk to me."

A groan of frustration tightened Luca's throat around his Adam's apple. If he hadn't squeezed her fingers as he made the animalistic cry, she would have left immediately. But when his fingers curled around hers and pressed into the back of her palm, she knew it was his way of doing the best he could—the only way he knew how.

"C'mon…" She tried again. "Fair is fair. You got *my* life story on my first day here."

When she sent him a playful wink she received a taut grimace in place of the smile she'd hoped to see.

"I was looking after my niece. Ensuring you weren't some lunatic Bea had sent my way."

Fran clucked her tongue. "First of all, Bea would never do that. And, second of all, I think you know I've encountered enough crazy in my life for you to feel safe in the knowledge I will pass no judgment when I hear your story."

Was that…? Had he just…? Was that the hint of a smile? No. He gave a shake of his head.

Frustration tightened in her chest. What would it take to get this man to trust her?

"Listen. Of all the people up here in this incredible, wonderful center of healing you've created, you seem to be the only one not getting any better."

She ignored his sharp look and continued.

"I'm probably the only one here who knows exactly what it's like to butt heads with their own destiny. My dad's due any day now and I'm already quaking in my boots. Please…" She gave his hand a tight squeeze. "Just lay your cards on the table and see what happens."

A rancorous laugh unfurled from deep within him. "Oh, *chiara*. If only you knew how apt your choice of words was…"

"Well, I *would* know if you told me." Despite all her efforts to rein in her emotions, she couldn't help giving the ground a good stamp with her foot.

Luca arced an eyebrow at her. "It's not a very nice story."

"Nor is mine. It's not like I'm made of glass, Luca. I'm flesh and blood. Just like you."

Luca's lips remained firmly clamped shut.

"You've already had my body!" she finally cried out in sheer frustration. "What do you *want*? Blood?"

CHAPTER FOURTEEN

LUCA WHEELED ON FRAN, his features turning dark, almost savage in their intensity. "I didn't ask for anything from you, *chiara*. Not one kiss. Not one cent. Remember that when you're gone."

Shock whipped anything Fran might have said in response straight out of her throat. She felt her mouth go dry and, despite the warmth of the summer's evening, she shivered as the blood drained from her face when he continued.

"Don't think I haven't seen it."

"Seen what?" Fran looked around her, as if the answer might pop out from behind a bush. She was absolutely bewildered.

"I *know* how you speak of Mont di Mare. How you've made this place into some sort of Shangri-la. A place where nothing can go wrong. Where everything is perfect and rose-colored. You don't get to do that. Not without knowing the facts."

Luca drew in a sharp breath, the air near enough slicing his throat as it filled his lungs.

What the hell?

After a summer of holding it all in, he couldn't contain his rage any longer.

Losing Fran, the clinic—perhaps even Pia if she saw the shell of a man he'd turned into—was more than he could take.

He began pacing on the outcrop where they'd stopped. And talking. Talking as if his life depended upon it.

"Thanks to my father's time at the poker tables, I am in debt up to my eyeballs. Worse. Drowning."

It was an admission he'd never made aloud.

He was shocked to see compassion in Fran's eyes when he'd been so brutal. Even more, they bore no pity.

It was what he had feared most. The pitying looks. He'd had enough of those at the funeral. The funeral in which he had buried his mother, his father, his sister and brother-in-law all in one awful, heart-wrenching day. A day he never wanted to remember, though he knew slamming the door shut on those memories only left them to fester. To rear their ugly heads as they were doing now.

He glanced across at Fran again. Surely she would shrink away from him at some point. As the facts of the story began to sink in. As the knowledge that *he* was to blame for everything that had come his way became clear.

Astonishingly, she seemed more clear-eyed and steady than he had ever seen her. As if his lashing out at her had been an unwelcome shock, but not unexpected.

"How did you open the clinic without assets?"

Fran's question pulled him back to the facts—however unsavory they were to confront.

"I had saved a fair amount when I working in Rome."

Her eyebrows lifted in surprise.

"Plastic surgery brings in a lot of money when you're willing to put in the hours. That, and some of the doctors here are actually operating as private practices, so they came with their own equipment. Thanks to Bea,

I learned about and applied for a few grants. Historic building restoration and the like. The rest…" He swallowed down the sour memories of learning just how far into penury his father had sunk. "Let's just say what's left of my soul belongs to the devil."

"I doubt that's true, Luca. You're too good a man to compromise your principles."

Surprisingly, Fran's face was a picture of earnestness rather than horror. As if she held out hope that the clinic could still be saved.

"Not me—my father. But I'm sure I can shoulder a large portion of the blame for that, as well. To cut a long story short—if I don't make a profit from the clinic very, very soon it will go to Nartoli Banking. My father leveraged the place."

"What will happen?"

"They'll repossess it." The emotion had drained from his voice now. "In a few weeks, most likely. Sell it to an investor, who will most likely raze the village, turn the site into a modern hotel. *Exclusive*, of course," he added with an embittered laugh.

He thought of Mont di Mare—the historic cottages and stone buildings, the gardens and archways—all of it being obliterated to make way for a glitzy glass-and-steel hotel aimed at the world's rich and careless…

"Is it essential to have the clinic here?" she asked. "I mean, it's obviously beautiful, and just the view alone is healing, but…could you not have set up the clinic in Rome?"

Fran's voice was soft. Nonjudgmental. She wasn't accusing him of making the wrong decision, just trying to paint a picture. She wanted to understand.

"Revitalizing the village had always been my sister and mother's dream," he finally admitted.

"As a clinic?"

He shook his head. "A holiday destination, summer homes—that sort of thing. They even toyed with the idea of trying to revamp it into a living, working village. One with specialized craftsmen—and women," he added quickly, when he saw Fran's lips purse and then spread into a gentle smile at his correction. "Similar ideas to what you had, minus the patients. A place where craftspeople could live and create traditional works of art and wares. Do you know how hard it is to find a genuine blacksmith these days?"

Fran shook her head, then quirked an eyebrow. "About as hard as finding world peace?"

He laughed. Couldn't help it. And was grateful for the release.

Fran lowered herself onto a broad boulder, her legs swinging over the edge as she looked out into the valley below.

Hands on his hips, he scanned the outlook, fully aware that this was most likely one of the last days he could call the view his own.

"This is the first time I've heard you speak about your family," Fran said when he eventually sat down alongside her.

"Pia is my family. I don't even deserve *her*."

He looked across in time to see Fran shake off his words, the hurt he'd caused because he wouldn't— *couldn't*—love her, too.

"I just meant—"

"I know what you meant," he cut in harshly. "I'm sorry, Fran. I know you're all about healing old wounds, making amends with your father and all that, but it's too late for me."

"How do you know that?"

He saw something in her then. A steely determination to see this through with him, no matter how ugly.

"You want the whole story?"

She nodded.

"All right—well, the beginning's pretty easy. Happy childhood. Wonderful mother. Doting father. They would've loved me to take up a bit more of the whole Baron Montovano thing, but they never pressed when they saw medicine was my passion. My sister and mother looked after things here. Had the vision. My father was a proud man. Passionate and very much in love with my mother. A few years ago, when his business ventures started going south along with the rest of the world's, he went into a panic."

"About what?"

"He became convinced he was going to die before my mother."

"Was he sick?" Fran asked.

"No." He corrected himself. "Or not that I was aware of. He and I weren't exactly close by then, and even if I'd asked him, he wouldn't have come to me for a medical exam."

"How do you know that?"

"Because he told me." Luca scraped his hand against the sharp edge of the stone he sat upon, not caring if it lacerated his skin. The cut would hurt less than the words his father had shouted in rage that night at the casino.

"You are the last person I would come to for help. The last person in the world."

"My mother and my sister were his world. He would've done anything for them."

"I bet the same was true for you."

"Don't speak of what you don't know, *chiara*. Do you know how he showed his love? His loyalty to his family?

By taking to the craps table. The poker table. Baccarat. Anything to try to scrape back the money he had lost in business. But instead of securing a healthy nest egg, he lost. Lost it all."

Fran's fingers flew to cover her mouth, but to her credit she didn't say a word.

"Just over two years ago I received a call from a casino in Monaco, asking if I could come and collect him. His pockets were empty and it was either me bailing him out or they'd put him in prison for the night."

He looked up to the sky, completely unadulterated by city lights, and soaked it in.

"I drove from Roma straight to Florence, where my mother and sister were. We decided to all go together. Show our support."

He kept his gaze on the sky. There was no chance he could look into Fran's eyes and get through this part of the story without completely breaking down.

"So we all climbed into the car and drove through the night to go and pick up my wayward father in Monte Carlo."

"You *drove*?" Fran asked incredulously.

"The things you do for love," Luca answered softly. He would have done anything for his father. Walked there if he'd needed to. Oh! How he wished he'd walked.

"What happened when you reached him?"

"He was furious at first. Blaming everything on me. For abandoning the family."

"By working in medicine?" Fran shook her head, as if trying to make sense of it all. "Didn't he know about the charity work you did?"

"No." Luca scraped his other hand along the rough surface of the granite. "It didn't suit my image for people to know, so I never really talked about it."

He tugged a hand through his hair, grateful for the deepening darkness. With any luck, it was hiding the waves of emotion crossing his face at the memory of his father eventually breaking down. Sobbing with relief and sorrow at the pain he had brought to his own family.

"Then we all piled back into my car." He laughed at the memory. They'd been jam-packed in that thing. Like sardines, his mother had kept saying. A motley crew, they'd been. Tearful. Laughing. Up and down the emotional roller coaster until they had all sagged with fatigue.

"Pia, you will be unsurprised to hear, was ever the diplomat. She kept everyone talking about what we were going to make for dinner when we got back to Italy. And it was somewhere around a very vibrant discussion about eggplant parmigiana—"

Luca stopped. This was the hardest part. Pieces of information still only came to him in fragments. His hands on the steering wheel. Entering the tunnel. The articulated truck crossing the median strip—

Mercifully, Pia's memory of the accident had never returned. He prayed, for her sake, that it never would.

"The truck driver must've fallen asleep. That route is renowned for it. Up and over the mountains. Lots of tunnels. We were all tired, too. I'd been driving all day. All night. It was why we'd forced ourselves to keep talking, inventing ridiculous recipes to try when we got home."

Luca felt his voice grow jagged with emotion. Each word became weighted in his chest, as if the words themselves were physical burdens he'd been carrying all these years.

"He just careened straight into us. There was nothing I could do!" The words scraped against his throat as though they were being torn from his chest.

Without even noticing her moving, he suddenly felt

Francesca's arms around him, and after years of holding back the bone-shaking grief of loss—nearly his entire family gone in one sickeningly powerful blow—he wept.

Luca hardly knew how much time had passed when at long last his breath steadied and the reddened edges of his eyes dried.

Fran had not said a single word through his outpouring. No trite placations. No overused sayings to try to soothe away a pain that could never be fully healed. Although now his silent grief had become a sorrow shared. It was Fran's gift to him. He could see it in her eyes, glistening with the tears she had not let herself shed, as he wept in the silvery, ethereal light of the moon.

"So that's where this came from?" Fran reached out and gently ran her finger along his scar.

He nodded, catching her hand beneath his own. He'd never thought of it as disfiguring. More as one of life's cruel reminders that he had debts to pay—both literal and figurative.

"If there's anything I can do—" Fran began, stopping abruptly when he dropped her hand as if it had scalded him.

Her touch hadn't. But her words had.

After all that didn't she see this was *his* burden to bear? His cross to carry alone?

"You've done more than enough, Francesca."

She blinked, and something he couldn't quite read had changed in her eyes when she opened them again. "I hope you're saying that in a good way."

"As best I know how. Now..." He pushed himself up, offering her a hand so that she could rise more easily from their mountainside perch. "I'd best be off. See my niece. *Buonasera.*"

He left a bemused Francesca at her doorway, not daring to let himself dip down and give her cheek a kiss. He'd said too much. Bared too much of his heart.

He had three minutes—the length of the walk between her cottage and his own—to pull himself back together. Make a man out of himself again before he saw Pia.

How would he tell her he was going to lose this place to the bank?

Again, his eyes returned to the stars, searching for answers.

God willing, he would never have to say a word.

Fran pulled a blanket over her shoulders and curled up in the window seat. The way her mind was buzzing, sleep was going to be a hard-won commodity. Nearly as impossible as it had been to say good-night to Luca.

Never before had she been so moved as when she and Luca had held each other and he'd finally given in to the years of grief he'd held pent up inside him.

If only—

No.

She gave herself a sharp shake, willing the tears forming in her eyes to disappear. If Luca could be so strong under such heartrending circumstances, she would strive to be the same. Never before had she held someone in such high regard. Never before had she felt such compassion, such love, for one man.

Even if he couldn't return her love he'd shown her the power of sacrifice. Sacrifices she was willing to make even if it cost her her heart.

Shivering a bit, she pulled the blanket closer around her shoulders, willing her body to recapture the sense of warmth she'd felt when she had held Luca.

She had half a mind to call Bea, desperate to brainstorm with someone. Come up with something, *anything* that would help save Mont di Mare from the bank. But Bea had enough on her plate without this to worry about.

Then the lightning-bolt moment came.

She *did* know one person whose entire life had been fueled by the betrayal of another. Who had poured his every energy into exacting revenge by succeeding in his own right.

Her tummy lurched, then tightened as her nerves collected into one jangling ball in her chest, but she picked up her phone anyway.

Courage.

That was what Luca had. In spades.

Strength.

She dialed the number. Took a deep breath…

Forgiveness.

Luca had so many reasons to let his heart turn black, and through everything all she had seen was compassion and—

"*Si, pronto?*"

Love.

"*Papa, è Francesca. Va bene?*"

CHAPTER FIFTEEN

"That was an excellent session, Giuliana. Are you pleased with your progress?"

Luca took a seat beside the girl as she wheeled her chair into the shade of the pergola after Dr. Torino had headed back to the gym.

"Si." Her eyes glistened with pride. "All the therapists and doctors here have been amazing. I can't believe how quickly I've gained in strength. Don't let Fran go back to America."

The smile dropped from his eyes. "I'm afraid I don't have much control over that."

"I'm sure if you asked her…"

Luca tsk-tsked and shook his head. "We're not talking about Fran right now—we're talking about you and your progress."

He didn't want Fran to go. But he was hardly going to beg her to stay on a sinking ship.

"Dai. Facci vedere i muscoli."

Despite his grim mood, Luca smiled as Giuliana pushed back her T-shirt and flexed her slender bicep.

He gave it an appreciative squeeze. *"Va bene*, Giuliana. You'll be winning arm wrestling matches soon."

This was the fun part. The satisfying part of being a doctor. Happy patients. Positive results.

"You're not finding the full days of rehab too tiring?"

Giuliana gave the exasperated sigh of a teenager. "No more than I'm supposed to!"

"Excellent. You're a star patient."

Giuliana giggled, waving away his praise. "That's not hard when there's only five of us. Besides—" she fixed Luca with a narrow-eyed gaze "—I have it on good authority you say that to everyone."

"Guilty." Luca shot her an apologetic grin. "You're all making me—the clinic—look really good."

"Ciao, Pia!"

Luca turned in the direction Giuliana was waving—something she hadn't been able to do when she'd arrived here—the smile dropping from his lips again when he saw Fran corralling his niece and her dogs into the large courtyard. Giuliana called out a greeting again, and Pia quickly changed course toward them.

Fran's eyes caught his but she didn't cross over. Not that he blamed her.

"Scusi, Dr. Montovano, Pia is going to show me some things with the dogs."

"No problem." Luca grinned—not that Giuliana was hanging around to see if he wanted her to stay.

"Dr. Montovano?" His administrative assistant appeared by his side with a note in her hand.

"Si, Rosa?"

"We've got a patient who would like to be transferred here. His parents, actually. They say their son has lost hope."

"We don't have room," he said by rote, giving his head a shake, though his mind was already spinning with ways to make it possible. It wasn't the money—though that would help. It was the hope part. When a patient had lost hope…

"They're asking for intensive. Maybe a month."

We may not have a month.

"Perhaps if he came for a day. A chance to see the other patients so he doesn't feel so alone," Rosa persisted.

"What's his case history?"

He shouldn't ask. Knowing more about the patient would make him want to help.

A shard of frustration tugged his brows together. His gut was telling him to say yes. The staff had already made it clear they would be fine working with more patients. It was simply a question of finding the room. He and Pia could move out of *their* house, but after so much disruption he hated to move her again.

Out of the corner of his eye he could see Fran approaching the pergola as the girls and the dogs disappeared, leaving gales of laughter in their wake. Fran's cottage was wheelchair friendly. Close enough to the clinic's hub to access all the facilities easily.

"It's just the three of them, you say?"

"Three of who?" Fran asked.

"A new patient and his parents," Rosa jumped in.

"No. *Not* a new patient. I'm afraid it won't work," Luca interjected. "There's nowhere for him to stay."

"How about my cottage?"

Fran looked between the two of them, as if they were both ridiculous for not thinking of it in the first place.

"You would give up your cottage?" Rosa's eyes lit with relief.

"Of course I would. Anything! I'd leave right now if that helped."

"And abandon Pia?" Luca shook his head. "Leave her with the job half-done—not to mention the other patients you've taken on—before your contract is up?"

Fran's eyes shot to his, striking him like a viper. Neither of them was talking about Pia and he knew it.

"I'm hardly *abandoning* anything. I only have a few days left anyway."

Of course she would leave. What had he thought would happen after last night? Had he really thought ripping his heart open and letting his whole sorry story pour out would keep her here? *No.* Quite the opposite. He hadn't thought at all. He most likely repulsed her now.

"I would *never* let my patients down," Fran shot back before he could get a word in. "I'm talking about the cottage. I can stay anywhere. The patients can't."

He waited for her to state the obvious. That he needed the money. He needed *her.*

"Rosa." He forced himself to speak calmly. "Would you please give us a moment to discuss Miss Martinelli's housing arrangements?"

"Of course, Dr. Montovano."

If he wasn't mistaken, Rosa gave the tiniest hint of a smile before she reluctantly headed back to the office. Italians loved a passionate fight, and from the speed of the blood coursing through his veins this was set to be explosive.

"So, what's your big plan? To camp out on one of the sun loungers? Or are you going to whip one of the cottages into shape with one of your feel-good projects?"

Luca knew he was being unreasonable. Knew there was bite in his bark.

"I'll stay in town. Commute in like the other doctors. Besides, with my father coming—"

"What?"

"My father. You know he's coming."

Luca shook his head. He remembered her mentioning something about a visit, but it hadn't really registered.

He couldn't believe Fran would humiliate him like this. Show a half-finished clinic to a man renowned for his exacting attention to detail. A man who with a few swift strokes of his keyboard could save the clinic from oblivion. Fran's father was the last person on earth he wanted crossing the entryway to Mont di Mare.

"Why would you do that? Why would you invite him here?"

Fran took a step away from Luca, as if the question had physically repelled her.

"He's my *father*. He wants to see the clinic. Meet the people I've been talking about all summer. You of all people should know how important family is."

Luca looked at her as if she'd slapped him. Her remorse was instant, but it was too late to make apologies. The warmth she had once seen in Luca's eyes turned into inaccessible black, his pupils meshing with his irises as if there would never be enough light for him to see any good in the world. Any hope.

His lip curled in disgust, as if by inviting her father here she had betrayed him. "What's the point in bringing him here if all you're going to do is leave? Showing Daddy what a good little girl he's raised?"

"You don't mean that."

"Oh, I do, *chiara*." He closed the gap between them with one long-legged stride. "Has this been *fun* for you? Playing at a mountainside clinic while the rest of us are struggling to survive?"

Fran opened her mouth to answer, then thought better of it. Her heart ached for Luca. Ached to tell him everything—but not in the state he was in now. Unbending. Proud. Hurt. There was hurt coursing around that bloodstream of his—she knew it—but it didn't change the facts. She loved him, but if inviting her father here meant losing Luca but saving the clinic, then so be it. Her father was coming whether Luca liked it or not.

"Tell the new patient to come." She forced her voice to sound steady.

"For how long, Francesca? Where's your crystal ball? A day? A week? How many days do you foresee here before I have to tell this miserable wheelchair-bound boy and everyone else here that they will all have to go?"

"Whatever you feel is best. Now, if you'll excuse me, I have a patient appointment to keep."

Fran forced herself to turn away and walk calmly toward the clinic, trying her very best not to let Luca see that her knees were about to give way beneath her.

She knew anger and fear were fueling Luca's hateful comments. Of *course* she wanted the clinic to flourish. She wanted everything in the world for him. She wanted *him*!

Couldn't he see it in her eyes? In her heart?

Leaving wasn't the plan. *Staying* was the plan. The dream.

But her father was a facts man. He needed to see things for himself. Touch the stone. Scour the books. Observe the work. He'd never invest in a dream he didn't think could become a reality. And for the first time since she'd rung her father and asked him to jump on a plane as soon as possible, she felt a tremor of fear begin to shake inside her, forcing her to ask herself the same question again and again.

What have I done?

CHAPTER SIXTEEN

LUCA RUBBED THE kink out of his neck. A night in his office hadn't achieved anything other than darkening his already-foul mood.

"They're just about to land, Dr. Montovano," a nurse called out to him.

He pushed up and away from his desk and strode toward the helicopter-landing site.

Against his better judgment, he had approved the new patient's arrival.

It was Francesca's doing. Of course.

Not literally, but he'd heard her voice in his head each and every time he'd tried to say no. If he was going to go down, he might as well go down in flames.

He looked up to the sky to see if he could catch a glimpse of the chopper. They usually headed in from Florence, but this sound came from the east. Nearer to the seaside airport.

Unusual.

It was all unusual. This hospital transfer was happening much earlier than normal.

He huffed out a laugh. As the patient's stay would no doubt be short, they could at least eke a few more sessions out of his early arrival.

See? He shot a glance toward the bright sky. *I'm still capable of seeing the silver lining.*

The whirring blades of the helicopter strobed against the rays of sun hitting his face. He closed his eyes against the glare, taking a precious moment to relish the fact that the clinic was still here to help. Might still make a difference.

A day? A week? He didn't know how long he'd have with this boy, but he would do everything in his power to show him that giving up without a fight was sounding a death knell. And dying young...? That wasn't going to happen on *his* watch.

By the time the chopper landed, he had realigned his features into those of a benign clinician. Just as well. The first face he saw was his patient's.

A scowling teenage boy who looked intent on proving that nothing and no one would improve his lot in life.

Luca stepped toward the helicopter with a grim smile.

Giancarlo Salvi. Seventeen years old. An able-bodied teen turned quadriplegic after a late-night joyride went horrifically wrong.

He took another step forward and saw the boy's scowl deepen. And why wouldn't it? Luca was able-bodied. Strong. Vital. *He* had the ability to walk toward things—and away from them.

The moment froze in Luca's mind—crystalizing as if it were a beacon of truth.

No matter how powerless he felt, he still had choices.

Energy shot into his limbs, and without further ado he helped the crew unstrap Giancarlo's wheelchair.

Destiny wasn't just something you haphazardly fell into.

Destiny was something you shaped.

* * *

Fran tucked herself behind a thick cascade of greenery near the pergola when she heard voices. The last thing she wanted to do was distract Luca during this crucial time. Or drag out the duffel bag she'd hastily jammed her things into before cleaning her cottage to gleaming perfection before the new family arrived.

She needed to get it to the car so she could meet her father at the nearby airport. He'd called a few minutes ago and asked for a ride. Something about the helicopter he'd chartered being delayed. The excuse sounded sketchy, but maybe it was his way of having some alone time before he saw the clinic.

A nervous shudder went through her. Once she'd brought her father here, Luca might well decide he never wanted to speak to her again. But if that was the cost of keeping the clinic alive, she could just about live with herself.

Fran let the stone wall behind her take her weight for a moment as she fought the sting of tears. When she'd invited her father here, to see if he thought the clinic was worth investing in, she'd thought she was doing the right thing. Now she was riddled with doubt.

Her father liked cars, not people. His passion wasn't health care. Or dogs. The only reason he'd said he would invest in Canny Canines was to finally bring his daughter home.

She swiped at her eyes when she heard voices on the other side of the wall. The last thing she needed was to have a member of the staff—or worse, Luca—find her blubbering away.

She tuned in to the female voices. A pair of nurses whispering something about the newly arrived patient insisting the helicopter must stay until he had deemed the place "worthy."

Fran's blood boiled on Luca's behalf. The place was *exemplary*!

Her jaw set tight as she tugged Edison in closer to her and listened more closely when the voices changed.

"This is where most of our patients like to spend their downtime."

Fran peered out from behind the froth of summer blossoms at the sound of Luca's voice. He was just a few meters away, guiding a teenage boy and his parents through the archway and out to the walled garden with the pool. This area always won people's hearts. An infinity pool on the side of a mountain overlooking the sea... What wasn't to love?

"You've got to be kidding me." Disdain dripped from the teenage boy's every word. "Your paralyzed patients hang out by the *pool*? Why? So they can see what everyone else gets to do for fun?"

Luca eyed the boy silently for a while. He didn't need to check Giancarlo's charts to know fear of failure was behind the boy's words. It was obvious that whatever treatment he'd been receiving had been palliative at best.

"Didn't your previous physio involve any pool time?" Luca asked finally. The bulk of his patients had done at least a trial run in a pool, if not an entire program of hydrotherapy.

"*Si*, Dr. Montovano." The boy's voice still dripped with disdain. "They just threw us quadriplegics in the pool and whoever bobbed up first won a prize."

"Giancarlo! *Amore*, he's trying to help." His mother admonished her son in a hushed tone, but her flush of embarrassment betrayed the frustration she was obviously feeling.

Despite himself, Luca felt for her. A parent trying to do her best in an already bad situation. His thoughts shot to Fran. She'd been doing the same thing. Taking a bad situation and doing her very best to make it better.

Why hadn't he given her a chance to explain?

"Not all patients are necessarily up to pool work. Isn't that right, Dr. Montovano? My son's concerns *are* valid."

Luca nodded in Giancarlo's father's direction and gave his chin a thoughtful stroke, trying his best to look neutral as he processed the parents' different approaches to their boy's disability.

The father was accepting his son's bitterness. Failure. As if it were a done deal.

The mother? He could see her love knew no boundaries. That she was willing to give anything a shot if it meant bringing back her little boy.

"Not all facilities are equipped to deal with patients in hydrotherapy scenarios. We're one of the lucky ones."

"Lucky enough to be on a mountaintop and hide all of us cripples away, you mean."

Luca stared into Giancarlo's eyes, not liking what he saw. The bitterness. Rage. The loss of hope. All reflected back at him as if they were mirrors into his own soul.

A movement caught his attention. Edison. The Labrador was running into the garden, chasing after a tennis ball.

"You let *dogs* roam around here?" Giancarlo still sounded irritable, but the tiniest bit of light in his voice and the flash of interest in his otherwise-dull eyes told Luca all he needed to know. He still had hope. Despite everything, the boy still had hope.

Luca looked up and saw Fran slowly walking toward

them, her hand making a sharp signal to Edison that he should sit in front of Giancarlo's chair.

The parents were looking between Luca and Fran for answers. Was this her way of asking him not to give up hope?

"*Buongiorno*. I seem to have lost track of my assistance dog." Fran unleashed her warm smile, instantly relaxing Giancarlo's parents.

The Fran Effect.

"*Per favore*. Allow me to introduce Francesca Martinelli—"

"Like the cars?" Giancarlo interrupted, the first hint of a smile discernible on his face.

"Exactly like the cars." Fran nodded. Then smiled.

Better than sunshine.

The next twenty minutes or so passed in a blur as Edison became the center of attention.

Giancarlo's parents watched, wide-eyed, as Fran and the assistance dog exhibited a wide array of skills. Holding the boy upright if necessary. Retrieving objects and placing them in Giancarlo's hands. Manipulating his electric wheelchair around hard-to-negotiate corners. Going for help if necessary. She was bringing smiles to the lips of three people who Luca was certain hadn't known much, if any, happiness in the months since their lives had been changed forever.

By the time Fran had finished with her display, the Salvis—including Giancarlo—were committed to staying.

"Let me organize one of the other doctors to show you around." Luca heard the note of caution in his own voice. Fran had performed a miracle and still he wasn't happy. What was wrong with him?

Once Dr. Murro had been found and was showing the Salvis around the facilities, Luca wheeled on Fran.

"What the *hell* do you think you're doing?"

Bewilderment swept across Fran's features. "What do you mean? I was helping! Didn't you want them to stay?"

"Not this way. Not when I don't know how long I can offer them treatment. Don't you see what you've done?"

"Offered him hope? Offered him a new way of looking at the world?" Defiance rang in her every word.

"Stop!" He spoke too harshly, too cruelly for someone who felt as if his heart was breaking.

Fatigue hit him like a ton of bricks. This couldn't go on. He only had so much energy, and what little of it was left would have to go to Pia and the clinic.

"Will you please just stop?"

Francesca looked at him, her eyes held wide as if a blink would shatter her into a million pieces.

In them—in those crystal-clear blue eyes of hers— he saw myriad messages. Confusion. Tenderness. Pain.

She turned away without a word, and as she disappeared around the corner he knew in the very core of his being what the universe had been screaming at him all these weeks—he was in love with Fran.

"Dr. Montovano?"

A knock sounded at Luca's office door. Enzo Fratelli, one of the physios, cracked the door open a bit wider, obviously hoping for an invitation to come in.

"Si?" Luca flipped over the pile of paperwork he'd been working on. No point in Enzo seeing all the red ink. Not before he'd found a way to tell the staff.

"We all want you to know we appreciate how much work you've been putting into getting the clinic up and running."

Luca pushed back from the desk, suddenly too tired to pretend any longer. "Is it worth it, Enzo? Really?"

He gestured for his colleague to sit down. He knew he'd given up a lot to come and work here—a life in Florence, assured work at a busy hospital.

"*Si, Dottore.* Of course it is." Enzo sat down, concern pressing his brows together. "What makes you doubt it?"

Money. Debt. The idea of doing this whole damn thing without Francesca to remind him of the bright side.

"What if I've been wrong?"

"About what?"

"The location. About having the clinic here at Mont di Mare."

"But that's half the draw. Surely you of all people would see that?"

Luca nodded, looking away from the appeal in the young man's eyes.

"I'm not saying the idea of the clinic needs to come to an end. Perhaps we'd be better off relocating to a city. Florence. Or Rome, maybe."

"I don't understand." Enzo shook his head. "This is your family's land, no? Your heritage." He opened his arms wide. "Being up here at Mont di Mare, breathing the mountain air, seeing the sea, being part of the sky, the meadows—all of it—is every bit as healing as the work I do in the physio rooms."

He tipped his head to the side, as if trying to get a new perspective on Luca. See him afresh.

"You've been working too hard, Dr. Montovano. Surely now that Francesca's father is here you can relax a little. Go enjoy a prosecco on the terrace—"

Everything inside him grew rigid. He'd not yet given himself a chance to process his feelings about Fran—about loving her—and now her father was here.

It didn't matter now whether or not *he* wanted her to stay. With her father here to influence—to persuade, see things through a cooler lens—everything would change.

"Where are they?" Luca strode out from behind his desk.

Enzo put up his hands and took a couple of steps back. "*Scusi, per favore, Dottore.* I thought you knew. She's showing him around the clinic now. Lovely time of day—seeing the sunset from up here."

Luca didn't hear what else Enzo was saying. He was running down the corridor, his blood racing so hot and fast he was surprised he could still see. It didn't matter. Blind. Breathless. However he found her, all he knew was one thing. He had to find Fran.

"Did you notice this, Papa? The date carved into the beam?"

Francesca watched as her father lifted his fingers and touched the date almost reverently.

"It's very beautiful, Francesca. How old did you say the village was?"

"It's medieval."

Francesca whirled around and all but collided with Luca. Her heart rate shot into hyperdrive and the power of speech simply left her. She'd been hoping Luca would stay holed up in the main clinic building, like he usually did, while she gave her father the grand tour. If her pitch was successful she could at least leave with a clean conscience, if not an unbroken heart.

"Scusi?" Fran's father turned, too. "You are?"

"Papa," Fran interjected, "this is Luca Montovano. Remember I told you about him? The clinic director. Luca, this is my father, Vincente Martinelli."

The men introduced themselves with a sharp handshake and the type of solid eye contact that seemed more gladiatorial than friendly.

"It's a delight to have you here, Mr. Martinelli," Luca said solidly, his eyes not affording her even the most cursory of glances. "I suppose Francesca has told you what a mark she has made here?"

Fran felt heat creep into her cheeks as the two most important men in her life turned toward her. She didn't like being the center of attention at the best of times, and it was all she could do to keep her feet from whipping around and pulling her away toward the wildflower meadows she'd grown to love so much. Wildflowers she'd never see again if her father took the bait.

"Of course." Her father gave Luca a discerning look. "Francesca has spent most of my time here so far singing your praises."

"Papa!" Fran protested. Feebly.

She knew as well as he did that she'd been completely transparent. Glowing like a love-struck teen despite every effort to present the clinic as an outstanding business opportunity.

"I was simply…simply making the point that the entire vision here at Mont di Mare is Luca's. From the cobblestones to the first-class clinic. None of this would exist without his insight. His…um…"

Stop talking, Fran.

No, don't!

This is your last chance.

And so she plowed on. Detailing the clinic's mission. The work they'd done so far. The work she would have loved to do if she could stay, but she knew with Luca's talent he'd surely find more therapists. The best, of course. Only the best.

Despite the charge of adrenaline coursing through

her, Fran saw that Luca's eyes softened as she spoke. The gentle light that warmed the espresso darkness of his irises got brighter and brighter as she carried on. Her eyes dipped to his mouth. Those beautiful lips she would never be able to kiss again.

Forcing herself to meet Luca's gaze, Fran charged ahead with her final appeal. If her father saw what she did in Luca he would do the right thing and accept her offer to leave today in exchange for starting a charitable foundation to support the clinic.

"Like yours, Papa, Luca's drive is pretty much unparalleled. In such a short time he has…he has… He's…"

Completely stolen my heart.

Luca's eyes widened slightly, his right eyebrow making that delightful little questioning arc she'd grown to enjoy watching out for whenever his curiosity was piqued.

"I've never seen anyone render my daughter speechless, Dr. Montovano. You seem to have made quite an impact."

"She's made a similar impression," Luca replied, his eyes never leaving hers as he spoke.

"Francesca is very loyal. Always has been," her father replied with a decisive nod.

And then Luca saw it.

The switch.

One moment Francesca was looking into his eyes as if her life depended upon it, and the next…

There wasn't a soul in the world except for her father. The very light in Francesca's eyes changed when her gaze shifted to her father. A steely determination replaced the gentle glow.

Thank goodness he hadn't dropped to his knees. Begged her to marry him as he wanted to.

We could do it. Together we could do anything we put our hearts and minds to.

This was his fault. He'd cut too deep to hold on to her affections. Been too harsh. She was a gentle soul who needed to be cared for as generously as she was generous in giving her heart to others. Again, he'd taken a bad situation and made it worse. *So* much worse.

The clinic had been meant to redeem him, not ruin him.

Luca's lungs strained against the pain. As if his heart was being ripped from his chest.

"Per favore," he finally managed. "Do continue with your tour. I wouldn't want you to miss anything before you both return to the States."

"Return?" Vincente turned to his daughter. "Haven't you spoken with him?"

Fran opened her mouth to try to explain but, much to her horror, her father beat her to it.

This wasn't the way it was meant to happen. She was supposed to be on a plane, heading far, far away from the man who had stolen her heart, before he knew she'd made one last-ditch effort to help.

"Si, Dottore," her father began. "My daughter, as you have obviously come to discover, is fueled by grand thoughts and ideas. She called me with a simple proposal."

"Which is…?"

Fran shivered to hear the chill in Luca's voice. She hadn't done it to hurt him. Far from it. She'd done it for *love*! Emotion choked the words in her throat and all she could do was watch, wide-eyed, as her father continued.

"Francesca said your clinic could do with a large financial injection. A way to get more rooms prepared for patients and increase cash flow. One of the ideas she suggested was to run her own business from here."

"Is this true?"

Luca turned to her, forcing her to meet his gaze.

Fran nodded, wishing the mountain would swallow her up and leave her in darkness. She was no business mogul. It was just an idea.

"It won't work. A single investment," her father continued, seemingly oblivious to the heartbreak happening right in front of him.

"Papa—no!"

"Hear me out, Frannie, I didn't get where I am today by being sentimental."

Fran's eyes darted toward Luca. He'd drawn himself to his full height, dark eyes flashing with emotion. He gave a curt nod. He'd hear her father out, but she knew any love he might have had for her was gone.

"Martinelli Motors isn't all about cars. Did you know this, Dr. Montovano?"

"I'm afraid I didn't. Fran hasn't told me much about you at all."

A hint of coldness shivered down Fran's spine. How could she? She barely knew her father.

"How would you feel about Francesca managing a charitable trust on behalf of Martinelli Motors here at the clinic? As well as her assistance-dog business."

"Papa?" A flutter of hope lit up Francesca's eyes while Luca remained stoically silent.

"Fran's been talking about starting a trust for ages, and I have to say I didn't put much stock in it. But now that I've seen the clinic, the passion with which my daughter approaches the business—"

"This is *not* her business," Luca interrupted.

"No, not now—but if I were to put money into it then she would, of course, become a partner."

"I think there's been a misunderstanding," Luca said, his eyes once again glued to Fran. "There is no part of this business that is for sale."

A pin might have dropped in a city two hundred miles away and Fran would have heard it in the silence that followed.

"Are you crazy?" Fran finally regained the power of speech, her eyes appealing to Luca to use common sense. *She* was the emotional one. Not him.

His refusal to answer made her even angrier. Now he was just being plain old stubborn.

"Papa. *Don't* let him refuse your offer. The clinic needs the trust. I will do anything to make that happen."

Much to her astonishment, her father raised his hand in protest. "I think Luca knows his own mind well enough. I'm not going to force the money down the poor man's throat."

Luca gave him a curt nod of thanks, then turned to walk away.

"Luca, please—wait!"

"I think I've heard enough." He began to stride toward the far end of the village.

"Luca, please," Fran pleaded once they were out of earshot of her father. "None of that went the way it was meant to."

He turned on her, chest heaving with exertion. Fran pulled herself up short, teetering on her tiptoes, reaching out toward him to try to gain her balance.

And that was when it dawned on him.

A truth so vivid it near enough brought him to his knees. He'd been fighting the wrong battle. Fighting a truth that had raged like a tempest within him from the day he'd laid eyes on her.

Love was about faith. Deep-seated belief. And trust.

Fran would never ask her father—a man with whom she was only just beginning to have a proper relationship—to pour money into something, *someone*, she didn't believe in. She saw something in *him*. Trusted *him*.

And here she was, after all the horrible things he had said to her, reaching out with nothing but love in her eyes.

He held out his hands to her and pulled her to him. With every fiber of his being he loved her.

He cupped her face with his hands and tipped his forehead to hers. "Francesca, I've been a fool. You aren't trying to take anything from me, are you?"

"Of course not," she whispered. "I love you."

"How?" His hands dropped to her shoulders and he held her out so she could take a good look at him. "*How* can you love me when I have been so horrible?"

A gentle smile played upon her lips before she answered. "Everything you do is motivated by love."

"And how do you come to that conclusion, my little ray of sunshine?"

"Because a lesser man would have given up long ago," she said, giving a decisive nod. Her voice grew clearer, stronger, as she continued. "A lesser man would've stayed in Rome. Put his niece in a home. Hidden from everything he was ashamed of. Instead you confront the things you hate most about yourself on a daily basis."

"I owe it to Pia—"

"You didn't owe her an entire *clinic*!" Fran said, the light and humor he so loved finally returning to her eyes.

"But her mother, her grandparents—it was *my* fault they were all in that car."

"It wasn't your fault the truck lost control. You didn't

make it cross the median strip. You didn't ask it to crash into you! I know it was awful, but it was *not* your fault."

Luca pulled her close to him, feeling her heart thud against his chest. He drew his fingers through her hair and asked aloud the question he'd wondered again and again.

"How can I deserve you?"

Fran pulled back, eyelids dropped to half-mast, and quirked an eyebrow. "You don't—yet."

"I beg to differ, *amore*, but you are standing in my arms."

"That doesn't mean we've made any decisions yet, does it?"

"About what?"

"About my business. Canny Canines. If you think I'm going to give it up just because you've won my heart you've got another think coming."

"Does this mean I'm going to have to go groveling to your father?"

Fran crinkled her nose. "I thought you didn't want his money?"

"I don't," Luca admitted. "But I *do* want something far more precious to him than any amount of money he has."

A twinkle lit up Francesca's eye. "Oh, yes? And what could *that* possibly be?"

"I think you know exactly what I'm talking about, Francesca Martinelli." He pulled back from her, folding her small hands between his as he knelt on the ground in front of her. "I would very much like it if you would consider becoming Francesca Montovano."

Fran's eyes filled with tears as she nodded. "Yes. Yes, please. I'd love to."

Luca rose to his feet, picked Francesca up and twirled her around, whooping to the heavens all the while.

When he put her down he tipped his head toward her and murmured, "As you're going to be staying awhile, I suppose it would be a good idea for you to agree with your father about the whole Martinelli Trust thing."

Fran's tooth captured her lower lip and he felt her fingers pressing into his hands.

"Do you mean it?"

"I can hardly refuse the opportunity to help needy children, can I?"

"Luca Montovano…" Fran sighed as she rose on tiptoe to give him the softest kiss he'd ever known, "I'm going to love you until the end of time."

He cinched his arms around her waist, pulling her in for a kiss so rich with meaning there was no mistaking how long he would love her in return.

"Forever and ever, *amore*. Until the end of time."

Two years later

"Dante!" Fran clicked her fingers, a proud smile lighting up her face as the dog padded off to the opposite side of the patio and returned with her padded shoulder bag.

"Is he getting so heavy that you can't get out of your chair?" Luca laughed, taking the diaper bag from their latest canine family member and handing it to his wife with a tender smile.

Fran gazed down into the eyes of her son—a teeny-tiny replica of his father.

"Pia's been bringing him to the gym. Getting the other patients to use him as a weight!"

She laughed at the memory of one of the poor girls straining to lift him to shoulder height, Pia leaning forward, her hands ready if he dropped more than a millimeter.

"I think he gains a kilo every other day!" She tickled the tiny tip of his nose. "Besides, why would I want to move when I have everything I need right here?"

"And what's that?" Luca asked, settling into the patio chair alongside Francesca.

"You know exactly what I mean, but as you've asked, I will tell you." Fran held up a hand and ticked off her list on her fingers. "A gorgeous man, a big furry dog, the most handsome son a woman could ask for and, of course, the view."

She reached out her hand, closing her eyes tight as the tickle of sparks that still tingled and delighted her each and every time she and Luca touched took effect.

"The view *is* rather spectacular," Luca said.

When she opened her eyes she saw he wasn't facing the mountains, nor the broad, lush valleys below them, not even the sea sparkling in the early morning sun. Luca—her husband, her love—was looking directly into her eyes.

* * * * *

ITALIAN DOCTOR,
NO STRINGS ATTACHED

KATE HARDY

CHAPTER ONE

FACE the fear.

Sydney faced the fear every single day of her life. Every day she made life-or-death decisions. Abseiling down the tower of the London Victoria hospital, to raise funds for specialist equipment for the emergency department, should be a breeze. She had a sheet full of sponsor signatures, with a large amount of money at stake. There was no question that she wouldn't do it. How could she possibly back out now?

But then she looked down. Over the edge. There was a white stone cornice and then...nothing.

For two hundred and fifty feet.

Back in the department, two months ago, this had seemed like a brilliant idea. Right here and now, she knew it was the most stupid, ridiculous thing she'd ever done. She sneaked another look at the edge, hoping that her fairy godmother was passing with some sparkly dust and the drop would look a bit less scary.

It didn't.

And there was no way that she could make herself walk backwards over the edge. OK, so she had a harness on, and a hard hat. The ropes were belayed, or whatever the technical term was, and the experts weren't going to let her fall. She knew that. All she had to do was go backwards over the edge and walk down the building.

But she still couldn't move her feet.

'It's OK, Sydney. You can do it. Just one tiny step back.'

One tiny step backwards. *Over the edge.* She couldn't even reply to the man who'd just spoken to her: the instructor who'd explained carefully to her just what she had to do to get off the top of the tower and go all the way down to the bottom. Her brain was refusing to process his name. Refusing to do anything.

Oh, help.

She couldn't step back. Couldn't step forwards, either, and let the team down.

Why, why, why had she agreed to be the first person down? Whatever had possessed her? Why had she thought it would boost her confidence in herself? She must've been mad. No way could she do this. She was *stuck*.

Then another man joined the instructor at the edge. 'Hi.'

She'd never seen him before. The part of her mind that wasn't completely frozen in fear thought how gorgeous he was, with eyes colour of melted chocolate, dark hair, and an olive complexion. He reminded her a bit of an actor she had a huge crush on and her friends in the department were always teasing her about.

'I'm Marco.'

And his voice was even more gorgeous than his face: just the hint of an accent, incredibly sexy.

He'd introduced himself to her. Now she was supposed to speak. But, just like her feet, her mouth was frozen and it wasn't going to let any proper words out.

'You're Sydney, yes?'

'Uh.'

Clearly he took the little squeak of fear as meaning yes. 'OK. What we're going to do now is sing together, Sydney.'

What? How on earth was *singing* going to help her frozen feet move?

'How about Tom Petty's "Free Falling"?' he suggested.

Not funny. *So* not funny. And just what any of her colleagues would've suggested. Clearly climbing people shared the same kind of dark humour as medics. *Falling.* Uh. She gave him a look of pure loathing.

He grinned. 'At least you're not doing this face down, *tesoro*. That's a bonus. And singing's going to take your mind off it and help you down, I promise.'

He sounded a lot more confident than she felt.

'If I start, will you join in?'

She managed a nod, and in return got a full-wattage smile. If her knees hadn't been frozen, they would definitely have gone weak.

'That's great, *tesoro*. You're going to sing with me. And you're going to keep your right hand behind your back, holding the static line, and just take one tiny step back. You'll feel yourself go down a little bit, but don't worry, that's fine—it's just the tension in the ropes letting you move. The line's going to take your weight. And then you move your right hand out to your side, and it'll give you the slack to start walking down. If you need to stop, just move your hand behind your back again. Got it?'

She nodded again.

'Excellent. Do you know the song "Walking on Sunshine"?'

She could almost hear it in her head, infectious and upbeat, a real summer anthem.

Another nod.

He smiled and began singing. To her amazement, he even hummed the intro, mimicking the tune of the brass section—and then she found herself joining in.

They got to the first chorus. 'One step back,' he encouraged during the bit where he was meant to sing the 'woh-ohs'.

Somehow she did it. Took a step backwards.

Everything lurched, but then it was stable again.

And he was still singing. Still keeping her company. Still with her.

She could do this.

Her voice sounded thready, but she was singing back. And she was walking. Not on sunshine, but against brick.

How she actually got down the building was a blur, but at last she was at the bottom. Her legs were shaking, so were her hands, and she could barely unclip the harness and move out of the way so the next person could abseil down the building and land safely.

'So are you going next?' the instructor asked.

'Me?' It had been a while since Marco had abseiled. But a building in the middle of London was going to be a lot safer than the last abseil he'd done at home, down the cliffs in Capri. Apart from anything else, they didn't have to worry about the tide coming in and causing problems with landing.

He glanced at his watch. Well, it'd be almost as quick as taking the lift. And nobody was going to notice any creases in his suit caused by the abseil harness once they were in the thick of things in the emergency department. 'I'm not on your list,' he warned, 'so it's going to put you off schedule.'

'Not as far off as we would've been if you hadn't talked Sydney down,' the instructor pointed out. 'So are you next?'

He wasn't technically part of the department for another half an hour, and he didn't have a sponsor form; but that wasn't a problem. He'd sponsor himself for the same amount as any of the other registrars had raised. He grinned. 'Yeah, I'm next. Thanks.'

It didn't take long to buckle on the harness. And going over the edge, he felt the whole adrenalin rush as he stepped backwards into nothing… It was the first time he'd really felt alive since Sienna's death.

By the time he reached the bottom of the tower, the rush had filled his entire body.

And the first person he saw when his feet touched the ground was Sydney. The woman he'd talked over the edge. The woman who'd been full of fear, and still looked slightly dazed.

He unbuckled the harness. 'Hey. Are you OK?' he asked softly.

OK? No. Sydney was still shaking all over. 'Yes,' she lied.

Then she made the mistake of looking up. It was him. Mr Gorgeous from the top of the tower. He'd just done exactly what she'd done, and he wasn't a nervous mess. He wasn't even breaking a sweat.

Get a grip, she told herself, and took a deep breath. 'Thanks for talking—well, singing—me down.'

'No problem.' He looked concerned. 'Are you sure you're all right?'

'I have to be—I'm on duty in a few minutes.' And she would be OK. She never let anything get in the way of work.

He touched her face gently with the backs of his fingers. 'I take it this was your first time?'

She nodded. 'And last. Next time one of our consultants gets a bright idea, I'm paying up and bailing out.'

He smiled. 'The adrenalin rush hasn't kicked in yet, then.'

'What adrenalin?'

'Look up,' he said softly.

She did, and saw someone slowly walking backwards over the top of the tower.

'You just did that,' he said.

'And I was stuck. Scared witless. I froze up there.' She shook her head. 'I didn't think I was scared of heights or anything like that. I've never frozen like that before.' Not even when she'd had the MRI scan and they'd told her the bad news. She'd managed to find a bright side. Up there had been simply terrifying.

'But you still did it. Which makes you amazing, in my book.'

'Amazing?' It had been a long, long while since someone had called her amazing.

'Amazing,' he confirmed. 'People like me, who do this for fun—we're not brave. The ones with real courage are people who do it even when they're scared, because they're doing it to make a difference. People like *you*.'

Sydney wasn't sure which one of them moved first, but then his hands were cupping her face and his mouth was brushing lightly against hers. Warm and sweet and promising—and then suddenly it spiralled into something completely different. Something hot and sensual and mind-blowing.

Or maybe that was what he'd meant by 'adrenalin rush'.

When he broke the kiss, she was still shaking—but this time for a different reason. She couldn't remember the last time someone had made her feel like this. And that in itself was incredibly scary.

'Now your eyes are sparkling,' he said softly.

'That's the adrenalin rush,' she said swiftly, not wanting him to think that it was his effect on her.

'Yeah.' He laughed. 'Well. Good to meet you, Sydney. And although I'd love to stay a bit longer and talk, I'd better go, because I'm starting my new job in less than twenty minutes.'

New job? It had to be at the hospital, or he wouldn't have been up the London Victoria's tower in the first place.

'Nice to meet you, too. Good luck with your first shift. Which department are you working in?' she asked.

'Emergency.'

'Me, too.' It suddenly clicked. *Marco*. She'd been too frozen with fear to take it in before. 'You're Dr Ranieri, our new registrar?' The guy on secondment from Rome.

He inclined his head. 'Though I prefer first name terms.'

'Sydney Collins. And I'm a much better doctor than I am an abseiler. Pleased to meet you—properly, this time.' She held her hand out for him to shake.

Clearly she was still wobbly from the abseiling, because her knees went weak again at the touch of his skin against hers and the memory of that kiss made her skin burn.

'So how long have you worked here?' he asked.

'Five years—since I qualified and did my two years' pre-reg training. It's a really nice department to work in. Everyone's great. Except possibly Max Fenton, who suggested we did this abseil in the first place.' She pulled a face. 'I think I've gone off him.'

Marco laughed. 'No, you haven't. He's a nice guy.'

'His wife's nice, too—Marina. Have you met her yet? She's Italian, too. She's working part time at the moment, and then she's off on maternity leave again in a couple of months.' She paused. 'So you've done a lot of climbing and abseiling?'

He shrugged. 'What can I say? I went through a phase of doing extreme sports.'

'You did that sort of thing for *pleasure*? Are you insane?' She shuddered. 'I'm going to have nightmares tonight.'

He just laughed, and Sydney looked at him. He really did have lovely eyes. And a beautiful mouth. Not that she should be thinking about that kiss. It hadn't meant anything; it had just been adrenalin whizzing through her system. She wasn't in the market for a relationship. Not any more. 'Do you sing many people down like that?'

'Not on an abseil, no—it's usually to distract little ones in the department, because it stops them being scared.'

'Fair point.' It was a technique she used, too. 'Though I normally get them to sing "Old Macdonald Had a Farm" or something like that.'

He laughed again. 'Ah, the song choice. I picked that

one because it's a happy song. It always makes me think of driving with the roof down on a summer day.'

Sydney looked at him and took in the quality of his clothes. It was a fair bet that he owned an open-topped sports car. Gorgeous to look at, a nice guy, and beautifully dressed: he was going to have women sighing over him everywhere he walked.

Though not her. She didn't sigh over men, any more. She'd learned the hard way that it wasn't worth the effort: the only person she could really rely on was herself.

'I take it you're meeting Ellen now?' On his first day, of course he'd be meeting the head of the department. At his nod, she said, 'I can show you to her office, if you like.'

'Thanks, that'd be good.'

Sydney Collins was absolutely gorgeous. Chestnut hair cut into a short bob, eyes the colour of the shallow bay near his family home in Capri, and a sweet, heart-shaped face. Better still, she didn't have the 'look at me' attitude that Marco disliked in women who spent hours on their appearance. Now that she wasn't panicking about the abseil, Sydney had turned out to be good company, lively and bright. He liked her instinctively.

And that kiss… He still didn't know why he'd done it; he wasn't in the habit of going round kissing complete strangers. The adrenalin rush from the abseil, maybe. But his mouth was still tingling, and he'd felt that zing between them when she'd shaken his hand. There'd been a look of surprise in her eyes, so he was pretty sure it was a mutual zing.

His head was telling him this was absolutely mad—he

wasn't looking for a relationship. He didn't want one. And yet his heart was saying something else entirely. That he hadn't felt a connection like this for so long: he should seize the moment and put some fun back into his life.

'Here we are,' Sydney said with a smile as they reached Ellen's office. 'No doubt I'll see you in the department later.'

'Sure. Thanks for bringing me here.'

'My pleasure. And thank *you* for getting me off the top of that wretched tower,' she replied. She smiled again, gave him a tiny wave, and headed off to the department.

So, this was it. Meeting the director of the emergency department again, and starting his new job. Six months of working in the busiest department of one of the busiest hospitals in London. And he relished the challenge.

He knocked on Ellen's door.

'Come in,' the director called. She smiled at him when he walked in. 'Have a seat. Was that Sydney I just saw with you?'

'Yes. She showed me the way here.'

'I gather you rescued her earlier.'

He blinked. 'Wow. The hospital grapevine here is *fast.*'

'It certainly is.' Ellen laughed. 'I guess it's one way of meeting your new team. Syd's not a registrar yet, but she's well on the way and she'll be a good support for you.' She gave him a speculative look. 'And I hear you have a good singing voice. You do realise you're going to get nagged into being part of the ED revue if we can get you to extend your secondment and stay past Christmas, don't you?'

He smiled. 'Not a problem. And maybe I can persuade some of the non-singers into forming a choir.'

'I have a feeling you might just manage that.' She smiled at him. 'Come on, let me show you round and introduce you to everyone.'

He'd met half the team when a trolley came round the corner, a paramedic on one side and Sydney on the other; clearly they were heading towards Resus.

He caught snippets of their conversation as the handover continued. 'Knocked off his bike...helmet saved him...broken arm...ribs...'

Given the situation, there was a very high chance that the cyclist would have a pneumothorax. And he'd dealt with enough cycling accidents in his time to be useful here. He glanced at Ellen. 'Mind if I...?'

'I was going to put you on Cubicles, to ease you in gently.' She spread her hands. 'But if you want to hit the ground running, that's fine by me. And you've already met Syd, so I don't have to introduce you. Go for it.'

'Thank you.' He quickened his pace slightly and caught Sydney up. 'Hey. Would another pair of hands be useful right now?'

'Considering that the driver of the car's due in the next ambulance, yes, please,' she said.

Within seconds Marco had swapped his suit jacket for a white coat. Although technically he was the senior doctor, he knew that Sydney had been part of the team for longer and knew her way round. 'I'll follow your lead.'

She looked surprised, and then pleased. 'OK. Thank you.' She turned to their patient. 'Colin, this is Dr Ranieri, our registrar. He's going to help me treat you.

We're going to sort your pain relief first and make you more comfortable, then we can assess you properly.'

He noticed that she didn't use Entonox; clearly she suspected a pneumothorax as well, so she was using a painkiller that wouldn't make the condition worse.

'Where does it hurt most, Colin?' she asked.

'My arm. And my ribs.'

Colin was definitely getting more breathless, Marco noticed, and finding it harder to speak.

Sydney listened to his chest. 'Decreased air entry,' she mouthed to Marco.

'Needle decompression?' he mouthed back.

She nodded.

His first instinct was to offer to do it, but he wanted to see how she worked; besides, given her throwaway comment about being a better doctor than abseiler, he had a feeling she needed to do this—that she needed to prove to him that she was good at her job and not some weak lightweight who couldn't cope. And he could always step in if she needed help.

'I'll hand you the stuff and keep an eye on the monitors,' he said.

'Thanks. Colin, I know you're finding it hard to breathe, so I'm going to put an oxygen mask on you to make it easier for you.' Gently, she put the mask on. 'At the moment, you've got air moving into the space around your lungs and it's causing pressure. I need to take it off; that means I'm going to have to put a needle in, but it's not going to hurt. Is that OK?'

Colin gave a weary nod.

Marco handed her a cannula.

'Thanks, Marco.' She smiled in acknowledgement,

and for a second Marco was lost in a mad memory about what her mouth had felt like against his.

But this wasn't the time or the place to think about that. They had a seriously ill patient who needed their help.

She inserted the cannula in the second intercostal space, withdrew the needle and listened for the hiss of gas. 'Great, that's it,' she said. 'Colin, now I need to put a chest drain in, to take off any fluid and gases that shouldn't be there and keep you comfortable.' She explained the procedure swiftly to him. 'I'm going to give you extra pain relief so you're not going to feel anything, but I need your consent for me to treat you.'

Colin lifted the mask away. 'Do whatever you have to. I'm in your hands,' he mumbled.

'OK, sweetheart. I promise I'm going to be as gentle as I can.'

Stella, one of the senior nurses, cleaned Colin's skin and covered it with sterile drapes. Marco handed Sydney the syringe and she injected local anaesthetic, prepared the chest drain and then inserted it. He was impressed by how smoothly and confidently she did it; Ellen had been spot on in her assessment of the younger doctor's skills.

He kept an eye on the monitors. 'Heart and BP are both fine. Do you want me to write up the notes as you do the assessment?'

'That'd be good. Thanks.'

She checked Colin over very gently and Marco wrote up the notes as she went. 'Suspected multiple rib fractures,' she said, 'but no sign of a flail segment. That's good news, Colin.' She checked the distal pulses and the sensation in his broken arm. 'I think you've fractured your elbow, so I'm going to refer you to our orthopaedic surgeon to fix that for you.' Finally, she took a sample for blood gases.

'OK, Colin, I'm all done here. I'm going to send you for chest X-ray so we can check out your ribs; I think you've broken several, but hopefully they're not complicated breaks. I also want to check out your arm properly for the surgeon. Is there anyone we can call for you while you're in X-Ray?'

'My wife, Janey.' He rattled off a number, which Marco wrote down.

'I'll call her,' Sydney promised.

'And I'll take you to X-Ray,' Marco said.

'Do you know where it is?' Sydney mouthed, so Colin couldn't see.

'I can read the signs,' Marco mouthed back with a grin.

She gave him the cheekiest wink he'd ever seen, and he was still smiling by the time he got to the X-ray department.

She was working on the driver of the car when he got back to Resus, and sent him off for observation for possible concussion. By the time she'd finished, Colin's X-rays were ready on the system for review.

'Want to look at these with me?' she asked.

'Sure.'

She peered closely at the screen. 'Hmm. Not all fractures show up on a chest X-ray, but it looks as if I'm right and it's not flail chest, so that's a good start.' She grimaced at the X-ray of Colin's elbow. 'That's a mess. It's going to need fixators. I'll refer him to the orthopods and warn them that he's already had a pneumothorax.'

She went back over to Colin. 'I've had a look at the

X-rays. The good news is that your ribs will heal by themselves, though it's going to be a bit painful for you over the next few days. But your elbow's going to need pinning, so I'm going to take you out to one of the cubicles to wait for the orthopaedic surgeon, and he'll take you to Theatre to fix your arm.'

Colin removed the oxygen mask. 'Janey?'

'She's on her way. And if you're already in Theatre by the time she gets here, our receptionists know to call me, and I'll take her up to the right waiting area and make sure she's looked after.'

'Thank you.' His voice sounded choked. 'I…'

She laid her hand on his uninjured arm to reassure him. 'It's OK. That's what I'm here for. You're going to be sore for a while, but it could've been an awful lot worse. Everything's going to be fine now,' she soothed.

The rest of the shift was equally busy, and Marco thoroughly enjoyed the rush and the challenge. Moving to London for six months was the best thing he could've done. There were no memories here, no ghosts to haunt him. And maybe, just maybe, he could finally start to move on with his life after two years of being numbed by guilt.

At the end of the shift, he saw Sydney outside the restroom. 'Hi.'

'Hi.' She smiled at him. 'So did you enjoy your first day?'

'Yes. You were right—it's a nice department.' He smiled back. 'And you're definitely a better doctor than you are an abseiler.' He'd liked the way she worked: confident, efficient, but most importantly putting the patients first and making them comfortable. Her people skills were top-notch. 'I was wondering—are you busy?'

She looked slightly wary. 'Busy?'

'If you're not, I thought maybe we could do something tonight.'

Her expression grew warier still. 'What, a welcome to the team thing?'

'No, just you and me.' He paused. There was a question he really had to ask before this went any further. 'Unless you have a significant other?'

CHAPTER TWO

SYDNEY'S head was telling her that this was a bad, bad idea. Going out with Marco—just the two of them. But she couldn't get that kiss out of her head. The way he'd made her feel, those little sparkles of pleasure running through her as his mouth had moved over hers. Maybe it was the adrenalin rush from the abseil still scrambling her common sense, but it had been too long since she'd let herself have fun.

He was only going to be at the London Victoria for six months. And he was asking her out on a date, not suggesting a long-term commitment. So on a need-to-know basis he didn't actually have to know about her neurofibromatosis, did he?

There was only one other reason she could think of why she ought to say no. 'We work together. It's usually not a good idea to date someone in your department,' she hedged. 'Things can get a bit—well, awkward.'

'We're both adults,' he said softly, 'and I think we can be professional enough to keep what happens outside work completely separate from what happens inside work.' He paused, keeping eye contact. 'So will you have dinner with me tonight?'

Clearly the adrenalin from the abseil was still

affecting her head, because Sydney found herself returning his smile. 'Thank you. I'd like that.'

'How about we go out now, straight from work?' he suggested. 'Then neither of us has to go home, dress up and drag ourselves out again.'

She looked at him with raised eyebrows. 'Marco, you're already way more dressed up than anyone else in the department. I hate to think what your definition of "dressing up" might be.'

He laughed. 'Before they retired, my parents designed clothes. My older brother and sister run the business now, and they tend to use me as a clothes horse—which is fine by me, because it means I never have to drag myself round the clothes shops, and my wardrobe's always stocked.'

'What happens if they give you something you really hate wearing?' she asked, sounding curious.

'They only did that when I dated their favourite model,' he said. 'To make the point that they didn't approve.'

'So you're an Italian playboy,' she teased.

'Sometimes,' he teased back. 'Actually, I'm starving. Where do you recommend we go?'

'Normally if I go straight from work it's to a pizza place or a trattoria.' She raised an eyebrow. 'Not that I'd dare suggest either of those to an Italian.'

He laughed. 'I'm not *that* fussy.'

'Do you like Chinese food?'

'I love it.'

'Good. Then I know just the place.'

The restaurant wasn't in the slightest bit romantic; it was very workmanlike, with bright lighting, but the food was terrific and Marco was glad that she'd suggested sharing several dishes. Well, apart from the fact that their hands kept accidentally meeting as they served themselves, because the touch of her skin against his was sending little flashes of desire up and down his spine—desire he hadn't felt in a long, long time. He had a feeling that she was affected in just the same way, because her pupils were huge; in this harsh lighting, he'd expect them to be almost pinpoint.

He really hadn't expected this. He couldn't even remember the last time he'd felt this attracted to someone. The times he'd dated during the past year had been in a failed attempt to forget Sienna, and the relationships had fizzled out by the end of the second date.

But there was something about Sydney. Something that felt different. Something that intrigued him and made him want to know more.

'So are you enjoying London?' she asked.

'Very much.'

'What made you decide to come to England?'

'It was a good opportunity,' Marco prevaricated. He could hardly tell her the truth—that he'd needed to get away from Rome. Away from the memories, away from the guilt. Two years of toughing it out had just worn him down, and all that trying hadn't stopped the bad feelings. At least here he didn't have to think about it all the time. He could simply block it out, because he and Sienna had never been to London and there were no memories of her here to haunt him. 'It's one of the busiest departments in one of the busiest hospitals in London. It'll be good experience for me and, when I go back to Rome, I'll have a better chance of promotion.'

Last time he'd been promoted, it had ended in heartache. In his life falling apart completely. Next time, he was determined it would be different.

He kept the conversation light until the meal had ended. 'Can I see you home?' he asked.

Her eyes widened slightly. Fear? he wondered. But why would she be afraid of him? Worried that he was taking this too fast, maybe?

'That wasn't a clumsy way of saying I'm expecting you to take me to bed just because I took you out to dinner tonight,' he said softly. 'You're female, and you had dinner with me, so I need to see you home safely. That's all.'

That made her smile. 'That's very gallant of you. Old-fashioned, even.'

'It's how I was brought up.'

'Nice manners. I like that.' She bit her lip. 'And thank you.'

He frowned. 'For what?'

'For not taking this thing between us too fast. I'm…' She took a deep breath. 'I'm not really used to dating. I've been focused on my career.'

'I'm not really used to dating, either.' He'd been in a relationship with the same woman since he was eighteen. Since his first day at university. Until the day two years ago when he'd taken that phone call and his world had fallen apart. 'And I've just started a new job in a new hospital.'

'And a new country,' she finished.

He nodded. 'So. This thing between you and me—no pressure. We'll just see where it takes us, yes?'

'Thank you. That works for me,' she said softly.

When they reached her flat, she looked at him. 'If you want to come in for a coffee, you're welcome.'

'Coffee meaning *just* coffee,' he checked.

She smiled, and he was glad to see a tiny bit of the wariness fade from her eyes. So had she had a bad experience with someone who'd pushed her too far, too fast? Was that why she avoided dating and concentrated on her career—why she'd thanked him for not taking this too fast? Not that it was any of his business; and now really wasn't the right time to ask.

He followed her into the kitchen, noting that her flat was small but neat. There were lots of photographs everywhere, and they were people who looked quite like her; clearly she was as close to her family as he was to his. Another thing they had in common.

'I'm afraid it's only instant coffee,' she said as she switched the kettle on.

'Instant's fine.'

She gave him a sidelong look. 'I bet you only have fresh coffee at your place.'

He laughed. 'Yes. But I've been either a medical student or a doctor for sixteen years, so I've learned not to be too particular. Coffee's coffee.'

'I do have something to go with it.' She rummaged in the fridge and produced a box. 'My bad habit.'

'Chocolate?'

'Better than chocolate,' she said with a smile.

He looked more closely at the packaging, and smiled as he recognised it. One of his own bad habits, too. 'Gianduja. I'm impressed. You're a woman of taste.'

She gestured to him to sit down at her kitchen table, and put some music on: a solo female singer, backed by guitar and piano, gentle stuff that he rather liked.

'How do you like your coffee?'

'Strong, no milk, please.'

She handed him a mug, and sat down next to him. But then they reached for a piece of gianduja at the same time and their fingers touched. He saw the sudden shock in her eyes, the way her mouth parted as if inviting a kiss.

And he really, really wanted to kiss her. Just like he had after the abseil. He needed to feel her mouth beneath hers, warm and soft and sweet and generous.

Except she'd thanked him earlier for not taking things too fast.

So, instead, he took her hand, pressed a kiss into her palm and folded her fingers over it.

'What was that for?' she asked. The wariness was back in her eyes.

'Because I'm trying very hard not to take this too fast,' he said. 'This is a compromise. A kiss that won't scare you off.' A kiss that wouldn't scare him off, either, if he was honest about it. The way she made him feel was unsettling, something he really wasn't used to. His head was telling him that this was a seriously bad idea; did he really want to put himself back in a position where he could lose someone? Hadn't he already learned that the hard and painful way? And yet there was something about her he couldn't resist. Her warmth. Her sweetness.

Colour bloomed in her cheeks. 'I feel like such a wimp.'

'About this morning. Just so you know,' he said, 'I don't make a habit of going around kissing complete strangers.'

'Neither do I.' The colour in her cheeks deepened. 'And I kissed you back.'

And he could see in her eyes that she'd enjoyed it as

much as he had. That she, like him, had mixed feelings: part of her wanted to see where this took them, and part of her wanted to run back to her safety zone. 'Tell me,' he coaxed gently. 'You feel the same thing, don't you? Something you weren't expecting or looking for, and maybe it scares the hell out of you because your head's saying you don't need the complications. But it's there and you can't get me out of your head—just as I can't get you out of mine, and I've been thinking about you ever since I first met you.'

He could see in her expression that she was thinking about denying it; but then she gave in. 'Yes,' she admitted, her voice husky. 'To all of that.'

He stroked the backs of her fingers with the pad of his thumb. 'I like you, Sydney. You're calm and you're good with the patients. I like that. And you're good company—well, when you're not stuck on an abseiling rope.'

She groaned. 'I'm never going to live that down, am I?'

'If I hadn't seen it for myself, I would've said it was a vicious rumour. Someone as calm and confident and efficient as you, panicking. But it's nice to know you're not really superwoman. That you have panicky moments, like the rest of us.'

She blinked. 'You're telling me that *you* have panicky moments? I'm not buying that one. I've worked with you. OK, so you let me lead, this afternoon, but we both know you have more experience than I do. You were being nice and trying to restore my confidence after the abseil.'

Oh. So she'd picked that up. 'Mmm,' he admitted.

'And I appreciated it. Because it worked.'

'Good.' He paused. 'Do you trust me as a doctor?'

'Yes.'

'Well, that's a start. And so's this.' He leaned forward and touched his mouth to hers. Briefly. Sweetly.

And the second he felt her lips part slightly, he was lost. He couldn't pull away. He gave in to the desperate need to kiss her properly. Within moments, she was kissing him back, her hands were cradling his face, and it felt as if stars were exploding in his head.

When he finally broke the kiss, they were both shaking.

This really wasn't supposed to happen, Sydney thought. *I wasn't supposed to be attracted to him. This was meant to be just putting a bit of fun back into my life. Seizing the moment. Enjoying a casual date. And now I'm way out of my depth, because I want this to go further—a lot further—and I think he feels the same way.*

Which means I'm going to have to tell him the truth about me.

Ice trickled down her spine. Down the scar. The physical reminder of the thing that had smashed up her marriage. The thing that had stopped her having a relationship since her marriage had broken up, because the scar on her back and the ugly patch of skin on her arm were constant reminders of Craig's betrayal and the reasons behind it, making her want to keep her distance. And there was no way she could bluff her way through it, because if she went to bed with Marco it would mean getting naked. That he'd touch her. Look at her. He'd either feel the scar tissue or see it for himself—and then he'd ask questions. Of course he would. Anyone would be curious. And then…oh, hell, then she'd have to be honest.

She really owed it to him to be honest now. So he knew exactly what he was getting into, if he started seeing her.

But the words stuck miserably in her throat and refused to come out.

'I'm sorry,' he said softly. 'Well, I'm not sorry for kissing you. I enjoyed it. But I *am* sorry for pushing you out of your comfort zone, for taking this faster than you're happy with.'

'I'm sorry, too,' she whispered. 'For—for being such a coward.'

He stroked her face. 'You're not a coward. I'm rushing you. So I'll go home now.' He took her hand again, kissed her palm and folded her fingers over his kiss, just as he had before. 'And I'll see you at work tomorrow.'

'OK.' She took a deep breath. 'Thank you for this evening. I enjoyed it.'

'So did I.' The expression in his eyes was so sweet, so gentle, that Sydney was close to tears. She ached to be able to trust. To be normal. To be whole.

But that wasn't going to happen. And somehow, she was going to have to find the right words to tell him tomorrow at work.

The truth.

CHAPTER THREE

'HEY, Syd!' One of the junior doctors met Marco and Sydney in the corridor on their way to Cubicles the next morning. 'Got a question for you. Who's the abseilers' favourite singer?' He grinned, looking pleased with himself. '*Cliff* Richard.'

She rolled her eyes. 'Pete, that's terrible.'

He laughed. 'I'll pay up my sponsorship at lunchtime.'

'Yes, and you can pay double if you make any more abseiling jokes,' she threatened, laughing back. 'Though I've got one for you. Two drums and a cymbal abseiled down a cliff. Boom, ba-doom, tssssh.'

'Oh, that's brilliant.' Pete gave her a high five. 'If I have any kids on my list today, I'm *so* going to use that one.'

Yet more things to like about her, Marco thought. Sydney didn't overreact to good-natured teasing, and she thought on her feet. The more he saw of her, the more he liked.

He knew that she liked him, too, from the way she'd responded to his kiss last night. Then something had spooked her. Bad memories, maybe? Perhaps he could get her to open up to him.

Though that made him the biggest hypocrite in the

world, because no way was he planning to open up and talk about Sienna.

Later, he told himself. Work, first.

Their first patient that morning was an elderly woman complaining of abdominal pain. It was a symptom common to a very wide range of conditions, making it difficult to diagnose what the problem was.

'Mrs Kane, I'm Marco Ranieri and this is Sydney Collins,' he said. 'We're going to find out what's making your stomach hurt, and make you much more comfortable. How long have you been feeling like this?'

'A couple of days. I wasn't going to bother you, but then it started hurting when the postman came, and he called the ambulance.'

'May we examine you?' he asked. 'We'll be as gentle as we can, if you can tell us where it hurts most.'

'Yes,' she whispered.

Gently, Marco examined her. There wasn't any guarding or localised tenderness: just general abdominal pain.

Sydney checked her temperature. 'You don't have any sign of fever, Mrs Kane.'

Which ruled out a couple of things, but he still had a few questions. 'I know this is personal, and I'm sorry, but may I ask when you last went to the toilet and passed a stool?'

Mrs Kane thought about it. 'A couple of days ago. I tried yesterday and couldn't,' she said.

Constipation could cause stomach pain; but Marco instinctively knew it wasn't that. There was more she wasn't telling them.

'Can I ask what you've eaten lately?'

Mrs Kane made a face. 'I haven't really been hungry.'

'Have you been sick at all, Mrs Kane?' Sydney asked.

'No. I thought I was going to be, yesterday, but then I had a drink of water and I was all right.'

'Again, I apologise for the personal question, but have you needed to wee more often?' Sydney asked.

'A bit.' Mrs Kane wrinkled her nose. 'But that's my age, isn't it?'

'Could be,' Sydney said with a smile. She caught Marco's eye. 'Quick word?' she mouthed.

'Mrs Kane, we just need to check something out, and then we'll come back to see you, if that's OK?' Marco asked.

At her nod, he followed Sydney out of the cubicle.

'I know appendicitis is much more common in teen-agers and young adults, but I have a feeling about this,' Sydney said.

'I agree. The presentation of appendicitis doesn't tend to be typical in very young or elderly patients—and if her appendix is retrocaecal, then it won't show up as pain moving from around her navel to the right iliac fossa.'

'And needing to wee more frequently—it could be an inflamed appendix irritating her ureter.'

'We're going to have to do a PR exam,' Marco said.

'It'd be more tactful if I do it,' Sydney said.

'Do you mind?'

She shrugged. 'That's what teamwork's for. Keeping our patient as comfortable as possible.'

They went back into the cubicle. 'Mrs Kane, we need to give you an internal exam,' Marco said, 'and then maybe a blood test and possibly a scan to give us a better idea of what's causing your pain—we want to rule out a couple of possibilities.' Diverticulitis and cancer were uppermost in his mind, though he wasn't going to alarm his patient by mentioning them at this stage.

'As an internal exam's a bit personal,' Sydney said. 'Would you prefer me to do it?'

Mrs Kane looked grateful. 'Thank you.'

'Marco, if you can excuse us a moment?' she asked.

'Of course. Give me a shout when you need me,' Marco said, and left the cubicle.

'Ow, that makes my tummy hurt,' Mrs Kane said during the exam.

Bingo: just what Sydney had expected to hear. 'Sorry, I wasn't intending to make it hurt. Let's make you more comfortable.' She helped the elderly lady restore order to her clothes and sit up. 'I think your appendix is inflamed and we're going to need to take it out.' She wasn't going to worry Mrs Kane by telling her, but elderly people were more prone to complications—and there was a higher risk of dying from a perforated appendix. 'Though sometimes we suspect appendicitis and it turns out that the appendix is perfectly healthy, so before I send you off to the surgeon I want to do a couple more tests, if that's OK?'

'Are they going to hurt?'

'You might feel a scratch when I take some blood,' Sydney said, 'but the scan definitely won't hurt.'

The blood tests came back with a high white cell count, and the CT scan showed Marco and Sydney exactly what they'd expected. 'Definitely an inflamed appendix,' Marco said.

They reassured Mrs Kane that the operation was done by keyhole surgery nowadays, so she'd recover relatively quickly, and introduced her to the surgeon, who also spent time reassuring her before taking her up to Theatre himself.

'Good call,' Marco said to Sydney.

'Thanks, but I could've been wrong—you know as well as I do how difficult it is to diagnose abdominal pain in elderly patients.' She shrugged. 'I just happened to read a few journal articles about it recently and they stuck in my mind.'

'Still a good call,' he said with a smile.

There was barely time for a break during the day; at the end of their shift, Marco caught Sydney just as she was leaving the hospital. 'What shift are you on tomorrow?'

'Late,' she said.

'Me, too.' He smiled at her. 'Do you fancy going to the cinema tonight?'

This was where she should make some excuse. Especially as she still hadn't found the right words to tell him about her condition.

But would it really hurt to see a film with him? And maybe afterwards they could talk. Was it so wrong of her to want just a couple more hours of fun, of enjoying his company, of enjoying being someone's girlfriend again? 'That'd be lovely.'

He took out his mobile phone and pulled the local cinema's details onto the screen. 'Drama or comedy?'

Given what she was going to tell him tonight, she could do with some light relief first. 'Comedy—if that's OK with you.'

'It's fine.' He consulted the screen. 'It starts at eight. Pick you up at half seven?'

'I've got a few things to sort out at home. Can I meet you there at quarter to?'

He smiled. 'Sure. I'll buy the tickets and you buy the popcorn.'

She smiled back. 'Deal.'

Even though the film was one she'd wanted to see and starred one of her favourite actors, Sydney found it hard to concentrate. Firstly because she still hadn't worked out a gentle way of telling him about the neurofibromatosis, and secondly because they'd finished the popcorn and Marco was holding her hand.

Just holding her hand.

How could such a light, gentle contact set all her nerve endings tingling? How could it make her whole body feel liquid with desire? How?

By the time they got back to her flat, Sydney was almost quivering with need.

She had to tell him. Now. Before things went any further. It wasn't fair to let him think there could be any possibility of a future between them, when she knew she had nothing to offer him.

'Marco—' she began as she opened her front door.

'I know,' he said softly.

He knew? What? How could he possibly know? The only people at work who knew about her condition were Ellen and the consultants, and there was no way they would've broken her confidence.

And then she stopped thinking as Marco cupped her face with his hands and brought his mouth down on hers. His kiss was soft, sweet and coaxing; every movement of his lips against hers made the blood feel as if it were fizzing through her veins. All thoughts of telling him were gone—until he untucked her shirt from her jeans and slid his hands underneath the hem, his fingertips moving in tiny circles across her back.

The second he touched scar tissue, he stopped. Pulled back. Looked at her, his eyes full of questions. 'Sydney?'

She blew out a breath and pulled away from him, wrapping her arms round herself like a shield. 'I'm sorry,' she whispered. 'I should've told you. I meant to tell you, but…' Her voice faded. How stupid she was to have wanted something she couldn't have. Hadn't she learned from the mess of her marriage to Craig? Her husband hadn't been able to cope with her condition; even though Marco was a doctor, would understand it more, it was still a big ask.

She closed her eyes, not wanting to see pity on Marco's face when she told him. And opened them again when he picked her up, carried her into the living room and sat on the sofa, settling her on his lap. 'Marco?' she asked, not understanding why he was still there. Shouldn't he be backing away as fast as he could?

'That feels like scar tissue,' he said softly. 'And, no, you don't have to tell me about it if you don't want to. I just wanted to be sure that I hadn't hurt you.'

It was the last thing she'd expected to hear, and it took her breath away.

'Sydney?' His voice was so gentle that it brought tears to her eyes—tears she quickly blinked away. She wasn't this weak, pathetic, needy creature. She was a strong woman. A damn good doctor. She'd just made the mistake of forgetting who she was for a little while and wanting something normal. 'No, you didn't hurt me. But thank you for—' The words caught in her throat for a moment. 'For being kind.'

'Kind isn't *quite* the way I feel,' he said.

'I meant to tell you.' She shook her head. 'Sorry. It was unfair of me to agree to date you.'

'Unfair?' He looked puzzled. 'How?'

'Because we can't really see where this thing takes us. I owe it to you to tell the truth—but I'd appreciate it if it didn't go any further than you.'

'Of course.' He frowned. 'You don't owe me anything, Sydney. But if you want to talk, I'm listening.'

She took a deep breath. 'I have neurofibromatosis type two. NF2 for short.'

He stroked her face. 'I'm an emergency specialist. I'm sorry, I don't know anything about NF2. What is it?'

'It's a genetic problem with chromosome 22,' she explained. 'It causes benign tumours to grow on nerve cells and the skin. And although it does run in families, it can also just happen out of nowhere, a mutation in the genes that takes years to show up.'

'One of your parents has it?' he guessed.

She shook her head. 'Neither of them are carriers, and my brother and sister had the tests—they're both fine. It's just me.' And how she'd raged about the unfairness of it, when she'd learned about her condition. One in forty thousand people had it. Why her? What had she done to deserve it?

Then the practical side of her had taken over, kicking out the pointless self-pity. Whining about it wasn't going to change anything. The best thing she could do was make herself informed, to understand what the condition was and how she could work round it to live as normal a life as possible.

'That's pretty tough on you,' he said.

'I'm fine,' she said, knowing it wasn't strictly true.

'So how did you find out?'

'I had back pain and nothing helped. Eventually I had an MRI scan to see if there were any lesions, and that's when they discovered the tumours pressing on my spine.' One of them had been the size of a grapefruit; and the operation had meant that she'd had to take some of her finals papers from her hospital bed. Not that she was going to tell Marco about that; she didn't want his pity.

'Which is why I felt the scar tissue on your back just now,' he said softly.

'Yes. The surgeon operated to remove the tumours, and they haven't grown back yet.' She dug her nails into her palm, reminding herself not to get emotional about it. OK, so the condition was incurable, but it wasn't terminal. It could be much, much worse; it just made her life a bit awkward, from time to time.

And it had blown her marriage apart.

'Are the tumours likely to grow back or cause you problems again?'

'Maybe; maybe not. I get a check-up every year to see how things are. I have a small schwannoma—what they used to call an acoustic neuroma—on both vestibular nerves, but the schwannomas are growing really slowly and they're not causing me tinnitus or anything, so my specialist says we'll keep on with a conservative approach.' She shrugged. 'So I'm fine.'

To her shock, he brushed his mouth against hers.

'What was that for?'

'For being brave,' he said simply. 'For telling me. And it won't go any further.'

And neither would their relationship.

She would've climbed off his lap, except his arms

were still wrapped tightly round her. She frowned. 'Marco?' Wasn't this the bit where he was supposed to walk out?

He kissed her lightly again. 'This doesn't change anything between us, Sydney.'

'Doesn't it?'

'No.'

She couldn't quite take it in. It had changed everything between her and Craig. Changed all their plans. Especially when they'd seen the genetic counsellor. Craig had panicked that the baby would inherit her condition; the counsellor had said that they could go for IVF and screen the embryo before implantation to make sure the baby hadn't inherited the chromosomal problem. Or there were other options: adoption, fostering. They could still have a family.

But Craig had stopped touching her after that day. Not just because of the risk of an accidental pregnancy: he'd called Sydney selfish for wanting a baby at all, because the chances were that her condition would worsen during pregnancy. The way he saw it, he'd be left carrying the burden of childcare and looking after her, too.

His voice echoed in her head. *You're so selfish. You haven't thought how it would affect me—how it would affect our baby. All you can think about is your need for a child.*

A child they'd both wanted. Or so she'd thought at the time.

She'd tried talking to him about adoption, but by then he'd looked things up on the internet, seen the worst-case scenarios and panicked. *How do you know the tumours won't turn malignant and you'll die? And then how am I going to be able to work* and *look after a child?*

He'd countered every argument she had. And then he'd moved into the spare bedroom, saying that he couldn't bear the sight of her arm. It had taken Sydney a long, long time to realise that it wasn't just because her skin was ugly enough to disgust him: for Craig, too, it was a physical reminder of their situation, and he simply hadn't been able to cope with it. And although she hadn't been too surprised when he'd moved out, she'd been shocked to hear his news only a matter of weeks later. News that felt as if someone had reached inside her, gripped her heart in an iron fist and ripped it out of her.

And she would never put herself in a position where someone could hurt her like that again.

'Sydney.' Marco's voice was soft. 'I take it that it did make a difference to someone else?'

She didn't want to talk about Craig. Not now. 'What makes you say that?'

'Because the sparkle's gone from your eyes. As if you're remembering something painful. Something someone said to you, something someone did, maybe. I'm not going to pry.' He kissed her lightly. 'But I'd like to see that sparkle back. The sparkle that was there last night when I kissed you, and tonight when we walked out of the cinema.'

A sparkle that had been there because, for those brief moments, she'd forgotten who and what she was.

Marco was being kind. But she was going to have to face the truth, and there was only one way to do that. Head on. She unbuttoned her shirt and slipped it down over her arm to reveal the large patch of skin covered with tiny nodules.

This was the bit where he'd walk away.

Marco could see it in her face: she was expecting him to be disgusted. To walk away. To fail the challenge.

So his guess had been right. Someone had hurt her badly. And Marco guessed that it went deeper than just that patch of skin. The man had clearly made her feel worthless as well as ugly.

'That's it?' he asked.

'Yes.'

Her eyes were a little over-bright, and he guessed that she was reliving past memories. And yet it was only a small part of her. Something that didn't bother him.

Gently, he reached out and stroked her skin. 'Does it hurt if I do this?'

'No.' Though her lower lip wobbled slightly, as if she was biting back the tears.

'Good. What about this?' He touched his mouth to the area where the nodules were.

'No.' Her voice was shaky, and he glanced up to discover that a single tear had spilled over her lashes and was rolling down her face.

'Ah, *tesoro.* I didn't mean to make you cry. I just wanted to show you that...' He shook his head. 'That this doesn't matter. It's surface. Moles, skin tags, birth marks, port wine stains—they're all common enough.'

She said nothing, but he'd seen the flicker of past pain in her expression. Whatever the guy had said to her, it had really hurt her. And it was about more than just her appearance, he'd guess. He would've liked to shake the guy, break his nose—except that wouldn't solve anything or make Sydney feel better.

He tried again. 'Nobody's perfect. Even a newborn baby often has milk spots or stork marks.'

'But not like this. It's *ugly*.'

That definitely didn't sound like the confident, bright doctor he knew from work; those were someone else's words. Her ex had clearly chipped away at her self-belief. 'Actually, no—it's just part of you. Just like a port wine stain would be.' And anyone who cared about her would accept it, not make a big deal out of it the way her ex obviously had.

He brushed his mouth against hers, and gently helped her back into her shirt. 'Just so you know, I'm not covering your arm up because I don't want to look at you or touch you—because I do want to look at you, Sydney. I do want to touch you. I'm covering you up for one reason only, and that's because right now I can see that you're uncomfortable with your skin being bared. I don't want you to be uncomfortable. I want you to be relaxed with me.'

She swallowed hard. 'I'm sorry. I'm being wet.'

'No. I've clearly brought some bad memories back to you, and I'm sorry for that.' He stroked her face. 'I'd guess that the person you should've been able to rely on let you down—and I'd guess it was when you were at your most vulnerable, say when you first found out that you had NF2.'

'Something like that,' she admitted. 'Though not when I first found out. Later.'

'I'm sorry he wasn't the man you deserved. But it's his loss, not yours.' Marco felt his lip curl in disgust. 'There's more to you than just your skin and your NF2, and beauty's much more than skin-deep.' He tightened his arms round her. *'Non tutti i mali vengono per nuocere.'*

'I don't speak Italian,' she said, 'so you've lost me there.'

'Every cloud has a silver lining,' he translated. 'We're both free. So there's no reason why we can't see where this takes us.'

'And this…' she gestured to her arm, though he guessed that really she meant the whole condition '…*really* doesn't matter?'

'It really doesn't matter,' he confirmed. Though there was one thing he needed to know. 'You said the tumours are benign. So it's not terminal.'

'Incurable, but not terminal,' she confirmed. 'And not contagious, either.' She took a deep breath. 'Though there's a fifty per cent chance of passing it on to a child. Just as well I don't ever want children.'

Her voice was light, but he'd seen something briefly in her eyes before she'd masked it—something that told him that it was a little more complicated than that. Just as it was for him; if things had gone to plan, he would've been a father now. Sienna would've been on maternity leave with their first baby.

It wasn't going to happen now, so there was no point in dwelling on just how much he'd lost. 'Noted,' he said softly. 'So if this thing between us takes us where I think it's going—where I'd like it to go—we'll be careful. Very, very careful.'

She looked completely taken aback. 'You want to…' she paused, as if searching for the right words '…go to bed with me?'

He could tell her in words, but he had a feeling that

the way her ex had undermined her would mean she'd find it difficult to believe him. So maybe there was a better way of explaining. He shifted her slightly on his lap, so she could feel his arousal for herself. 'Does that answer your question?' he asked.

Colour bloomed in her face. 'Oh.'

'Good.' He caught her lower lip briefly between his. 'But I'm not going to rush you into anything tonight. Let's have fun getting to know each other.'

For a moment, he thought she was going to back away. But then she stroked his face, a look of wonder in her eyes. 'Yes.'

He stole a kiss. 'You won't regret this, *tesoro*,' he promised. He'd make sure of that. 'And now, I'm going home. While I still have a smidgen of self-control left. Because, even though I'd really like to take you to bed right now, I think you need a little more time to get used to the idea.'

She nodded. 'I'm sorry.'

'Don't apologise. It's not a problem.' He kissed her again. 'I'll see you tomorrow. *Buona notte*.'

CHAPTER FOUR

THE next day, Sydney was smiling all the way in to work; butterflies were doing a happy dance in her stomach at the thought of seeing Marco. She still couldn't quite believe that someone as gorgeous as Marco had even given her a second glance, let alone wanted a relationship with her. Especially now he knew the truth about her. Yet there had been no pity in his eyes when he'd looked at her, no disgust or abhorrence about how ugly her arm was. Not like the way it had been with Craig.

Dared she take the risk and let herself believe that?

Maybe if Marco didn't want children of his own, this could work out, because then the effects of NF2 on her pregnancy wouldn't be an issue, the way they had been for Craig.

She knew she was rostered on to Cubicles again for the first part of her shift; so was Marco, and her pulse beat just a little faster at the thought. But when she walked into the staffroom and he greeted her with a casual, 'Hi', the butterflies all sank again. She'd expected a little more warmth to his smile. So did this mean he'd spent the rest of yesterday evening looking up NF2 on the internet and now he felt the same way as her ex-husband—that she had nothing to offer him, no future except unwanted complications?

But she did her best to keep a professional smile on her face and treat Marco just the same as the rest of her colleagues. No way was she going to let anyone realise what an idiot she'd been.

Marco glanced at her. 'We'd better go and do the handover in Cubicles, Sydney.'

'Sure.'

As soon as they were out of earshot of the others, he said, softly, 'Can I see you tonight after our shift, *tesoro*?'

She was about to make a slightly sharp retort when she looked into his eyes. They held the extra heat that had been missing in the staffroom, and then she realised that she was letting her past get in the way. She'd assumed that Marco's reactions would be just the same as Craig's. That he'd back off because she wasn't perfect. But Marco wasn't Craig. She'd just been completely unfair to him, judging him by someone else's standards.

'Everything OK?' he asked.

'Yes. Sorry. Wool-gathering. Yes, I'd like that.'

'Good.' And the expression in his eyes was everything she could have wished for.

She dealt with her first case; her patient had tripped on the kerb on the way to work. Her ankle had hurt slightly at the time, and she'd thought she'd just twisted it, but by lunchtime she'd hardly been able to put weight on it.

'I think it's a sprain,' she said when she'd finished examining the ankle, 'but because you can't put weight on your ankle I'm going to send you for an X-ray to make sure there isn't a tiny fracture.'

While she was waiting for the X-ray results to come through, she headed back to Reception to collect her next patient; on the way, she overheard a deep voice saying, 'Wow, you were a very brave girl. Does it hurt now?'

A slightly wobbly childish voice confided, 'It's a bit sore.'

'OK, sweetheart, I can do something about that, but first I need you to make a fist for me.'

Clearly there was some damage to the little girl's hand, Sydney thought, and Marco was checking for nerve damage.

'That's great. Well done. Can I ask you to help me a bit more?'

'Ye-es.'

'There's this song, but I can't remember the words and I need your help.'

A moment later, a beautiful tenor voice began singing 'Old MacDonald Had a Farm'.

So he was using his distraction technique again, was he? Sydney couldn't help smiling. And she was slightly disappointed to discover that he'd finished singing when she called her first patient back again to put an elastic bandage on her ankle and give her advice about resting her ankle and doing gentle physio exercises.

The shift flew by; but finally she handed over to the night shift. Marco was waiting for her by the restroom. 'I heard you singing, earlier,' she said.

'Ah, to the little girl who'd been bitten by a dog. The wound was infected, so I had to clean it and give her a tetanus shot, as well as antibiotics. I thought it might be wise to start the distraction technique early.'

Marco was excellent at distraction. She knew that, first-hand. 'So did it work?'

He smiled back. 'It helped that I had a different song. I was getting a bit bored with my repertoire.'

'"Incey Wincey Spider" is a good one—as long as the child isn't scared of spiders, that is.'

'I don't know that one. You'll have to teach me.' He raised an eyebrow. 'I'm happy to pay your fees in kisses.' He glanced around, then stole a kiss. 'That's on account.'

Sydney swallowed hard. 'I thought you might have read up on things last night and changed your mind.'

She meant it to come out lightly, but the neediness must've shown in her face, because he said softly, 'I read up on things, yes, but nothing's changed. I just didn't think you'd like the hospital grapevine running overtime about you. That's the only reason I didn't kiss you hello. Properly.' He smiled. 'Well, that and the fact that kissing you would shoot my concentration to pieces and we had patients to see.'

'I hadn't even thought about the hospital grapevine.' But she was glad that he had. When her marriage to Craig had collapsed, the news had been round her old department in what felt like seconds, and she'd hated the fact that people were talking about her. Even though she liked her colleagues, she didn't want to be the subject of gossip.

'So how about I cook dinner for us?'

She blinked. 'You cook?'

He laughed. 'Italian men are very good at three things. Singing, cooking, and...' He drew nearer and whispered in her ear, 'Making love.'

She felt the colour flood into her face and heat coiled

deep in her belly. Was that what he was planning tonight? Making love with her? Anticipation, excitement and fear mingled, sending a shiver down her spine. And they grew stronger as they headed back to his flat.

'Um—can we stop off at the shops so I can buy some wine?' she asked.

'There's no need, *tesoro*. I have wine.'

She coughed. 'Someone insisted on seeing me home last night because that was the way he was brought up. And I was brought up to take flowers, chocolates or wine as a gift if someone's cooking dinner for me.'

'Fair point.' He smiled at her. 'But I'd still rather not stop. If it makes you feel better, maybe you can cook me dinner some time.'

He clearly wasn't going to budge, so there was no point in making a fuss about it. 'OK,' she said, keeping her tone as casual as his.

'Good.'

He led her up the steps to his front door and unlocked it, then ushered her inside and shed his suit jacket. 'Come and sit in the kitchen with me and have a glass of wine. It won't take long to make dinner.' He paused. 'Before I start—are you vegetarian?'

'No. I like most foods—with the exception of Brussels sprouts.' She grimaced. 'My mum always insists that we eat three with our Christmas lunch, because it's traditional.'

He laughed. 'That sounds like a challenge. And I bet I can serve you sprouts and you'd enjoy them.'

'And the stakes are?'

His eyes glittered, and her heart missed a beat. She'd just offered him a challenge. And she was pretty sure that his answer was going to involve sex.

He bent to nuzzle her ear. 'Loser...'

Her mouth went dry, and she could barely breathe.

'...makes pudding.'

Now, that she hadn't expected. And she didn't know whether to laugh, be embarrassed or kiss him, he'd tipped her so completely off balance.

He gestured to the chair next to the small bistro table in his kitchen. 'So, can I pour you some wine? Red or white?'

'I don't mind—whatever goes best with the meal.'

'White,' he said, and took a bottle from the fridge. He poured them both a glass, then lifted his own in a toast. 'To us.'

'To us,' she mumbled, her stomach in knots. A man like Marco Ranieri must be used to dating gorgeous women. She was flawed. Would she live up to his expectations?

'Of course you will.'

Sydney was horrified. 'Oh, no. Please tell me I didn't say that out loud.'

'You did.' He leaned down to kiss her lightly. 'And I'm glad you did, because now I know what's worrying you. Yes, I've dated gorgeous women. And you happen to be gorgeous, so there's no change there.' He lifted a hand to forestall her protest. 'And, yes, I know you have some nodules on one tiny patch of skin.'

Tiny? It was huge, the reason she couldn't even wear a short-sleeved T-shirt.

'I'm not that shallow, *tesoro*,' he said softly. 'I'm interested in the whole package. And I might point out that the ancient Persian rug-makers always wove a flaw into every rug, because nothing is ever perfect.'

She blew out a breath. 'Sorry. That was *really* wet of me.'

He looked thoughtful. 'No. In your shoes, I think I'd find it hard to trust. And you have no idea how good it makes me feel that you're taking a chance on me.' He smiled. 'And now I'm going to feed you.'

'Can I give you a hand with anything?'

'No, you're fine. Just chat to me.'

Sydney thoroughly enjoyed watching Marco cook; he was deft and efficient. Not to mention very easy on the eyes, particularly when he got rid of his tie, undid his top button and rolled his sleeves up. In a suit at work, he was gorgeous; but, here and now, slightly more dishevelled, he looked touchable. Mouthwateringly so.

And dinner was far better than she'd expected: a perfectly presented *tricolore* salad, pasta with pesto, chicken *parmigiana* with steamed green vegetables, and then strawberries and the nicest ice cream Sydney had ever tasted. 'That was fantastic,' she said. 'And you must let me do the washing up.'

'No chance,' he said with a smile.

'Territorial about your kitchen, are you?'

'No. I can think of better uses of our time.'

Her heart skipped a beat at the heat in his eyes.

He made coffee—using a proper espresso machine, she noticed with amusement—and then ushered her through to his living room. She noticed the state-of-the-art TV, music system and games console dominating the room; but there were also full bookshelves, and a guitar propped against one wall.

'Do you play classical or pop?' she asked, indicating the guitar.

'Both. My parents made me have music lessons at

school. I moaned at the time, but I'm glad they did. It's a good way of getting rid of stress.'

'Would you play something for me?'

'Later, sure.'

There were photographs on the mantelpiece; she gestured towards them. 'Can I be nosey?'

'Of course.'

She set her coffee on the low table and took a closer look at the photographs.

'Your parents, your brother and sister?' she guessed, seeing the family resemblance immediately.

'Yes. My brother, Roberto, and my sister, Vittoria. Roberto's the one who runs the business side of things, and Vittoria's the designer—she's incredibly talented.' He came to stand behind her and wrapped one arm round her waist, drawing her back against his body. 'That was taken last summer, in my parents' garden at Capri.'

Overlooking the sea. 'I don't think I've ever seen a sea so blue,' she said.

'Capri's something else,' he agreed. 'I trained in Rome, and I stayed there when I qualified because there were good opportunities there, but I always think of Capri as home. It's where I grew up.' With his free hand, he gently replaced the photograph on the mantelpiece, then turned her to face him. 'Sydney. I know I'm rushing things, but I've been dying to do this all evening and I don't think I can wait any more.'

He kissed her, his mouth sweet and soft and coaxing as it moved against hers; and then, when he deepened the kiss, it felt as if stars were exploding in her head.

Sydney had no idea when or how he'd manoeuvred them over to the sofa, but the next thing she knew she was sitting on his lap, her hands were thrust through his hair, and he'd slid his hands under the hem of her long-sleeved T-shirt and was stroking her abdomen. The more he touched her, the more she wanted him to touch her. And she really, really wanted to touch him. She untucked his shirt from his trousers and began to explore his skin. It was so soft under her fingertips, and yet his body was lean and muscular; clearly he looked after himself. She felt him unsnap her bra, and then he rolled so that she was lying on the sofa and he was kneeling between her thighs.

'You feel gorgeous,' he said as he nuzzled her abdomen. He gradually kissed his way higher; she slid her hands back into his hair and urged him on as his mouth found one nipple. It had been so long, so long since someone had touched her like this, made her feel so amazing...

And then she became aware that he was lifting her slightly so he could take her T-shirt off.

Meaning her arm would be bare, in full view.

She waited for him to recoil. Except he didn't. He kissed her lightly. 'I'm sorry, *tesoro*, I'm rushing you. I'll stop.'

'Yes. No.' She grimaced. 'Sorry, I'm a mess—I'm not used to feeling this way.' She stroked his face with a shaking hand. 'And you're so perfect.'

Perfect? If only she knew the truth about him, Marco thought. But, if she did, he knew she'd put the barriers straight up between them again. And he wouldn't blame her. She'd had a rough time over the past few years and she needed a man she could rely on. He was far from being Dr Reliable—he'd let his wife down in the worst possible way. And how did he know that he wouldn't let Sydney down, the way he'd let Sienna down?

'Nobody's perfect,' he said lightly. 'Certainly not me.'

'Marco, I...' She swallowed hard. 'I do want you. I do want this. But...'

He knew what she wasn't saying. That she felt self-conscious. Awkward. Embarrassed.

'I might just have a solution. And it's because I want you to relax with me, not because I have issues about your skin or your NF2—just so you're clear on that, I don't have any issues at all.' Except commitment issues. Been there, got it badly wrong, and never wanted anyone to pay that kind of price again. But keeping this relationship light and fun didn't mean he could just be selfish and ignore Sydney's needs.

He sat up, finished unbuttoning his shirt and took it off. 'How about I close my eyes while you take your top off and put this on?'

Colour slashed over her cheekbones. 'I'm sorry. I'm being ridiculous.'

'No, you're tense. And I want you to feel amazing, not worried.' He stole a kiss. 'One thing, *tesoro*. Leave the shirt unbuttoned. That way, your arm's covered so you don't feel awkward, but I still get the pleasure of seeing you.'

He'd lied about not being perfect, Sydney thought. Because he'd come up with the best possible solution to her worries. And she really, really appreciated his sensitivity. 'Thank you.'

'Tell me when I can look,' he said softly, and the heat in his gaze sent a thrill down her spine.

Swiftly, she stripped off her T-shirt and bra, then slid his shirt on, like a jacket. It still held the warmth of his body, and she could smell his clean, masculine scent. It felt like being held, being treasured, and tears pricked her eyelids.

'OK,' she whispered.

He opened his eyes and sucked in a breath. 'Wow. Do you have any idea how incredible you…?' He made an impatient gesture with his hand. 'Oh, forget talking.' He pulled her into his arms, kissed her hard, then scooped her up and carried her to his bed.

Sydney was aware of deep, soft pillows and cool, smooth sheets against her skin; but as soon as Marco touched her again the world telescoped down to just the two of them.

She shivered as he undid her jeans and stroked her midriff. He nuzzled his way up to her breasts, and teased her nipples with the tip of his tongue. 'You're gorgeous,' he said. His voice was just that little bit deeper and huskier, telling her that he was as turned on as she was.

Gently, he eased her hips off the bed so he could draw the denim down over her hips. He stroked every centimetre of skin he uncovered and followed it up with kisses as he pulled her jeans down over her thighs, past her knees, over her calves—then started at the hollows of her ankle-bones and kissed his way upwards again.

By the time she felt his mouth grazing her inner thighs, she was quivering. Desperate. It had been years and years since she'd felt like this, a burning need that couldn't be quenched. 'Marco? I need you now,' she whispered. 'Before I implode.'

He stripped in seconds, and retrieved a condom from

his wallet. And then he knelt between her thighs. 'Are you absolutely sure about this, *tesoro*?' he asked.

In answer, she reached up and kissed him.

Slowly, slowly he eased inside her.

She'd forgotten how good this could be—and Marco was more than good. Every touch, every kiss, every caress stoked her desire until she felt as if she couldn't hold on any more. She didn't make a single protest when he gently took his shirt off her, meaning they were completely skin to skin—because that lumpy patch on her arm didn't matter any more. Her legs were wrapped round his waist, he was kissing her, and then her climax hit and everything felt as if it had just gone up in flames. She cried out his name; in answer, his mouth jammed over hers, and she felt his body shuddering against her as he reached his own climax.

He was still holding her when she finally floated back to earth.

'Let me go and deal with this. I'll be back in a second.' He kissed her lightly.

She leaned back against the pillows, hardly able to credit what had just happened. They'd just made love, and he'd kissed her and touched her all over. There was no need for her to feel shy with him. He accepted her for who she was. What she was. Flaws and all. And that was what made the tears so hard to hold back: it had been so, so long since she'd felt this way. Years.

Marco returned to the bedroom, naked and looking completely comfortable in his skin. He took one look at her, sighed, and slid into bed beside her. 'Come here.'

When he pulled her into his arms for a cuddle and stroked her hair, the sweetness of the gesture made her crack. She tried really hard to blink the tears back, but they escaped anyway, dripping onto his skin.

'What's wrong, Sydney?' he asked softly.

How could she explain it? He'd made her feel attractive for the first time in years, and she was finding it overwhelming.

'Did I hurt you?' he asked, looking concerned.

'No.' He'd been gentle. Protective. He'd made her feel amazing. 'I'm just being pathetic.' She dragged in a breath. 'Sorry. It's just…it's been a long time since anyone made me feel this good.'

'If it helps,' he said softly, 'it's the same for me.'

Why would a man like Marco have been single for years? she wondered. He was good company, he was kind, he was more than easy on the eyes—any woman would consider herself lucky if he was hers. 'How come?' The words were out before she could stop them; she bit her lip. 'Sorry. That's prying.'

'It's OK.'

No, it wasn't. She could feel the tension radiating through him. She shifted so that she could stroke his face. 'I'm sorry for bringing back bad memories. Break-ups can be hard.'

'It wasn't a break-up.' A muscle worked in his jaw.

The pain in his eyes made the connection for her. Single, but not because of a break-up; that had to mean something much more final. Her heart contracted sharply. Obviously they'd been happy, and the bottom had dropped out of his world when his partner had died. 'She must've been very special.'

'She was.'

'I won't push,' she said softly, 'but if you ever want someone to listen, I'm here.'

'Thank you.' But none of the tension in his body was gone. If anything, it was worse. He pulled away. 'I'll make us some coffee. The bathroom's next door. Help yourself to what you need. I'll be in the kitchen when you're ready.' He pulled on his jeans, then practically fled from the room.

Oh, hell. She hadn't meant to trample all over his feelings and bring bad memories back for him. She'd shower, then she'd apologise.

Once she'd showered and dressed, she restored order to the crumpled bedclothes, then joined him in the kitchen. 'Sor—' she began, but he shook his head.

'It's fine. I'm sorry. I find it…' he paused and spread his hands in an eloquent gesture '…hard to talk about what happened. But I guess I owe you the facts.'

'You don't owe me anything,' she said softly.

'My wife was killed in an accident, two years ago.' His expression was bleak.

What did you say to someone in the face of such devastation and unexpected loss? She didn't have a clue, but silence would definitely be the wrong thing. All the words she could think of were inadequate—but they would have to do. 'I'm sorry. That's tough, losing someone so young.'

He shrugged. 'Tough things happen to everyone. You just have to deal with them.'

She had the strongest feeling that he hadn't really dealt with it. That coming to London had been an attempt to block out the memories and he still hadn't come to terms with his loss.

He poured her a coffee and added milk. 'Is this OK? Not too strong?'

Clearly he didn't want to talk about it any more. Sure. She'd respect his boundaries. 'It looks fine. Thank you.'

'Good.' He paused. 'So you've lived in London since you joined the London Victoria?'

'Since I was eighteen. I trained in London.'

'So you know the place well.' His smile was slightly forced. 'While I'm here, I'd like to see London properly, and the best way to do that is with someone who knows it. I was wondering if you'd like to be my tour guide, maybe.'

Whether he meant as just a friend, or whether they were still going to see where this thing between them was going, she wasn't sure. But she kept her tone light. 'Sounds like fun. Though where I take you depends on what you like. Museums, theatres, parks…'

'The lot. Definitely the London Eye at night,' he said. 'And all the scientific museums.'

'It's years since I visited them. I'm probably not going to be much cop as a tourist guide,' she warned.

'Then we can explore together. And it'll be even more fun, because it'll be new to both of us,' he said. 'We can make a list and tick things off. Places you've always wanted to see, too, but never got round to visiting.'

Making new memories together, to replace the old bad ones. That definitely sounded good to her, whether he was offering simply friendship or something more. 'That,' she said, lifting her coffee cup, 'is a deal.'

CHAPTER FIVE

By the weekend, Marco and Sydney had worked up a wish-list of places to visit between them; and she realised that she'd forgotten how much fun it was to plan a day out with someone.

She was working an early shift on Saturday while Marco was off duty, so he met her from the hospital after her shift.

'How was your day?' he asked.

'Full of Saturday morning DIY accidents. Hammered thumbs, slipped chisels, and one guy who'll take the five seconds to put on a pair of safety goggles next time he drills something, because it'll save him a trip to hospital and a wait in Reception until we can irrigate his eye to get the tiny bit of plaster out, and then eye drops while we check his scratched retina.' She raised an eyebrow. 'Not to mention the eyepatch and antibiotic drops for the next three days.'

'Ouch. You've just reminded me why I always pay someone to do things like that for me.'

She laughed. 'You must be the first man I know who's admitted to not being able to do DIY.'

'Life's too short to be pompous—and I'd rather spend

my free time doing something I enjoy,' he said with a grin. 'Are we still on for Kew Gardens?'

'We certainly are.'

It didn't take long to get there on the tube and Sydney enjoyed strolling hand in hand through the gardens with Marco.

'It's very pretty,' he said.

'I love this time of year, when the spring flowers are out.' She gestured to the blue carpet of the 'glory of the snow'. 'And these are my absolute favourite.'

'Very English,' he said.

She laughed. 'Maybe you're thinking of the bluebells, and they're at their best at the end of next month—and I'm so going to take you to see English woodland.'

He stooped to whisper in her ear, 'As long as I get a kiss under every tree.'

A thrill went down her spine at his words. She still couldn't quite believe that he enjoyed kissing her—but the glitter in his eyes convinced her. As did the lightest, sweetest, most teasing brush of his lips against hers. 'That's on account.'

The thought of how he'd kiss her later, in private, turned her knees weak.

'So spring's your favourite season?' he asked.

'It's a tie between that and autumn—I love crunching through the fallen leaves on a frosty day.'

'And that would be what, October time? I'm adding that to our list,' he said.

'How about you—what's your favourite?'

'Early summer,' he said, 'when all you can smell in my part of Italy is blossom from the lemon and orange groves.'

'It sounds beautiful.'

'It is. There's nowhere else in the world where I'd rather live.'

His voice was full of passion; and yet he was here in London. Trying to get away from his memories, perhaps? 'What made you choose England?'

'The opportunity to expand my knowledge.'

'Did you ever consider doing a stint with Doctors Without Borders?'

He froze. Oh, hell. The worst possible question she could have asked.

Though it wasn't Sydney's fault. He hadn't told her what had actually happened to Sienna. Sydney wasn't the sort to come out with thoughtless comments or trample on people's feelings. Besides, it was an obvious question to ask an emergency specialist who'd talked about wanting to broaden his experience.

Yet he couldn't bring himself to tell her the truth. To drag up all the pain, the loss, the memories he was trying to keep locked away.

'I thought about it,' he said, forcing himself to keep his tone light, 'but it didn't happen.' This was his cue to ask her whether she'd ever thought about working for Doctors Without Borders, he knew—but he wanted to get off the subject as fast as possible. 'So what's your game plan? Registrar, consultant, head of department?'

'Pretty much. Though I'm also tempted by the teaching side. I like the idea of helping to train new doctors, to give them confidence in their skills and teach them how to see their patients as people, not just as conditions that need to be fixed.'

He nodded. 'Fair point. And I think you'd be good at that. You're calm, you're unflappable, and they'll learn a lot of patient skills by shadowing you.'

To his relief, she didn't push it when he changed the subject back to Kew; as they walked through the gardens, hand in hand, his tension began to ease.

When the first spatters of rain hit them, they headed for the café to take shelter.

He glanced through the window at the sky. 'It looks to me as if it's set in for the day. We'll have to see the rest of Kew another time, I think. Unless you don't mind getting drenched?'

She laughed. 'Are you telling me you're fussy about your hair getting wet?' She reached over to ruffle his hair. 'Actually, you look quite cute like that.'

'Like what?'

'Dishevelled.'

He leaned closer and lowered his voice. 'I can think of a very pleasant way of getting dishevelled…but we might get thrown out of the café, so we'll have to take a rain check on that.'

'Ah, but this isn't rain,' she corrected with a grin. 'It's an April shower.'

He caught her hand and raised it to his lips. 'Shower. That's a nice thought, too.'

He wanted to have a shower with her? Her eyes widened. 'Marco, I…'

'Don't worry, *tesoro*,' he said softly. 'I'm not going to push you into doing anything that makes you feel uncomfortable. Although one day, I assure you, I'm going to make love to you in a shower. *Allora.* What's next on our list? We need something indoors.' He took his mobile phone from his pocket and browsed through the notes they'd made together. 'How about the National Gallery?'

'Good idea. That's a really easy journey from here.'

When they reached central London again, it stopped raining for just long enough that Marco could admire the bronze lions in Trafalgar Square, and then they headed for the gallery.

'Let's go and see the Constables first,' Sydney suggested. 'I love the one with the rainbow over Salisbury Cathedral.'

He dutifully admired them, then took her in search of the van Goghs. 'I have to admit, the Constables were pretty enough, but I prefer these,' he said. '"The Sunflowers" is one of my favourites; it's really good to see the real thing instead of a print.'

She smiled at him. 'I half expected you to be waxing lyrical over the Italian painters.'

He laughed. 'It's not the nationality of the painter that matters; it's whether the painting speaks to me.' How long had it been since he'd visited an art gallery? Or maybe it was more that you never really explored the city where you lived unless you were showing someone around. He and Sienna had been wrapped up in their work and in each other. With Sydney, it was different. And he was enjoying being carefree for once, just having fun and keeping things light.

They wandered round until closing time, stopping here and there to admire a particular painting, then headed back to her flat. It was Marco's turn to wait in the kitchen, sipping a glass of wine, while she made dinner; he was surprised by how much he enjoyed the domesticity. And how much he'd missed it.

'I should've asked you to bring your guitar,' Sydney said. 'It would've been nice to hear you play while I'm cooking.'

'Next time we're at my place, I'll play for you,' he promised.

The food was excellent, but best of all was the pudding.

'I was expecting today to be a bit summery,' Sydney said as she opened the fridge door, 'so I'm afraid this doesn't quite suit the weather. I made it this morning before my shift, though I really should've made you a traditional English pudding—apple crumble and custard or something.'

'This looks nice,' he said as she placed the bowl on the table. 'Trifle?' The top looked like fresh cream, decorated with strawberries.

'Sort of.' She gave him a seriously cheeky smile. 'It's an English twist on a classic Italian pudding. I know strictly it's not tiramisu unless there's coffee in it, but it's the same principle.'

'So what's in it?'

Her eyes sparkled with mischief. 'Guess. If you get it wrong, you have to pay a forfeit.'

'Oh, yes? And if I get it right?'

'Then you choose the forfeit.'

He grinned. 'Sydney Collins, I like the way your mind works.'

She spooned some of it into a bowl for him, and he tasted it. 'Very nice. There's definitely a real vanilla pod, cream and mascarpone. But I can't quite work out what you've soaked the sponge fingers in. Orange juice? White wine?'

'Orange juice, yes; wine, no. So you owe me a forfeit,' she said, looking pleased.

He stood up, caught her round the waist and kissed her lingeringly. 'Will that do?'

'Very nicely.'

He was pleased to see that her cheeks were pink and she was slightly breathless. 'So what's the missing ingredient?'

'Raspberry liqueur.'

'It's a very nice combination.' He finished his dessert. 'Can I be greedy?'

'Help yourself.'

'The problem is, I want you as well.' He scooped her onto his lap and kissed her. 'Though there is a solution.'

'Which is?'

'I take you to bed. And then, afterwards, we eat the rest of the tiramisu.' He paused. 'In bed.'

'That's so decadent.' But she was smiling. 'I like the way your mind works, too, Dr Ranieri.'

'Take me to bed, Sydney,' he said huskily.

She slid off his lap, took his hand and led him to her bedroom. It was a gorgeous room with duck-egg-blue walls, teal curtains and matching bed-linen; the pile of silky cushions on her double bed was covered in a peacock-feather design—strong and vibrant, much like Sydney herself, he thought appreciatively.

She closed the curtains and put the bedside lamp on low. This time, to his pleasure, she let him undress her, though he noticed that she flinched when he took off her long-sleeved T-shirt and bared her arm. To reassure her, he kissed the lumpy patch of skin, then drew her close. 'That wasn't pity, by the way. Like I said, it's the whole package I'm interested in. I like who you are, Sydney, and I like the way you look. I like the way you taste. And I really like the way you feel.'

He skimmed the flat of his palms down her sides, moulding her curves. 'You turn me on in a big way,' he said. He picked her up and laid her on the bed, then tipped her back against the pillows and kissed his way down her body. He loved the fact that he could make this bright, sweet woman wriggle beneath him and make her eyes go hot with desire.

He put on a condom to protect her, then covered her body with his. He couldn't remember the last time it had felt this *right*, the way it did with Sydney. She wrapped her legs round his waist, and he pushed in deeper. She gave a little sigh of pleasure and tipped her head even further back, offering her throat to him. He couldn't resist drawing a path of hot, open-mouthed kisses down her soft, sweet skin. She drew him closer still; Marco could feel the change in her breathing and knew that she was close to climax.

Well, he wasn't ready yet—and he wanted to really blow her mind.

So he slowed everything down. He withdrew slowly, until he was almost out of her, then eased back in, pushing deep, putting just enough pressure on her clitoris to make her gasp.

'Marco—you're driving me insane— I need…' Her breath hitched.

'Open your eyes,' he said softly. 'Look at me.'

She did, and he quickened his pace again. He could see the exact moment that she climaxed and let himself fall over the edge with her.

Afterwards, she lay curled against him.

'Want me to go and get the tiramisu?' he asked.

'No, I'll do it.' She climbed off the bed and belted a silky dressing gown round herself. He half expected her to leave it on when she returned with the bowl and two spoons—but, to his pleasure, she simply handed

him the bowl and took off the dressing gown. Without
flinching. The fact that she was starting to trust him
really warmed him.

Though quite how he was going to get himself to
trust her enough to tell her the truth about Sienna's accident, he wasn't sure. He didn't want to see the disappointment in her eyes when he told her just how badly
he'd let his wife down—and then make the connection
that he'd end up letting her down, too. No, he'd wait.
Let himself enjoy this just for a little while longer. And
then he'd find the right words.

CHAPTER SIX

OVER the next few days, as well as being in tune with each other outside work, Marco found that he was perfectly in tune with Sydney at work, too. She had good instincts and wasn't afraid to ask questions to get the full picture; and she was so empathetic that patients warmed to her and opened up to her.

At Wednesday lunchtime, the paramedics brought in a girl with acid burns to her hands. 'This is Jasmine. She has acid burns to her hand and arm. It happened at school.'

'It wasn't an accident. Leona did it on purpose,' the girl said, her voice hard. 'She's jealous of me. She said she'd make sure nobody ever fancied me again because the acid would burn my face and make me ugly.'

'The other girl's coming in a separate ambulance,' the paramedic continued. 'The police want to talk to them, once you've finished treating them.'

'Do you know what kind of acid it was?' Sydney asked.

'Dilute hydrochloric acid, according to the teacher. I checked there wasn't any metallic contamination and the teacher had them both wash their hands under running cold water. We continued irrigating her skin in the ambulance,' the paramedic explained.

'Thanks. We'll take it from here,' Marco said. 'Can you check the other girl, when she comes in?' he asked Sydney.

'Sure.'

'Jasmine, I'm Dr Ranieri,' he said to the girl. 'I'll check you over, then give you some pain relief before I start treating the burn.'

When the other ambulance came in, the paramedic introduced the other girl to Sydney and did the handover.

'Leona, I'm Dr Collins. If you can let me have a look at your hands, then I'll give you some pain relief. Can you tell me, were you wearing anything else when this happened? A jumper or anything?'

Leona shook her head and bit her lip.

'OK.' Sydney looked at the girl's skin. It was reddened and blistered, though clearly it had been irrigated thoroughly. She gave the girl pain relief, then checked the PH value of her skin. 'I'm just making sure that all the acid's off your skin before I treat you,' she said. 'With a burn like this, your skin is at risk of infection, so I'm going to put some antibiotic cream on and a dressing.'

'Thank you,' the girl whispered.

Her face was still pale; maybe it was simply that she knew that she was in severe trouble and was worried about the consequences of what she'd done to the other girl. But something didn't feel quite right. Given that this girl was meant to be the one who was aggressive and made threats, how come she was so quiet now and not brazening it out? And Jasmine, who was meant to be the victim, hadn't seemed frightened or upset. There had been a hardness in her voice, too.

But, more than that, there was something else that raised Sydney's suspicions that all wasn't quite as it seemed.

'You'll need to come back and see us in two days, so we can see how you're healing. I just need to have a quick word with my colleague, and then I'll be back to see you. Will you be OK to stay here?'

Leona nodded.

Swiftly, Sydney walked over to the cubicle where Marco was treating Jasmine. 'Can I have a quick word?' she asked.

'Sure.' He excused himself to Jasmine.

'Meg, can you keep an eye on Jasmine for us and make sure she doesn't leave the cubicle or anyone else go in, please?' Sydney asked one of the staff nurses, keeping her voice low.

At Meg's nod, she took Marco to the kitchen, where she knew they wouldn't be overheard.

'What's the problem?' he asked.

'There's something not right about this—I don't think Leona threw acid over Jasmine.'

He frowned. 'How do you mean? They both have acid burns.'

She handed him a plastic cup. 'Imagine this was full of liquid and you were going to throw it over me. How would you stand?'

His frown deepened, but he held the beaker as if he were about to throw the contents over her.

'Now, I can see what you're going to do, or maybe you've told me that you're going to throw that in my face and it's acid—so I put my hands up to protect myself, like this.' She demonstrated holding her arms up to protect herself, with her inner arms facing towards him. 'And if I try to knock the beaker out of your hand, to stop you throwing the contents over me...' She lowered her hands and traced her fingertips over the top of his hand at base of his thumb. 'It's going to spill here, and along here.' She traced further, along the side of his arm.

'That's where my patient's injuries are,' Marco said quietly. 'And if you put your hands up like that to protect yourself, some of it's going to splash over your inner forearm.'

'Which is where my patient's injuries are,' Sydney confirmed.

'So the story we've got is completely the wrong way round. Why's Jasmine claiming it was Leona—and, more to the point, why's Leona taking the blame for it?' Marco asked.

'That's what I can't work out. But I wanted to run my theory by you before I talked to her,' Sydney said.

'I agree with you. Go and see what you can find out from her, and I'll have a quiet word with the police, tell them what we think.' Marco blew out a breath. 'What a mess. Poor kid. She's the one who gets hurt and then the blame's lumped on her as well. My guess is, it's bullying that went further than either of them expected, and now neither of them knows what to do.'

Sydney returned to the cubicle. Leona's face filled with fear as the curtain twitched back, and relaxed again when she recognised the doctor who'd treated her.

'Are you OK?' Sydney asked gently.

Leona nodded.

Sydney sat next to the girl on the bed. 'We need to

talk. I know you didn't throw the acid over Jasmine,' she said softly. 'She might be claiming that you did it, but I know you didn't. So what's the real story?'

Leona remained silent, her face white.

'If someone said they were going to throw acid in my face,' Sydney said, 'I'd put my hands up to protect myself. And maybe I'd try to knock the beaker out of her hands. And if that happened, my injuries would be exactly where yours were. If I tried to throw the acid over someone, and they defended themselves, my injuries would be exactly where Jasmine's are. That's what I wanted to discuss with my colleague, and he agrees with me.'

Hope flared in Leona's eyes, and just as quickly died again. 'It's no use. They'll all back her up and say I did it.'

'Who will?' Sydney asked gently.

'Everyone in the class.' Leona dragged in a breath. 'Jasmine's the most popular girl in our year. Nobody's going to take my word over hers.'

'I do,' Sydney said. 'So does Dr Ranieri. And he's telling the police what we think, right now. When they investigate something, they take account of physical evidence as well as verbal.'

Leona shook her head. 'Who are you going to believe? She's rich and she's pretty and she fits in.'

'She said you were jealous of her,' Sydney said thoughtfully.

Leona swallowed. 'She said she was going to throw acid in my face so I'd be covered in scars and even uglier, and then Sean wouldn't talk to me any more.'

'Is Sean your boyfriend?'

'No, he's hers. He was only talking to me, that's all.

He likes the same music that I do. We were talking about the new single by our favourite band. Of *course* he wouldn't fancy someone like me. I'm not pretty enough.'

I'm not pretty enough. The words echoed in Sydney's head. Exactly how Craig had made her feel, because of the lumpy skin on her arm and the scar on her back. Ugly. And it wasn't just the physical appearance—it was what it stood for. The fact that she was abnormal, a woman with nothing to offer.

Though Marco was teaching her to see things a different way.

'Everyone's got different ideas of what's pretty and what's not,' she said softly. 'And sometimes if people tell us we're ugly, we believe them when it isn't true.'

'I'm not trendy like Jasmine. Mum can't afford to buy me fashionable stuff.'

'And, when you're a teenager, that's tough.' Sydney could still remember the awkwardness of those years. 'But as you grow older, trust me, things change. People see you for who you are, not what you wear. Real beauty isn't about looks, it's about who you are and how you treat others.' She paused. 'You're not ugly, Leona. Far from it. And you don't have to put up with anyone who tells you that. That's bullying, and it's wrong.'

'Who's going to stop her? Last time I told, school didn't believe me. She got one of her friends to lie and say I was trying to get her into trouble. The teacher said it was her word against mine and we should both stop being so silly.'

'But she carried on being nasty to you?'

Leona didn't answer, but Sydney could see the pain in the girl's eyes. No doubt she'd had to put up with plenty of spiteful comments and name-calling.

'Something to think about,' she said softly. 'When a bully's feeling weak, they pick on someone else to make them upset.' Which was exactly what Craig had done with her, blaming her for the end of their marriage. Maybe he hadn't intended to bully her, but he'd felt weak and helpless, and the only way round it for him had been to make her feel guilty for something she had no control over. 'And if they're successful in upsetting someone, it makes them feel powerful, so they keep doing it. If you stand up to the bully, they lose their power.'

'I did stand up to her. And look what happened.' A tear trickled down Leona's face. 'I can't go back to school. Not after this.' Her breath hitched. 'And my mum's going to kill me.'

'Your mum,' Sydney said, 'will be horrified that someone's tried to hurt you.' She put her arm round the girl's shoulders. 'I promise, we'll get all the problems stopped. Remember, you're not the one who started this. It's not your fault, and you're not going to be in trouble for something you didn't do.'

In reply, Leona burst into noisy tears, which Sydney guessed were of relief. She drew the girl closer and held her until the sobs subsided.

'Thank you,' Leona whispered. 'I didn't think anyone would believe me.'

'I do. And we're going to get this sorted out.' Sydney patted her shoulder.

The curtain twitched back, and a woman who looked like an older version of Leona came in, looking terrified. 'Leo! Oh, thank God you're not badly hurt.' She wrapped her arms round her daughter.

'I'll leave you together,' Sydney said. 'The police

are waiting to talk to you whenever you're ready. If you need anything, just ask for me or Dr Ranieri.'

At the end of their shift, Marco and Sydney were both drained.

'That poor girl,' Sydney said. 'Jasmine's been picking on her for years. Her mum had no idea and feels so guilty, poor woman.'

'But she knows now, and the school can do something to stop Jasmine's behaviour,' Marco said. 'Especially now the police are involved. They said it's assault intending to cause grievous bodily harm, so she's in serious trouble.' He raised an eyebrow. 'Just as well for both of them that the acid was more dilute than she thought it was—and that there wasn't any metallic contamination. And the teacher acted fast to irrigate their skin and stop the damage getting worse.'

'It's bad enough—Leona might still be left with scars.' Sydney bit her lip. 'And I was the biggest hypocrite in the world. I told her that beauty's about more than looks.'

'Uh-huh.'

'That's your cue,' she said, 'to say "I told you so".'

'There's no point. You already know it's true.' He took her hand and squeezed it. 'For the record, I think you're beautiful.'

'Thank you.' She squeezed his hand back. 'So are you.'

The following Saturday was bright and sunny, and Marco picked Sydney up in a convertible sports car.

She eyed it. 'You bought this just to use while you're in England?'

He laughed. 'I'm not quite that extravagant. It's a hire car.'

'Which you didn't really need to hire. We could've used my car, you know.'

He wrinkled his nose. 'I'm Italian. I hate being driven.'

'That's got nothing to do with being Italian and everything to do with having a Y chromosome,' she retorted, making him laugh again.

'It's a gorgeous day, *tesoro*. Why would you want to be stuck in a tin can when you can feel the wind in your hair?' he asked, and pushed a button to take the roof down.

'Oh, you show-off,' she teased. Though, to his pleasure, she admitted that the drive to Hampton Court was enormous fun and she was glad he'd hired the car.

'So this is Henry the Eighth's favourite palace,' he said as they walked from the car park and he saw the house for the first time. 'It's a gorgeous building.'

'Garden first, while it's still sunny?' she suggested.

'And the maze. Did you know it's one of the oldest hedge mazes in the world, and it takes twenty minutes to reach the centre?'

She blinked. 'You've been reading up on it?'

'And the house,' he confirmed. 'That way I get the most out of my visit, because I know what I'm looking at and what to look out for. So I also know that we can get to the centre by keeping our right hand on the hedge all the way. It's not the shortest way and we'll still come across dead ends, but we won't get lost.' He smiled. 'And I have plans for the dead ends.'

As in kissing her in every one until she was breathless and her eyes were sparkling.

Once they'd had their fill of the gardens, they headed for the house. Marco shivered as they walked through the long gallery. 'For a warm day, it's really cold in here.'

'Maybe that's because it's supposed to be haunted by Catherine Howard,' Sydney said. 'She was under house arrest and escaped her guards—she ran down here to find the king and plead for her life, but she was caught and dragged back through here to her rooms, screaming all the way.'

'Poor woman.'

'Apparently people tend to feel cold and uncomfortable in the same place,' Sydney mused. 'So maybe you just found the bit she's supposed to haunt.'

'More like it's caused by air currents from the concealed entrances. People know the story, so when they walk into a column of cold air they think it's for supernatural reasons, not scientific.'

'So you don't believe in ghosts?'

'Sometimes,' he said, 'you see what you want to see.' He sighed. 'I guess that's one of the reasons why I left Rome. I kept seeing Sienna, except when I got closer I realised it was just someone who looked a bit like her. Someone who had the same hairstyle or the same body shape or wore the same scarf.'

'I know what you mean. And all the memories in a place, coming back to you when you least expect it and making you wish things could be different. That's why I left my last hospital,' she said. 'I hated seeing the pity in everyone's eyes. Here, they don't know the details—just that I used to be married—and nobody makes a big deal about it.'

'It's a lot easier to cope in a new place without any

memories,' he said. 'You can't change the past. You can't undo what you've done—or do what you've left undone.' It was the nearest he could get to a confession of the truth. For now.

As if she understood, Sydney squeezed his hand. 'All you can do is try to move on. Remember the good stuff and learn to let the bad stuff go.' Her smile was wry. 'Which I guess is easier said than done.'

'I guess we're both trying,' he said. 'Sorry. I didn't mean to make our day full of shadows.'

'I know.' Her fingers tightened briefly round his again. 'Come on. Let's give ourselves a break here and enjoy the rest of the house.'

He forced himself to smile, and by the end of their tour of the house had managed to shake his sombre mood.

When he'd driven them back to London and parked outside Sydney's flat, she said softly, 'I was wondering... We're both off duty tomorrow. Do you want to stay tonight?'

He was tempted. Severely tempted. Waking up with her in his arms, in the morning... But that would be taking their affair up to the next level. He couldn't do it. 'Sorry, I need to get the car back.' He could see in her expression that she was going to suggest following him to the hire-car place in her car and picking him up. 'And then I have some things to sort out back at my flat.' It wasn't true, but it was a kinder way of letting her down. He wasn't rejecting her. He just couldn't do this. The guilt and the fear were too much for him right now.

'Sure.' Her voice was bright and breezy, but he'd caught the glimmer of disappointment in her eyes. He hated himself for it; but he also knew that if she knew the truth about him she'd be even more disappointed. It was better this way.

'I'll see you tomorrow, *tesoro*,' he said. 'If it's dry, we'll go down the river to the Thames Barrier, and if it's wet we'll look at our museums and galleries list.'

'Sure. Goodnight,' she said, and kissed him lightly. 'See you tomorrow.'

He waited until she'd closed her front door behind her, then drove the car back to the hire place. When he let himself into his empty flat, he half wished he'd taken Sydney up on her offer. She was right about needing to move on. And, with her, he was beginning to feel that maybe he could find happiness again.

Yet there was a voice in his head saying, *What if?* What if he let himself get close to her, fell in love with her—what if he lost her, the same way he'd lost Sienna? Could he really face going through all that pain again— the days of numbness, of feeling trapped in a flat, grey world where everything had lost its meaning? Days when he'd forced himself to go through the motions, made himself smile reassuringly at his patients when all the time the grief locked inside him had made him want to howl out the unfairness to the sky.

He'd sworn he'd never let himself get into that position again.

And yet he was drawn to Sydney's warmth. The sparkle in her eyes—a sparkle that he'd put there. He enjoyed her company. And the zing of attraction between them when they made love... Part of him couldn't help thinking that life was short and you should just take happiness where you could find it. He was being given a second chance of happiness—one he didn't really deserve, but he was being given it anyway. So maybe he should grab that chance with both hands.

Maybe.

CHAPTER SEVEN

ON TUESDAY afternoon, Sydney was working in Resus when the paramedics brought in a girl who'd collapsed at her sixth-form college and was confused and disoriented. The girl wasn't up to answering questions, but luckily her best friend had come with her.

'Ruby, what can you tell me about Paige?' Sydney asked.

Ruby bit her lip. 'She's been worrying about being fat. She won't touch anything with carbs in it, because she says carbs make you fatter.' She looked anxious. 'I don't think she's been making herself sick, but she's not eating properly. She's said for ages she's got stomach ache, and I thought it was because she's hungry.'

The girl's breath smelled musty and of pear drops; plus there were definite signs of dehydration. Her pulse was weak, and her heart rate was more rapid than Sydney was happy about.

'Do you have any pain anywhere?' she asked.

'Tummy hurts,' Paige mumbled.

Hunger, some kind of infection, or something else? Sydney wondered. 'OK, I can give you something to help with that. First of all, I'm going to put an oxygen mask on you to help you breathe more easily, and then

I'm going to put some monitors on you to help me diagnose what's wrong.'

Quickly, she put Paige on oxygen and hooked her up to the monitors so she had continuous readouts of her blood pressure and heart rate, as well as her ECG.

There was something else she needed to know, and she thought she might get the true answer from Ruby. 'Sorry, I'm going to have to ask you something awkward,' she said. 'Whatever you tell me stays with me, and you're not going to be in any trouble, but I need to know the truth because it'll affect the treatment I can give Paige. Do you know if she's had any alcohol recently?'

Ruby shook her head.

'Has she been taking any kind of drugs? Something the doctor gave her, or something she bought at the chemist's?' She paused. 'Or even something recreational—as I said, you won't get into trouble, but I need to know the full details so I can give Paige the right treatment.'

'She doesn't do drugs. She doesn't even smoke.'

'That's good. Thank you for being honest with me.' She turned back to Ruby. 'I need to take some blood from you so I can send it to the lab, and I need to do a finger-prick test. You might feel a sharp scratch, but that's all. Is that OK?'

Paige nodded weakly.

Just as Sydney had suspected, the finger-prick test showed high blood glucose levels.

'Ruby, I'll need to ask you to wait outside for a little while so I can do some more tests,' she said. 'Do you know if anyone's managed to get in contact with Paige's parents?'

'Yes, her mum's on her way.'

'That's good. And she's very lucky to have a friend like you.'

'Is she going to be OK?'

Sydney gave her a reassuring smile. 'Yes.'

Ruby looked visibly relieved. 'When she collapsed, I thought…'

Sydney patted her shoulder. 'I know. And it's been tough on you—but you did all the right things. Look, there's a drinks machine round the corner. Go and get yourself a hot chocolate, and then you can come back and see Paige.'

'Thank you.'

'Paige, can you hear me OK?' Sydney asked.

The girl nodded without opening her eyes.

'You're very dehydrated, so I need to put a drip in your arm to give some fluids. And I'm going to need to put a catheter in so I can measure your fluid input and output and check how your kidneys are doing. Are you a diabetic?'

Paige shook her head.

'Is anyone in your family diabetic?'

Again, a shake of the head.

Once the catheter was in, Sydney was able to test a urine sample; as she'd suspected, it contained ketones and sugar. Was it because, as Ruby said, Paige had been starving herself? Or was it undiagnosed diabetes, brought to crisis point?

She needed a second opinion.

'Dawn, would you mind staying with Paige while I have a quick word with Marco?' she asked.

'Sure,' the staff nurse said.

To her relief, Marco was between patients.

'I need to pick your brains,' she said. 'What do you know about DKA?'

'Diabetic ketoacidosis usually happens when diabetes isn't controlled—and that often happens before it's diagnosed,' Marco said. 'It's more common in younger patients, it's twice as common in women as in men, and it's sometimes brought on by an infection or another illness.'

'I have a patient with what I think is DKA. The glucose levels in her blood and urine are high.' She took him quickly through the case. 'According to her best friend, Paige has been starving herself, so that might have tipped the balance.'

'It's all pointing to DKA, with those glucose and ketone levels.'

'She's dehydrated, so I'm getting fluids into her. Not too fast, because I don't want her to go into cardiac failure or end up with cerebral oedema. I'm planning to add insulin next, then check her potassium levels, and I'm keeping her on a monitor for ECG, heart rate and blood pressure for the time being.'

'Good plan. I take it her parents are coming in?'

'Yes. Her best friend says that her mum's on the way.'

'Do you want me to get in touch with Endocrinology so we can get a diabetes expert down to talk to her mum, and get the ball rolling on a proper diagnosis and treatment for the diabetes?'

'If you don't mind, yes, please—I want to get back and keep monitoring her.'

'Leave it with me. Call me if you need anything else,' Marco said with a smile.

'Thanks.' Sydney returned to her patient, feeling lighter of heart. Marco was utterly reliable and believed in teamwork; she knew he wouldn't forget to do something he'd promised.

Over the next couple of hours, Paige's condition improved, and Sydney was happy to admit her to the endocrinology ward for overnight monitoring. 'The nurses there are very experienced and they'll be happy to answer any questions you have about diabetes,' Sydney told her. 'And, when you're newly diagnosed, of course you'll have questions—they won't think you're being silly. It's their job to make sure you understand your diabetes and how to manage it so you keep well.' She smiled at her. 'And you're lucky you've got a friend like Ruby.'

'She's the best,' Paige whispered. 'I'm so going to buy her chocolates. Except I won't be able to eat any of them with her.'

'That's true, but you can still share other things. You take care now.' She patted Paige's shoulder.

When her shift ended, she went up to see how Paige was doing, and was pleased to see that the girl seemed brighter.

'I forgot to say thank you. For helping me, and being kind,' Paige said. 'And the nurse—sorry, I can't remember her name.'

'Dawn. That's what we're here for,' Sydney said, touched, 'but I'll tell her. I'm glad you're on the mend. The best days of all are when I can do something to help and my patients get better.' She paused. 'Ruby was worrying that you weren't eating properly. You'll need to be careful, in future, because if you don't eat properly you're at risk of your blood sugar going all over the place and making you feel very ill.'

'The dietician's coming to see me tomorrow,' Paige said. 'I don't want to feel like I did this afternoon.'

'So proper eating from now on, yes?'

Paige gave her a wry smile. 'Yes.'

'Good.' Sydney smiled at her. 'I'll let you get some rest.'

When she went back down to the restroom, Marco had already left. But he'd also left a message on her phone: *I'm cooking tonight. Text me when you're on your way M x*

She texted him back. *Leaving now, will bring pudding with me S x*

She called in to a supermarket on the way to his flat and bought a fresh pineapple and some seriously good vanilla ice cream.

Marco met her at the door and kissed her lingeringly. 'Fresh pineapple. What a treat. I take it you went up to see young Paige?'

'Yes. She's on the mend and knows she has to eat properly in future—and thank you for your advice.'

'All I did was confirm what you already knew.' He slid his arms round her and drew her close. 'Ellen says you have the makings of a brilliant registrar, and she's right.'

'I'm not there yet. I still have a bit to learn.'

He kissed her. 'And you're humble with it—one of the things I like about you.'

'Thank you.' She smiled at him. 'So how was your day?'

'OK. It was my day for arm injuries. Sprains, bangs and a dislocated elbow from a toddler who fell over in the supermarket and wouldn't let anyone touch his arm. I ended up going through my whole repertoire of songs before he'd let me put his elbow back in place. I sent him off with a big smile and a shiny sticker.'

'Oh, bless. You're so good with the little ones.' Then her smile faded. What an excellent father Marco would make. But that was yet another reason why this thing between them couldn't be more than temporary; she wouldn't be able to give him children. Not without a lot of risks—and it just wasn't fair to expect him to shoulder those risks.

She forced the thought away and enjoyed her evening with him, curled up on the sofa together watching a film.

'On Friday, you're on an early, yes?' he asked.

'Yes. Why?'

'Because we're going out.' He paused. 'Dress up.'

Dress up. It wasn't something she did very often. Most of the time, when she went out with friends, the dress code was smart casual. Long-sleeved tops and jeans were fine. And it had been ages since she'd been to a wedding or a christening.

She looked through her wardrobe that evening when she got home; there were a couple of long-sleeved dresses, but they were too everyday.

Help.

At least tomorrow was Thursday, late-night shopping evening, so she'd be able to get something—but she wouldn't have time to look in many shops. A quick trawl on the internet found her a gorgeous long-sleeved lace dress, in a retro sixties look with black lace over a contrasting lining. She scribbled down the relevant details, then rang the shop during her break the next morning to see if they had it in her size. Amazingly, they did, and they agreed to put it by for her. After her shift, she sent Marco a text: *Gone shopping for girly stuff, see you tomorrow S x*

When she tried the dress on, she found it was a bit shorter than she'd usually wear, but Marco had been definite when he'd asked her to dress up. And anyway her legs were reasonable, it was just her arm, and the lining of the dress covered that. It was perfect. She had a pair of black patent-leather court shoes that would go brilliantly with it; and it was warm enough in the evenings now that she wouldn't need a coat or even a wrap.

Marco wouldn't even give her a clue where they were going; anticipation and excitement buzzed through her all the next day. He was picking her up at seven, so she dashed home after her shift and took the time to dry her hair properly and put make-up on.

Marco felt his jaw drop as Sydney opened the door to him. 'Wow, you look amazing. I mean, not that you normally don't look nice. But...' He shook his head and smiled. 'Wow.' The high heels and the length of the dress made her legs look as if they went on for ever. And she'd gone for the barely-there kind of make-up that he knew took a lot of effort.

'I scrub up OK, do I?'

'More than OK.' So much so, that he couldn't help yanking her into his arms and kissing her. Thoroughly. He pulled back to smiled at her, then grimaced. 'Sorry, you'll have to redo your lipstick. There isn't a scrap of it left.'

She just laughed, looking pleased.

He glanced at her shoes. 'We won't be walking very far, but are you OK to walk in those?'

She smiled. 'Marco, I'm thirty years old. I know better than to buy shoes I can't walk in.'

'Not necessarily. My sister Vittoria's heading for thirty-five and she buys impossible shoes.'

'She's a dress designer, so she's allowed to. I'm a doctor. I know how good flat shoes are.'

He laughed and kissed her again, then led her to the taxi.

She repaired her lipstick just before the taxi pulled away. 'So where are we going?'

'The London Eye—I've booked us tickets.' Not just tickets, but he was looking forward to seeing her face when she found out.

The taxi dropped them off on the South Bank; they walked across to Jubilee Gardens, where the London Eye was all lit up as dusk started to fall. Marco led her to the fast-track entrance. 'I hate queues.'

The capsule had two champagne cocktails waiting for them.

'Marco? Why are there only two glasses?' she asked, sounding puzzled.

'Because there are only two of us. We have a private capsule.'

She looked shocked. 'This must've cost you a fortune.'

He flapped his hand dismissively. 'Money's not a problem, *tesoro*. And I wanted to enjoy this just with you.'

Her eyes narrowed. 'Oh, no—is it your birthday and I've missed it?'

He stole a kiss. 'No, my birthday's in March—there's no particular reason for this. It's just something I wanted to do and I wanted to share with you. And really don't worry about the money. When my parents retired, they bought me a flat in Rome in lieu of a share of the business, so I'm not exactly poor.'

'Thank you—and now I know why you wanted me to dress up.'

'Absolutely.' Though he hadn't finished, yet.

They watched as London spread out before them, lit up and beautiful. When their capsule reached the very top of the Eye, Marco kissed her; there was a sweetness and an intensity in his kiss that sent a thrill all the way through her. She'd never, ever done anything like this before, and it was just amazing.

'Thank you,' she said when they reached the bottom. 'That was incredible. I feel like a princess, totally spoiled.'

'My pleasure, *tesoro*. I enjoyed it too. And the night isn't over yet—we still have to eat.'

'Dinner's my bill,' she said immediately.

'No.'

'Marco, you paid for the London Eye trip—and it was more than just a normal flight, it was really something special. The least I can do is buy you dinner in return.'

'No. This is my evening, and I want to spoil you. So no arguments, OK?'

Dinner turned out to be in a very swish restaurant in the middle of the city—with a chef whose name she recognised immediately. 'This place has a Michelin star!'

He shrugged. 'And? I like good food.'

'Don't you have to book a table ages in advance?'

'I struck lucky. There was a cancellation.' He smiled at her. 'Now, stop worrying—just enjoy.'

Their table was by a window with an amazing view over London. The food was fabulous, and at the end they shared a tasting plate of the chef's signature puddings. After some of the best coffee and *petits fours* she'd ever tasted, they took a taxi back to her flat.

'That has to be the best evening I've had in years,' she said.

'Me, too,' he said. 'I'll always think of tonight when I think of London.' He touched his mouth to hers. 'London, and you.' He undid the zip at the back of her dress and traced the line of her spine with his fingertips; she shivered, arching her back and tipping her head back so he could kiss the hollows of her throat.

'Turn round,' he said softly, and she did so.

He gently slid her dress off her shoulders, then kissed his way down her spine as he eased the material down over her hips. Her dress fell to the floor and he smoothed his palms down her thighs. 'I want to touch you, Sydney. Taste you.'

He was still on his haunches when he turned her to face him, so his face was level with her navel; he laid his cheek against her abdomen. 'You're so soft and you smell so sweet.' He brushed kisses across her skin, working his way up; she shivered as he straightened up, wanting more.

He traced the lacy edge of her bra and drew one shoulder strap down, and then the other, before kissing his way along her exposed skin. 'So soft, so smooth, so kissable.'

She shivered. 'How come I'm in my underwear and you're still dressed?'

'Because you haven't taken my clothes off yet.' His

dark eyes glittered with pleasure. 'I'm in your hands,' he whispered. 'All yours.'

'All mine,' she repeated. For now. And she was going to make the most of it.

She removed his tie, then undid the buttons of his shirt; she took her time, retaliating for the way he'd undressed her so slowly. She could feel his breath hitch as the pads of her fingertips teased his skin. Good. She wanted him to be as turned on as she was, as desperate for her as she was for him. Finally, she pushed the soft cotton from his shoulders, letting it fall to the floor.

She leaned forward and pressed a hot, open-mouthed kiss against his throat; he arched his head back, giving her better access, and closed his eyes in bliss as she nibbled her way across his skin.

Her hands stroked over his pecs, his abdomen. 'You look like a model from a perfume ad.'

'Is that right?'

'A really, really sexy perfume ad,' she said.

It was enough to snap his control. The next thing she knew, they were both naked, she was in his arms, and he was carrying her through to her bedroom.

He gently laid her on the bed and switched on the lamp.

Then he froze.

'What's wrong?'

'Condom. It's in my wallet. Give me two seconds.'

Yet more proof that Marco wasn't like other men; he knew she was on the Pill, but he also knew that she was adamant about avoiding any risk of pregnancy, so he hadn't complained about her request to use an extra form of protection.

He came back with the little foil packet, and the

desire in his eyes was so strong that it made her catch her breath.

'Sydney.' He kissed her throat, nuzzled the hollows of her collarbones; in turn she was stroking him, touching him, urging him on.

He moved lower, took one nipple into his mouth and sucked. Within seconds, her hands were fisted in his hair and breathing became much, much more difficult. He moved lower, nuzzling her belly, and slid one hand between her thighs; she couldn't help a needy little moan escaping her.

'You feel hot,' he whispered as he cupped her sex. 'Wet.' He skated a fingertip across her clitoris.

'Now, Marco,' she whispered. 'Please now.'

He didn't need her to ask twice; he ripped open the foil packet, rolled the condom on and slid inside her. She wrapped her legs round his waist to draw him deeper.

'You feel amazing,' he whispered.

'So do you.' Her voice sounded shaky.

'OK?'

'Very OK. You send me up in flames.'

He lowered his mouth to hers in a warm, sweet, reassuring kiss.

Pleasure spiralled through her and it was as if he could read her mind; he slowed everything right down, focusing on the pleasure and pushing deeper, deeper. Slow and intense and so incredibly sexy that her climax splintered through her, shocking her by how fast and how deep it was. As her body tightened round his, it pushed him into his own climax; and it was like nothing she'd experienced before, a weird feeling of being at one with the universe.

He stayed where he was, careful not to crush her with

his weight and yet clearly not wanting to move and be apart from her. And it felt like a declaration. Neither of them said a word, but she could see in his eyes that he felt it, too. Things were changing between them. Could they start to believe in the future?

CHAPTER EIGHT

AT THE team quiz night out at the local pub, the following weekend, Marco ended up sitting next to Sydney. By the end of the evening, his arm was resting casually across the back of her chair.

'So how long have you two been an item?' Dawn asked.

Sydney felt her eyes widen; automatically, she glanced at Marco. How were they going to get out of this without telling a pack of lies?

'Don't deny it. You've both gone red—even you, Marco, the King of Cool,' Dawn teased with a smile.

'We're just good friends,' Marco protested.

Pete laughed. 'Which everyone knows is a euphemism for seeing each other.'

'Looks as if we've just been busted,' Marco said, sounding resigned, and drew Sydney closer.

'We were trying to avoid the hospital grapevine,' Sydney explained.

'*Nobody* can avoid the hospital grapevine,' Pete said. 'At least, not for long. And now we know why you two are so in tune at work.'

'That,' Marco said, 'is because we're both observant.'

'No, it's more than that—half the time you second-guess each other,' Dawn said. 'Pete's right.' She smiled. 'And you're good together.'

'Yeah. She's not bad.' Marco ruffled her hair.

'Neither's he, for a clotheshorse,' Sydney retorted, and everyone laughed.

Afterwards, when everyone was breaking into little groups to travel home together, Marina Fenton caught her arm. 'I'm so pleased for you, Syd. He's a lovely guy, and it's about time you found someone who'll treat you properly.' She paused. 'I take it he knows?'

Sydney knew what she was referring to—Marina was one of the few people who knew about her NF2— and nodded. 'He says it doesn't bother him.'

'Which is just how it should be.' Marina hugged her. 'That's brilliant.'

'Don't start planning wedding bells or anything,' Sydney warned. 'We're just seeing where things take us. Having fun. And I'm fine with that.'

'You don't have to justify yourself to me, Syd,' Marina said. 'As long as you're happy.'

Marco and Sydney walked back to his flat with their arms round each other.

'Are you OK with our colleagues knowing about us?' Marco asked.

'Yes. They're a nice bunch. I don't think they'll give us a hard time.'

'Good.' He let them into his flat. 'Can I get you a glass of wine?'

'Could I be really middle-aged and have hot chocolate?'

He smiled. 'There's nothing middle-aged about chocolate. And you've a way to go anyway before you're middle-aged—I'm not middle-aged, and I'm two years older than you are.' He made a mug of chocolate for her, and coffee for himself.

'So are you going to play something for me?' she asked, gesturing to his guitar, when he ushered her into his living room.

'Sure. What do you want, pop or classical?'

'Classical, I think, please. Something mellow.'

He played her a couple of pieces she recognised.

'Was that Bach?' she asked.

'One of the lute suites,' he confirmed.

'You're really good. Did you ever think about being a musician rather than a doctor?'

He shook his head. 'It's my way of relaxing more than anything else. I wanted to be a doctor from when I was about…oh, twelve or so. I liked the idea of being able to fix things.'

She wasn't surprised; he'd tried to fix her, too. And so far he'd made a pretty good job of it. He'd healed a lot of her scars.

'How about you?' he asked.

'We're not really musical in our family. I sing along with the radio, like most people do, but that's as far as I go.'

'Sing with me?' he asked.

She wrinkled her nose. 'I'm not good enough.'

'We're not making a record,' he said with a smile, 'we're having fun—and anyway, you forget that I've already heard you sing.' He played the beginning of 'Walking on Sunshine'.

She groaned, remembering the way he'd sung her through the abseil. 'Marco, I'm not in the mood for something energetic.'

'Even if I'm not going to make you walk backwards off a tower?' he teased.

'Even if,' she said, smiling.

'OK. Something soft. Do you know this one?' He played the opening of a ballad that had topped the charts a couple of years before.

'I only know the chorus,' she admitted.

'That'll do.' He got her to join in with the chorus, and Sydney was surprised to discover how much she enjoyed it. He segued into another ballad whose chorus she knew. And then he sang another one she didn't know at all, but the lyrics brought tears to her eyes.

'Hey, I didn't mean to make you cry.' Marco propped the guitar back against the wall and then sat beside her on the sofa. He scooped her onto his lap and held her close.

'Sorry, I'm being wet again—but that's such a lovely song. The words are just gorgeous.' All about his girl-friend being amazing, just the way she was—the kind of acceptance she hadn't had from Craig, but Marco could've been singing that song just for her because that was exactly how he treated her. As if she was amazing, perfect, just the way she was.

She stroked his face. 'And your voice is fantastic.'

'Thank you.' He kissed her, his mouth soft and coaxing, and then he deepened the kiss and she felt desire flooding through her veins. She didn't protest when Marco carried her to his bed.

Later that month, a sickness bug hit the hospital. The departments were all running on a skeleton staff, who all worked crazy hours to try and cover for colleagues who'd been laid low with the bug.

Halfway through Sydney's shift, she knew she'd fallen victim—her head felt hot and any second now...

She excused herself to her patient, bolted for the nearest toilet, and just made it to the sink before she was violently sick.

No way was she going to be able to finish treating her patients. And the last thing she wanted to do was to give a virus to someone on top of whatever medical problem they already had. She splashed her face with water, cleaned up the bathroom and then, taking a kidney bowl with her in case the sickness caught her unawares, went in search of Ellen.

One look at her, and the head of department sighed. 'You've got it, too, Syd?'

'Yes. Sorry.'

'Go home. I'll arrange cover.'

'I've got a patient with an ankle injury in Cubicles. I apologised to him before I dashed out, but—'

'The last thing he needs is for you to fix his ankle and send him home with your bug,' Ellen interrupted gently. 'Go home. I'll sort it and let everyone know where you are. Don't come back until you're fully over it, OK?'

'Thank you,' Sydney said gratefully.

She just about made it back to her flat before she was sick again. The only thing she was fit for was grabbing a bowl to be sick in, a glass of cold water, and falling into bed.

She slept for most of the afternoon, and then she was aware that her entryphone was buzzing.

Clutching the bowl, she staggered towards it. 'Yes?'

'Buzz me in,' Marco said.

'No. I've got the sicky bug.'

'And I have the constitution of an ox—as well as rehydration sachets and paracetamol. Buzz me in.'

She couldn't face arguing, so she did what he asked.

'*Tesoro*, you look terrible,' he said when he walked in the front door, carrying a bag of what looked like groceries and a laptop case. Frowning, he laid his fingers against her forehead. 'And you're burning up. Did you take paracetamol?'

'No.'

'I didn't think you would've done, somehow,' he said dryly. 'Medics are the worst patients. Go back to bed. I'll bring you some through in a moment.'

She could hear him moving around in the kitchen, doors opening and closing and the chink of a glass. A few moments later, he came in with a cool flannel and a glass. He gently wiped her face.

'Thank you,' she whispered. 'That feels better.'

'Good. Now, take these.' He gave her two paracetamol tablets. 'I don't need to tell you why.'

To bring her temperature down. Obediently, she took the tablets.

'And now you need to drink this.'

She took a mouthful and pulled a face. 'That's vile. Oral rehydration solution?'

'Because you've been sick, your electrolytes are out of balance, and you know as well as I do that flat fizzy drinks contain way too much sugar and not enough salt and it doesn't work. This stuff does. Keep taking little sips. *Bene*,' he praised as she did what he asked.

He made sure her pillows were comfortable and settled her again. 'You have a bowl? Good. Back in a moment.'

This time, he brought her cool water with a slice of

lime. 'It'll make your mouth feel a bit nicer,' he said. And he'd brought her a pile of magazines. 'I wasn't sure what you liked, so I got you a selection.' He rested his hand briefly against her cheek. 'But if you don't feel up to reading, just rest. I'm going to cook you something light.'

She shook her head, her stomach already protesting at the thought. 'I'd rather not.'

'I promise, *tesoro*, you'll be able to keep this down. Now rest.'

She leafed through the pile of magazines. He'd meant it when he'd said he'd bought a selection: a celeb magazine; a glossy women's magazine; a satirical magazine; and a scientific journal. And it really touched her that he'd made so much of an effort.

Not feeling quite up to reading, she closed her eyes and rested. A few minutes later, Marco reappeared with a tray.

'Chicken soup. Not home-made, I'm afraid, but it's from the deli round the corner from my flat, which is the next best thing. It's light and it's nourishing.'

'Thank you.' She looked at it. 'Marco, it's so kind of you, but I really don't think I can face it.'

'*Tesoro*, you need to keep your strength up. And this is the perfect thing. Just take one mouthful,' he coaxed.

In the end, she managed half a bowl.

'Rest, now,' he directed. 'I'll bring you a drink in half an hour.'

'Marco, I can't expect you to spend your evening here.'

'I'm staying,' he said. 'Because I want to look after

you. And I have my laptop with me, so don't worry, you're not holding me back from anything.'

She blinked. 'You're staying?' Was he saying what she thought he was saying? Taking their relationship to the next stage? 'Tonight?'

'Mmm-hmm. It means I'll need to leave a little bit early in the morning, so I can change at my place—but I'm staying with you until you're better.' He stroked her hair. 'Now, rest. Call me if you need me.'

He was just doing the decent thing and looking after Sydney while she was ill, Marco told himself as he went into the kitchen and ate his own soup. He'd do the same for any of his colleagues.

He told himself the same thing at three o'clock next morning, when he was wide awake, his body curled protectively round Sydney's—and he knew he was lying to himself. He hadn't spent the whole night with anyone since Sienna; the fact that he was here in Sydney's bed had nothing to do with the fact that she was ill, and everything to do with the fact that now he had an excuse to stay.

Part of him wanted to flee from the intimacy, because this was nothing like the casual, fun fling he'd expected it to be. And yet part of him desperately wanted to stay, rather than go back to the lonely life he'd led for the past couple of years. Here, with Sydney in his arms, it felt so right...

But was he kidding himself? If things came to the crunch, would he end up letting her down the way he'd let Sienna down? Could he trust himself to do the right thing for her?

Right then, he had no answers. But he took comfort

in the warmth of her body next to his, her regular breathing, and finally he fell asleep.

Once Sydney had recovered from the bug—which Marco, true to his predictions, didn't get—things didn't quite go back to normal. Because Marco found himself spending more nights at Sydney's flat than at his own. He didn't move in officially; though he kept a spare toothbrush and razor at her flat, and brought a change of clothes if he was working an early shift, simply to make life easy for them. And occasionally at weekends Sydney stayed at his flat, though again she didn't keep more than a spare toothbrush in his bathroom, or brought a change of clothes with her.

It was still a fling, Marco told himself. And they were still working their way through his list of must-sees in London, including walking Beatles-style over the zebra crossing in Abbey Road and getting a passer-by to take their photograph, visiting the Tower of London to see the ravens, seeing all the fascinating specimens in jars at the Hunterian Museum, and then going to see the oldest operating theatre in Europe, in the roof of St Thomas's church.

'It's stunning to think that two hundred years ago surgeons could do an amputation in less than a minute,' he said. 'And with a huge audience.'

'They didn't have much choice, with no anaesthetic or antiseptic available, and having an audience like this while they worked was the only way they could teach their students. Lucky for our patients that it's not like this now.' Her tone was light, but something in her expression told Marco that he'd just touched on a sensitive subject. Of course. She'd had operations to remove tumours on her spine. Two hundred years ago, she wouldn't have survived the invasive procedure.

He slid his arm round her and held her close. 'OK?' he asked softly.

'I'm fine.' Though she sounded just a little too bright and breezy for his liking.

In the middle of the week, he was surprised when she had breakfast with him in her dressing gown. 'Are you on a late today?' he asked.

'No. Day off. Errands to run,' she said. 'I'll call you later, OK?'

She was being evasive, but Marco didn't push it. 'OK.' He kissed her lightly. 'I have to run or I'll be late for my shift. Have fun doing your errands. Dinner at my place tonight?'

'That'd be lovely. I'll text you if I'm running late.' She smiled. 'You know how it is—queues and waiting.'

'Can't you do whatever it is online?'

'No,' she said, but she didn't elaborate.

He found out why, later that evening, when she arrived at his flat.

'Get all your errands done?' he asked.

'For another year,' she said.

He frowned. 'What do you mean, for another year?'

'It was my annual check-up.'

She'd told him she had errands. Not quite how he would've described medical procedures. 'If you'd said, I would've come with you.'

She flapped a dismissive hand. 'Honestly, there was no need. I'm used to it, and there's an awful lot of waiting around. You wouldn't have been allowed in with me for the scans, in any case.'

'I could still have sat in the waiting room with you, kept you company.'

'It's OK. I had a book with me.'

His curiosity got the better of him. 'So how did you get on?'

'I had a scan of my brain and spine, balance tests and eye exams. Just to see what the changes are from last year, and whether we need to act or keep a watching brief.' She smiled. 'There's no change from last time on the schwannomas on my vestibular nerves. So I'm good to go.'

'Well, I'm glad about that. But I wish you'd told me.'

'It's just routine. Nothing scary.' She kissed him lightly. 'Don't fuss. Can I give you a hand with dinner?'

It amazed him, how brave and matter-of-fact she was about it all. But if he told her how remarkable she was, she'd dismiss it. He contented himself with returning her kiss. 'Sure you can. And we need to plan where we're going this weekend. Didn't you promise me some bluebells?'

She smiled. 'Yes. And I remember you promised me, something, too.'

A kiss underneath every tree. He remembered. 'And I always keep my promises.' Well. Almost always. The one time he hadn't… He pushed the thought away. That had been then. This was now. And he needed to be fair to Sydney.

CHAPTER NINE

Two weeks later, Sydney woke feeling out of sorts. She'd slept badly; maybe she'd grown too used to Marco being there at night, because the bed felt too big without him, and she felt lonely when she woke on her own—which was utterly ridiculous and made her cross with herself for being so daft. Yes, they'd become closer since they'd been outed as a couple at work, and more so since he'd looked after her when she'd had the vomiting bug, but it was still only a fling between them. It would be stupid of her to read anything more into it than that.

But she didn't feel herself all morning.

'Are you all right, Doctor?' one of her patients asked as Sydney examined her injured hand.

'Fine, thanks,' Sydney lied through gritted teeth. She could hardly tell the poor woman that her perfume was so strong that it was making Sydney feel queasy.

'You look a bit pale.'

Because she was trying to keep down the nausea. Oh, don't say the sicky bug had returned. Though she wasn't aware of anyone else going down with it again. 'I'm fine,' she fibbed again, and forced herself to concentrate on suturing the nasty gash.

She was still feeling rough in the afternoon. In the

ladies', she adjusted her bra. Maybe it had shrunk in the wash, or something, but it felt too tight and her breasts were sore. And she was going to have to cut back on the amount of water she was drinking, because these trips to the loo were getting ridiculous.

Her breath caught as she thought about it. Sore breasts, feeling sick, frequent micturition… Then she shook herself. Of course she couldn't be pregnant. She was on the Pill, and she and Marco used condoms as well for extra protection. They'd been very, very careful not to take any risks. Babies weren't on the agenda.

And yet she'd had that sickness bug, which would've affected the Pill. Supposing one of the condoms had been faulty?

No. She dismissed the idea as totally far-fetched. How rare was it that there was a problem with a condom? She was probably just feeling premenstrual, that was all.

But the thought wouldn't go away. Every time she said goodbye to one patient and walked down to Reception to collect the next, the question slid insidiously into the front of her mind. Was she expecting Marco's baby?

She was glad that her shift wasn't the same as Marco's today; she needed a little bit of time to get things straight in her head. Starting with buying a pregnancy test in a supermarket at the end of her shift, so she could prove to herself once and for all that she wasn't pregnant and she was just premenstrual and hormonal and grumpy.

She let herself into her flat, put the box on the kitchen table, and made herself a cup of tea. It tasted absolutely awful. Obviously the milk was out of date and she hadn't noticed, because she'd spent the last two nights at Marco's flat instead of at her own. She poured the cup of tea away, got rid of the milk and then picked up the box. Time to settle things and find out the truth.

The test took only a few seconds. She put cap the on the stick and checked the display: one blue line, so she knew that the test was working. The second blue line gradually appeared, and she sagged in relief. Just as she'd hoped. Not pregnant. Now she could stop worrying and get on with her life.

She washed her hands and was about to put the test in the bin when she noticed something and went cold.

The test result couldn't have changed from negative to positive in the space of a few seconds. It just couldn't have done.

But the lines were very dark and very clear, telling her that the worst thing possible had happened.

She was pregnant.

Bile rose in her throat. What on earth was she going to do?

She *couldn't* have a baby. The odds were way too high that the baby would inherit her neurofibromatosis. One in two. The toss of a coin. How could she gamble with a child's health like that? Worse still, if the baby *was* affected, the geneticists wouldn't be able to tell her how severely the baby would have the condition. And the baby might be much more severely affected than she was herself. How could she condemn her child to a life of struggling with mobility and learning difficulties?

She sank to the bathroom floor and drew her knees up to her chin, wrapping her arms round her legs and resting her chin on her knees. It felt as if the bottom had just dropped out of her world, and she was too numb to cry.

Pregnant.

How would Marco react when she told him? OK, so he'd been brilliant with her when she'd been ill. But a short-lived bug wasn't at all the same thing as a pregnancy with possible complications; and in turn nine months of pregnancy wasn't the same as eighteen years of bringing up a child—with or without a disability. Marco was great with kids at work, but that was all part of his job: it didn't mean that he wanted children of his own. Besides, he was the kind of man who liked Michelin-starred restaurants and open-topped sports cars. That hardly went with the kind of lifestyle involving babies and toddlers, sensible cars and family-friendly restaurants with high chairs.

Though he was also a good man, the sort of man who believed in doing the right thing. If she told him she was expecting his baby, she knew he'd offer to change his plans to go back to Italy and he'd stand by her. But she didn't want him to stay with her out of a sense of duty. It'd be fine, at first, but eventually he'd start thinking of the plans he'd put on ice for her. He'd feel trapped, and he'd start to resent both her and the baby for holding him back.

She spent a miserable evening thinking about what to do next—and, however hard she tried, she just couldn't work out what was the right thing to do. Even writing down the pros and cons didn't help. There seemed to be a mile-long list of cons for every option, balancing out the pros.

When the phone rang, she picked it up without thinking, glad of something to distract her from her thoughts.

'Hi.' Marco's voice was warm, and it felt like a hug;

she had to fight back the tears. 'I've just finished my shift. Have you eaten yet?'

'Yes,' she fibbed. She'd been too upset and miserable to eat. And now she was way past hunger.

'OK. If I bring pizza with me, can I come over?'

The idea of pizza made her feel sick, but she said brightly, 'Sure. See you in a bit.'

'Ciao, tesoro.'

Well, she needed to talk to him about it. It might as well be sooner than later. The longer you put things off, the worse the situation became—whether it was a rusty patch on a car, a leaking tap or a medical condition. Better to sort things out as early as possible.

But, when he arrived, she found that all the words had dried up.

And the scent of the pizza made her feel really, really queasy.

'Are you OK?' he asked, looking concerned.

This was it. Her cue to tell him.

Except how did you tell your fun, flirty lover that things had just got a whole lot more serious?

'Just tired,' she mumbled.

'Do you want me to go back to my place?'

Yes. No. Both, at the same time. She couldn't answer.

He frowned. 'Sydney, are you sure you're all right? I know you said your check-up was all clear, but if you've got a tumour that's suddenly decided to grow and started pressing on a nerve and is causing you problems…'

'No.' But that was a real possibility for the future. Pregnancy would affect her condition. The tumours were likely to grow more quickly—and the ones on the vestibular nerves could affect her balance as well as her hearing. She'd be no good at work—she'd keel over all the time. And how unfair would that be on her colleagues? 'I'm just tired,' she fibbed again. *She had to tell him. Now.* But she couldn't find the right words.

'Go to bed, *tesoro*. I'll clear up in here when I've finished, and then I'll join you.'

But she couldn't sleep, even with Marco's arms wrapped round her. She kept plumping her pillow up and shifting to get a more comfortable sleeping position, but it didn't work. She tried willing herself to go to sleep, but that failed, too. Counting sheep was useless.

In the end, not wanting to disturb Marco, she slid out of bed, pulled on her dressing gown, and went to sit in the kitchen. She left the light off so it wouldn't wake him, and sat there in the dark with her elbows propped on the table and her chin resting on her hands.

Pregnant.

With complications.

How was she going to tell him?

She shrieked as the kitchen light snapped on—she'd been so lost in her thoughts and worries that she hadn't heard Marco come in.

'Things obviously aren't OK, *tesoro*, or you wouldn't be sitting here alone in the dark, in the middle of the night.' Marco came to sit beside her. 'You look worried sick. And now I'm worried about you, so will you please tell me what's wrong?'

'I...' A tear leaked out before she could stop it, and she dashed it away.

'Whatever it is, we can sort it out.' He wrapped his arms round her. 'Just tell me.'

She was shaking too hard to talk, trying desperately to keep the tears back.

'Sydney, talk to me. Please.'

She dragged in a breath. 'I don't know how to tell you.'

'You had a letter from your consultant? They made a mistake with the tests?'

'No, nothing like that.'

'Then what, *tesoro*?'

She closed her eyes as she forced the words out, not wanting to look at him and see the horror in his face. 'I'm pregnant.'

Pregnant? Sydney was *pregnant*?

Marco stared at her in utter shock.

She couldn't be.

Given her condition, they'd had to be really careful about contraception. Even though she was on the Pill, they'd used condoms as well, just to be safe. There was practically zero chance of her conceiving.

Except she'd had that sickness bug.

And condoms—rarely—could fail.

And it only took one sperm to fertilise an egg. The only one hundred per cent reliable method of contraception was abstinence.

She was pregnant.

'I'm going to be a father.' He said the words slowly, testing them out.

A father. He'd planned to start a family with Sienna, after their stint at Doctors Without Borders. Except then she'd died in the flash flood and he'd shied away from the thought of ever settling down and having a family. How could he be so selfish as to want that for himself, when Sienna would never have that chance?

'A father,' he said again, still not able to take it in.

'I'm sorry,' she whispered.

He wasn't going to let her take the blame. 'It takes two to make a baby.'

A baby.

Their baby.

'How pregnant are you?' he asked hoarsely.

'I don't know. It's early days.' Her breath hitched. 'I felt funny today. Everything smelled. My tea tasted disgusting. I thought I was premenstrual.'

'But you did a test?'

She closed her eyes. 'I thought it was negative,' she whispered. 'And then I looked again…and it was positive.'

Pregnant.

With his baby.

And Marco suddenly knew exactly what to do, because now everything was clicking into place. 'It's OK, *tesoro*. We'll get married.'

'No.'

He stared at her, shocked. 'What do you mean, no? You're expecting my baby. Unless… Were you thinking…?' He couldn't quite bring himself to say the words. She'd said a while back that she didn't want children. Was she really thinking of having a termination?

She was shaking again. 'There's a fifty per cent chance that this baby's inherited my NF2—and it's a variable condition. You can't tell how badly any individual's going to be affected. I'm reasonably OK, but supposing the baby's affected much more badly than I am? Tumours in the brain can cause fits, vision problems, difficulty with balance. Or spinal tumours on the neck might make it hard for him to blink or smile or swallow. Or he might have spinal tumours like mine, except they might develop at a much younger age—he could end up in a wheelchair. And it's all my fault.'

He could see the panic in her face. And she was thinking about the worst possible scenarios. He needed to get some balance into this, right now. 'There's also a fifty per cent chance that he or she will be absolutely fine.'

'But we don't *know*, Marco. We don't know anything. It's not like an exam, when you know whether you've worked hard enough and you've got a pretty good idea how you did. This is completely out of my—*our*—control.'

He forced himself to say the words. 'So you want a termination?'

She swallowed hard. 'I've been thinking about it all afternoon. How can I destroy a life? It's not what I want. I can't do it. And yet I'll never forgive myself if I've passed this—this *disease* on. Whatever way I look at it, I'll be doing the wrong thing. I can't kill our baby. But I can't… I can't…' The words choked off.

He wrapped his arms round her. 'I don't know what to say. Except it's my baby too, and we'll get married and deal with this together.'

'That's your sense of responsibility talking. It's not fair to you.' She dragged in another breath. 'I don't want you to do what you think is the right thing, and end up resenting me and the baby for holding you back and making you change your plans.'

'I wouldn't resent you.'

'Maybe not right now, you wouldn't. But how do you know how you'll feel in a year's time, five, ten?' She shook her head. 'We've never discussed the future. I mean, this thing between us—we never made each other any promises. We said we'd just see where it takes us.'

'We have—and it's brought us here. It's given us both something we've never expected.'

'I never even asked you if you wanted to have a fam—' Her voice broke.

He stroked her face. 'Yes, I did. Sienna and I were going to try for a family after we'd worked at Doctors Without Borders. And then...' He sighed. 'After she died, I put it out of my head. Even when I started to date again, it wasn't something I let myself think about. It seemed wrong, planning a future when she didn't have one any more.' He drew her close. 'This feels as if I've been given a second chance at happiness. A chance to have that family I always wanted.' He paused. 'Except you don't want children. You told me that weeks ago.'

Her eyes filled with tears. 'I wasn't being completely honest with you about that. I...I did want children. I wanted to feel a baby growing inside me, those little flutters when the baby first kicked, even the heartburn and the backache. I wanted it all. I told myself it was fine being just an aunt, but it wasn't true. I envied my sister and my sister-in-law like mad. Seeing a new life, knowing you've created it—it must be so amazing.'

'So what made you change your mind about wanting children?' he asked softly.

'The NF2.' She dragged in a breath. 'I asked my consultant what it meant for the future. He said if we had IVF we could screen the embryo before implantation and make sure the baby hadn't inherited my NF2. And pregnancy...it can affect my condition. You know as well as I do, pregnancy hormones can affect a lot of medical conditions, make things speed up or slow down.

In my case the tumours can grow faster or larger. They can cause extra problems with nerves. And as soon as Craig found out the risks, he was dead against the idea of having a baby.'

'What about adopting a child?'

'Or fostering. I suggested it. He refused flatly. It was as if something just shut off inside him. He said he didn't want a family. Ever. And that I was selfish to want a child.' She bit her lip. 'Except he wasn't telling me the whole truth, either. A month after he left me, I found out he'd moved in with someone else.' Her voice was so cracked, Marco could barely make out the words. 'And she was three months pregnant with his baby.'

Marco swore. 'And he made you believe that the break-up of your marriage was your fault, when all the time he'd been unfaithful to you?'

'It *was* my fault,' she said, looking desperately sad and tired. 'If I'd been normal, if I hadn't had NF2, he wouldn't have needed to look elsewhere. He wouldn't have needed to find someone who could give him a baby without complications.'

'No *way*,' Marco said firmly. 'He wasn't man enough to give you the support you needed, when you needed it. He didn't deserve a bright, warm, gorgeous woman like you—and you are gorgeous, Sydney, you really are. Inside and out.' He paused. 'I'm not so sure that I'm good enough for you, but I'll do my best to be.'

She frowned. 'Not good enough?'

He couldn't tell her now. She had enough to deal with. But he'd explain later. And in the meantime he'd try his hardest to give her the support she needed, the support she deserved. 'It takes two to make a baby. And I'm going to support you. Starting with going with you to see your consultant and seeing if things have changed since you last thought about starting a family.'

'Five years ago. Just before I started here.'

'Medicine changes, *tesoro*. Maybe there are new answers now. But if there aren't, it doesn't matter, because I'll be here.'

'But you're going back to Italy in three months' time.'

'Was,' he corrected. 'I can extend my secondment.'

'But I thought you really missed Italy.'

He shrugged. 'The situation's different now.'

'But—'

The only way he could think of to stop her talking and make her see that he really did want to be here was to kiss her. For long enough that they were both breathless.

'Things change,' he said softly, 'and you have to learn to compromise to deal with the changes. We're going to have to roll with this. Right now, we're both shocked and in a place where we don't have a clue what we do next. But sitting here in the middle of the night, getting upset and not being able to make an informed decision, isn't going to be good for either of us.' Or the baby, though he didn't quite dare add that. 'We're both on early shift tomorrow. We need to get some sleep. Come back to bed, *tesoro*. I don't have any answers right now, but maybe if we sleep on it we'll be in a better place to make decisions tomorrow.'

She nestled closer. 'I know you're right. I just wish…'

'We'll work it out,' he said. 'Together.'

Though, he didn't get much sleep that night, and he was pretty sure that Sydney was faking it, too. Her breathing wasn't quite deep and even enough to be that of genuine sleep.

Quite how they were going to work this out, he had no idea. It scared the hell out of him. Even apart from his fear of letting himself love someone and lose them again, the way he'd lost Sienna… He'd let his wife down, and now he was being given a second chance. Would he end up letting Sydney down, too? Or could he get it right, this time?

The only way to find out was to give it a try.

And he was going to give it his very, very best shot. To give Sydney the family she deserved and the love she deserved. Somehow.

CHAPTER TEN

NO LEMONS. No ginger. No peppermint teabags—nothing that would settle Sydney's stomach. In the end, Marco gave up looking through the cupboards and the fridge. He put some dry crackers on a plate and filled a glass with water, then took them in to Sydney.

'How are you feeling?' he asked.

'OK.'

Considering that she was pale, with dark smudges under her eyes, he didn't believe her.

'You?' she asked.

'Fine.' It was just as big a lie, and he could see from her expression that she knew it, too. 'Eat your crackers. They'll stop you feeling sick.'

'Thank you.' But she only nibbled at them. And she crumbled one of them completely.

He sat on the edge of the bed and took her hand. 'You're brooding about something. Talk to me.'

'When I had my annual check-up, I had an MRI scan.' She bit her lip. 'And pregnant women aren't supposed to be scanned in their first trimester, because of the risks to the baby.'

'OK. Firstly, it's early days and you had no idea that you were pregnant, so don't blame yourself. Secondly, it's a theoretical risk. The chances are, everything's absolutely fine.' He squeezed her hand. 'I know you're worried, and I know why you're worried. But, until we've talked to the consultant, we're coming from a position of ignorance and we're probably scaring ourselves over nothing.'

'I know,' she said, sounding miserable. 'But I can't help it, Marco. The fear's like a fog all around me, and I can't fight my way through it.'

'Talk to your consultant today,' he said. 'Get an appointment. I'll come with you.' He kissed her lightly. 'And we'd better get moving, or we'll be late for work.'

And, because babies and children were uppermost in her mind, it seemed that it ended up being Sydney's day for treating them. A toddler with a bead stuck up her nose; another who'd cracked her head against her grandmother's piano hard enough to have a deep gash needing stitches; a young lad who'd fallen over on the playing field and stretched out an arm to save himself, ending up with a Colles' fracture.

But the one that really got to her was the five-year-old who'd gashed his arm.

'I'm going to clean it, then put some magic cream on it to numb it,' she said to him, 'and then I'll be able to stitch it up and you'll be absolutely fine.'

The little boy was convinced that it was still going to hurt, and screamed the place down. But the cut was too long for her to be able to glue it or use skin closure strips, so there was no alternative to stitches.

'Sweetheart, the doctor's not going to hurt you. She's going to make you feel better,' his dad said, cuddling the child. 'And do you know how I know? She's magic.'

The little boy continued roaring his head off.

'Watch. She's so magic that I can make a coin appear from behind her ear.' He opened both hands wide, to show his son that they were empty, then clicked his fingers behind Sydney's ear and produced a coin. 'See? She's magic. So the magic cream she put on your arm will definitely work.'

At that, the little boy became calmer. 'Are you sure, Daddy?'

'Yes, sweetheart, I'm sure. Everything's going to be just fine.' His father stroked his hair back from his tear-stained face, and the little boy gave him a wobbly smile.

'What a gorgeous smile,' Sydney said. 'Did you feel that?'

'Feel what?'

'I just put the first stitch in,' she said.

The little boy looked at his arm, to check that she was really telling him the truth. 'But it didn't hurt.'

'Your dad's right. It's magic, so it won't hurt,' she said with a smile, and finished suturing the cut. 'There we go. All done. And I think you deserve a bravery sticker.' She took a small sheet of stickers from her pocket. 'Do you want to choose one?'

'Thank you,' the little boy whispered, and chose one of a lion with a plaster on his nose.

'If there's any sign of infection, you'll need to bring him back in.' She quickly went through the signs of infection with the little boy's father. 'Other than that, come back in a week or so and we can take the stitches out. And I promise that doesn't hurt, either.' She ruffled the little boy's hair. 'Well done for being so brave.' She smiled at his father. 'And I was very impressed with the magic trick.'

'I normally use them on the kids at school. If we've had a good day, I'll do a couple of magic tricks at the end of the day,' he said.

She could imagine Marco doing something like that. Learning magic tricks to delight his child, and comforting him and distracting him the way this little boy's father had just done. It made her heart ache. Would they get the chance to be a family? Could this work out? The questions spun round and round in her head, and she was no closer to finding an answer.

She managed to get an appointment to see her consultant, later that afternoon, and Marco came with her.

'Well—congratulations,' Michael Fraser said. 'You didn't say anything the other week.'

'Because I didn't know I was. We didn't exactly plan this to happen,' Sydney said. She took a deep breath. 'I've read up on NF2 in pregnancy.'

'No doubt scaring yourself silly in the process,' Michael said wryly. 'Worst-case scenario, yes, your tumours might grow faster—particularly the ones on your vestibular nerves, so you might start getting tinnitus and some hearing loss. But you also might sail through this pregnancy with nothing more than any other pregnant women faces—morning sickness, backache and indigestion.'

Marco's fingers tightened round hers. 'How will you know if Sydney's condition changes?'

'We'll monitor her more regularly. I'll book you in for more appointments with me, Sydney,' Michael said, 'and I think, rather than using your GP and midwife for antenatal care, I'm going to refer you to Theo Petrakis in the maternity department here.'

She nodded. 'I know Theo. I've sent patients up to him before.'

'So you already know how good he is.' Michael looked pleased. 'Hopefully that will help to reassure you a bit.'

'Yes. As long as keeping an eye on me doesn't mean sending me for more MRI scans.' Sydney swallowed hard. 'The one I had the other week—'

'Is highly unlikely to be a problem for the baby, if that's what you've been reading up about. So try to put it out of your mind and stop worrying about it,' Michael cut in gently.

'What worries me the most,' Sydney said quietly, 'is whether the baby has NF2. There's a fifty per cent risk of inheriting it.'

'We can test for that, when you're fifteen weeks—I assume you know what an amniocentesis involves?'

'Technically.' She shrugged. 'Obviously I haven't been through it myself or done the procedure on anyone else.'

'Because you work in a different speciality,' Michael said. 'If the chromosome is affected, we can't tell you how severe the condition will be—but at least you'll be able to prepare yourselves. Remember, though, a fifty per cent chance of inheriting it also means a fifty per cent chance of *not* inheriting it.'

Again, Marco squeezed her hand, as if to say, *See? It's going to be fine.*

'I'll see you in a month, and in the meantime I'll book you in with Theo. You know where I am if you have any questions—if you're worried about anything at all, just come and see me. Either or both of you.'

'Thank you.' Sydney blew out a breath when they left Michael's office. 'I'm scared, Marco.'

'I know, *tesoro*.' He kept his fingers firmly laced through hers.

'Supposing the baby's affected?'

'You're building bridges to trouble. You said earlier, it's not like an exam, when you have a rough idea how well you've done. This is something we can't change. Try to focus on the fifty per cent chance of the baby not having NF2.'

'I'll try.' Though it was easier said than done. It was easier at work, when she had to focus on her patients and had no time to think about anything else, but when she was off duty it loomed uppermost in her mind.

Marco did his best to distract her. He continued to work through his list, taking her to the Aquarium and London Zoo and the Planetarium. And all around them, Sydney saw families. Babies and toddlers enchanted by the brightly coloured fish. Preschoolers laughing in delight as they walked through the butterfly house. Older children trying the hands-on exhibits and marvelling over the 4.5-billion-year-old meteorite.

Families.

Something she wanted so badly.

Was it so much to ask? 'No, it's not too much to ask,' he said.

She blinked. 'Did I just say that out loud?'

'No, but it was written all over your face. Longing.' He twined his fingers through hers. 'It's not too much to ask. And we're lucky, Sydney. We've been given something very, very special—the chance to be a family together.' He gestured to the people around them. 'I see them and I think, this is what it's going to be like for us.'

'What if…?' She couldn't quite bear to speak it out loud. In case she tempted Fate.

'Then we'll deal with it. I'm not saying it's going to be easy—whether our baby has NF2 or not, it's not going to be plain sailing all the time. We'll have our problems, just like all parents do. But we'll deal with it.' He smiled at her. 'Because we'll be together. And we can lean on each other.' His eyes glittered. 'Just so you know, I'm terrified that I'm not going to be a good enough father. So you're going to have days when you're going to have to reassure me, just as I'll have days when I'll need to reassure you that it's OK not to be perfect, either.' He shrugged. 'I guess we just have to take things as they come. And that's worked for us so far, hasn't it?'

'Yes,' she admitted. He hadn't said he loved her, just as she hadn't said that she loved him. But she looked forward to being with him, and she was pretty sure it was the same for him, too. So maybe he was right, and they just had to relax and take things as they came, and just trust each other to be there.

Sydney's first appointment with Theo Petrakis was hugely reassuring.

'I've looked after several mums who've had NF2. I won't lie to you and say it's going to be completely problem-free—you're a doctor and you know what your condition means. You're a high-risk mum, so you're going to be seeing me once a week, and we're going to keep a close eye on your blood pressure. But there's a pretty good chance you're going to have a healthy baby and a reasonably good pregnancy.' Theo smiled at her. 'I can put you in touch with some of my mums, if you like. Having a support group of people who understand because they've been there can really help.'

'Thank you. I'd like that,' she said.

'So. First things first. I've asked Ultrasound to fit you in for a dating scan.' He looked at Marco. 'I hope you've got tissues with you. If you haven't, I'd advise you to go and buy some.'

Marco frowned, mystified. 'Why?'

'Put it this way, even though I've seen hundreds of scans before, the first time I saw my own baby on the screen, I had to blink back the tears. It's incredibly moving. Like nothing you can imagine.'

Half an hour and three glasses of water later, Marco and Sydney were called in to the ultrasound suite. Sydney held his hand tightly as the ultrasonographer squeezed radio-conductive gel over her abdomen and ran the transceiver head over it.

'We have a good picture,' she said.

Marco stared at the screen, watching the tiny foetus whizzing around inside Sydney's womb, its tiny heart beating so strongly…

And the last of the barriers he'd put up round his heart simply collapsed. Theo had warned him that this was moving—but he hadn't said the half of it. It blew Marco away. This was his child. His baby. His and Sydney's. A tiny life that they'd made together, curled up inside her. A little miracle they hadn't asked for but they'd been given.

Protectiveness surged through him, shocking him

with its intensity. He'd never, ever felt before that he would willingly lay his life down for someone else—but he'd do it for this baby. And it was terrifying.

'Marco, you're hurting my hand,' Sydney said softly.

'Sorry.' He released his grip. 'That's…that's…' He was lost for words. How could he explain how amazing this was, to see their unborn child? It was as if he'd just been dropped into a slot—and it fitted. Felt *right*.

'You're seven weeks,' the ultrasonographer said as she finished taking measurements. 'So you'll be having a Valentine's baby.'

Marco couldn't think of anything he wanted more.

Though he could see the conflict in Sydney's face. The longing. Clearly she wanted this baby as much as he did, felt that same surge of protective love for their child. But he also knew that she wouldn't be able to relax completely, wouldn't be able to let herself give their child all that deep, deep love she felt, until she was absolutely sure that the baby hadn't inherited her condition. Not because she was prejudiced against disability—he'd seen the care she'd taken with disabled patients in their department—but because she wouldn't ever be able to forgive herself for passing on that disability. She'd always blame herself.

How could he make her see that it didn't matter? That they'd both love their child, no matter what, and they'd be able to face the problems and cope with things together?

Maybe it was time he told her the truth about Sienna. Faced up to things himself: he, too, had spent years not being able to forgive himself. It was a risk: once she knew the truth about him, she might not want him there any more. But he was going to fight for her. Because she was worth it.

At the end of their shift, Marco looked serious.

'Is everything OK?' Sydney asked.

'I need to talk to you about something.'

A flicker of fear ran through her. Was this where it all went wrong and history repeated itself? Had Marco had time to think about it and decided that the complications would be too much for him?

'Sure,' she said, trying to sound neutral.

'Let's go to the park. Find a quiet spot.'

The worry and anticipation grew as she walked with him through the park, found a quiet spot by the lake.

'You were honest with me,' he said, 'about what happened with Craig. And I need to—to be honest with you about Sienna.'

'You don't have to tell me anything.'

'I want to,' he said simply. 'Because I don't want any more barriers between us. And I'll warn you now, it's not good.' He dragged in a breath. 'And afterwards, when you know...I'll understand if you change your mind about me.'

She frowned. 'Why would I do that?'

'Because it's my fault that Sienna died.'

No way. She didn't believe that for a second. But he clearly needed to tell her the truth, and the least she could do was be there for him and not judge, the same way that he'd been there for her when she'd told him about Craig. She reached over to take his hand. 'I'm listening,' she said softly.

'I met her when I was a student. It's a cliché, but I fell in love with her the first day we met. Well, what an eighteen-year-old thinks of as love. We studied together, we worked together—and we knew we wanted to be together. We got married the week after we graduated.'

What an eighteen-year-old thinks of as love. Sydney knew how that felt. OK, so she'd met Craig when she was twenty, but it had been the same thing for her. That rush of passion, the joy, the hope. And they hadn't even waited until she'd graduated before they'd got married. They'd thought they'd be together for ever. *For richer, for poorer, in sickness and in health...* What a joke that had turned out to be.

But it had obviously been different for Marco. It really had been, *until death us do part.*

'I worked in the emergency department, and Sienna was a paediatrician. We both thought we'd got all the time in the world to start a family, so we concentrated on our careers. Then she saw this documentary, and she couldn't get the pictures out of her head. She told me she wanted to do a stint at Doctors Without Borders, so she could help people and make a real difference. And I knew what she meant—I liked the idea, too. It was why I became a doctor, to make things right. We planned to do a year with Doctors Without Borders, then come back to Italy and start a family.'

No wonder he'd gone all distant on her when she'd asked him if he'd thought about working for Doctors Without Borders. She squeezed his hand.

'But then I was offered a promotion. It meant I'd be working with one of the best emergency specialists in Italy. I'd learn such a lot—I'd be able to give so much more to my patients. So if I delayed that year out at Doctors Without Borders, just for six months... Could I be that selfish and put my career first, knowing how much she was looking forward to working with me for Doctors Without Borders?'

Sydney knew what she would've done in those circumstances. Told him to stay and that they'd do their Doctors Without Borders stint later. 'What did Sienna think about it?'

'She saw how much I wanted to do it. So we compromised. I'd take the post, stay in Rome for six months, and then I'd follow her.' He closed his eyes. 'Three months into her service, there was a flash flood, and she was killed.'

He'd said she'd died in an accident. Sydney hadn't pushed for the details—but now she knew how tragic it had been. Sienna had died while trying to help people. Sydney stroked the pad of her thumb over the back of his hand. 'I'm so sorry.'

'The worst thing is, if I'd been out there with her, the way I was supposed to be—instead of being selfish and following my own needs—it wouldn't have happened.'

'How do you work that one out? Marco, nobody can stop a flash flood.'

'But I would've been able to keep her safe,' he insisted, 'so she wasn't risking her life.'

'Has it occurred to you,' she asked softly, 'that if you'd been there you might've died as well?'

He shook his head. 'I let her down.'

'No. She talked it over with you and you found a workable compromise—which is exactly what I would've done, too. OK, I didn't know her, so I can't say how she would've felt, but I *can* tell you how I would've felt in her shoes. I know what a good doctor you are, Marco, and the promotion would make you even better because you'd learn so much from the specialist. So I

wouldn't have resented you for not going straight out
to Doctors Without Borders with me; I would've been
proud of you for making the right decision for your
patients and your career.' She met his gaze. 'You know
when I told you about me, and you said that nothing had
changed? Well, the same goes this time round. You're a
good man, Marco Ranieri. And I...' There was a huge
lump in her throat. Did she tell him she loved him?
But right now she didn't think he'd hear what she was
saying. It'd be just words. 'I couldn't ask for a better
father for my baby.'

He looked bleak. 'How can you say that? I put my
own needs first. I was selfish.'

'You weren't selfish. You didn't tell her not to go.
You didn't stand in her way. And if she hadn't died, you
would've gone out there exactly as you agreed to do—
you wouldn't have made excuses.' She sighed. 'Marco,
you're expecting the impossible from yourself. Even
if you'd been there, you couldn't have saved her. Yes,
it was tragic that she died so young—but sometimes
things just happen in life that we can't fix and wouldn't
stand a chance of fixing.'

'I've tried to tell myself that,' he said.

But clearly, Sydney thought, he hadn't been able to
believe it.

'I went through all the stages of grief. Denial that she
was dead, anger that she'd been taken, bargaining that
if I could have her back, I'd give so much to the world.'
He blew out a breath. 'And then depression. Missing
her so much that it was a physical pain. For six months,
it was like living in the shadows. I moved house, but it
didn't help—I saw her everywhere I went. Like a ghost.
She haunted me. In the end, my sister dragged me out

to lunch and told me that if I wanted to follow Sienna to the grave, I was going the right way about it. That, yes, it was terrible she'd died so young, but she knew Sienna and knew she wouldn't want me to waste my life the way I was doing, that she wouldn't want me to destroy myself.'

'I didn't know Sienna, so I can't speak for her,' Sydney said, 'but I'm with your sister on that. If Craig and I...if he'd been the man I thought I fell in love with, and I'd died when they operated on my spine, I wouldn't have wanted him to spend the rest of his life alone and mourning me. I would've wanted him to find someone else who loved him as much as I did. I would've wanted him to be happy.' She paused. 'Supposing it was the other way round for you—would you have wanted Sienna to spend the rest of her life alone, mourning you, no joy in her life?'

'No. I'd want her to...' his breath hitched '...to have a family who loved her.'

'There you go, then.' She stroked his face. 'That's the last stage of grief. The one you didn't talk about. Acceptance. Knowing that you can't bring her back, and nothing you could've done would've saved her. That it wasn't your fault. And that it's time to move on.'

He sighed. 'I did what Vittoria suggested. I went out. I dated. But I never let anyone close. And I couldn't get rid of the guilt—I felt so responsible. I still do. If I'd gone out there with her, or if I'd persuaded her to wait until I could go with her... So many times, I begged for time to turn back just a few short months, to give me a second chance to make things right. I used to dream of it—and then I'd wake alone.' His expression was bleak. 'It was like losing her all over again.'

'So you weren't really ready to date again,' she said softly.

'Not then, no. I felt I let Sienna down, and I lost my faith in myself.' He looked at her. 'And then came to London and I met you, and the world suddenly seemed like a different place. There weren't any memories to haunt me in London. I could enjoy just being with you. Having fun.' He paused. 'Though, if I'm honest with you, I feel a bit guilty about that. I can't even see Sienna's face any more. I can't remember what her perfume smells like. I can't remember her voice. And she was my *wife*.' He looked anguished. 'I loved her for more than a third of my life. How can I forget her just like that?'

'Because you haven't seen her for more than two years. And memories fade, on the surface. But she's still here.' Sydney put her hand over his heart. 'Exactly where she should be. Exactly where she'll always be— because part of you will always love her.'

He frowned. 'And that doesn't bother you?'

She shook her head. 'She was part of your life before you met me. I don't expect you to scrub out every memory of her and get rid of every photograph, because that's totally wrong. She helped to make you who you are now. A man who's kind and caring. A man who notices problems and fixes them quietly, without expecting lots of fuss and praise for his efforts.'

He looked at her, as if unable to believe she really thought that of him.

'It's true. And the way you make me feel—you make me feel different, too. That evening we went to the London Eye, I felt like a princess.'

'That's how I want you to feel, always.' He bit his

lip. 'I know I'm asking you to trust me, and trust's hard for you after what Craig did to you. You've been let down badly before. And I've let my partner down badly before, so I'm hardly the best person to trust. It scares the hell out of me that I'm going to let you down when you need me most.'

'You're not going to let me down.' She felt the tears fill her eyes. 'Marco, you've been there for me and supported me every minute since I told you about the baby. You've come to all my appointments with me, you've held me when I can't sleep. I couldn't ask for anything more.' She took a deep breath. 'Remember what you told me about just taking things as they come? I think you're right. Maybe that's what we need to do right now.'

'None of it matters, as long as we're together.' He wrapped his arms round her. 'I'll try my hardest not to let you down.'

'I know. And that's all I want,' she said softly.

CHAPTER ELEVEN

BUT Sydney was still waking up in the middle of the night. Every time Marco woke to find the bed empty, he knew where she'd be. In the kitchen, sipping a glass of water and trying not to bawl her eyes out. And every time, he just scooped her up, sat down and settled her on his lap, holding her close and willing her to take strength from him.

'I'm sorry. I'm trying not to brood.' She gulped. 'I just wish…'

He knew what she wished. That this baby had been planned, the embryo had been screened and she could relax and enjoy her pregnancy, without worrying that she'd passed on her condition. Even though it wasn't her fault that the gene had mutated, and it took two to make a baby, planned or accidental.

'IVF isn't an easy option, you know,' he said softly. 'And sometimes it takes several cycles until it works. One of my sister's friends went through it, and she ended up having seven cycles of treatment over three years. Vittoria says it nearly destroyed her.'

'And this is destroying me,' Sydney whispered. 'Waiting and wondering, and praying that I haven't passed on my bad chromosomes. That I haven't taken away our baby's quality of life.'

'You haven't taken away our baby's quality of life,' he reassured her. 'If he or she has NF2, for all we know, it might even be milder than you have it.'

'It's three weeks until the amnio,' she said. 'And then a two-week wait until we get the results.' She looked bleak. 'It feels like a lifetime. I just want to know. To be *sure*.' She bit her lip. 'I want this baby. I do. I don't even have the words to describe how I feel—how much I love this baby. But at the same time I'm so scared, Marco. So scared that everything's going to go wrong. That the complications are all going to be too much. I just wish…'

'I know, *tesoro*.' It wasn't easy for him, either, seeing her eaten up with fear like this. This was a time when they should be enjoying the new life they'd made, making plans, choosing nursery furniture and looking at first toys and books and tiny outfits.

He needed to distract her.

And he could only think of one thing that might work.

He had a quiet and very confidential discussion with Ellen, the next day. To his relief, she agreed with him.

'Aren't you getting up for work?' Sydney asked on the Friday morning.

'Change of duty,' he said with a shrug.

As he'd hoped, she assumed that he was on a late. The second she'd left for work, he leaped out of bed, showered and dressed, then packed for both of them. Luckily she was very organised and had a file where she kept important paperwork, so he was able to locate her passport quickly. He booked the taxi, then had just enough time to make one essential purchase before taking the taxi to the hospital with their suitcases at lunchtime.

Sydney had just seen her last patient before her break when Marco walked into the department to find her.

'Ready for lunch?' he asked.

She looked surprised. 'You came in early just to have lunch with me?'

'Something like that,' he said with a smile. Only better.

'Aren't we going to the canteen?'

'Nope.'

She frowned when she saw the taxi. 'Marco? What's going on?'

'I'm kidnapping you.'

'But you're on a late, and I still have half a shift to do.'

'I'm on a day off, and you're on leave as of...' he glanced at his watch '...about five seconds ago. I'm taking you away for a few days,' he said. 'Completely away from here. You need a break, and I know the best place in the world to relax.'

'But—I'm on duty.'

'No, you're not. Ellen's changed your duty. You're not due back until Thursday next week.'

She blinked. '*Ellen* changed my duty?'

'She's worried about you, *tesoro*,' he said softly. 'I knew you'd told her about the baby, so I had a quiet word with her the other day. And she agrees with me—a break will do you good, help to take your mind off the situation.' He smiled at her. 'And we have a taxi waiting to take us to the airport.'

'Where are we going?'

He refused to be drawn. 'I'll tell you when we're about to board.'

'Marco, I…'

'Just enjoy this, *tesoro*,' he said softly. 'You have a lot you're worrying about and you need distracting. And this is the best way I can think of doing that.'

'But—I haven't packed.'

'I packed for both of us. If I missed anything, then I'll get it for you at our destination,' he told her.

'I don't know what to say.'

He kissed her lightly. 'You just say "Yes", and get in the taxi.'

It wasn't until they got to check-in that Sydney finally found out where they were going. 'Naples.'

'That's the nearest airport to Capri.' He was taking her home. To *his* home.

'I've booked us into a hotel in Sorrento.' He squeezed her hand. 'I thought staying with my parents might be a bit too much pressure for you. Though we do need to call in and see my family while we're in Italy,' he added, 'or they'll never forgive me.'

He'd thought of everything. 'Marco, I…' She felt the tears well up.

'Don't cry, *tesoro*. Everything's going to be fine.'

Their flight was on time, and he'd arranged a hire car at the airport. 'My sister's using my car while I'm in England, and it's not fair of me to demand it back at zero notice,' he said. 'I suppose we could've taken the train, but I love the drive round the coast.'

She smiled. 'And trust you to make it an open-topped car.'

'Well, it'd be a pity to waste the sunshine,' he said

with a grin. He drove them out of the city. 'Look to your left.'

A huge mountain loomed over them—and then she realised what it was. 'Vesuvius?'

'Yes, and you can see her from the whole peninsula. She'll follow us all the way to Sorrento. We can walk up the volcano later in the week, if you like; there are stunning views from the top.'

Sydney enjoyed the drive, despite the road being so twisting and narrow. The view was spectacular, with houses scattered on the cliffside leading down to a perfect turquoise sea. When they arrived at the hotel, she found that he'd booked what she suspected was the honeymoon suite; it was right at the top of the hotel, secluded, with its own balcony and stunning views over the sea.

'Is that Capri?' she asked, gesturing to the island in the distance.

'Ischia. Capri's a little further round to the left.'

When she unpacked, she discovered that he'd packed everything she would've put in the case herself. There was enough time to shower and change before dinner on a terrace overlooking the sunset; and the food was fantastic.

'Marco, thank you for this. Though I ought to p—'

'No,' he cut in, second-guessing her, 'this is my treat. You're not paying for *anything*. We're having a few days away where we don't have to think and we don't have to worry—just the two of us, no pressure, so we can relax and enjoy it. It's the complete opposite of London, here—slow and easy, not rush, rush, rush.'

When they made love that night, his touch was very tender, very sweet. He undressed her slowly, stroking her skin as he uncovered it and following the path of his hands with his mouth. He cupped her breasts and teased her hardening nipples with the pads of his thumbs until her breathing grew uneven, then dipped his head and took one nipple into his mouth, teasing it with his tongue and his teeth until she slid her hands into his hair, urging him on.

'Marco, I need you now,' she whispered.

He gently laid her on the bed against the pillows, stripped off his clothes in a matter of seconds and let them lay where they fell. 'Now?' he asked.

In answer, she drew his head down to hers and kissed him, hard.

Slowly, slowly, he entered her, keeping eye contact all the way; the sheer desire in his expression made her melt. She wrapped her legs round his waist, pulling him deeper. All she could think of was him, the way he made her feel. His kisses were sweet yet intense at the same time, giving and demanding in equal measure.

As her climax hit, she cried out his name; she heard his answering cry, muffled against her shoulder.

He was holding her so tightly, as if he'd never let her go. It had never been quite like this before; was it because they were here, in Italy, or was it because things were changing between them again? Had he finally come to terms with his own nightmares? She didn't want to spoil the moment by asking him. But as she relaxed in his arms she held on to the thought that maybe, just maybe, he was falling in love with her, the way she was falling for him.

They were on the top floor and nobody could see into their room; he'd left the curtains open, and she could see the stars against the inky sky. *Star light, star bright, first star I see tonight...* The old rhyme echoed in her head. And she knew exactly what she'd wish for. To be a real family, with Marco and their baby—without the spectre of NF2.

For the first time in weeks, Sydney actually slept properly, and the next morning at breakfast she felt more human than she had for ages. The nausea had gone; traditionally, this was the time when women bloomed. And here, away from their usual routine, and with Marco being so tender, she felt as if she was really blooming.

'No coffee for me, thanks,' she said to the waiter. 'Just orange juice will be lovely.' Especially as it was freshly squeezed.

'Do you mind if I have coffee, or is the smell too much for you?' Marco asked.

'It's fine.'

'Grazie, tesoro.'

While Sydney stuck to toast, plain yoghurt and a juicy-looking nectarine, Marco indulged in the pastries. 'This is one thing you definitely can't find in England.'

'What, cake for breakfast?' she teased.

'*Pasticiotti*, if you please—I can never decide between the lemon ricotta and the vanilla filling.'

She eyed his plate. 'So you have both.'

He grinned. 'It's a proper Italian breakfast. I'll work it off in the pool, this afternoon. I thought I'd take you to Vesuvius this morning, if you'd like a walk. It's not too strenuous, and if we go now we can avoid the hottest part of the day.'

'That'd be lovely.'

He drove them back towards Naples, then turned off up a very narrow and twisting road; there was barely enough room for the cars and buses to pass each other, and there were several places where Marco had to reverse to let a bus through.

'I'm glad you're the one driving, not me,' she said feelingly.

At last they reached the car park. 'The air gets a bit thin, so just say if you need to stop. We'll take it steady,' Marco said.

The path looked as if it went in wide zigzags and didn't slope too sharply; but clearly appearances were deceptive because there were two people handing out stout sticks at the bottom of the path.

'I thought you said it wasn't strenuous?' she asked.

'It isn't that bad, but can be a bit slippery underfoot, with all the little bits of lava on the path. The sticks help you keep your balance.'

They sat down on one of the benches halfway up the path to look out over the Bay of Naples and the stunning view. The slopes of the volcano were covered in trees and bushes with yellow flowers.

Strange to think this was a live volcano they were walking up; right now it seemed just like any other mountain. But when they got to the top, she could smell the sulphur and see the yellow deposits on the far side of the crater. Then she looked down into the crater and saw little puffs of smoke. 'Wow—that's actually steam coming from the vents!' It was as if she understood the real power of nature for the first time; that crater had been filled with hundreds and hundreds of tons of rock, and it had all been blasted out by the force of the eruption. 'This is awesome,' she said, 'in the true sense of the word.'

He smiled. 'It's been a while since I came here, but I know what you mean. My parents brought us here when we were small, and I can still remember the first time. It just blew me away.' He laughed. 'Pun not quite intended. And, of course, I had to have an ornament made out of lava. I still have the little salamander somewhere.' He bought one for her at the souvenir stall at the top of the slope. 'He'll remind you of Vesuvius.'

They were on their way back down the slope when they saw a small child who'd clearly fallen over and grazed her knees. Her father was looking anxious and her mother was frantically looking through her bag—for plasters, Sydney guessed, and the worried look on the woman's face told her that the hunt was unsuccessful.

She tugged at Marco's hand. 'I have plasters and wipes—but if they don't speak English I'll need you to translate for me.'

'Of course, *tesoro.*'

They went over to the parents; Marco established that they were Italian, and explained that he and Sydney were both doctors. While she took the wipes and plasters from her bag, Marco soothed the child and sang an Italian song—a tune she recognised, but she had no idea what the words were. The child clearly knew it as she joined in, her high voice harmonising with Marco's rich tenor.

Gently, she cleaned up the little girl's knees. This was what it would be like to be a family with Marco. She could imagine him singing with their child, the way he was with this little girl. He'd make such a great dad. They'd make a great family, because this baby really would be loved. So much. By both of them.

'*Mille grazie,*' the little girl's mother said.

'*Prego,*' Marco answered with a smile.

Despite the stout stick, Sydney nearly slipped on the

way down; Marco caught her arm to stop her falling. 'OK?' he asked.

She smiled at him. 'I'm fine. Thanks for rescuing me.'

'No problem.' He smiled back. 'When you were patching up that little girl's knees, you went all dreamy for a moment. What were you thinking?'

'That you're going to make such a great dad. You'll sing our baby's tears away.'

He laughed. 'I'll certainly give it a go. And you're going to make a great mum. Practical and kind and warm and…our baby's going to love you so much.'

Maybe, she thought. If she could only keep her fears at bay.

'It's going to work out, *tesoro*,' he said softly. 'Whatever happens, we'll cope—because we're together. Trust me.'

Looking into his dark, dark eyes, Sydney believed that she could trust him. That maybe, just maybe, he was right.

Once they were safely down at the bottom and had handed in their sticks, Marco drove them back to the hotel. 'It's the hottest part of the day. Definitely time for a siesta.'

She was grateful for the break, especially as the room was air-conditioned; and the nap really revived her. In the evening, Marco took her to a restaurant with a fabulous terrace overlooking the sea—and inevitably in the shadow of Vesuvius. The food was fabulous, and she was delighted to discover that the ice-cream sundae she'd ordered came shaped like the volcano, with sparklers on the top. 'How lovely!'

'So is the distraction working?' Marco asked.

She took his hand across the table. 'Thank you, it's helping a lot—and you're right, this is a beautiful part of the world.'

'It's the most romantic place in Italy,' he said. 'Though I admit to being a tiny bit biased.'

'I love it here,' she said. 'I can see why it means so much to you.' And to think that he was choosing to stay in London, with her, rather than coming home to Italy… it was humbling, and at the same time it made her feel warm inside. Cherished. *Loved*. He hadn't actually said the words, but he didn't need to. It was in the way he acted towards her. The way he made time for her. The way he encouraged her to focus away from her fears and towards the deep, deep love she felt for their baby.

On Sunday morning, they had another lazy breakfast. 'Should we visit your parents today?' she asked.

He shook his head. 'No way are we going to Capri on a Sunday in the middle of summer. I'd rather wait until tomorrow; it'll be less crowded and a much more comfortable journey.'

They spent the day pottering about; Sydney sat on one of the recliner chairs under the orange trees and watched Marco swimming in the hotel's pool. She wasn't surprised that he was attracting admiring glances from the other women around the pool; he really was gorgeous, and his smile was enough to make any woman's knees go weak.

She found herself wondering, would she have a little boy who looked like him? Or a girl with his beautiful dark eyes? Then she realised that she automatically cupped one hand over her abdomen—just like any other pregnant woman, wanting to protect her unborn child. Cherishing it. Bonding with the little life growing inside her.

Later that day, they wandered through the old town, hand in hand; they could hear someone singing.

'My dad used to sing that when I was small. *Torna a Surriento*.' He began singing along with it, his beautiful tenor in counterpoint to the baritone.

'That's lovely,' she said when he'd finished.

'It always makes me think of here,' he said.

She found herself relaxing and almost, *almost* able to forget her worries—sitting in a café with Marco, drinking freshly squeezed orange juice, and trying the *sfogliatelle*, crispy pastries filled with a mixture of ricotta cheese and lemon. And a walk along the marina before dinner, as the sun began to set, was just perfect.

On Monday, they caught the hydrofoil over to Capri, and took the funicular railway through the lemon groves up to the main part of the town. Marco bought flowers and chocolates in the main square, then found a taxi to take them to his parents' house. She was amused to see that the taxi was open-topped, albeit with a striped awning to protect the passengers from the sun.

'Marco, I don't speak any Italian,' she reminded him when the taxi pulled up outside the address Marco had given to the driver.

'That's not a problem. Everyone in my family speaks good English. And we're not staying all day, *tesoro*— just for a little while, to say hello.'

As the taxi pulled up, nerves swamped her. 'Marco, have you told them that you and I are…?' She hadn't told her family about the baby, yet. Or her closest friends.

'No, I haven't. They know we're friends. Colleagues.

That you need a break. That's all they need to know. They won't pressure you,' he said. 'I promise.'

He paid the taxi driver, then ushered her into the house. A spaniel came bouncing up to them, barking, and Marco crouched down briefly to make a fuss of him. '*Tesoro*, this is Ciccio—who's an old softie and just makes a lot of noise to pretend he's a tough dog.'

The spaniel rolled over to have his tummy rubbed, his ears flopping over his face, and Sydney couldn't help smiling.

'Marco, *amore*!' An elegantly dressed woman who was clearly Marco's mother came into the hallway and hugged him warmly.

Marco introduced them swiftly. 'Mamma, this is Sydney. Sydney, this is my mother, Zita.'

Zita hugged Sydney, too. 'Very nice to meet you.'

'You, too,' Sydney said shyly.

'Is this your first time in Capri?'

'Yes.'

'Then you must make Marco take you to Monte Solaro. The views are amazing. Come and sit in the garden with us. Can I get you a cold drink? Juice, sparkling water?'

'Juice would be lovely, thank you.'

'I'll get it, Mamma,' Marco said. 'Sydney, go and sit down.'

Zita introduced Sydney to Salvatore, Marco's father—who was very much an older version of Marco—and then Marco appeared with a tray containing glasses and a jug of juice.

The garden overlooked the sea, with the inevitable view of Vesuvius; bougainvillea grew everywhere, as well as beautiful blue trumpet-like flowers that Zita told her were morning glory.

Talking to Marco's parents was as easy as talking to her own, Sydney discovered; they had the same warmth and kindness she liked so much in Marco.

Ciccio barked again and dashed off into the house; a couple of moments later, two more people joined them.

'Sydney, this is Vittoria, my sister; and Roberto, my brother,' Marco said, greeting them both warmly. 'Vittoria, Roberto, this is Sydney.'

They, too, spoke English and included Sydney in the conversation as if they'd known her for years, instead of only just having met her. Exactly as her own family would be with Marco, and Sydney felt a throb of guilt at keeping him such a secret. Especially given her pregnancy.

Zita insisted that they all stay for lunch, which they ate in the garden. 'Proper Caprese food,' she said. 'Ravioli filled with *caiotta*, parmesan and marjoram; *chiummenzana*…' she gestured to the bowl of tomato sauce '…salad, bread. Help yourselves.'

'This is fabulous,' Sydney said after the first mouthful.

Zita looked pleased. 'I grow my own herbs, and Salvatore grows the tomatoes.'

They finished with *torta caprese*. 'It's traditional—almond and chocolate cake,' Marco told her.

'And it's fantastic. Thank you so much,' Sydney said.

'*Prego,*' Zita said with a smile.

Although she hadn't allowed anyone to help her prepare lunch, Zita did allow Vittoria and Sydney to do the washing up afterwards.

'It's the first time I've seen Marco happy since—' Vittoria stopped abruptly, looking worried.

'Since Sienna?' Sydney asked lightly.

Vittoria's eyes were wary. 'He told you about her?'

'Yes. And it's so tragic that he lost her like that.'

'She was lovely. Very warm and sweet, kind.' Vittoria smiled wryly. 'Which isn't very tactful of me, singing her praises to you.'

'That's not a problem,' Sydney said. 'Actually, that's what I thought she was like. I wouldn't expect him to choose someone cold or selfish.'

'No.' Vittoria regarded her. 'I know it's the first time we've met, but you have a lot in common with her. The same warmth, the same kindness. And I'm glad my brother's found someone who'll love him the way he deserves.'

Sydney felt her eyes widen. 'He told you?'

'He didn't need to. I could tell by the way you look at each other.' Vittoria held up one hand. 'I promise, none of us will say anything until he's ready to tell us officially. We'll be tactful. But I'm glad. I've been so worried about him, especially since he left for England. His emails are always cheerful, and so are his phone calls, but unless you can see someone's eyes…' She shook her head. 'I worried that he was really unhappy, but he was putting on a brave face because he was trying to stop us worrying.'

Sydney couldn't help smiling. 'You always do worry about your family. I'm the same with my brother and sister—even though I'm the baby out of the three of us.'

'I hope we're going to be friends,' Vittoria said.

'So do I.'

'Good.' Vittoria hugged her warmly. 'And he's a good man. He'll make you happy.'

He already does, Sydney thought. *He already does.*

'Mamma's right, I should show you Monte Solaro before we go back on the hydrofoil,' Marco said when they took their leave—and when Zita had pressed several wrapped slices of the *torte caprese* on them.

They took another taxi to Anacapri and then joined the queue for the chairlift.

As Sydney watched the people at the front of the queue, she realised that the bar across the chair wasn't locked in. 'Are you sure it's safe?'

He looked at her. 'Ah. I forgot you were scared of heights.'

'I'm not scared of heights. It was just walking backwards into nothing that spooked me. But in England that bar would be locked in. Safely.'

'It's fine, *tesoro*. Just hold on to the side of the chair if you're worried. Do you want me to go first?' he asked.

'I...' She thought about brazening it out, and gave him a wry smile. 'Yes, please. So you're there to meet me at the other end.'

He smiled. 'The views are worth it, *tesoro*, I promise.'

The slope seemed gentle at first, then suddenly became very steep—but as the ride progressed, she found herself relaxing more. By the time she arrived at the top, she was no longer gripping the side of the chair with white knuckles.

Marco was waiting for her; he took her hand and walked with her over to the railings.

'Wow. You're right, this is stunning.' There was a

sheer drop below them. 'It feels like looking over the edge of the world. And the colour of the sea… It's beautiful, Marco.'

Marco's hand closed round the box in his pocket. 'The edge of the world,' he said. 'The perfect place. Sydney…' He took a deep breath. 'I like you.'

'I like you, too.'

He shook his head. 'That's not what I meant to say. So stupid. I had all the words in my head. I rehearsed them for ages—and they're just *gone.*'

'What words?' She looked mystified.

'I…I like you. I like the way you're gentle with patients and you're patient with me. I like the way you think on your feet. I like the way you see the good in people.' She'd seen the good in him when he hadn't been able to see it himself. He kept his gaze fixed on hers. 'I like waking up with you, your smile being the first thing I see in the morning. I like going to sleep with you, the warmth of your skin being the last thing I'm aware of at night. And you make me want to be a better man.'

'Oh, Marco.' Her eyes glittered with tears. 'You don't need to be a better man. You're fine just as you are. You remember that song you sang me, that night?'

He remembered. About her being amazing, just the way she was.

'That goes for you, too,' she said softly.

It gave him enough hope to continue. 'I know this might seem fast, but I've known for a while how I feel about you.' He took a deep breath. 'I want to be with you, Sydney. I want to make a family with you, be with you for the rest of our days.' He dropped down on one knee and took the box from his pocket. 'I love you, and I want to make a life with you—and, God willing, our baby. Will you marry me?' He flipped the lid on the box.

She looked at the ring—a princess-cut tanzanite in a simple platinum setting—and a tear slid down her cheek.

'Sydney?' *Please don't let me have misjudged this. Please don't let her say no*, he begged silently.

'You love me?'

He nodded. 'I knew, that night on the London Eye. I guess I was still a bit in denial—I was still a bit of a mess—but I knew you were special. That you really meant something to me. I'm not going to forget Sienna or dismiss what we had, but you've helped me lay all the ghosts to rest. I'm ready to move on, and you've shown me that it's possible to be happy again. That happiness is there, and all you have to do is reach out and grab it with both hands. We can do that. Together.'

'You really want to marry me,' she whispered.

'Because I love you. Not because of a sense of responsibility. I love you, I love our unborn child, and whatever we face in the future I know we'll cope with it because we belong together.'

'After Craig, I never thought I'd risk my heart again,' she said. 'I never wanted to put myself in a place where I'd be vulnerable, where someone could hurt me. But you...you're different. I can trust you. You've been there for me every time I've needed you.' She took a deep breath. 'I love you, too. And I want to be a family with you.'

'So that's a yes?'

'That's a definite yes.'

He took her hand, kissed her ring finger, then slid the ring onto her finger. Then he stood up, picked her up and whirled her round. 'You've just made me the happiest man in the world.' He paused. 'My family liked you, by the way. A lot.'

'I liked them, too.' She smiled ruefully. 'I really should introduce you to my family. I guess I just didn't want to say anything until…'

She didn't have to finish. He knew what she meant. Until they knew the amnio results.

'We can keep it quiet for a while longer, if that's what you want. I won't take it personally,' he said. 'I know how you feel about me, and that's the important thing.'

She slid her arms round her neck and kissed him. 'I love you, Marco, and I'll be proud to be your wife.'

CHAPTER TWELVE

BACK in England, when she was at work Sydney wore her engagement ring on a chain round her neck, tucked underneath her clothes so it was close to her heart. And every time she caught Marco's eye in the department, they shared a private, special smile.

One afternoon in Resus, Sydney had a case where she really needed a more experienced view. She went in search of Marco. 'Can I borrow you for five minutes? I need you to review some X-rays with me, please,' she said.

'Sure.' He came over to the computer with her and she pulled up the files.

'My patient Aiden is a trainee acrobat—he's seventeen years old. He did a handstand yesterday and fell on his left shoulder. It still hurt today, and he said it felt as if everything was pushed forward, so he came in to see us. I put him in a collar to immobilise his neck before sending him to X-ray. It's definitely a broken collarbone, but I'm not happy about treating this one with a sling.' She blew out a breath. 'It's a really bad break.'

He looked at the screen. 'It looks as if the bone's almost through the skin—and if the bone gets exposed to air, he's at risk of getting an infection. You're right.

We can't just strap his arm up, the way we'd normally treat a break there. Call the orthopods and get them to reduce the fracture and pin it.'

'He said his back hurt, so I asked X-ray to do his back as well.' She pulled up the next file. 'Fractured sacral bone, by the look of it.'

'He's not going to be able to train for a couple of months,' Marco said, 'or he's at risk of stopping that fracture healing and making it worse. Have you done a CAT scan to check his neck for injuries?'

'That's happening right now. I wanted to review these X-rays with you while he's in the scanner—the poor kid's had enough waiting about.'

A few minutes later, Aiden was wheeled back in.

'You've definitely broken your collarbone, Aiden, and it's quite a bad break so we're going to need to send you up to the surgeons to have it pinned,' she said. 'The good news is, the scan you just had done shows that there's no injury to your neck, so you're probably feeling the pain from the break rather than anything else.'

'So, once it's pinned, I can go back to training?' he asked.

'Sorry, no,' Marco said. 'You've also fractured your sacral bone, at the base of your spine. So it's not a good idea to train until that's healed, which will be about the same time as the pin's removed from your collarbone— and that will be about nine weeks.'

'*Nine weeks?*' Aiden looked aghast. 'But the troupe's in a big competition in two weeks' time. I have to be there. It's my big chance. I can't miss it.'

Sydney took his hand and squeezed it. 'If you don't let your bones heal properly, there's a chance you might make things worse—and then it'll take a lot longer to heal. And if the fractures are bad enough, you might never be able to do acrobatics again.'

He went white. 'But—it's all I ever wanted to do. Since I was tiny.'

'I know it's hard,' Marco added, 'but sometimes you have to look at the bigger picture. It's better to miss one opportunity now and then excel at the next one than to try to do things too soon and for it all to go wrong.'

Sydney said quietly, 'I've called the surgeon down, Aiden, so as soon as he's here I'll introduce you to him and he'll talk you through how he's going to pin your collarbone. He won't be long. Is there anything we can get you while you're waiting, and do you want me to call anyone to give you a bit of moral support?'

'I... No. Dad's going to be so mad at me. I've messed up my big chance.'

'You'll get another chance,' she comforted him. 'And your dad's going to be disappointed for you, but I'm sure he's going to be more worried that you're hurt and in pain.'

'You don't know Dad,' Aiden muttered.

Marco frowned. 'Aiden, do you want to talk to us about that fall?'

The boy grimaced. 'What's there to say? I overbalanced and ruined the routine.'

'Did anyone hit you when you made a mistake?' Sydney asked gently, guessing immediately what Marco had been driving at. Was the break from a fall—or from being struck by something?

'No. Dad never uses his fists.' The boy looked shocked enough for her to believe him. 'But words... they stay with you a lot longer. In your head.' Aiden bit his lip. 'He already thinks I'm useless because I'm not as good as he was at my age.'

'Maybe,' Sydney said softly, 'this is a chance to think about what you really want to do. Do you want to be an acrobat for yourself, or just to please your dad? Because you can't live out someone else's dream, love. It won't work, because your heart won't be completely in it, no matter how much you want to please that person.'

'I'm never going to be as good as he was.'

'Then maybe your talents lie in other directions,' Marco said. 'My father was a fashion designer. But I was never interested in clothes, and he was fine about me becoming a doctor.'

'You're lucky,' Aiden said feelingly.

'Can your mum talk to your dad for you?' Sydney asked.

'She went off with someone else. I haven't seen her since I was ten.'

'If you want me to talk to your dad, that's fine,' Marco said. 'And I'll explain to him that if you over-train while you're still healing, you'll never be able to do acrobatics again.'

'And then what will I do?' Aiden asked bleakly. 'I'll have no job, no home—because he's not going to let me stay if I'm not part of the troupe.'

'Maybe we can help with that,' Sydney said. 'I can have a word with social services and see if they can get you somewhere to stay and some careers advice.'

'No. I don't need any of that. I'm going to be an acrobat,' Aiden said, looking panicky.

'OK, love. Try to relax, now. I'll be back to see you in a bit with the surgeon,' Sydney said.

Marco followed her out of Resus. 'Poor kid,' he said. 'That's hard for him, not having anyone he can rely on.'

The same position she'd felt herself to be in, until she'd met Marco.

'Maybe I can have a word with his dad,' he mused.

'This might be one of the things you can't fix,' Sydney warned.

He shrugged. 'Even so, I can try.'

It was one of the things she loved about him: the way he *cared* so much. And if anyone could fix this situation, Marco could.

On the Monday, Max came into work all smiles. 'Carly has a baby brother. Nearly four kilos, mum and baby both doing well—and, no, we still haven't decided on a name.'

'Congratulations,' Marco said, shaking his hand warmly. The more so because he could identify with the relief on Max's face that mother and baby were both fine. It would be the same with him, worrying about Sydney during labour.

'Thanks. If any of you want to go up and visit Marina, I'm sure she'd be delighted to show him off.'

Just as Marco knew that Sydney so desperately wanted to show off their own baby. But she was still keeping things quiet until after the amnio, not wanting to tempt fate. Please, he begged silently. Let this all be OK. For her sake.

'Are you busy at lunchtime?' Sydney asked.

'Not if my favourite doctor wants to have lunch with me.'

'Not *lunch*, exactly,' she said. 'You know I organised the department's collection for the baby?'

'Yes.' He also knew that she was superstitious about things and wouldn't buy a gift until the baby had arrived safely.

'I'm going to buy the baby's present at lunchtime, and I wondered if you wanted to come with me.'

Marco guessed exactly what that was code for. Sydney was itching to look at things for their own baby, but was being equally superstitious and refusing to choose a thing or even decide on a colour for the nursery until they'd had the amnio result. He was in no doubt that she loved their unborn child, but he knew the fear was still holding her back. All he could do was be there, hold her when the doubts got too much for her, and gently remind her that love would get them through anything. 'I'd love to come with you,' he said softly.

He was surprised at how much he enjoyed helping her choose the departmental gifts for Marina and Max's newborn.

'This stuff's so beautiful,' Sydney said wistfully.

'I know, *tesoro*. Not much longer to wait, now. And then you get to do whatever you like with my credit card.'

She laughed. 'But you'll come with me? Help me choose things for our baby?'

He drew her into his arms and kissed her softly. 'I wouldn't miss that for the world.'

At the end of their shift—and when everyone had signed the card and sighed over the gorgeous baby clothes Sydney had chosen—they headed up to the maternity department. Marco held Sydney's hand very tightly as they were let into the ward.

Marina was sitting up in bed, cuddling the baby, when they walked in.

'Hello! Come to see my gorgeous boy and have a cuddle?' she asked.

'You bet.' Sydney handed the parcels to Marco, sat on the bed next to Marina and cradled the baby in her arms.

Marco's heart turned over. He could just see her holding their own baby, her face full of love, and it moved him so much he couldn't speak. He just handed the card and the neatly wrapped gifts to Marina.

'From the department? Oh, thank you!' She opened the parcels, exclaiming in delight over them; but Marco had eyes only for the baby. Ever since the moment he'd seen their baby moving on the screen of the scanner, he melted whenever he was near a baby.

'I always forget how tiny they are when they first arrive,' Marco said, crouching down next to Sydney and touching the baby's hand. How tiny and perfectly formed. The baby yawned, and he couldn't help smiling.

'And how warm they are. That special baby smell,' Sydney said.

He could hear the slight wobble in her voice, and he knew what she was wondering. Was this how it would be for them?

'Do you want to hold him, Marco?' Marina asked.

He couldn't resist. 'Oh, *piccolo*,' he crooned softly, taking the baby from Sydney and cradling him. He knew exactly what Sydney had meant by the warmth, the weight, the special baby smell. And how he wanted to hold his own and Sydney's baby like this. He caught her gaze, and knew she was thinking exactly the same thing. How much she was looking forward to the moment when she first held their baby.

'So how far are you?' Marina asked.

Sydney blinked. 'How far am I what?'

'It's OK. I'm not going to tell anyone. Well, except Max, obviously, but I'll swear him to secrecy,' Marina added. 'Congratulations.'

'How did you know?' Sydney asked.

'The way you held the baby,' Marina said simply. 'The way you looked at each other.'

'It's that obvious?' Marco asked.

'To me, yes, because I've been there myself. I haven't heard any rumours, yet.'

'I'm fourteen weeks,' Sydney said. 'And not really showing that much.' Especially as she was wearing baggy clothes to hide the slight bump.

'The blooming stage.' Marina smiled at her. 'So does that mean we're going to have a departmental wedding?'

'Better come clean,' Marco said ruefully.

Sydney fished out her engagement ring to show Marina. 'Obviously it's against health and safety to wear it at work.'

'And you're keeping it to yourselves for now. Is that why you whisked her off to Italy, Marco?'

'Partly.' Not that he was going to elaborate on the other reason.

'That ring's absolutely gorgeous. Have you set a date?'

'After the baby arrives,' Sydney said. 'We were thinking a spring wedding.'

'It sounds perfect,' Marina said. 'I'm so pleased for you both.'

'Thank you.' Regretfully, Marco handed the baby back to her. 'We'd better let you get some rest.'

'Plus we're being greedy—everyone else in the department is desperate to come up and see you,' Sydney added. She kissed Marina's cheek. 'Well done. He's gorgeous.'

'Irresistible,' Marco agreed, handing the baby back to Marina.

'See you both later,' Marina said with a smile.

Marco took her hand as they left the ward. 'That's going to be us, in a few months. With our own little miracle.' There was a huge lump in his throat. 'I can hardly wait.'

'Me, too,' Sydney said, squeezing his hand. 'Me, too.'

He kissed her. 'We'd better get back to work. I happen to know that Aiden's back in for a check-up this afternoon—and his dad's going to be with him. I think I need to have a word.'

'The man sounds like a complete bully.'

'It's probably insecurity.' Marco shrugged. 'His wife left him, so Aiden's all he has left—and he's probably terrified of losing his son.'

'Which is why he's pushing him away like this, making him feel that he's useless?'

'Some people believe that if you tell someone they're rubbish, they'll fight back to prove you wrong.'

'More like, their self-esteem will drop.'

'But someone who's that scared isn't going to see that. Let's hope he'll listen to me.'

At the end of their shift, Marco and Sydney walked home together, their arms wrapped around each other.

'How did you get on with Aiden's dad?' she asked.

'He just needed someone to point out to him that if he pushed his son any harder right now, Aiden would end up in a wheelchair and resent him for taking away his mobility as well as his career.'

'So he's going to back off?'

Marco nodded. 'I think young Aiden's got the chance now to find out what he really wants to do. If that's acrobatics, fine; if it isn't, he'll still have a home and his dad will support him in whatever he wants to do.'

She stroked his face. 'I'm so glad you're one of life's fixers.'

'Sometimes it works.' He kissed her lightly.

When they made love that night, it was more intense than Sydney had ever felt before. This time, as Marco's body surged into hers, he whispered, 'I love you.'

'I love you too,' she whispered back, adding silently, *for always*.

CHAPTER THIRTEEN

THE day of the amniocentesis, Sydney couldn't concentrate on anything. She put chilli instead of cinnamon on her morning porridge; she stood staring into the fridge, clearly having forgotten what she wanted in the first place; and Marco could barely get a proper sentence out of her.

By the time they got to the waiting room, she was as white as a sheet.

He took her hand. 'Try not to worry, *tesoro*.'

'I can't help it.' She bit her lip. 'And I hope we don't have to wait too much longer. I'm dying to go to the loo, but if I do I'll have to drink more water and we'll have to sit here for another half an hour.'

The receptionist called her name, and she started.

His fingers tightened round hers. 'You're not alone. I'm here,' he said.

'I know.'

But he could feel her shaking.

She lay on the couch, and the ultrasonographer took her hand. 'We're just going to take a tiny bit of amniotic fluid from around the baby so we can grow the cells. You'll just feel a sharp scratch. OK?'

'OK?' she whispered.

'Well done.' The ultrasonographer smeared radio-conductive gel over Sydney's abdomen and then ran the transceiver over it.

Marco glanced at the screen; the baby was moving about a lot, clearly picking up on Sydney's worries.

'Try to relax,' the ultrasonographer said.

But he could see in Sydney's eyes that panic had set in. She was worrying about all the maybes. 'Remember that Sunday morning we walked through Sorrento?' he asked. When she nodded, he began to sing *'Torna a Surriento'*. And eventually the tension in her body seemed to ease and the baby stopped moving about quite so much.

The ultrasonographer inserted the needle and took the fluid. 'All done.' She smiled at Marco. 'You have a lovely voice. Your baby's really going to enjoy bedtime lullabies.'

'So we hear in two weeks?' Sydney asked.

'Two weeks. I'm afraid it does take that long to grow the cells and analyse them.' The ultrasonographer patted her hand. 'I know it's hard, but try not to worry. And try to rest for today and tomorrow, OK?'

Marco took Sydney back to her flat.

'So are you going back to work now?' she asked.

'No. I'm taking the time off with you.'

She frowned. 'Marco, I'm not going to start rushing around doing things.'

'I know, but if you're on your own you'll start brooding. I'm not going to make you have bed rest for the next two days, because I know it'll drive you crazy, but I do want you resting. Put your feet up, *tesoro*. We're going to watch a pile of comedies and play board games and do crosswords together.'

'You're going to keeping me occupied, hmm?'

'As much as I can.' He stroked her face. 'Waiting's the hardest part of anything. But we'll get through this.'

Her face was filled with sadness. 'What if…?'

'We'll deal with it when it comes. Don't build bridges to trouble,' he said softly.

It was easier for both of them to keep their minds occupied at work—until the day when the results were due. They both slept badly the night before, and the atmosphere in the flat was full of tension. Sydney dropped the jar of decaf coffee, which smashed on the kitchen floor; Marco burned the toast; and his jaw ached so much that he was convinced he'd been grinding his teeth in his sleep.

The tension rose with every second that ticked round. When would they get the call?

The phone rang, and she grabbed it. 'Yes. No. Look, I'm sorry, I know you're only doing your job, but I'm perfectly happy with my electricity provider and I'm expecting an important call. Please go away.' She hung up. 'I can't believe I got cold-called today, of all days.'

'They're just doing their job, *tesoro.*'

'If the hospital was trying to ring me when I took that call—'

'Then they'll try your mobile next,' he reminded her.

But her mobile phone didn't ring. And neither did the landline.

Every time they glanced at the clock, thinking that surely a quarter of an hour had passed, they were shocked to discover that it was only a few seconds.

Then the phone rang again. Sydney fumbled as she tried to grab it, dropped the phone and cut off the connection. 'No!' she howled, and checked the display to see who had called.

'Number withheld. It has to be Theo's secretary.'

She rang the number. 'Engaged,' she said, her mouth thinning. She redialled. 'Still engaged.'

'Sydney, if she's talking to someone else, she'll be a couple of minutes. She'll probably try you next,' Marco said gently, trying to calm her down—all this stress wasn't good for her or for the baby.

Sydney redialled again; this time, she got through. 'Hello? It's Sydney Collins. Were you just trying to ring me? Yes.' She paused. 'Yes. I see. Thank you.'

She put the phone down and promptly burst into tears.

'Sydney?' Clearly she'd just heard the news she didn't want to hear. Why else would she be crying her eyes out? Marco wrapped his arms round her. 'Oh, *tesoro*. I know that right now it feels like the end of the world. But we don't have to make any decisions today. We have a little while to work things out.'

'It's OK,' she sobbed. 'It's OK. Chromosome 22. It's *normal*.'

It took a moment for what she's said to sink in.

The baby didn't have NF2.

And then he picked her up, whooped and swung her round in a circle. 'That's fantastic!'

So everything was going to be all right now. Sydney wasn't going to crucify herself any more over whether she'd passed her genetic problem to the baby; now she knew for sure that she hadn't, she could relax into her pregnancy and really enjoy it.

She touched his cheek. 'Marco, you're crying,' she said in wonder.

'Because I'm relieved—not that it would've been a problem for me if the baby had NF2, but because you're not going to blame yourself any more for something that isn't your fault. And I'm happy. And I love you very, very much.'

That weekend, Sydney took Marco to meet her family. And they liked him as much as Marco's family had liked her. Her parents and sisters-in-law were charmed by his good manners, her brothers indulged in good-natured banter about football with him, and her nieces persuaded him to play endless games with them.

'He's lovely,' Sydney's mother said when she managed to get her daughter to herself in the kitchen. 'So much better for you than Craig ever was. Why have you been keeping him a secret all this time?'

'It's complicated,' Sydney hedged. 'And I didn't want to say anything about the baby until I had the amnio results back. Just in case—' her breath caught '—I'd passed on the NF2. I couldn't forgive myself if I had.'

Sydney's mother hugged her. 'Oh, darling. I hate to think that you've been going through all this on your own.'

'I wasn't on my own. Marco supported me.'

'Why didn't you tell me?'

'Because I didn't want to burden you.'

Sydney's mother gave her a rueful smile. 'I'm your mother. You'd never be a burden to me, darling. Though I do understand how you felt—I've been there myself. When you were first diagnosed, your father and I blamed ourselves. I went over and over what had happened when I was pregnant with you, just in case I'd done something that caused it.'

'Mum, it wasn't your fault, or Dad's. It was a genetic mutation. Pure chance.'

'And it wouldn't have been your fault, either, if the baby had it too,' Sydney's mother said softly. 'But I'm glad for your sake that it's all worked out.'

'Me, too,' Sydney said. 'I didn't think it was possible to be this happy.'

Marco's family was equally delighted by the news of the baby and their engagement. When Marco told them, Sydney could hear the shrieks of joy even though he hadn't switched the phone through to speaker mode.

'They want to talk to you,' Marco said with a grin, and handed her the phone.

Ten minutes later, when Sydney hung up, she was slightly dazed.

'What?' Marco asked.

'I think we've just been organised. Your sister's making me a wedding dress and she's flying over next weekend with fabric swatches and designs for me to choose. And, um, your parents and your brother are flying over with her, so they can all meet my family.'

'Ah.' He grimaced. 'Sorry. They're Italian. They like everything big and noisy. I'll tell them to back off.'

She shook her head, smiling. 'No, it's lovely, feeling part of a huge extended family. It was never like that with Craig. It was always made very clear that I was just an in-law.'

'You definitely won't be that with my family. You're one of us,' Marco told her. 'An honorary Italian.'

She smiled back. 'Which is wonderful. Everything's just perfect.'

And it was. Marco's and Sydney's families never

stopped talking the entire weekend, swapping stories and showing each other photographs and laughing. Everyone at work was delighted for them when they announced the news about their engagement and the baby. And when Sydney felt the very first kick inside her, her joy was overwhelming; this was everything she wanted. Just perfect.

Until she became aware that her hearing had dulled rapidly on her left side. She could only work out what patients were saying if they were close to her—and noisy social situations were next to impossible.

She tried telling herself that it was winter, she had a bit of a cold and it was just slightly inflamed Eustachian tubes affecting her hearing; but when she heard the soft, high-pitching ringing in her ears, she knew.

Tinnitus.

So the schwannomas on her vestibular nerves were growing and starting to cause problems.

That evening, after work, she sat on the sofa next to Marco and took his hand. 'We need to talk.'

He frowned. 'What's up?'

'I have a problem.'

He scooped her onto his lap and rested his hand on her bump. 'What kind of problem, *tesoro*?'

'I'm getting tinnitus. I think… I think it's the vestibular schwannomas. They must've grown and started pressing on the nerves.'

He stroked her face. 'So would that be part of the reason why you slept through the alarm this morning?'

'I *was* tired and I slept like a log last night. But…' She sighed. She had to be honest with him. 'I probably didn't hear the alarm. I had a patient today—I couldn't hear half of what he was saying. It didn't help that Cubicles were particularly noisy and his voice was soft. And I do have a bit of a cold. It might be just that.'

'But you're worried, and that's enough for me. We'll see Michael and find out what's going on and what the options are.'

She bit her lip. 'I can't help remembering what Craig said—that I'm selfish for wanting this baby, knowing that the pregnancy hormones can make my condition worse.'

Marco said something very pithy about Craig. 'You're not selfish at all. Look, your NF2 is part of you, and we're in this together. It doesn't change the way I feel about you or about our baby. He wasn't planned, but he's very much wanted.'

'I know.'

'But sometimes it's hard to forget the most hurtful words,' he said. He kissed her swiftly. 'Thank you for trusting me. For not shutting me out.'

'I might have to rely on you quite a lot,' she warned.

'I'll be here.' He kissed her again. 'Always.'

To her relief, Michael fitted them in the next day. 'We can do an MRI of your head and it won't affect the baby,' he reassured her. 'And we need to do some acoustic tests to see how badly your hearing's been affected.'

But his face was grim as he showed them the results on his computer screen after the scan. 'Bad news, I'm afraid, Sydney. The left schwannoma is growing faster than the right. You're going to need surgery—either through microsurgery or gamma knife—or you risk losing your hearing in that ear completely if the tumour puts too much pressure on the acoustic nerve and damages it.'

'I'm not having surgery while I'm pregnant—and absolutely no to the gamma knife.' She blew out a breath. 'I won't expose the baby to radiation.' She lifted her chin. 'I had months of worrying myself sick over whether the baby's inherited my NF2. I'm not going to spend the rest of my pregnancy worrying over whether the baby's been affected by anaesthetic or radiation or anything else.'

'It's Sydney's call,' Marco said. 'I'm backing whatever decision she makes.'

'I'll be fine. If the worst comes to the worst, I still have hearing in my right ear. And maybe we can use the gamma knife to shrink the tumour after the baby's born,' Sydney said.

Michael nodded. 'OK. We'll keep monitoring you. In the meantime, try not to worry.'

Afterwards, Sydney bit her lip. 'Did I do the right thing, Marco? Should I have opted for surgery?'

'*Tesoro*, it's your call,' he said gently. 'You know the risks and you know the options. I meant what I said. Whatever you want to do, I'll back you all the way.'

'If I lose my hearing…' She dragged in a breath. 'I think we should get a baby listener with flashing lights, so I can see when the baby's crying if I can't hear.'

'For during the day, that's a good idea. At night, I'll wake, so you don't need to worry,' Marco said. He stroked her hair. 'What about your back? I've noticed you standing with your hands pressed into the small of your back.'

She smiled. 'That's something that just about every pregnant woman does. It's completely normal pregnancy backache. And, believe me, I remember what the other sort of back pain felt like,' she said feelingly, 'so I know the difference. I'm fine. It's just my hearing.'

Just. She was so brave, Marco thought. And he was incredibly proud of her.

To both Marco and Sydney's relief, the rest of her pregnancy passed without any more complications. Sydney's hearing worsened a fair bit more, but she had no other worrying symptoms.

Two days before the baby was due, she woke in the night, feeling slightly uncomfortable. She managed to turn over and go back to sleep, but by breakfast-time she realised what was happening. 'Marco, the baby's coming.'

'Contractions?' He went white. 'How often?'

'Twenty minutes apart. I think.'

'I'll ring the hospital.' He punched in Theo's number; the conversation was brief, and then he rang Ellen to say he needed cover for the day because he was going to be at Sydney's side for every second of labour. 'Theo says come in when your contractions are every ten minutes, and Ellen sends her love,' he reported.

Gradually over the morning, the contractions drew closer together. The second they were ten minutes apart, Marco drove Sydney in to the hospital.

'OK?' he asked as they headed into the maternity unit.

She nodded.

He could tell by her expression that she was being brave. 'You're nervous, *tesoro.*'

'I know we did all the classes and we know all the breathing, but…'

'It will be fine,' he reassured her. 'And I'm not leaving your side.'

'I'm excited as well as nervous. I can't *wait* to meet our baby,' Sydney said.

He smiled. 'Me, too.'

Theo examined her, did a quick check of the baby's heartbeat, then smiled in satisfaction. 'Everything's fine. I'll leave you in the capable hands of Iris, our senior midwife. Any worries, call me.'

Marco rubbed her back with every contraction and got her walking around the ward. And then finally Sydney was ready to go into the delivery suite. Marco coached her through the breathing and made no protest when she gripped his hands and dug her nails in.

'One last push,' Iris encouraged. And then they heard a cry and she smiled. 'You have a beautiful baby boy.'

'Niccolo,' Sydney said. 'His name's Niccolo.'

Iris weighed him and checked him over. 'Perfect Apgar score,' she said as she handed the baby back to Sydney.

Sydney was so tired—and yet so happy at the same time. She wanted to yell from the rooftops how happy she was, even abseil down the tower of the London Victoria. And the sudden rush of love she felt for their baby was stronger than she would ever have believed.

Marco's eyes were glittering with unshed tears; she knew that, like hers, they were happy tears.

'He's so beautiful. He looks like you,' she said softly.

'Our little miracle. I'm so proud of you both.' His voice was thick with emotion. 'I love you, Sydney.'

Once they were back on the ward, there seemed to be a constant stream of visitors wanting to congratulate them and see their beautiful baby. Sydney's entire family; Max and Marina; Theo and his wife, Maddie; Michael; and every doctor and nurse from the emergency department. So much love and so many good wishes for them, Sydney thought happily. It just didn't get any better than this.

CHAPTER FOURTEEN

SYDNEY had agreed with Michael that a month after her son was born she'd have the gamma knife operation on the tumour. Fergus Keating had asked one of his former colleagues, Amy Ashby, to come to London and help with the operation; Amy was an expert in gamma knife surgery and had set up a specialist neurology treatment centre in Norfolk. Sydney liked her immediately. 'I feel safe in your hands,' she said.

'Good. That's how it should be.' Amy looked thoughtful. 'Sydney, I have to be honest with you—I can't promise it's going to do the trick and get your hearing back completely. If there's too much damage to the nerve, you might need an auditory brainstem implant before you can hear properly again on that side. But I'm hoping that in a couple of weeks' time you'll have healed enough for it to make a difference.'

'That's good enough for me,' Sydney said.

The day after the operation, Marco strolled into his wife's hospital room, carrying the baby in his arms. 'I think Mamma might just be ready to come home, Nico,' he told the baby.

Sydney was sitting on the bed, case packed, tapping her fingers impatiently. 'I've been ready for *hours*.'

'Sorry. Somebody wanted his breakfast. He yelled the place down because I wasn't heating the milk fast enough for him. And *then* he decided to be contrary and take his time about drinking it. Apparently I'm not as good as you, when it comes to breakfast.'

He handed the baby over to Sydney, and she held him close, breathing in his scent. 'Oh, I missed you, *bambino*,' she said softly. 'And I missed your daddy. I could've come home last night, but, oh, no. Daddy said I had to stay in, just in case.'

'Easier than having to rush you here in an ambulance,' Marco said dryly.

'There was no need to be so cautious. I was fine. Amy and Fergus are brilliant surgeons. I can go back to completely normal activities today.' She gave him a rueful smile. 'Though I will admit to having a bit of a headache.'

'You had a cage screwed to your head and then radiation beams zapping you. Of course you have a headache.'

'The cage bit was done under an LA, so it didn't hurt, and I didn't feel a thing during the gamma knife stuff.' She rolled her eyes. 'You know that. You were there with me.' She kissed the baby. 'Nico, Daddy's such a fusspot.'

'Of course Daddy fusses. You're both important,' Marco informed the baby. He sat down next to Sydney and kissed her. 'Have they given you anything for that headache, *tesoro*?'

'Yes. I'm just waiting for Fergus to sign the discharge form.' She bit her lip. 'When he and Amy called in to check up on me last night, after you left, they had a chat with me about the scan. They say my left vestibular nerve is too damaged for me to get much of my hearing back in that ear, but they're confident the right-hand schwannoma's going to shrink over the next couple of months—enough for me to hear really well again in my right ear.'

'That's a bonus.' He stroked her cheek. 'We'll manage just fine with Nico. And there's always the possibility of an ABI later for your left ear.'

She nodded. 'I'd hate not to be able to hear Nico's first words properly.'

'You will,' he promised. 'And think of all the other firsts we have to look forward to. The first tooth, the first steps, the first day at school, the first driving lesson...'

She laughed, just as Marco had intended her to. 'I'm surprised you didn't go up to the first grandchild!'

'That, too. We have *plans*. A whole lovely life ahead of us.' Marco stole a kiss. 'I'm going to see where Fergus has got to. And then we're going home. The three of us.'

Their wedding day was the brightest day in May that Sydney could ever remember. She was full of smiles as she arrived at the register office in the car with her father. She and Marco had arranged with the registrar to be interviewed separately before the ceremony, because both of them wanted to stick to the tradition of not seeing each other on their wedding day until the wedding itself.

'OK, love?' her father asked.

She smiled. 'More than OK. I don't think I've ever been this happy.'

The beautiful white stone building with its imposing steps, moulded doorway and filigree work in the arch above the double doors was familiar to her from newspaper photographs of the rich and famous. As she drew nearer she could see that there were rose petals scattered on the steps; clearly someone had already been married here today, starting a new life together full of hope. Just as she and Marco were facing a new life together full of hope.

She sorted out all her side of the paperwork with the registrar while the guests were being seated, and then it was time for her to enter the room. Both their families were there waiting for them, along with their closest friends—including Marco's, who'd flown over from Italy with his family.

She'd forgotten that Marco's friends had been in a band with him in their student days—but they'd brought guitars with them, and performed a quiet, acoustic version of 'Walking on Sunshine' as she entered the room. The song he'd used to sing her down from the abseil, the very first time they'd met—and so appropriate, because that was exactly what it felt like as she walked towards him. When he turned round to watch her walk towards him, the sheer love on his face made her heart skip a beat.

Both of them meant every word when they made their vows.

When the registrar gave him permission to kiss his bride, he kissed her lingeringly. 'I love you. And you've just made me the happiest man in the world.'

There was a huge lump in her throat, but she managed to say, 'And I love you, too, Marco. So much.'

The wedding meal at the hotel they'd booked was

wonderful—the room was full of laughter and smiles, and there was none of the awkwardness between the different sides of the family that she'd noticed at weddings she'd been to in the past. The evening reception was a lot bigger; in the emergency department, you got to know so many people from other departments, and it seemed that half the hospital wanted to share their day.

'Time to hit the dance floor,' Marco said.

The song they'd chosen was the one Marco had played to her about how amazing he thought she was. And it was even better because she could hear him clearly, thanks to the gamma knife surgery. She wasn't going to miss a single tiny bit of her wedding day.

'You're amazing, too,' she whispered at the end, and kissed him.

She paced herself with the dancing during the evening, but towards the end she was starting to feel tired. She didn't admit it, but Marco clearly noticed.

'Time to sneak off, *tesoro*,' he said.

'Don't we have to say goodbye to everyone first?'

'It'll take the rest of the night to do that. Everyone will understand.' He smiled at her. 'And I kind of want you to myself. Especially as Nico has two sets of grandparents on hand to spoil him—and we have the honeymoon suite.'

A ripple of desire slid down her spine at the expression in his eyes. 'Now, that sounds tempting…'

When they reached their room, he opened the door, then picked her up to carry her over the threshold, letting the door click closed behind them. He set her back on her feet in front of the four-poster bed and turned the lights to low.

'You look lovely, *tesoro*.'

'Thanks to your talented sister.'

'Not just the dress. You look lovely anyway. And now you're all mine.' He took off her bolero jacket and hung it up, then slowly unzipped her dress, kissing every inch of skin he uncovered. And Sydney didn't flinch when he finally removed her dress, baring her arm, because she knew that he loved her exactly as she was. The lumpy skin was no longer a badge to remind her not to trust. It was just a part of her—and Marco's love had taught her to accept that.

She thoroughly enjoyed undressing him, too. 'I see what you mean. You looked stunning in that suit—but it's just window-dressing. Because you're gorgeous anyway.'

'You've made me so happy,' he said, holding her close. 'I love you, Dr Ranieri.'

She loved the sound of her new name on his lips. 'I love you, too, Dr Ranieri. For the rest of our days.'

* * * * *

COMING SOON!

We really hope you enjoyed reading this book. If you're looking for more romance, be sure to head to the shops when new books are available on

Thursday 7th February

To see which titles are coming soon, please visit

millsandboon.co.uk/nextmonth

LET'S TALK
Romance

For exclusive extracts, competitions
and special offers, find us online: